NO PLANNING FOR LOVE

A MONSTERA BLUFF NOVEL

BOOK ONE

KATIE HAYPENNY

ISBN-13: 978-1-968941-01-7

Edited by: Kate Seger

Cover art by: @linda.noeran

Interior art by: @lanabanana.art

Author portrait by: @willdahlias

Library of Congress Control Number: 2025914491

Printed in the United States of America

No AI was used in the writing of this book.

This book is dedicated to my husband, who would always encourage me to write, even when I didn't think it was in the cards for me. Life dealt me a good hand when I met him.

CONTENT WARNINGS

Be aware of spoilers below! This steamy, plot driven novel includes:

*Cheating (In the past – not between the MCs)
*Panic attacks
*Explicit sexual acts between consenting adults
*House fire
*Assault to FMC (Held down forcefully – not by MMC)
*Physical injuries to both MCs (That are fully healed! This is a HEA, after all!)

CHAPTER 1
CARA

Rain patters on my windshield as I drive down an unnervingly empty road carved through an endless salt marsh. My gaze is drawn to the marsh grasses dancing in the wind, the rhythm affirming its life amidst the harsh landscape. The hypnotic motion appears to beckon me ahead, urging me to keep moving forward. Until the tempo is disrupted by chaotic wind gusts, pulling me out of the daydream. Breathing deep, I refocus on the long swath of road ahead.

Before long, a sign appears in the distance. Finally, some confirmation I'm heading in the right direction. "Welcome to Monstera Bluff." The friendly announcement rings ominously to me—a reminder I have no idea what's in store for me in this unfamiliar place. That I'm only here because I've lost almost everything along the way. My home. My career. My heart. Laid to waste by a lying, cheating man. A tale as old as time.

As I pass the rustic roadside welcome sign, the rain thickens, and storm clouds deepen ahead, blotting out the sky. The wind whips up, singing a false lullaby, inviting me to be swept away. But I need to ground myself, stay strong, like the marsh grasses around me weathering storms that try to snap them, yet they still stand tall. Especially now, as the next chapter of my life is set to begin.

"Welcome to your next mistake," I mumble to myself, reasonably skeptical of this serendipitous opportunity.

Thinking back to that fateful job interview that brought me here, I still can't believe how perfectly timed it had been. The very day after I'd decided to leave my mess in Atlanta, Monstera Bluff Mayor Clancy Evermane's email had appeared in my inbox. Despite its oddly personal nature and my initial suspicions that it was spam, something had compelled me to respond. The video interview that followed had been almost surreal. Not just because of the mayor's unexpected good looks —which I firmly filed under "off limits" given my track record with bosses—but because of how thoroughly he knew my work, right down to papers I'd published in grad school nearly a decade ago. We'd clicked immediately, sharing similar visions for sustainable urban development, and his offer to make me Monstera Bluff's first city planner had come within minutes of our two-hour conversation ending.

Maybe I should have questioned why a small-town Georgia mayor had sought me out so directly, or why everything seemed almost too perfect. But after the year I'd had, running from Chicago only to land in another bad situation in Atlanta, I'd been too desperate for a fresh start to look this gift horse in the mouth.

Clancy sent detailed directions on how to get here, claiming GPS couldn't find the way. At the time, I thought it was preposterous, so I tested his theory on Google. He was right; it didn't recognize any address in the town. As if it existed in a digital black hole.

With the destination ahead, I unlock my phone and reread his instructions. They seem simple enough, and I make a mental note to watch for the next turn-off.

Information about the town itself is scarce, though it does, in fact, exist—despite some of my doubts at first. I'm certain I'm not being catfished, but everything feels a little odd. In life and work, I'm meticulous—dotting every I and crossing every T—but now I'm anything but prepared to arrive in Monstera Bluff. *If any celestial being out there in the universe can hear me, please don't let me rush headlong into my own Deliverance. As soon as I hear a banjo, I'm out.*

My tires screech on the wet pavement as some unseen force slams into me, shoving me against the seat. Fearing I'm going to drive into the marsh, I slam on the brakes. The small trailer I'm hauling behind me wobbles alarmingly. Somehow, I manage to roll to a stop in the middle of the road. Tears fill my eyes and my throat constricts as I choke on unexpected sobs.

The worst, most miserable times in my life flash on repeat in my brain—*struggling to hear her last shallow, shuddering breaths over the incessant beeping and chattering of the hospital. The perfect engagement ring, shining and stunning, on another woman's finger. The force of the impact, the crunch of metal, pain spearing through my body.* The memories rise sharply, like they only just happened moments ago, jagged and raw. I've already lived through them, and though they still haunt me, they're usually nothing like this waking nightmare taking me right back there.

Something is very wrong with me that a welcome sign could send me into an all-consuming tailspin. Why did I think a job in podunk Monstera Bluff would solve anything? Nothing in my life is salvageable. Why keep trying? I would turn the car around and never think about this place again if I could. Cosmic joke's on me, though. I have nowhere else to go.

Feeling so alone, I weep as I relive each horrible, life-altering experience. The weight of these unwanted memories could drown me in the marsh. I attempt my calm breathing exercises—deep breath in my nose and out my mouth, holding my hand to my belly, rinse and repeat. How could things go so wrong in my life? Why did I let myself get desperate enough that this was my only option? Thoughts of self-doubt swirl in my head, but I try not to let myself sink further into despair.

I give up on breathing exercises and place my hands at the top of the steering wheel, resting my head there for several minutes, attempting to still my thoughts and empty my mind. The tears streaming down my face eventually subside. "Just get through this," I whisper to myself as a hiccup painfully convulses my chest. Eventually, I regain my calm, exhaling long and sad, wiping my wet, puffy eyes with the back of my hands. The wind has stilled in the time I've been sitting here, no longer calling out to me. The storm has lulled for now.

Knowing I can't roll into town a complete mess, I try to pull myself together, staring out the window, numb and depleted after my meltdown. A vast emptiness is left inside me where those emotions ballooned and burst, now wrung out of me, making me feel so insubstantial I'm about to blink out of existence from the inside out.

The tears eventually dry from my face. Even though I'm not holding up traffic—not a single car has driven by—there's no point in waiting here any longer, putting off the inevitable. Feeling ready enough, though still very much worse for wear, I drive slowly so as not to miss any signs of civilization. My destination must not be too far ahead, but the wild, stark surroundings tell a different story. The land looks untouched. Coastal Georgia should be much more populated. But since exiting I-95, there have been few signs of life on this narrow road, just a dingy old gas station some miles back that someone couldn't pay me to step into. Soon, a wall of lush pine trees looms in the distance, the primeval forest drowning the road in its shadow. An occasional driveway tunnels through the dense tree line, leading into hidden-away properties. Every so often my eyes catch movement behind the forest's darkened boundary. "Are those deer?" I wonder aloud, but the road-shy creatures don't allow me a good enough glimpse to know for sure. I let up on the gas pedal anyway, not wanting to test my abysmal luck.

An upcoming intersection looks like it should lead to the main road into town, yet my instructions are very clear to keep going. It's obvious I'm being led the long way, keeping me to the outskirts of town. I'll put my trust in them for now since I'm basically driving blind. I need to meet up with my landlady first and get settled into the apartment in her carriage house before I can explore any further.

A few turns later, the blue mailbox from my instructions comes into view. I pull into the driveway, which splits into a small parking area to the right and a wide circle, connecting back up with itself to the left. A fountain decorates the center of the circle. The landscaping is controlled chaos of plants and flowers, wild but well-maintained. I park in a spot next to a pristine vintage Jeep Wagoneer. My small SUV looks bland in comparison.

The main house sits behind the circle drive looking very grand— way more picturesque than anywhere I've lived before. I'm no architect, but it looks like it was built in a Greek Revivalist style in the nineteenth century. The large, square, two-story structure is painted white with

French blue shutters adorning tall windows and a centered front door in the same hue—all very symmetrical. Porches on both levels feature pillars running the full height to the overhanging roof. The first-story porch is open except for the pillars. The second story's has an ornate railing and a centered oval decorative window. The ceilings above each level are painted in the traditional haint blue, which I learned about during the short time I lived in Atlanta. The carriage house where I'll be staying is painted similarly, though the structure is much more modest and sits off a sidewalk from the parking area. It looks surprisingly big. Well, it may be the right size, considering the scale of this estate.

A woman sitting on a porch swing at the main house stands up and makes her way toward me, her movements so graceful she's practically gliding. She waves her hand in welcome, so I do the same. As she reaches me, I'm captivated by how striking she is. Effortlessly elegant. She wears a sleeveless tea-length navy blue shift dress with a slight flare. It looks flawless on her lithe, statuesque figure. Deep garnet red hair—a hue that shouldn't be natural, yet the richness of color shows that it is—runs long and thick halfway down her back with a white forelock on each side of her part. Practically glowing, her smooth ivory skin shines like a pearl, with only some laugh lines to reveal her maturity. I was under the impression she'd be a decade older than me but she looks nearly untouched by age. Her bright violet eyes glitter, the light catching them like cut gemstones. She's a dazzling vision, the likes of which I've never seen. Like a bee to a flower, she draws me in.

"Cara! I'm so glad you made it. Welcome! I hope the directions weren't too confusing," she greets me with a languid drawl in a bright, pleasant tone. Her smile widens as she thrusts out her hand for me to shake, her affability nearly at odds with her poise. And yet, the instant I take her hand, I sense her inner vibrancy runs even deeper. "I'm Ada Mayweather, a member of the town council. I'm so very happy you accepted the job in the mayor's office and that you're already here. You'll be staying in my carriage house for as long as you'd like." She motions to the building behind us.

My stare seesaws between her and her house, almost at a loss for words, though I do my best to recover. "It's lovely to meet you, Ada. Thank you so much for hosting me. I'm grateful to you and the mayor for being so generous. I appreciated the thorough driving directions. There's no way I would have made it otherwise. My phone was useless," I reply a touch too formally. She seems genuinely kind, but I can't help feeling inferior in my sloppy but comfy outfit and a bare face still hot from crying.

"Do you live here alone?" I ask without thinking, my wrung-out emotions making small talk a challenge.

Ada chuckles at my question. "Oh yes, just me and my two cats in this dusty, old house. It's been in my family for generations. I know it's much too ostentatious for just little old me, but I can't stand to part with it. I was... married... once, so it hasn't always just been me. But that was a long time ago."

My stomach sinks at my unintended rudeness, like I was prying. I nearly cut her off, words spilling out of my mouth in awkward horror. "I'm sorry, I should have worded that differently. I was wondering if anyone else lives on the property, like other tenants."

She waves it away in good humor. "Oh, don't worry yourself. The gossip mill loves to brew a tempest in a teapot around here, so it may as well come from me. He and I were like fire and frost, more than you could ever know, and we just weren't meant to be together in the end. I've been on my own in this house for a long time. I've never rented out the carriage house before. Just had occasional guests stay there. So, it'll be nice to have some long-term company." Her eyes grow misty, but she quickly blinks it away.

It's obvious there's more to the story, but I'm not going to veer from inadvertent into intentionally rude territory if I can help it. So I hold my tongue, only intoning in sympathy and agreement.

To my relief, she drops the subject and continues, "I've become a bit of an ambassador for newcomers in recent years. I don't know all of what Clancy told you, but I gather this is a leap in the dark for you without knowing what to expect here in Monstera Bluff."

It's an opening to finally learn a little more about this town. "We talked shop more than anything else. But he explained that the town has a population of about twelve thousand and growing. He needs me to help plan for expansion so it can maintain its livability and character. I think we'll work well together. I'm embarrassed to admit I tried to do more research on the town, but I hit a lot of dead ends. I would love it if you could tell me more." I sound overeager. Her mouth quirks, like she's on to me.

Her eyes gleam playfully as she tells me, "Look at me about to talk your ear off. Such a bad hostess. Why don't I show you the carriage house so you can unpack a bit and freshen up? It's just after lunch, so knock on my door in an hour, and we can have sweet tea and talk some more. Then I will take you into town."

I inwardly groan and try to school the disappointment on my face. She knows exactly what she's doing! Ada walks toward the carriage house. "Lead the way," I mutter to the back of her head.

Ada unlocks the door, and we climb the steps to the second story, where the kitchen opens into a great room with enough space for distinct dining and living areas. It's blessedly air-conditioned, furnished but uncluttered, and remodeled at some point in the last decade. It was designed with clean lines and simplicity in mind. Luckily, the result is very homey. The large kitchen island will make prepping meals a breeze. And the oversized couch and chair in the living room look soft and cozy. The excess of windows makes the great room surprisingly bright. Refinished wood flooring seems to be the only original feature left, not that a carriage house interior would have much to salvage. I let out a sigh of relief. I really had been worried about the state of my rent-free apartment, which was included as part of my compensation package.

I can't hide the smile on my face when Ada turns to me. "Not bad for an old garage, right?" she jokes.

"More luxurious than any apartment I've lived in, to be honest!" I'm delighted by it.

She smiles, looking gratified, as we walk further into the space. "The kitchen is stocked with basics, but you'll still need to go grocery shopping. I hope the furniture is to your liking. The dining table may be a little small, but there's a leaf to extend it if you ever need to. Through the hallway is the bedroom, and across the hall is the bath. There's a linen closet at the very end of the hallway with a washer and dryer. I trust you won't get lost in here." We both giggle as she concludes the brief tour.

She places keys on the kitchen island. "Truly, I hope the apartment will suit you. In case you ever need it, I've included a key to my front door on the keychain. Generally, I leave the door unlocked, but you never know. If you ever have any issues, just call or text me. I left my name, cell number, Wi-Fi password, and our address on a note on the fridge."

After thanking her for everything, she leaves me to my own devices. There's a lot to do in the hour until I'm due at her house.

I haul in everything from my little SUV, but I leave the trailer for later. Sweat drips down my back after the repeated trips up and down the stairs carrying boxes and bags. It's still quite hot and humid even though it's a fall day. For the last trip up the steps, I reach for the overnight bag I packed, knowing it'll take time to sort through everything. I'm glad I have a couple nice outfits ready to go because this now-sweaty athleisure outfit won't cut it for first impressions. I head to the bathroom, finally ready for a shower. The early morning drive and hoofing it up and down the staircase so many times has really taken it out of me.

My reflection in the bathroom mirror makes me wince. My eyes are still red-rimmed from crying, and my formerly artfully crafted messy bun is now just plain messy. I look as disheveled as I feel. My face is pink and sweaty from exertion. The dark circles under my eyes look deeper than ever. The woman in the mirror barely resembles me. Too gaunt. Too exhausted. Too pitiful. Just a shell of who I was, looking as lost as I've felt since Mark entered my life.

Ten Months Ago

"Cara, do you have the proposal for the State Street project almost finished? I need it in my inbox before you leave."

Victoria Hansen, Vice President of Hansen Company, calls out to me from her office as I walk past. Based on how she interacts with me at work and oftentimes outside of it, no one would suspect I've dated her son, Mark, for years. "I'll have it to you by the end of the day, Victoria,"

I respond automatically as I turn around and backtrack to her office door.

"I expect it to dazzle. Don't disappoint me. Otherwise, I'm not sure I can pair you with Mark anymore," she warns with a rictus smile.

I hurry back to my cubicle, knowing it's going to be a very long day. The deadline was supposed to be end of day tomorrow, so I'm not sure why Victoria's asking for it today other than to make my life difficult. I counted on that extra day to make the bid proposal for the Chicago DOT's newest South Loop bike lanes worthy of the multi-million-dollar budget behind it. Even though it should break all sorts of HR rules, Mark is now my boss, and he's supposed to be heading up this project. But I haven't seen him all day to inform him of the revised deadline. He's been out of the office a lot this week, and I have no clue why.

After lunch, there's still no sign of him, so I send a quick text. "Victoria wants State today not tomorrow. Want to approve the draft before I send it?"

He's been slow to respond to me recently, so it's no surprise when it takes him over an hour. "I told you to run with this one on your own. I don't have time with my new responsibilities as director to hold your hand on a straightforward project. Associates shouldn't need oversight like this. If she needs it today, then do what you have to do to get it finished."

If I had wrapped this up without reaching out to him beforehand, he'd have been mad about that instead.

It makes me want to throw my phone, but I just roll my eyes and make the mistake of replying, "As a junior, I'm following protocol for my role."

I look over at the master's in urban planning and design diploma hanging on the cubicle wall beside my desk. When we got together after meeting in a sustainable urban development course, Mark pushed me into joining his family's civil engineering firm. I started here as soon as the ink dried on that framed piece of paper. At the time, he was excited we'd get to be junior associates together, the new generation at the firm.

"Get a grip, Cara. You've worked here for eight years. You know what to do." His name is listed as the main contributor to the bid proposal, but he hasn't read a word of it. As the boss, he can get away with it. I'd love more than anything to work for the city's planning and development office, but I'm stuck here, stagnant, not getting the credit due to me in an entry-level role. Victoria made me sign an iron-clad non-compete when I started, and my urban planning career in Chicago would be dead in the water if I left. And even if I could, I'd probably see Mark even less than I do now.

Wiping an errant tear threatening to roll down my cheek, I type, "I'll have to stay late, but it'll get done. I'll copy you on my email with the finalized version."

"That's my best girl. We'll talk later." I drop my phone on my desk and rub my temples.

Finally wrapping up my work, I email the document to Victoria and Mark and head out for the night. It's already after nine and I'm the last person in the office. I call Mark as I wait for the elevator, and he picks up after a few rings. "Hey, I haven't seen you all day. Can I come over tonight?"

Mark clears his throat and whisper-speaks into the phone. "Hey babe, bad time. I'm doing some schmoozy event for my parents. You know they've been asking me to step up even more. But I'll see you tomorrow at the office."

The distance between us has grown with each of his promotions, not just professionally but emotionally, too. I miss the old Mark, the one I fell in love with, more and more every day.

Catching myself zoning out in the mirror, I pat my cheeks, trying to wake myself up. In record time, I unpack my toiletries and clothes from my overnight bag, pull the scrunchie out of my hair, undress, and hop in the oversized shower. Anticipation speeds me along, even though I'd love to linger under the spray. Maybe I'll do that tonight when I can finally relax. My hair will have to air dry since I don't have time to do much else. Hopefully, it'll form nice waves. Minimal makeup highlights my eyes and lips. I slip on my white maxi dress with cap sleeves, a fitted bodice, and a tiered skirt. The material is thick and luxurious to the touch. It's one of my favorites. Naturally, I slip on inconspicuous shapewear shorts underneath in case we walk around. Chafing is no joke in the humidity.

Checking the time on my phone again there's only a few minutes to spare, but then I remember I haven't checked in with my best friend since yesterday as I finished packing. Rose is giving me space. That's her style. She and I met in Chicago on one of my earliest projects at Hansen Company. It needed input from the Chicago Transit Authority, and she was the project manager assigned as my contact. We have a lot in common. Not much family support, and as a result, we had to figure it out on our own from a young age. Her mom is older and in chronic frail health. My mom is... well, not in my life. And, of course, we share a passion for urbanism that borders on obsession. We've been inseparable ever since.

I quickly text her. "Made it in one piece, mostly. Drive wasn't bad. The carriage house is surprisingly nice. Meeting up with my landlord soon, and then I'll probably wander around town."

In mere seconds, she responds, "Mostly? Hope that doesn't mean anything too bad?" I cringe, knowing I should keep that emotional collapse to myself. She'd be too worried. "Spill everything when you have a chance! And don't fall into any time loops or black holes while you're out!"

She's been salivating over the mystery of the place and cracking jokes about it since I told her about the job. *Does the Roswell of Georgia need a downtown revitalization? Or do the lizard people need some traffic calming?* Beneath the silliness, I could tell she was nervous about my move to Monstera Bluff, Georgia, since we couldn't find anything about the town. Her increasingly outlandish theories helped lighten my mood. Weirdly enough, her jokes made me feel optimistic about finally making a difference in a community and getting the credit I deserve for my work, *even if you and Bigfoot himself have to duke it out to eliminate single-family zoning.* She just shrugged when I suggested maybe I could win him over with a persuasive presentation instead.

"Once I settle in, we'll plan your visit! I miss you so much. Especially today," I type, still feeling a pang of guilt about moving away from her earlier this year. But she understands and doesn't hold it against me.

"You can't keep me away! I should have visited you after the drive out to Atlanta, at least to help you pack again. I feel so guilty. Six months is too long without seeing your gorgeous face in person. Texts and calls are no substitute!" She follows her message with a string of crying emojis. "Plus, I think you might need me asap when you find out the town is overrun with slimy swamp monsters created in a top-secret government lab. The two of us could take on the creature from the black lagoon."

I bark a laugh at her ridiculous text message. She's been my rock for a long time, but she stepped up for me during this difficult year. Rose is so supportive without being overbearing. She's a whopping two years older than me but has always had her life together like a real adult. When we met, she was already stable in her career, working in the transit planning field. To the envy of everyone she knows, she lives in the most amazing apartment, cheap and spacious, on a quiet street walkable to the train. The unit is utterly beautiful, with tall ceilings and wood floors, full of natural light, and a small yard where she plants flowers. She says she'll never move out—no other Chicago apartment could compare. In her words, "They'll have to cart my cold dead body out of there." I don't blame her. If my life had been different, I'd have been content to live out my days in a cozy place with a garden. One day, perhaps.

Most importantly, though, she was self-confident, even when we were both still in our mid-twenties. Always so independent and living life on her own terms. She tries to tell me that she doesn't have everything going for her. She points to her abysmal love life as proof. Though she hasn't wasted years of her life on a scummy cheater like I have.

"A side of grits is probably the slimiest thing I'll encounter today. But you never know with all these swamps around here. Gotta run! I'll call you later." I send it before shoving my phone in my purse. I'd love to chat more with Rose right now, but time is short. I zip my purse, put on my strappy sandals, and head out the door to meet with Ada.

Walking on the sidewalk from the carriage house to the main house, I admire more of her property. There are neighbors nearby, but the house has a surprising amount of privacy. Live oaks drip with Spanish moss. Magnolia trees stand tall. The front yard fountain gurgles pleasantly. Its tranquil scene feels like stepping back in time. The perfect place for some much-needed peace in my life. Though as beautiful as it is, it's a lot of house and yard for one person. Maybe that's why she offered to let me stay here.

I knock on Ada's door, and she swiftly opens it. "Come in, welcome to my humble abode!" she bids with a wink as she moves aside and waves me in.

The two-story foyer is breathtaking. Light and bright with a glass chandelier catching every ray of sunshine, sending a sprinkle of rainbows across the room. Double doors to grand rooms open on either side toward the front of the foyer. The base of an elaborate curved staircase sits past the doors on the left side and wraps high around the wall to the right side. I'm spinning, appreciating every detail.

"Wow, this place is magnificent."

She smiles. "My ancestors seemed to have a flair for the dramatic, but I can't complain. Let's have our sweet tea in the parlor. My, do you look as pretty as a peach in that dress! I love it!" I blush at the genuine-sounding compliment. It's flattering coming from someone as sophisticated as her.

She ushers me into the parlor and pours us sweet tea from a crystal pitcher sitting on a tray atop a coffee table. I would expect the room to be filled with musty antiques, but it's decorated in an understated style. We take seats opposite each other on her long brown leather couches with a beautiful patina—old but not worn. The room is a sea of dark green, with the walls and ceiling painted. Board and batten wainscoting reaches halfway to the ceiling, which boasts decorative crown molding. A lush oriental rug covers the antique wood floor. A wide gray marble fireplace yawns open on the inside wall. I wonder if its twin sits on the other side in the next room, as is so often the case in these old mansions. Simple cream curtains long enough to brush the floor keep the room from looking too dark. It fits my first impression of her elegance. I instantly feel comfortable.

"So, Cara, you're coming from Atlanta? Did you grow up there?" she asks around her sip of iced tea.

"I was only there for around six months," I explain carefully, keeping my voice light. "I really needed a change of scenery in my life, but it turns out Atlanta wasn't a good fit for me, work and otherwise. Normally, I don't leave jobs so quickly."

"It is such a big city. Maybe that was part of it?" Ada guesses.

Shaking my head, I answer honestly. "No, I lived in Chicago my entire life before that. So I'm used to a big city, it's the only life I know. I just couldn't connect with the people and the place. That made things... difficult after a time. And I didn't necessarily have a plan for where to go next, and then I ended up with the job offer here. It's a big change, but I'm excited." Thankfully, she accepts that explanation.

"I think you'll like it here. It's a tight-knit community. You'll meet a lot of townsfolk through your work. I promise we're friendly and won't bite unless you ask," she responds with a tinkling laugh. I paste a smile on my face, unsure what she means.

Deflecting any more uncomfortable questions about myself, I try to steer our conversation to her and the town. "What do you do beyond serving on the town council?"

"Well, I run the family business, an apothecary shop downtown. I'm there most days when the council isn't demanding my time." She hums airily, almost amused, at something that I haven't caught the meaning of.

"An apothecary?" I wonder, unsure of what that could be. "Do you sell things like medicine and beauty products?"

"Yes, and more. It has almost everything you could need," she answers ambiguously.

"Are there a lot of shops downtown? I can't wait to see it, get a better sense of the place. I think I missed all of it on my way in," I press.

"Let's talk about the elephant in the room. I can tell you're fit to bursting to hear all about Monstera Bluff. And now that you're here, this conversation cannot wait much longer." Ada hesitates, fidgeting. Her earlier breeziness is absent, supplanted by this charged moment. "This is a unique town, and we very much prefer to keep to ourselves for reasons that will become clear to you. We are not unfriendly, but we feel we must protect what we have. I think you may need to see the town for yourself to understand."

I stare at her, mind racing to every possibility, none of them good. My body feels shaky with alarm that I'm about to be thrust into a situation I'm wholly unprepared for. A normal place wouldn't need to operate in secrecy. What did I get myself into?

"I'm also trusting that you will help protect us, too. We wouldn't have brought you here if we didn't think you could handle this information. That said, you may need time to come to terms with everything, so I encourage you to do so without worrying if I'll be offended," Ada explains, careful with each word. She waits for my response, so I force a stiff nod in agreement.

I don't know if that's a promise I can honor, but I guess I have to try.

CHAPTER 2
CARA

Ada ushers me out of the house, leading me to the Wagoneer parked by the carriage house. She must sense my reluctance to leave with her because she lightly guides me by the back of my arm to keep me moving. "You look as jumpy as a cat on a hot tin roof. C'mon, I swear you'll be just fine. You may even like it here," she claims.

Honestly, it doesn't make me feel any better—just the opposite. Like she's about to induct me into a cult. I want no part of this.

I'm tempted to jump into my car and peel out of here, never looking back. But then I'd have no job, no money, nowhere to go. My bank account is running low enough that I'm not sure I can afford a deposit on a new apartment. Maybe I was brought here because they somehow knew I'm too broke to leave. Against my better instincts, I get into the car with her. I'd be so mad if any of my friends did something this stupid, but here I am doing it anyway. It occurs to me that Rose and my other friends who know about my move would have no way of finding me if something were to happen. I clutch the armrest like my life depends on it.

Pulling out of her driveway, she maintains a slow pace, like we're on a leisurely Sunday drive. It seems a little aimless, but I have no doubt this is planned, like my route into town. The neighborhood streets are quaint, lined with looming crape myrtles creating a canopy of prolific red, pink, and purple flowers. Shouldn't this be a little late in the season for those blooms? Some white picket fences round out the idyllic scenery in front of me. Though the houses aren't nearly as grand as Ada's, most are large. Many seem excessively tall, enough so the proportions seem way off. Some have massive front doors that stand out on an otherwise tall but classic style of construction.

In one front yard, I spot a little dog running toward the open arms of its owner. At least, I think it's a dog. Except it's on two legs and wearing clothes. The blonde woman scoops up the gray dog in her arms and then smiles and waves at us as we're about to drive by. Ada flutters her hand at them. The woman points at us, saying something in her dog's ear, getting its attention. And the little dog sees us... and waves, too.

I lurch forward in my seat, craning my head to try to keep them in my sight as we drive away. "Did that dog just *wave*?" I gasp in disbelief.

Ada glances at me non-plussed. "Oh, that's not a dog. That's her little boy."

My jaw drops, and I shake my head incredulously. "Her little boy, are you sure? Do you mean she's a *dog mom*, like, to a pet?"

"Very sure it's her son. He looks just like his father," she answers placidly, though with a noticeable quirk of her lip.

Before I can grill her any further, we pass a couple walking down the sidewalk, holding hands, absorbed in each other's company. They don't pay any attention to us. It would be otherwise unremarkable, except they're both green. Unmistakably vibrant green. It's so realistic that it looks wrong, sending a shudder through me. My unease spikes as if my mind can't reconcile what it's seeing.

"Um, are those people wearing costumes? Is there an early Halloween party?" I babble.

"There's no party happening today that I know of." She's unfazed by the strange sight.

Blinking over at her, I can't hide my fear any longer. I demand, "What is going on here? What is..." My questions devolve into a horrified screech as a giant blue and black moth dips just above the windshield. It had to be the size of a person, if not bigger. Holy shit, just how big are the insects in this part of the country?

"Cara! Cara, you're okay. You're safe. Calm down, please. That's just Frederick... being Frederick. While I don't appreciate his aerial acrobatics so close to my automobile, he's usually quite the sweetheart," she explains, patting my arm to soothe me.

I jolt away from her. This is so far from being okay. Molding myself against the car door, as far from her as possible, I repeat my question, "What is going on here? What... is this place?" My voice comes out as a choked whisper. My lungs feel too small, like I can't breathe deeply enough. It's suddenly so hot and cramped in this space. I start to sweat. I want to crawl out of my skin just to get the air I need, and yet I don't dare open the window or try to get out of the car. This town isn't safe.

Ada pulls into a parking space, surrounded by other cars, so we must be somewhere more public. This isn't a comforting thought. I'd rather go back to my apartment and hide. She frowns and cranks up the air-conditioning, pointing the vents right at me while I continue to suck in every breath. Ada sighs and looks at me wanly. "Well, hon, I had no intention of giving you such a fright. This was all a bit of a gamble, but I needed you to see this with your own eyes because just hearing it from me, you'd never believe it. And I can't say that I've ever had the pleasure of revealing this information to anyone, because I haven't. Until now. Monstera Bluff is... is a safe haven, a sanctuary for folk you may think of as... monsters. I prefer to call them Whispered Folk, though they go by many names."

"Monsters are real?" I croak. The world tilts on its axis, and my brain can't orient to this new perspective. My eyes furiously dart between Ada and the sidewalk in front of the car. And there they are. Monsters. Some unrecognizable. All frightening. My heart thuds too hard in my chest at being so near them. An ancient, reptile brain self-preservation fight or flight instinct kicks in. I want to run away so badly, but I desperately hold still, praying they won't notice me.

She gives a sympathetic smile. "Monsters are real. They are sentient, free-thinking, intelligent, and sociable, just like humans, some even more so. I know this is a lot to take in. There's no rush, so just take your time."

I pinch myself to make sure I'm awake. Wishing this nightmare wasn't my real life. "Why would you bring me here? I could probably handle a cult, but not this! I thought my life couldn't get any worse. I knew this was a mistake. I am so, so stupid! Why does this always happen to me?"

I hug my arms into myself, wanting to curl up and disappear. I cried so much earlier that now I can't muster a single tear despite my near hysterics. Emotions are stuck in my body with no way to escape. Finally, I meet Ada's gaze again, she's been watching me with compassion in her eyes, taking no joy in my reaction. In a moment of clarity, I realize she was given the unenviable task of blindsiding me while also talking me off the ledge.

After a prolonged silence, staring at the impossible scene in front of me, Ada severs it. "Please understand you have nothing to fear from us. Consider that some folk here may be quite scared of you. You represent the most dangerous thing in the world to them—humans. Even if their appearance seems strange, they are our neighbors and friends."

"What are you? What is Clancy? How do monsters exist?" My shrill voice rises with each question, working myself up even more as my mind reels. "We're still in Georgia, right? How come no one knows about you? I have service on my phone. You must have the internet because the mayor had a Zoom meeting with me."

Ada hoots in laughter, startling me. "Well of course we're in Georgia! We do exist in the same world as you. Always have. But we conceal our town with strong magick. We do sometimes need to interact with humans who don't know about us. People exactly like you. We rely on the human world a bit for things we can't do or make ourselves. Like Wi-Fi. And Zoom. Monstera Bluff is not a scary place, and we are all people—well, for the most part."

My eyes bug out in shock. She gestures placatingly. "Don't worry yourself, please. It's one of many sanctuary towns and outposts across North America where Whispered Folk can live and be safe, though this one seems to be becoming more popular lately, and we have an influx of new residents. The town needs to expand, which is why we need you and your talent."

"But I saw Clancy and he's human! He was wearing a shirt and tie!"

I cry out, aware of how full-on crazy that sounds. But at least this turn to the absurd is helping me cope, knowing I've already interacted with some type of monster, even if he looked fully human to my eyes.

"How much did you see in that interview?" she shrewdly asks, her mouth curling into a knowing smile.

"Um, his shoulders and head?" I reply slowly, unsure of everything I thought I knew.

"Well, there you go. He only allowed you to see a narrow view of him. He's a clever one, if you couldn't tell. And to answer your question about me, I'm a witch, and my coven has always protected this town." The pride in her voice is unmistakable.

"You're a witch?" I say in disbelief. She nods emphatically, as if through her willpower alone, she can force me to come to terms with all of this. And honestly, she's probably the only reason I'm not in a fetal position right now.

"Magic is real. Like magic tricks?" I ask dumbly.

"No, it's *magick* spelled m-a-g-i-c-k. It's altering the laws of nature at will," she describes as if that would clear up the confusion. Oh so carefully, she reaches her hand toward me like I'm a skittish animal and warmly clasps my shoulder. "I know this information must be shocking, but you are accepting everything quite well," she tries to appeal to me.

I am not accepting anything well. In fact, I'm freaking the fuck out.

"Okay, so is Clancy also a witch?" I grasp at straws, wishing she'd just tell me. He could be some hideous creature.

"You'll see what Clancy is when we meet with him. We can't ruin all the fun now, can we?" she teases. I beg to differ on her definition of fun.

I'm about to confront this new reality... and meet real live monsters. I'm still too overwhelmed, too panicky. Ada seems to be following my line of thought and suggests, "Why don't we sit a spell in the air conditioning? I'm going to text Clancy to let him know we're nearby."

She begins texting as I stare at monsters walking by, living their lives. Mostly I have no idea who or what I'm looking at. I've grown both terrified and ashamed because, as Ada says, these are just people, too. There's a mom and two kids with snake tails in place of their legs... slithering by. I'm sure they're not actual snakes, right? Oh my god, I bet there *are* lizard people here, too. Rose was right! She'll shit a brick when she hears about this. Can I tell her about this?

A tall, muscular bull man carries a crate of vegetables down the block. Oh fuck, is that a minotaur? Does that mean Greek myths were real? My brain can't compute these thoughts right now. Some winged and feathered bird creatures walk by from the other direction. Can they fly? Are they descended from dinosaurs? Whatever they are isn't in my vocabulary. Anything I know is from pop culture and mythology, which is fiction... I thought. This is very much real life and I'm dreading everything about it.

Ada interrupts my twisting thoughts, "Clancy is at the Midnight Mystic, our twenty-four-hour coffee shop. It's popular, you'll like it. He's in a meeting, but he says we're free to join them." She smiles at me encouragingly. I nod my head and tell her I'm ready, even though it's a complete lie. I start to open the car door with clammy, shaky hands but pause for a moment to fix my face and hair in the mirror to meet my boss. I won't make that mistake again after arriving at Ada's a total frazzled mess. I step out of the car and smooth my dress. It's more to calm my frayed, weary nerves than anything.

Out of sheer luck, there's a break in the pedestrian flow of monsters on the sidewalk in front of us. I step onto the curb and follow Ada. We walk down the block, and I barely register my surroundings. I'm sure this main street is charming. Its design and features are literally my bread and butter. But I have no idea. My brain has shut down beyond basic function at this point. My eyes scan from monster to monster, and I put as much distance as possible between us as I walk past. Some seem human, like Ada, but looks can be deceiving, apparently. I really hope I'm not the only human here.

Ada stops me with a hand to my shoulder. I must be on autopilot, too focused on staying away from monsters. She holds open a door and I mindlessly step inside. The crowd noise rattles my brain, agitating me. My eyes take a few moments to adjust from the bright sunshine, leaving me standing frozen in fear of what's around me while blinded.

Once they finally adapt to the dimmer interior, my eyes immediately catch sight of a familiar, too-handsome face nearly head and shoulders above the crowd. His golden tan, deep brown eyes, and thick, blonde chin-length hair are unmistakable. Clancy sees me instantly, a huge smile splitting his face. He waves us over to a very roomy corner where he's standing. I move toward him but nearly stumble over my feet, arrested at the unexpected sight of him. He's riding a horse? Oh my god, where is the rest of the horse? Where is the rest of Clancy?

His human torso, covered in a fitted black t-shirt, connects to... a horse body. It's a light yellow-gold color. Behind him, a tail *swishes*. And it's the same blonde shade as his hair. I force my eyes back to his broadly grinning face, toothy and genuine, so I don't stare too indecently.

Ada's hand on my shoulder firmly pushes me forward. Only then do I notice someone next to him. Oh fuck, he's frightening, like a demon incarnate full of teeth, claws, horns, and wings. But his skin is a dark lavender gray hue instead of the red my imagination expects. My steps stutter again as shock blooms painfully in my chest, straining my ability to breathe. These two are contrasts in light and dark. Friendly and hostile.

The devil monster stands broad and tall, though not as tall as Clancy. He only wears a pair of well-fitted jeans on his brawny body, which I guess are popular with everyone, even a gray demon. I would laugh at the incongruity of it all, but I'm too stunned. No shoes, no shirt, no service must not apply in this coffee shop. Good lord, I need to get a grip and keep my wandering thoughts in line before I say something stupid.

When I finally meet his eyes, he stares back with a grim expression, mouth pressed into a thin line, like he's sizing me up in equal measure. His wings snap back even tighter than they already were. The movement makes me gulp in nervousness. Ada says I have nothing to fear, but he's intimidating, scary, everything she insists this place isn't. I can't help but wonder why he's part of my welcoming committee. His demeanor tells me I'm anything but.

My flight instinct flares up, but Ada nudges me toward him and Clancy. It feels like it took five minutes to walk across the room, but it was probably just five measly seconds. My legs are dead weights as my mind screams at me to run. I dig my heels in when I'm several feet away, unable to force myself any closer.

"Clancy, our newest resident has arrived!" Ada announces cheerfully as she finally releases me.

Clancy beams. "Cara Bishop! Mother Earth in all her glory, I'm so happy to finally meet you in person!" Clancy greets me with the most genuine enthusiasm I've ever heard. His sonorous voice fills the room, drawing unwanted attention to me. Even so, his smile is infectious, coaxing a small, albeit reluctant, one from me as well.

He's even more disarming in person than he was in our video interview. He steps forward and extends a large, strong hand down to me from his significant height. Slowly, I reach mine toward it. He grips it tightly, giving a friendly shake. Surely mine are clammy and gross, but he doesn't miss a beat. "I bet you never thought you'd be working for a centaur in a town full of inhuman inhabitants, but life is funny that way, and we're so glad you're here. You arrived at the perfect time. Meet Benoit Garde-Pierre, owner of Guardian Construction. His business has a lot of contracts with the town, so you'll be working together closely."

I peer anxiously at Ben-wah-something-something, barely comprehending his name, as I'm stunned to learn I'll have to spend time with him. My face falls at the thought.

While extending his hand, his gravelly voice simply states, "Call me Ben."

It's barely human. Much too large, with only three fingers and a thumb tipped with terrifying claws. Very slowly, I step forward and do the same, holding my breath in anticipation of getting sliced by them. Instead, he gracefully grasps my hand, holding it. His warm, textured skin feels... sort of nice. I exhale shakily, my body drawing breath again in relief. I blink up at his face, meeting his intense midnight blue eyes, a stunning complement to his skin color. "Ben," is the only response I can muster.

He briefly locks eyes with me before letting go, breaking the spell.

As I step backward away from Ben, I bump into someone and let out an involuntary screech. Embarrassed, I turn around with apologies on my lips, only to come face to chest with a brick wall of a man. I gawp at his unusual tawny skin and long dark green hair. His proportions are off, his arms too long and his facial features too wide and exaggerated.

He nods in acknowledgment and moves on as I babble incoherently, an apology never quite coalescing into real words.

As the strange man leaves, I survey the crowded space, fear too tightly wound within me to give more than a cursory glance at anyone. Turning back to the group, Clancy and Ada don't seem to be paying attention to my unease in such close quarters with monsters. But Ben does. His dark blue gaze studies me with keen awareness, a judgmental look affixed to his face. He doesn't interact with me further.

"Mayhap you will find comfort in knowing that monsters love caffeinated beverages as much as humans. This isn't the only coffee shop in town, but it's the busiest. You'll never have to do without in Monstera Bluff," Clancy informs me as he takes a swig from a cup on a table next to him.

It dawns on me quite suddenly. Oh my god. "Monstera Bluff. Is the name a joke?" I accuse, swinging my head to look at some of the bizarre and impossible beings near me.

"Yes, it is. And now you're in on it." Ada claps her hands in delight that I've figured it out.

"I thought maybe one of the founders was a little too into house plants," I wheeze as Ada and Clancy chuckle. Ben remains silent.

"You've got gumption, Cara. I'm so happy to see it. Ada told me she's brought you up to speed on what makes our community unique. Not that you could miss it in here," Clancy says as he gestures around the room. "You are still standing on your own two feet, so I call that a win, considering how new the world of monsters is to you. I'm sorry to have kept you in the dark about something so fundamental to this community, but everything else we talked about remains true, so I hope you won't hold it against me. Your talent will be a boon to this town. And your work in the human world will translate well here."

These compliments feel unearned, especially since I can't picture staying here. "Thank you, Clancy. I appreciate your confidence in me. I'm still in shock. Um, I'm sorry if I'm being rude. I need time to get used to everything." My stilted speech sounds unconvincing, even to my ears.

"Cara, you are doing fine. Just take deep breaths if you ever feel nervous," Ada tells me with a quick squeeze to my shoulder.

They're mollifying me with these compliments. Handling me with kid gloves. Ben continues to watch all of this, his face frozen in derision. No doubt he's angry at being forced to work with me. I have a feeling we'll never get past this bad first impression. I wish I hadn't met him today. Maybe if I had met a few other monsters before him, I wouldn't be so scared. I'm sure it's offensive. But what's done is done. It may not be Ada and Clancy's plan, but embarrassment is going to quash my fear before anything else.

"I will. Thank you for the advice," I tell my feet.

"That's why she's the first stop on the welcome wagon! C'mon, let's get you oriented with the town. I'm sure you still have a lot of questions. It's a good thing I have a lot of answers, and I could talk a gate off its hinges!" Clancy's jovial tone forces my eyes back upward to see him flashing me his brightest smile yet.

"Do you want anything before we leave, hon? I need some coffee," Ada offers as we walk toward the door.

"Honestly, I don't think I could handle it right now," I admit, unsure if my stomach would keep it down. Her expression turns apologetic.

As Ada heads to the counter, I overhear Ben discreetly arguing with Clancy, trying to extricate himself. "I have another meeting, so I'll be off. We can talk about certain developments tomorrow," he grits out through clenched teeth.

"The only meeting you have, my friend, is with me. So please be so kind as to *hold your horses* and we will talk about everything on your mind." Clancy smirks, unwilling to entertain Ben's protests. Ben rolls his eyes, clearly unhappy with Clancy's request. As Clancy walks away to join Ada, who's waiting for her drink, he begins talking to her animatedly about something. Ben and I are left alone, separately.

I chance a look at Ben when it seems like his attention is elsewhere. He stares out the windows with arms folded across his expansive chest and a pensive expression settled over his features. I'm able to watch him uninterrupted for a minute.

His skin looks like a stone surface—the word lithic pops into my brain, something I read long ago in grad school—the way the light catches on it. His face is rectangular, with sharp-edged cheekbones and a

Roman nose that makes him look severe. The ridge above his eyes is pronounced enough to give the impression of eyebrows, though it doesn't seem like he has any. Two horns at the top of his forehead curve backward on his bald head.

Though proportioned like a human man, there are a lot more inhuman features I hadn't noticed yet. His ears are pointy, and a long tail emerges from a slit in the back of his jeans. His bare feet have three clawed toes with another claw at his heel, raptor-like but more substantial, with the same coloring as his skin. He looks like an apex predator through and through.

The whole picture of him is jarring, beastly. He's scary to me, but not just because he's some kind of monster. He also clearly doesn't like me, and I guess I don't blame him. I've been timid, rude, openly staring. This is the worst-case scenario for my people-pleasing tendencies. Preoccupied in my own thoughts, he catches me inspecting him. It's just my luck. I blush, mortified, turning away quickly. Out of the corner of my eye, I sense that his gaze stays on me for a while, heavy and deliberate. Then he turns away blankly as if nothing interesting could be gleaned from the sight of me.

My face still feels warm as Ada links her free arm through mine, escorting me out of the coffee shop. She holds a paper cup in her other hand. "We pride ourselves on the downtown, all it has to offer for our community. I hope you find it equally delightful," she leans into me and gushes. I attempt an enthusiastic nod, though no memory surfaces of walking down the street on the way in here, erased by bone-deep, overwhelming panic.

Stepping outside, finally viewing it with seeing eyes, I realize that the downtown area is picturesque and surprisingly bustling. The main street, separated by a grassy tree-lined boulevard, looks to be several blocks long, comprised of two- and three-story buildings on each side. Most appear to be mixed-use, with businesses on the ground floors and apartments or offices above. It's immediately clear that many of the buildings' proportions are taller and larger than normal—like those houses I noticed earlier. I guess monsters like Clancy and Ben can't be ducking under every doorway they step through.

A surprising number of buildings boast stone facades, possibly limestone, as well as some wooden and brick structures tucked between them. The streets are full of activity, with pedestrians crowding the sidewalks. Every visible storefront is occupied. This town could be the poster child for downtown revitalization if it wasn't so... secret and full of monsters. It's a shame. Whatever strategies they've put into practice with their need to be self-reliant could probably be applied to other small- and medium-sized towns. The long-dormant academic in me would love to write a case study. Though their circumstances are so unique, there could still be lessons to learn from this thriving community.

Clancy leads us at a leisurely pace down the street, passing many businesses, cute shops, and restaurants. I wonder if he's given this impromptu tour before because he seems well-practiced and exceptionally knowledgeable. Everything he points out is punctuated by the clip-clopping of his hooves on the sidewalk.

When passersby get too close, I tense up, holding myself tighter, weaving down the sidewalk in an absurd dance to avoid them. I try not to cower, but it's difficult to control. My hands clutch at my heart at times. I make a point of lowering them, forcing them down toward my sides. As soon as I'm distracted, they're back in place near my chest.

Throughout all of this, I attempt as many questions as I can, though I'm still too distracted by the monsters around us to fully concentrate on Clancy's explanations of the workings of the town. I notice that most parking spaces are occupied even though it's a weekday afternoon. Most cities would install parking meters to take advantage of the activity.

"Does the town generate any revenue from parking?" My voice scrapes as we walk too close for comfort to a woman...with furry pointed ears and antlers. Ben extends a quick, friendly greeting to her as she passes, the first glimmer he's capable of anything but surliness.

Clancy begins to answer, "No, the town hasn't explored that option yet, though we have experienced an increase in traffic in the business district..." But he's interrupted as a tall, voluptuous, human-looking woman in a tight, low-cut dress rushes up to us. She flirtatiously brushes her thick, waist-length, jet-black hair behind her shoulder, pushing her chest out a little in the process. The brazenness is nearly comical, yet I don't dare make a peep.

"Clancy! I'm so pleased my application will be up for a vote at the council meeting next week. You have been so helpful. I'll have to think of something especially fitting to repay you." She simpers as she looks him up and down.

"Marieke, it was my pleasure to help. You don't owe me anything. I only want to see you succeed. It will be a benefit to the community. May Mother Earth grant you many blessings for your new business," he compliments her with a dashing smile, his charm ratcheting up a few notches higher, if possible.

"Stop by after the spa opens for any service on the house. I'll be sure to take extra good care of you, but you already know that. See you soon," she promises suggestively as she squeezes her hand up and down his forearm, batting the eyelashes framing her large brown almond-shaped eyes.

As the woman struts away, my jaw practically hits the pavement beneath me. I catch Ada rolling her eyes and shaking her head as Clancy looks back to check her out as she walks away. Ben barely seems to notice her, almost looking bored at the interruption. Not that she bothered to acknowledge the rest of us anyway.

"Clancy has quite the fan club. I'm sure you'll learn that after spending time with him. He's quite the popular male among the eligible females here," Ada teases. "Clancy, surely she didn't need your help applying for a business license?"

"My door is open to everyone, Ada," he reminds her. "Even to a flirtatious selkie in need of some encouragement to follow her dream."

Ada laughs. "That she is! Well, let's get a move on before he's propositioned by the next damsel in not-much-distress."

A shrill giggle erupts out of me. I didn't even know I was holding it in. It causes both Clancy and Ada to crack up, diffusing the tension of the ridiculous moment. Soon, we find our rhythm again, with Clancy continuing the grand tour. He points out how the business district extends down the intersecting side streets, so I'll have to work up the courage to explore them. Someday. Ada happens to mention her friend lives in the garden unit below the record shop we just passed by.

"So, are all the buildings here zoned for mixed use?" I contemplate as I look back and notice the stairs leading down to the semi-subterranean dwelling.

"We have land use consideration but no official zoning. It doesn't need to be defined, as we don't have any restrictions, except that light industrial operations cannot be operated in the downtown business district. Ben here can tell you that while his company's office is nearby, he doesn't store heavy equipment or materials there"—to which Ben curtly nods. "However, the town council does have to approve how land is newly developed, so they can determine if the proposed use is appropriate for its location," Clancy expounds helpfully.

Unfortunately, I barely have a chance to ask more questions. Clancy's attention is often waylaid as almost everyone we pass greets him or Ada. Ben inclines his head and offers a few hellos but is subdued compared to those two. I get some blatant stares, but most passersby give me a friendly smile or nod. Maybe they don't realize I'm a human. Or perhaps the presence of the mayor and a town council member prevents me from receiving overtly negative attention. It doesn't alleviate my nerves that I'll have to interact with monsters without them at some point.

Watching these monsters streaming through the busy sidewalk, I still don't know what most of them are. In my mind, I relate everyone to any obvious animal characteristics. Oh, there's that snake family again, and the youngest is having a temper tantrum. A bi-pedal wolf is getting into a pickup truck that needs a serious wash. A goat-legged man with a twitchy little tail is putting a sticky note on the door of a shop and locking it. A foxy lady—in the most literal fur-covered sense—struts down the sidewalk, giving Clancy a saucy, knowing smile and a wink. Clancy sounds... and looks... like a horse. Okay, he mentioned he's a centaur, but the point remains. I understand it's my mind trying to make sense of what I'm seeing, but I imagine that's actually quite mean of me? I'm worried it will be hard to see them as just people when my brain screams otherwise at me. This is going to be a "me" problem, and I need to get over it fast if I decide to make a life here.

Eventually, we reach town hall, facing the end of the street we just traversed, overlooking the downtown. If this is where I get to work, it'll be the least bitter pill to swallow in all of this. There's an inviting plaza in front with benches shaded by rows of live oaks. The building itself has a limestone exterior like many of the other downtown buildings, but it's built on a grander scale. Three towering stories feature ornate decoration like window surrounds and wide eaves at the flat roof line. I hope the interior is just as beautiful. Most importantly, there's an overfull bike rack near the building's entrance. Ah, it warms my heart to see it. And gives me the idea of asking Ada if she has a bike I could borrow. On clear, cooler days, it would be a great way to commute.

"Ladies, Ben and I must beg leave to go over some construction proposals. It was an absolute joy finally meeting you in person, Cara. Why don't you arrive here at nine tomorrow morning and we can get you settled into your office? There's a town council meeting next week, so there's a lot to go over before then," Clancy suggests, and I agree to the plan.

He shifts to Ada and, with a lowered voice, remarks, "Let's have a conversation tomorrow afternoon about that issue with Councilman Samuels." Even with so little context, the look that passes between them underscores its seriousness.

Ben furrows his brow in a way that I'd generously call brooding. "Why don't we get on with looking at those proposals, Clancy, and let them continue with their day." Ben then turns to us, "Ada, good to see you as always."

He regards me for a moment, finally settling on, "Cara." I guess he has nothing else to say to me.

We finally part ways, and Ada directs us toward the other side of the main street. Once we're out of earshot, she startles me with a loud bark of laughter. "Ben was in rare form today. He's always moody, but something must be stuck in his craw."

"I think it was me," I confide, unable to hold my tongue.

"Well, I don't see how that could be," she reasons. I feel wretched and it must show on my face because she grabs my arm, stopping us. "Listen, Cara, you are being far too hard on yourself. You learned a life-changing secret. Give yourself some grace and understanding that it will take time to accustom yourself. I'm not going to hide our community from you, but there will be an adjustment period, and it's okay if you're still uncomfortable," she sympathizes.

I nod my head, tears burning my eyes. They escape down my cheek before I can stop them. In a gentler tone, she soothes, "Don't let a grump like Ben make you cry. Don't let him make you feel like your best isn't good enough."

I know all too well I shouldn't cry over someone like him, but it's easier said than done.

Three Years Ago

My eyelids droop, and a headache from excessive caffeine has lodged itself firmly behind my eyes. It's another extraordinarily late night at the office, and Mark and I are working hard to finish a plan for transforming a busy four-lane intersection into a traffic circle. Victoria promised it to a client with way too little lead time.

"Mark, I think we need to keep this one simple. Victoria would rather us float that idea to the client later than hold up this proposal." I struggle to keep the weariness out of my voice. It's nearly eleven, and I'm beat. We need to wrap up for the night.

Mark sneers at me, "You think you're the only person who knows how to do this. Well guess what? I'm the engineer on this project, not you. And it's my name at the top of our letterhead. This isn't your decision to make."

I put my hands up in a pacifying gesture. "You're right. You have more say than I do in this project. I didn't mean to suggest otherwise. I'm just tired. I'll get another cup of coffee."

We continue working on a section outlining his idea to incorporate enhanced pavement marking patterns that he thought of earlier today, and it seems like we've moved past our disagreement. Another hour and a cup of coffee later, I'm nearly falling asleep at the conference room table.

I must be too quiet because Mark finally notices. "Is this too boring for you? You always do this. It's like that Winnetka project. You act like you're the only one who can come up with a good idea. And now you're doing it again."

His outburst jars me awake. I'm not even sure how to approach his anger. He's spinning in circles at this point. That Winnetka project was years ago. I don't know why he's hung up on it. It wasn't a big deal and certainly not my fault. The client wanted to keep the renovation of a train station within a very specific scope, and Mark wanted to incorporate a redesign of the features on its exterior, which was a much bigger and more expensive project. I let him know we should leave them out of the initial documentation, but they're great ideas to propose later as a future phase of development. He disagreed, so we kept it in, and we very nearly lost the contract. Victoria chewed my head off, too.

"Mark, let's focus on finishing this up. I'm awake, I swear." I try to calm him.

"You mean you don't want to hear about how you treat me like you're better at this than me. You can't even stay awake to help. Take a good look at yourself and figure out why you're like this." He's yelling now, and I acquiesce because I just want to make it home before the workday starts tomorrow.

"You're right. I'll do better, I promise. You have my full attention," I say as contritely as possible. He finally seems satisfied, and we get back to work. These blowups come out of nowhere, and I can't tell what sets him off. They only started recently. It must be the extra pressure his parents put on him. I understand that. I don't want to make it worse for him.

I get home at dawn without time to do anything but shower, put on a clean outfit, and eat some breakfast before I'm due at the office again. My stomach is sour and I feel like hell after the all-nighter. But I'm at my desk early enough to take a final pass at the proposal and email it to Victoria before she arrives. Mark takes a personal day, and I don't hear from him at all. But his words repeat in my mind. *You act like you know it all every time we work together. Take a good look at yourself and figure out why you're like this.* There has to be a better approach I can take. I don't want to miss out on any time with him, even if it's working on a stressful project.

As I suspect, the client accepts the proposal... mostly. They decline to include Mark's pavement marking idea. They say there isn't enough evidence that it will prevent potential traffic conflict to justify the extra cost. I will never mention it to him again.

Ada and I resume our stroll. We pass Midnight Mystic from the other side of the street, and I feel a pit of anxiety in my stomach just looking at it.

She must notice, acknowledging, "I'm sorry you had to take the long way around to get here. Clancy and I didn't want you to see any of this before I had a chance to talk to you. I'm sure you understand why. I live quite close to downtown, though you may not have realized that on your way in."

"How do you keep this place a secret?" I ask, still unbelieving.

"Lots of ways. Digitally, we have Whispered Folk who specialize in scrubbing any internet footprint. We restrict our connections with the human world, limiting it to interactions that gain goods and services to improve our quality of life. Physically, my coven maintains the protective wards made of powerful and sophisticated magick around the area."

I gasp, "Wards? Like barriers?"

She looks alarmed by my clamoring response. "Yes, it's attuned to only affect humans and Whispered Folk. You should have felt a little unsettled, worried, a sudden need to get home. I knew the moment you arrived and let you through, hopefully without effect. Those of us who work on it can feel when it's breached without an enchanted travel amulet to let them pass through without disturbance."

Despair brushes beneath the surface of my skin. "Yeah, I felt it. I thought I was having a mental breakdown."

She looks distraught, her hands wringing. "Oh, I'm sorry, hon. I never meant that to happen. You must be unusually sensitive to its magick because the first effect is mild. Initially creates a niggling feeling to get you to turn around. It grows much stronger the further you go, compelling you to leave until it becomes both mentally and physically painful to remain. We don't like that first line of defense to wallop someone too hard. Could be they're just lost or turned around. I swear I let you through right away. I'm so sorry that happened."

"I'll be alright," I mumble without conviction. The dredged-up past opened a gaping wound, slicing through any healing from those painful experiences. So much progress decimated through sheer bad luck.

CHAPTER 3
BEN

My latest project for the town has been a pain in my tail... to put it nicely. The town council voted to expand some roads and left the details to me and Clancy to sort out. They pat themselves on the back for a job well done. Check off a box on their to-do list and move on. But they are always loud and clear when they don't like something about the finished product. Well, a few of them, anyway. My business wouldn't be as successful without my contracts with the township, but they're all a mixed blessing. I'd rather manage my company without playing politics.

I'm checking out the progress on the construction site—currently a dusty clearing—and I'm not happy with it at all. "What am I not seeing?" I mutter to myself, pacing the edge of some rebar installed by the crew yesterday. I can feel it in my bones. Something isn't right with the plan Clancy and I drew up. The team is following it precisely, and I don't fault them, but I need to rethink my approach. I'm lost in thought when Clancy calls me.

"I've got big news, Ben, a surprise, really. I know we already had our business meetup this week, but this can't wait. You have to hear about it today. Meet me at one this afternoon at the usual spot," Clancy insists before I even have a chance to say hello.

"Ashes, Clancy, we just met yesterday. Can you tell me now over the phone? Or at the pub tonight?" I reason with him, but I can already tell he isn't going to back down.

"Absolutely not. This requires face time, as soon as possible. Plus, I'm the mayor, so you can't argue with me," he jokes.

"I don't think *anyone* would agree with you on that," I point out, knowing well he gets an earful every day.

Clancy's a bon vivant, but he's wickedly smart and a great mayor. He has something up his sleeve if he's called an emergency meeting with me at Midnight Mystic. The coffee shop caters to both the day and night crowds with all types of palates. My palate isn't so unusual. I always order black coffee. Both of us feel cooped up in our offices and like to escape when we can. It's a good meeting point.

When I arrive a while later at Midnight Mystic, he waves me over, looking unusually giddy, making me even more apprehensive about the news he's itching to reveal. He's already ordered me coffee and hands it to me like he's trying to butter me up. I know whatever is going on will annoy me.

"Is this a bribe?" I eye him suspiciously.

"Can't a male buy his best friend coffee? Ben, this is what you wear to meet me? I thought you were in the office today. You couldn't even wear a shirt?" he rebukes flippantly.

Glancing down at myself, I wonder what he's talking about. My work jeans aren't even dirty, and I don't always wear a shirt, even when I'm in the office. "I'm sorry. Is this a date, Clancy? You need to properly ask me out next time so I wear the correct attire. And no, you know construction work doesn't really get done in an office. I was out at the site when you called," I scoff.

"Well, it could be a date... if you play your cards right." He chuckles much too deviously. Oh fire and ashes, what is he going on about? I cross my arms, readying myself for his so-called news.

"You'll never guess what I did." Clancy lights up. He's practically vibrating in excitement. It must have been killing him to wait a couple hours to tell me. "I was able to rearrange my budget, so I hired a city planner." He regales me with the story about the human he interviewed and hired in secret. "And she's beautiful, Ben. I can't wait for you to meet her." He laughs at whatever imagined meeting plays out in his mind. I don't even want to know.

At some point during his long-winded speech about her qualifications and progressive approaches to urban design, I can't hold back any longer. "Fire burn it to ashes, Clancy! I get we could use some help, but bringing an unknown human here who doesn't know about us? You can't just do that... it's simply not done and for good reason! This was reckless, especially coming from you. What if she turns out to be a threat?" I try to keep my voice steady, but my anger seeps in.

"Tell me how you really feel." He snorts. Clancy has a knack for pushing my buttons in a way that only someone you've known for your entire life can. I pinch the bridge of my nose to keep my headache at bay.

I take a deep breath, regaining my composure. "You know as well as I do that we must remain guarded against the human world. Now more so than ever. Did you even think this through? You're opening us up to so much unnecessary risk. What about her friends and family? A mate? What will she tell them? What if they want to visit? It risks too much exposure. You should find someone else."

"Ben, you wound me." He sighs, melodramatically holding his heart. "Of course I thought of all of this! I'm not that irresponsible!" I grunt in disagreement, and he laughs me off. "But what I didn't get to tell you yet was that I found her through the Seer. It wasn't happenstance. Though I did have to Google her to figure out who she is and how to contact her. It's not like Darla's sight can exactly peek into her phone and give us her number. And let me tell you, she is the real deal. She's meant to be here, Ben. I know you don't want to believe it even though it's coming straight from the horse's mouth, but you can't deny Darla," he ribs, his face smug.

He's got me there. If Darla says the human is supposed to be here, then it's the truth. Her visions are often timely and paramount. When someone seeks her guidance—like Clancy says he did—there's no guarantee she can help. Not everything sparks her gift, so this human's arrival must be auspicious. But what Clancy doesn't want to admit is that her sight can be ambiguous, opaque, never revealing the full story. We can't know what twists and turns her vision will take us on if we heed it.

I let out an irritated grunt, feeling more petulant than I should. "Fine, you know I won't dispute Darla. But I still don't like it. We were doing just fine managing our projects."

Clancy shrugs off my disapproval. He pulls his phone out of the leather bag slung across his chest and types out a brief text. Apparently, his attention has wandered. I roll my eyes and wait for him to finish.

He looks up from his phone, beaming, though Mother Earth knows why. "You know that dog won't hunt. We've been struggling lately, and you can't deny it. This is for the best, Ben. We can't keep going the way we are. These public works projects take up too much of my time when I should be shaking hands and kissing babies," he quips, cracking up at his own joke.

"But in all seriousness, I mostly did this for you. You deserve to work with someone who can design these projects more skillfully so we can focus on more important things. Maybe she can take some of the heat from the town council too." He knows how much they can get under my skin.

"Do they know about this human?" I ask, dreading the answer.

He has the courtesy to look sheepish. "Uh, no, except for Ada. But this is part of my budget, so I don't need their approval. I only told Ada before you because she would need a place to live. Ada offered her carriage house apartment."

The headache has now lodged itself painfully behind my eyes. "Alright, I'm mostly upset that you didn't bother to include me in this plan until it was over and done with. I'd like to have some say in your big ideas that upend my work." I rub my eyes to try to relieve the pressure. It's not working.

"Town council is going to have a field day with this." There's a weariness in my voice I can't hide. I don't want to fight with Clancy. He's confident in his actions, which makes him a great leader. But sometimes, being part of the blowback of these unilateral decisions, especially as his closest friend, stings more than it should.

Clancy claps me on the shoulder. "Ben, good buddy, you were at the front of my mind during all of this. Just trust me."

I shake my head, not believing a word. "Fine, Clancy, we'll see how this goes. When does she start?"

He checks his phone again. "Oh, any minute now," he tells me, grinning like the Cheshire Cat.

The bell on the coffee shop door jingles as it opens, making me glance over. A human-looking female drifts inside, looking completely lost, capturing my attention immediately. She's illuminated from behind by the afternoon sunlight streaming through the doorway. A glowing goddess—haloed, bright, and beautiful—her ripe, curvaceous form outlined beneath her white dress begs to be worshiped. Dark wavy hair falls past her shoulders. Her alabaster skin shines in the light. Time stills while I watch her stunning form. My cock stirs at just the sight of her, proof of my hot-blooded, unexpected attraction.

It seems time has stopped for her as well, but not because of me. Her generous, rosy mouth has fallen open, her doe eyes wide on her heart-shaped face, like she's surprised to be here. Her eyes sharpen on Clancy, of course. Many females have this reaction to his handsome face. The attention he receives has never bothered me much before. But something is different about this female. Jealousy jabs me hard in the ribs, and I growl in frustration at myself.

I'm mired in this thought for only an instant when I see Ada Mayweather behind her, guiding her forward. Ah, so the goddess is our new planner. Clancy waves them over. He must be delighted. This timing couldn't be more perfect for his scheming. I'm still watching her when she finally notices me. She blanches in fear, barely able to look in my direction. Mayhap I don't always look friendly, but I am not a frightening male. Her reaction seems excessive.

Oh. Of course. Clancy hid the truth from her. She's shell-shocked. I've never encountered a human so very new to learning about our existence, so I'm not sure how it usually goes. But this does not seem right. Her fear is genuine. I'm the monster that goes bump in the night in her eyes. Fire and ashes, it's a terrible idea to bring her to a crowded place right now. Clancy and Ada are doing her a disservice, and it angers me I've been dragged into it.

"Clancy, our newest resident has arrived!" Ada presents her to us after nudging the poor female as close to us as she's willing to go. She's about to jump out of her skin.

"Cara Bishop! Mother Earth in all her glory, I'm so happy to finally meet you in person!" Clancy booms, laying on his signature charm and convincing her to shake his hand. "I bet you never thought you'd be working for a centaur in a town full of inhuman inhabitants, but life is funny that way, and we're so glad you're here. You came by at the perfect time. Meet Benoit Garde-Pierre, owner of Guardian Construction. His business does a lot of work for the town, so you'll be working together closely."

I finally catch her mesmerizing eyes and hold them. Cara Bishop. Her name didn't stick with me earlier. I search the hazel depths for anything telling me who she is, then extend my hand in greeting. A refusal would gut me, though I would try not to hold it against her. She stares uncertainly at it for too long, but to my surprise, connects our hands, her silky skin on mine exquisite.

"Call me Ben," is all I can manage, my throat suddenly dry. Her eyes return to mine, and I don't want to let go of her.

"Ben," she greets in a soft, hesitant voice. I need to give her the gentle introduction that Clancy and Ada have not afforded her, so I force myself to release her hand and stay quiet during their conversation. I don't want to overwhelm her any further.

However, my intentions don't change that we're in the middle of a community hub. Midnight Mystic could be a crash course on Whispered Folk; everyone comes here. Naturally, Wyck bumps into her... he needs to pay better attention to where the ashes he's going. I suppress a snarl as I watch her flail and fluster, obviously alarmed by him. This immersive introduction to Monstera Bluff is not the flawless plan Clancy believes it to be, treating this macabre meet and greet like it isn't the most shocking experience of her life.

We finally make to leave the coffee shop. I can't stomach witnessing her fear any longer, so I pull Clancy aside and try to make up a plausible excuse. "I have another meeting, so I'll be off. We can talk about certain developments tomorrow," I snap at him, not hiding my frustration.

"The only meeting you have, my friend, is with me. So please be so kind as to *hold your horses,* and we will talk about everything on your mind," Clancy brushes me off, with a signature pun no less, smug in his delusion that my presence is both required and necessary.

He makes his grand plans with an iron will. A benevolent puppet master of those around him. And this scenario seems to be playing out to his exact design. He'll never let me leave until it suits him. So I give in, despite my unabated reservations. Clancy is lucky that I trust him because he has never acted so foolhardy. I'm rattled by the potential consequences... and by the enchanting human he brought into this mess.

Gazing out the window, woolgathering about Cara, I feel her eyes on me. I'll indulge her curiosity for a bit before I let on that she's caught. Clancy and Ada have unwisely left her unattended, but she remains in my peripheral vision. If anyone gets too close, they'll quickly learn their intrusion is unwelcome. I must be an oddity to her, one she may never feel comfortable with. Between that and my undeniable pull to her, it will be a strained working relationship.

Eventually, her candid perusal feels too weighty against my soul, so I turn to her. She flushes crimson as she abruptly turns away, pretending to study some artwork on the wall beside her. Well, two can play that game. Taking my time to drink her in, I realize I may never have this chance again. Cara would be breathtaking if she weren't so awash with fear. But if she possesses a fraction of the talent Clancy claims, why would she accept a job here? What happened to her that made her agree to move to a tiny town she knew nothing about on short notice? She's less outright panicked than when she first arrived, but her complexion looks haunted. She isn't here in Monstera Bluff by choice.

Her presence will not go unnoticed. Certain members of the town council will hit the roof when they find out a human was hired and brought here under their noses. It'll be a bumpy ride for a spell, and I'm not looking forward to it. She's innocent, unaware of what is to come. I school my face of any reaction, but guilt eats at me so I return to looking out the windows. I can't help but wonder what her presence will mean for me, my life, and my work. Clancy's mischief has thrown a wrench into all of it.

Finally, Clancy and Ada rejoin us so we can leave. Walking away from the coffee shop allows Cara to relax a little. Her spine extends straighter. Her eyes shine brighter. But I still make a point to give her space, never walking next to her. As Clancy engages with her about the town, she perks up considerably.

"Did the town choose angled parking to accommodate higher density?" she observes. "Were other orientations considered?"

"The spaces were first painted only a decade or so ago, and this seemed to be easiest for drivers. I wasn't in office then, but I believe the town council pushed for it since townsfolk parked so haphazardly. There was an influx of automobile purchases around then since it became easier to use the internet to source them," Clancy explains.

She's barely able to ask a question about parking revenue before Hurricane Marieke—as I like to call her—approaches. She only has eyes for Clancy, totally ignoring anyone else when he's around. I've met few females as persistent for Clancy's affection as her, even though she knows they'll never be mates. She doesn't truly like *him* all that much— just his status and what it can do for her. They both know it. But Clancy loves female attention—craves it, even from someone as annoying as her. It takes all my willpower not to roll my eyes before she finally leaves. Luckily, Cara seems to have found the interaction comical.

Her personality emerges as we walk, and I'm glad to see it. It's not my place to add to their conversation. But I do make sure no one gets too close to Cara as I stay ahead of her. It seems like the whole town has chosen this moment to walk down the street. Ada snickers as I scowl at a group of teenage brownies known to be troublemakers, daring them to even breathe in her direction. I don't want her hiding again because someone has gone out of their way to scare her.

It takes an age, but we finally cross to the plaza in front of town hall. Cara's soft gasp as she admires the building is sweet-sounding. Her appreciation of its beauty satisfies me. It's one of the first construction projects undertaken by my forefathers, leading them to found the construction company I now operate. I hope she'll find joy working in such a beautiful building.

I lock eyes with Clancy, making sure I have his attention. "Why don't we get on with looking at those proposals, Clancy, and let them be on their way," I press. An understanding passes between us as he nods.

I turn to Ada. She should take better care of Cara the rest of the day. I can't say that right now, but I try to infuse that meaning in the look I give her as I say, "Ada, good to see you again."

And then, finally, I look into Cara's wide eyes. Uneasiness reflects back at me, so I keep it brief. "Cara." A flash of distress crosses her face. Clancy waves, and we turn our separate ways.

When we enter the building, Clancy smacks my arm. "What's with you, Ben? You couldn't even be civil to her? That was not what I'd call playing your cards right, buddy."

I stand incredulous. "Civil? You mean participate in that charade by pretending she wasn't scared out of her mind? Especially at Mystic? Fire and ashes, something's going on with you. Don't turn this on me!"

He holds up his hands in a pacifying gesture. "Fine. Fine, you're right. But you could have said more than two words to her. You're so damned prickly sometimes." He runs a hand through his hair, an anxious habit.

He leans in and fiercely whispers, "There's something I couldn't tell you earlier about the Seer's words. It must stay between us. Let's get to my office first."

We walk silently down the hall, and Clancy shuts his office door behind us. I sit facing his desk as he stands behind it. He rubs his hands together, looking concerned. "Before you shred me with your claws, I know we overwhelmed her, and it was on purpose. Ada and I agreed this was the best approach. I hoped she'd embrace that human expression 'fake it till you make it,' and I'd say she did a fine job, considering."

"That's a *horse shit* explanation. She can't turn off her survival instinct," I interject.

"Well, she must. Because Cara needs to accept it quickly." Clancy's voice sobers.

I growl in frustration. "What does this have to do with the Seer?"

"I approached Darla as soon as I reckoned I could hire someone. They had to be the perfect candidate to hire under the nose of the town council. Still, I didn't have high hopes Darla's gift would be able to help me. The question seemed too insignificant. I asked her, 'Who should I bring here as the city planner?' I couldn't believe it triggered a vision—maybe it was how I phrased it? I'll never know. She told me to seek out Cara Bishop, formerly of Chicago. 'She needs to find her place quickly, or there will be no place for her at all.' That last part is exactly how she worded it," Clancy explains, as serious as I've ever heard him.

I'm stunned, reflecting on the weight of the Seer's words. "That sounds ominous."

Clancy nods. "My thoughts exactly. So I couldn't risk coddling her too much." We look at each other with the somber conclusion there's something more at stake than we currently understand.

"Do we tell her?" I float, unsure of how to proceed.

"Absolutely not." Clancy's hand slices through the air like he's cutting off my line of thought. "It may mean nothing bad, but there's no way to know at this point."

This information validates the approach I took with Cara today. I'll shield her from anything or anyone who would cause her fear—including me. I feel resolute in this decision. But Clancy and I aren't done here. There's the matter of Councilman Samuels and his merry band of naysayers, the perennial thorn in Clancy's side. "So what will you do about the council when they discover your dirty little secret?"

Clancy barks a laugh. "Just leave that to me. Cara will swoop in here and take charge. She'll justify her hire through her own words and deeds better than I could. But anyone who says otherwise will have to go through me. I'll handle them, especially at Tuesday's meeting."

I appreciate his protectiveness toward her. I'd expect nothing less, but it's good to hear after everything that's transpired today. It's Wednesday. We have just under a week until all hell breaks loose—on the official minutes, no less.

Even while Clancy and I discuss other town business, all conversation leads back to Cara. "With your blessing, I'm putting her on Howling Road. I don't feel good about it, now that it's started. I won't move ahead on any incomplete projects she'll want a say in," I inform Clancy, having no doubt he'll agree with me.

As soon as Clancy told me about her, I made the decision to halt work until Cara figures out the missing puzzle piece. Even though I wasn't aware of his plan to hire her, thinking back on our planning sessions, it's obvious he pulled himself back on this project. At the time, I thought he was too wrapped up in other issues to give it due deliberation, so I finalized too many aspects of this project without him. It's probably why it feels inadequate for the town's needs.

Clancy's face splits into a toothy, knowing grin. Ah, this is another exactly what he wanted to happen. The male has an uncanny ability to orchestrate people's lives. He could almost give our dear Seer a run for her money.

"Great idea," he lauds, knowing full well I see his handiwork. "My blessing is no longer needed. This is Cara's realm now, and I consider our priorities aligned. Come by tomorrow just before lunch. I'll be sure to include the current plan with her orientation materials so she'll be ready to meet with you. You'll have the whole afternoon to put your heads together. I think you'll make quite the team." He waggles his burnished gold eyebrows and chuckles to himself. I shake my head and refuse to dignify his innuendo with a response.

"It's time we wrap up. I should head over to the site and let the crew know to shut it down for now." I stand up to leave, having had my fill of his scheming today. "Until tomorrow, Clancy." I glance over my shoulder as I open his office door. He looks pleased as punch with himself.

He calls out to my back, "Tomorrow's a new day and a new beginning with our clever city planner. And wear a damn shirt this time!" I hear his self-satisfied chortling as I walk down the hall.

Clancy can be a test sometimes. I've long endured his penchant for meddling. Since we came of age, he's pushed me at females. When he drags me to social gatherings, he calls me his "official wingman." Such human nonsense. The joke cracks him up to this day. Well, he certainly doesn't need my help. He casually dates many females, with even more throwing themselves at him. To his credit, he's been subtler about it since he took office as mayor.

Some females catch my eye, though I would never consider someone he's been with—eliminating them as a possibility in my mind—making my pool of potential mates here low. His preoccupation with setting up me and Cara is puzzling. Her situation is complicated. Fear is no foundation for romance, and he admits he saw her reaction, too. Besides, her easy manner with Clancy tells me her interest would lie elsewhere, with someone more pleasing to the human eye. I can't compete with that.

Exiting the building, a fortifying breath of fresh air helps clear my mind. Mother Earth knows I'd love nothing more than to take flight and leave behind the stress of the day. Everything in life feels lighter when soaring through the air. But today's events have me anchored to the ground. I should drive to the construction site since carrying tools isn't practical while airborne. My truck, parked near the Mystic, is in front of me before I know it, distracted by the day's events replaying in my mind —Cara in the lead role. I head over to let the crew know what's going on and that they'll be reassigned by tomorrow. There's no shortage of work since we're the only major construction company in town. I'd love to move on to the next job as well, but I have to face this one, and Cara, head on tomorrow.

CHAPTER 4

CARA

"Would you like to visit my shop?" Ada suggests after she hands me a tissue to wipe my eyes.

The answer is obvious. "Of course!"

"It's just on the next block. Normally, I'd be there today, but I had a very good reason to take a day off," she explains with a wink.

Maybe it will lift me out of my dark mood. If she's a witch, will she have *magickal* items there? The possibility makes this strange new world of monstrous creatures seem more fun than frightening... almost.

A wooden sign hangs above her shop with the name "Mayweather Potions and Panacea." We step inside the long, narrow shop, and it's a feast for the senses. It smells pleasantly herbal. A small sitting area is arranged next to a large front window. Antique wooden shelves overflowing with jars and other vessels full of ingredients line the walls, nearly reaching the overly tall ceiling. A rolling ladder attaches to a track above the shelves. The walls and ceiling are painted a deep eggplant color. Natural light spills in from the large windows at the storefront. Six hanging lanterns that look Middle Eastern in origin illuminate the rest of the store in golden hues.

A long wooden counter runs down one side of the store. Another shorter one in the back displays tools resembling a chemistry set. Maybe she makes magickal potions there. A young woman with caramel skin and thick dark hair pulled back in a high ponytail stands behind the side counter. She greets us warmly.

"Sunny, thanks for covering for me. This is Cara. She just moved here today and will be working for the township. Cara, this is Sunny, my shop assistant and potions apprentice." Ada acquaints us before she ushers me to the sitting area. As we sit, I realize I'm exhausted, but I won't waste this opportunity to talk to Ada alone. If I thought I had a lot of questions before, they've increased a hundred-fold.

"What do you actually sell here? I thought you meant you ran a pharmacy before," I delve in, needing some answers for any peace of mind.

"Mostly potions, alchemical ingredients, amulets, enchanted items, and the like. We do sell a little of everything, that was true," she clarifies. My mind boggles at all that would entail.

"If I wanted to buy something, what would you suggest?" I ask, trying to understand what magick can do.

"I'll walk you through the shop one of these days to get the full picture. Not that you would need any of it, but you could permanently change your hair color. Grow it as long as you want. Our skincare can smooth wrinkles. Add freckles or remove them. A glamor could change one of your features, like your eye color, or even your entire face or body. But not everything we sell is about changing one's appearance. You could buy an enchantment to shrink an object and then return it to its original size when needed—or vice versa. So popular when moving houses. We have permanent and temporary magickal adhesives. Enchantments that attract dust and dirt particles in your home. Some substances like stone, metal, and wood can be strengthened or even changed to something else with a coat of the right potion. An amulet can warm or cool the air around you, no matter the weather. Those are very popular in the summer," she explains with a laugh.

It dawns on me that I'm sitting in a shop full of wonders.

"What type of magick can you do? Do you use wands or something to make magick?" Witches in stories always seem to have wands.

"No wands or brooms or any nonsense like that." She laughs. "We use spells and incantations that are generally spoken or involve extreme mental focus and may require certain ingredients or elements to be present. My strengths are in transfiguration magic, so changing the appearance and structure of objects and substances, sometimes making them more potent. My magick favors certain elementals, specifically air and earth, altering them at a molecular level, transforming them from the inside out."

An antique metal bowl sits on the coffee table between us. Ada points to it so I watch as she recites, "What's old is now new, let its shine show through." Within a few seconds, all signs of tarnish and age peel off and vanish into thin air. The bowl is now so shiny I can see my reflection in it. My jaw drops. It's so surreal. I can scarcely believe I saw her do that, even something so simple.

"I've always loved a weathered look. Perfect is overrated," Ada declares, before reversing it with a few more words. "Show your age in full, once bright now turns dull." It ages a hundred years again before my eyes, the oxidation spreading across its surface like a liquid before drying. "I've been told vinegar does the same thing, but I find magick to be a little easier."

"Unbelievable!" I marvel. "Can you still do magick if you can't speak for some reason? Like if you lose your voice?"

"Certainly, though mayhap not as powerfully if someone is used to speaking a spell or incantation, but the words are mostly a guide or an intention to focus our magick. They are also very personal. So, for instance, if Sunny wants to do the same thing, she'd speak her own version of it because her magick is different than mine. Part of harnessing our magick as witches is learning the words and phrases that focus it best. We can still think through these spells, use our inner voice, if our mind is cleared and full concentration is possible. It takes practice, though! Our minds are just as busy and cluttered as yours," she acknowledges.

"Wow, I still can't believe magick is real," I utter, as I turn my attention back to the shop, taking in every detail. "You must be very busy if you have this shop, sit on the town council, and welcome newcomers like me."

"Yes, idle hands as they say..." My eyebrows raise in alarm. "I'm kidding! But yes, I'm busy as a bee. I like it when my days are full." Her response sounds rote, like she must say it all the time. My mind wanders to her mention of an ex-husband earlier. I wonder how he fits into all of this. But it's not my business. She'll tell me more if she wants to.

"I was considering how I would explain Monstera Bluff to you, and maybe I should start from the beginning. How does that sound?" My wandering mind snaps back to attention at her words.

I waste no time in my response. "Absolutely. Maybe that will answer some questions I was about to ask."

She takes a deep breath, and I can tell I'm in for quite the tale. "My ancestors, the Mayweathers, settled early in the colony of Georgia when it was still the property of the British crown. As you may be able to tell, witches could hide in plain sight easily enough, so we lived in human communities across the colonies for many generations. But it was a necessity for witches and their covens to remain discreet. You may remember some infamous trials from your history classes... Those humans, mostly female, were innocents caught up in religious fervor."

"Did the witches know what was happening to these women?" I gasp.

"They knew about it, yes, but there wasn't much they could do unless they could help an accused human flee," she explains, looking grim. "From what I've read, my ancestors, as well as other covens, were wracked with guilt. But they were also scared for their own well-being. Don't make the mistake, though, of thinking established religions are always anti-magick. They look the other way when it suits them. But if they get the slightest whiff of magick that isn't directly benefiting them, they can turn vindictive. It taught my ancestors to be cautious to safeguard not only themselves, but also others who may be caught in the crossfire."

"Why does that not surprise me?" I roll my eyes. "But how did you end up here in coastal Georgia?"

"This large swath of land the town sits on was purchased by my ancestors in the late eighteenth century. It had been a farm at some point. But my family's coven had no use or desire for something of that scale, so they established their own small settlement here with only subsistence farming, fishing, and an orchard. They let the rest of the land go wild. Goods were traded with nearby human settlements during this time. For a while, that was the extent of their regular interaction with the human world. It turned out to be a smart move on their part because not many humans were familiar with the land after so many generations had passed, so it's been easy for them to overlook, even now. I can't say for certain if it was on purpose, knowing they would eventually open their settlement to other Whispered Folk, but nevertheless, that's what happened. And they were able to do it without much difficulty." She shrugs like it was no big deal.

"Did the witches at the time actually bring monsters here?" I ask, baffled at how monsters could be snuck across an ocean.

"My family maintained ties with witches in England, where they hailed from. Through them, we also had contact with communities of Whispered Folk across Europe, Africa, and other parts of the world. They acted as middlemen, spreading the word about us. Many Whispered Folk needed a place to go as the human population exploded, war and conflict spread, and the Industrial Revolution changed and polluted the landscape. That said, we obviously couldn't take everyone, even if Whispered Folk populations are minuscule compared to humans. But we offered to provide sanctuary for families or clans of various Whispered Folk who needed safety. Many declined, deciding to stay where they were despite hardship. Some went elsewhere in this wide-open countryside to establish their own communities. But many accepted our offer, and the town of Monstera Bluff was established," Ada pauses, letting her history lesson sink in.

Her story drives my curiosity, but my mind is racing, struggling to accept everything I'm learning. Monsters are real and live among us! There's magick *for sale* a few feet away from me! My perception of the world has been turned on its head today. There's an alternate history no one even knows about. I have so many questions that they muddle together, making it hard to parse through and know where to begin. But her family seems central to this place, at the very least. And I need to learn everything I can about the town. "Your family has done so much. You have every right to be proud of them. Is all your work meant to keep up the family legacy?" I ask earnestly, gesturing around the shop.

Ada smiles softly, and her attention drifts for an instant. "Yes, but it's not the burden it may seem. My house, the shop, and staying active in the community are enmeshed in the fabric of my being as a Mayweather. I could no more leave one than tear out a piece of my soul. I rejoice in it. It keeps me tied to this place and to past generations of my family."

"Are there other Mayweathers here?" I wonder aloud.

"No, I'm the only one left in Monstera Bluff." She sighs. "We were once a large family with many branches, but that changed in more recent generations. Some moved away decades ago. Some died young or without heirs. Life was hard in past centuries, even for witches. I was my parents' only child. And they passed away unexpectedly some time ago."

"I'm so sorry about your parents, Ada," I say sorrowfully. "Do you have any family you're close with?"

"Thank you. I do have aunts, uncles, and cousins, but they have never lived here and don't have the connection to the community I do. So now the Mayweather lineage in Monstera Bluff continues in me," she explains, her tone melancholy.

"Are there other founding families that still live here? Did Clancy's family move here early on?" I ponder.

She chuckles. "Is it that obvious? He and I have that in common—we often feel the weight of this community on our shoulders. It's sort of a Monstera Bluff tradition that an Evermane or a Mayweather takes office as mayor. Though I've never felt the calling for it, the town council is more than enough for me. Clancy comes from a large family. The Evermanes and other centaur clans were among the first Whispered Folk to move to North America from the British Isles. They chartered ships to travel here, if you can believe it. Our ancestors had known each other for a very long time before that."

"Centaurs on ships? How is that possible?" I gasp in disbelief.

"Horses were brought over on ships by the Spanish. I gather it wouldn't be dissimilar. If Clancy were here, he'd make a joke about not having sea legs." She cracks herself up at the thought.

I giggle. I can almost imagine him saying something like that too. "Clancy is a bit of a character. How long has he been the mayor?"

"Clancy's father was the longtime mayor but retired a few years back. Clancy assumed the mantle and ran for office. He just started his second term earlier this year."

I lean forward in my chair. "He seems like a natural-born politician. If it weren't for, well, his being a centaur, he'd be a political darling in the... human world. When I first talked to him in our interview, I couldn't help but think he'd have voters wrapped around his little finger." I smile that I had puzzled out his character so quickly.

She claps her hands in delight. "That he does! Clancy has verve and energy that's authentic. It's a big reason why the townsfolk are enamored with him. But don't let that sunny disposition fool you. He's a strategist at heart. Every decision he makes has a motive and moves toward a bigger plan. He's wily and intelligent, though some only see his outward persona as the charming golden boy and don't give him his due credit. You'll see he has a few adversaries on town council." She shakes her head in annoyance.

"What about Ben... Benoit? And his family? What is he?" I attempt nonchalance, but Ada sees through it.

"Oh, Ben. He was being colder than a well digger's butt in January," she jokes—reminding me of *colder than a witch's tit*, making me wonder what *that's* about—"Pay him no mind. He can be reserved, but it comes off as unfriendly at times. He should have tried harder, knowing how new you are to town. The Garde-Pierre clan and other gargoyles came from France and originally settled in what was then the Louisiana Territory. His branch of the family moved here several generations ago."

"Ben's a gargoyle? I thought he was a demon!" I croak.

Ada practically shrieks in laughter and smacks the arm of her chair. "Well, he certainly earned that impression, didn't he?"

Before I lose my nerve, I probe, "Was it rude of me to ask what he is? What monsters Whispered Folk are? I really don't know much about them other than what's in movies and folklore."

She smiles at my awkwardness. "I appreciate this question more than you know. You want to be sensitive about it when you talk about Whispered Folk. Well, there are many, many kinds of Whispered Folk, so it will take a while to get up to speed. As to whether it's rude—like any personal question, the answer is both yes and no. I think it depends on how you approach it. For the most part, everyone will be happy to talk about themselves. But you can always ask me or Clancy anything you might be uncomfortable asking someone directly. We know you're very new to this, and we'll be happy to help you."

I hum in acknowledgment. "It's just... I bumped into a guy with green hair at the coffee shop. What was he?"

"Oh, that's Wyck. Nice young male, but very shy. Quite the tech whiz. He's a troll," she offers.

"Like from under a bridge?" I blurt out.

She slaps her knee and howls in laughter. "They don't all live under bridges... well, not anymore. Maybe that's a good example of what you shouldn't say when you meet someone!" My embarrassment must show, so she tries to contain herself. "I'm just larking around! Goodness gracious, you're easy to tease!"

I'm not sure if she's teasing about my assumption or if they do, in fact, live under bridges. I'm too self-conscious to ask.

Ada's eyes sparkle in mirth. I'm not trying to be funny, but apparently, my naivete is entertaining her. "I have another silly question," I venture to ask, not knowing when to quit. "Your eyes are stunning. They look violet, like Elizabeth Taylor's eyes supposedly were. Was she a witch, too?"

This sends her over the edge. "Well, I declare you are a true delight, hon. Now, she's no Mayweather, but she was certainly bewitching!" Ada gives a conspiratorial wink and dissolves into a fit of giggles, and I can't help but follow suit.

We chat lightheartedly for a while longer. Customers flit in and out, but Ada still gives me her undivided attention as Sunny helps them. I haven't been observing them too closely, but there are some I simply can't ignore. One customer wanders in for a potion, an extraordinarily short, blonde-bearded man... and instantly, I know in my heart of hearts that he's a gnome. He has to be. I hope his name is David. I watch as he leaves. "Was that a gnome? They're really *real*?" Ada nods and laughs at my fervor.

Soon after, a rust-red, bare-chested, hairy giant with oversized hands and feet comes in, ducking under the already tall doorway. He and Sunny converse, and she hands him a necklace, which he slips over his head. He immediately shimmers out of existence, and in his stead, a tall but human-height man stands in his place. I'm caught off guard by the sight, and I nearly screech, hands flying to my mouth just in time to contain the noise.

Ada looks at him and shrugs. "He's an ogre, one of the larger species of Whispered Folk. Not too many around these days, though a few live on the outskirts of town. He's an example of someone who couldn't enter the human world without significant magickal assistance. Even with the disguise amulet, it's hard to pull off. The enchantment is uncomfortable, like a too-tight second skin, I've been told, so usually they're only worn when necessary and for a short time," she explains so offhandedly as if it isn't breathtakingly, earth-shatteringly amazing.

Her simplified explanations help me reconcile with this strange new world around me. It also doesn't hurt that her store has a very comfortable, welcoming vibe. Maybe that's magick, too. Nevertheless, I could spend the rest of the day here. My thoughts occasionally drift back to Ben, though, and I really wish they wouldn't. Am I so hung up because he doesn't like me? Because he makes me nervous, representing an otherness I'm still coming to terms with? Probably a bit of both.

At the next opening in our conversation, I interject, "Are Clancy and Ben friends? They seem close even though they seem like very different... people." I end my question kind of lamely, not wanting to offend. Ada politely ignores that part of it.

"Absolutely, those two are thick as thieves, have been since they were kids, though you wouldn't expect it based on their personalities. But they are very similar in the ways that count. Both are very loyal to their friends, family, and the community. They're completely dependable and honest. And both have good hearts, though *one* of them is very good at hiding it. He keeps most everyone at arm's length. I'm not sure he shows many people other than Clancy and his family his true self. I wish he'd let the rest of us in on what's going on inside that bald noggin a little more often," she confesses with genuine affection. Her eyes dart to the window behind us. "Well, speak of the proverbial devil... or should I say demon?"

My eyes follow as Ben walks by without seeing us. He certainly cuts an imposing figure striding down the sidewalk.

Like a sign I'm becoming inured to magick and monsters, my stomach growls ferociously like a hungry beast, much to my utter humiliation. I immediately spread my hands across my midsection, as if that could tame it and keep the offensive sound inside.

"Well, it looks as if I've been remiss in my hostess duties again. That sounds like quite an appetite. Why don't we grab a bite to eat? I can finally show off the culinary delights this charming little town has to offer."

We step outside her shop, and she leads me to an already bustling restaurant across the street. "The Roaring Wood is probably our most popular restaurant if you don't count Midnight Mystic. It's farm-to-table, supported by Taurus Farm just outside of town, as well as some... Whispered Folk-friendly farmers in the region," she explains.

Ada checks her phone. "It's a little early, but I nearly qualify for the 'blue hair special,' so let's head inside," she suggests with a self-depre-cating grin.

"No, Ada! That can't be true!" I squawk in protest, dismayed she believes herself to be practically elderly.

Mirth dances in her eyes. "Oh, it's truer than you believe! My days as a vivacious young witchling on the prowl are long behind me. And there's nothing wrong with that! Being an old maid suits me just fine."

She's so disarming it makes me chuckle. "Well, Ada, you are what the young people would call 'adulting goals.'"

She throws her head back in laughter. "Well, if the young people like you have spoken thus, I will accept it."

I hear the buzz of activity inside the restaurant before I can see it. Stepping inside the threshold is like entering a friendly forest picnic. The tables are carved from giant logs with a pedestal base in the center, and the round top is the cross-section of the trunk, showing all the rings. Sturdy, elegant wicker chairs with colorful cushions provide a cozy complement to the tables. Living ivy and branches are woven in patterns along the ceiling, with fairy lights shining through like sunlight from above. The neutral wood elements are balanced by colorful cushions, linens, and tableware, so every-thing still feels bright and whimsical. It would be a cute place for brunch or a romantic date spot late at night. Despite the odd hour, the place is packed.

The hostess, whose skin has a bluish hue and ears resemble fish fins, greets me and Ada. She stares a little too long at me, probably trying to figure out who and what I am. *Hello, my name is Cara. I'm your new human neighbor.* I should put a sticker on and save everyone the trouble. We sit at a table in a front window where bright natural light illuminates the room. Good for people watching, if that's what you're into, but it only makes me feel exposed. I clam up, subtly trying to breathe slowly through my nose and out my mouth. Ada notices but, thankfully, doesn't comment.

With trembling hands, I pick up the menu and try to get lost in it to forget about my surroundings. Every item on it sounds seasonal and fresh. My eyes bug out at the prices... not because of how much they are but because of how little, like something out of a bygone era.

"This food would be more than triple the price in Chicago or Atlanta... or anywhere!" I exclaim.

"Cara, you're not in Chicago anymore..." She snorts. "Massive profit may not be as important here as it is in the human world. A rising tide lifts all boats. And in more practical terms, the overhead expenses are undoubtedly much less, so it's easier to make a living running a restaurant without price gouging."

That seems plausible, though a place as beautiful as this wouldn't be cheap to create and maintain.

"You know, we have a weekly farmer's market where you can buy a lot of the same produce used here. We'll go sometime. It's on Monday evenings, so both the day and night crowd can attend," Ada casually mentions, like that last part wouldn't set off warning bells.

"Oh, um, the night crowd?" I squeak, trying to remain composed.

"Oh yes, there are nocturnal Whispered Folk who start their days when the sun sets. They are all perfectly harmless like everyone else around you. Now that it's getting dark earlier, you'll see them more often. It's why a lot of businesses are open twenty-four hours or have a set of daytime and nighttime hours. Nothing to be concerned about," she informs me over her menu.

I gulp in a few breaths, thinking about who and what else could possibly come out at night as I try to focus on the menu again. Oh god, every horror movie takes place at night. All the scariest things come out then. Do I need to be worried about vampires? Ghouls? Zombies?

Werewolves? Oh no. I already saw a wolf child. And a wolf man. No no no.

Our server, human-looking except for her enigmatic golden cat-like eyes and scary sharp teeth, greets us, and we place our order. I'd love a stiff drink or several—bourbon neat, preferably—but my emotions are still unsteady, and I don't want to risk ending the day with a worse impression. No more weepy meltdowns for me today, please. I opt for water and a golden beet and goat cheese salad. Ada recommends getting a bread plate, too, so I oblige, because who am I to turn down bread?

It comes with thick slices from a perfectly crusty, slightly sour, naturally leavened loaf, as well as squares of decadently chewy, rich focaccia. I groan at my first bites of each.

"Good, huh? We certainly won't let you starve here," she says between bites of her own delicious-looking meal of chicken dumplings.

I can picture myself coming back often. This is some of the best food I've had in a long time. I wonder if all the restaurants here are this spectacular.

I haven't been able to afford a fancy meal ever, probably. It was always Mark's treat when we were dating, one generosity I could count on with him. Though he insisted we only go to expensive and exclusive restaurants, which I didn't always enjoy, I did learn a lot about food and cuisine from them. It's heartening to know I can pay my own way at a restaurant like this and eat a more satisfying meal than any I ever shared with him.

Four Years Ago

Today is Mark's and my five-year anniversary, and it seems like a momentous one. Sometimes, he'll go a little over the top with gifts— often more expensive than meaningful. Honestly, what I want more than anything is to finally move in together. I'm nearing thirty, and all my long-coupled friends are either engaged or married by this point. I know not everyone follows the same timeline, but I feel like this would make so much sense in our lives. He insists I live in a luxury building in the South Loop, close to both him and the office, so my rent is more expensive than I can afford with my salary. And I don't have help from my family like he does. It doesn't leave much at the end of the month to put into savings after all my other expenses.

I'm at my desk when he stops by with a dozen plush red roses. "Mark, these are gorgeous! Thank you!" I gush as he hands them to me. I push my nose into the center of a bloom and luxuriate in its fresh, sweet scent.

"Not as gorgeous as you." He pecks my cheek as he affectionately squeezes my upper arms. "I've got to run to a meeting. I'll swing by at six so we can go out to dinner. I have a surprise for you!" he tells me hastily as he pulls away, giving me his most dashing smile.

I wave him away with a love-drunk grin and then return to basking in the sight and smell of the immaculate bouquet in my hands. A card is attached to the brown paper wrapping, with twine holding it in place. I unfold it, realizing right away this isn't Mark's handwriting. It's his assistant's. Other project leads don't have assistants, but that's what nepotism can do for you. "Happy anniversary to my best girl." Such a small detail, but it ruins the gift. My stomach roils in hurt and anger. Did she make the dinner reservations, too? Did she have to remind him about the anniversary? I thrust the flowers away from me and toss them haphazardly on my desk. I'll find a vase in the office kitchen for them later. I don't care if they start to wilt.

Concentration eludes me the rest of the day. But the clock ticks slowly, so I do my best to get as much work done as I can to fill the long hours. What kind of surprise does he have for me tonight? Could it be moving in together? I've been trying to bring it up for months, but he doesn't give me many opportunities for heartfelt discussion. I don't bother with dropping hints, subtle or otherwise, anymore. It hasn't worked. And I'm not sure if he's been ignorant of my attempts or just plain ignoring them.

When the hour finally arrives, I double-check my hair and makeup in the bathroom mirror. I don't have enough time to stop home to freshen up, so I brought a nice cocktail dress and lingerie in my gym bag to change into, as well as a curling iron and hairspray to fix my limp hair. I look pretty good, considering I just worked a ten-hour day. I return to my desk to wait for Mark, pushing down my bruised feelings, not wanting to ruin the night. The roses sit in a vase at a far corner of my desk. I turn my back to them and check my phone to see if there's any message from him. All day long, coworkers were ooh-ing and ahh-ing over them. The plump blooms do look expensive, and no doubt they came from a fancy florist. But each mention of them cuts me a little deeper. Hopefully, they won't last long, so I can get them off my desk.

Mark insisted we go to a newly minted Michelin-star restaurant in the West Loop. I guess he had to plan this in advance to get a reservation. It's blown up since the announcement. A high school friend of mine who is a sous chef at an upscale restaurant in the city even had a hard time getting in with her connections. When I let her know where we're going tonight, she told me it's a place to be seen more than a place to enjoy. Not what I would choose, but Mark's been talking about it all week, so I'm excited to at least share the experience with him. I love good food and going to restaurants, of which there is no shortage in Chicago, but I don't need to go somewhere so obscenely trendy and expensive.

I'm scrolling on my phone when I notice Mark approaching. He looks handsome in his expensive, tailored suit. I feel underdressed compared to him. He folds me into an embrace, kissing my earlobe—something he does when he says he doesn't want to mess up my makeup. Reaching my arms around his neck, my body molds into his, and I feel my anger and tension escaping me. I breathe in his neck, a hint of aftershave still evident after the long day. The press of his belt and the ridge of his groin into my lower belly warms me all over. No matter what else is going on, being held tightly in his arms cures everything.

"Are you ready?" he murmurs intimately in my ear.

"Always." I smile with love in my eyes.

Mark orders a car, and we're at the restaurant in no time. Minimalist dark wood-paneled walls and dim lighting from giant bowl-shaped over-head hanging lights result in more darkness than atmosphere. The low-backed black leather chairs are a missed opportunity for creativity, given the table is also black, as are the cloth napkins... Everything just feels excessively devoid of color, austere to a fault. A little soulless.

We're seated right away and given menus. My jaw drops at the prices, and I'm glad he's paying. We order the wine pairing for the multi-course meal and talk about our workdays. We don't have any projects together right now, so he's telling me about developments for the firm I haven't heard about yet. They're good to know from a professional perspective, but this is hardly conversation for an intimate anniversary dinner. We only see each other a few times a week outside of work, so it reminds me how lonely it feels when we barely interact at the office.

I try to play the part of supportive girlfriend, but I can't help but let a wan smile slip when he's telling me about a potential client he seems particularly passionate about. He notices it immediately and cuts off his story. "Cara, what's going on? Why the face?" he asks, perplexed, a hint of annoyance in his voice that I've interrupted him.

"Oh, nothing really. Just thinking about how much I miss you when you're so busy." I reach over and squeeze his hand, rubbing my thumb across the top. He looks pleased by that and squeezes back. I can't help but wonder what his surprise is. "I've been looking forward to this all day. I'm so curious about what else you have in store tonight." My eyes are half-lidded as I try to telegraph my desires to him. A romantic dinner. A long, lust-filled night in bed. An invitation to stay there, indefinitely.

"You look like you want dessert before dinner, Cara," he says, desire deep and dark in his voice.

"Only with you, Mark," my finger lightly paints small circles along the inside of his wrist.

"We have plenty of time for that later." He takes my hand and threads our fingers together, effectively ending our flirtation. I want to pull him across the table to me and make later happen now, but that would be uncouth in such an exclusive restaurant where people are dropping obscene amounts of money. He lets go of my hand, and I sense a shift in his tone and body language immediately. "I wanted to talk to you about something and tonight seems like the perfect time for it."

This about-face makes me uneasy, but I try not to let on to avoid more censure. "My parents are fast-tracking me so I get to experience all levels of the business before taking over. They're going to announce another promotion for me next week." He beams at me, like this is the best news in the world. And for him, it is. But it sucks the amorous feeling right out of me, hollowing out the hope in my chest. "Well, what do you think?" he follows up, looking at me expectantly.

I can tell he's peeved he's not receiving the desired reaction from me, the fawning praise. I give a tight, genial smile so utterly fake it feels painful plastered on my face. "That's great news, Mark. Congratulations." He's satisfied and proceeds to talk on and on about it, as if he can't tell that each word feels like a stab in my heart.

Finally, I interrupt his monologue after dessert is brought to our table. I haven't tasted any of this overpriced, overhyped meal. It's all sawdust, heavy and flavorless, in my mouth. "If you're going to be so much busier, why don't we think about moving in? I'll barely see you otherwise." I carefully shape each word, not wanting to reveal the emotions his "surprise" has wrung out of me.

"Babe, you know I like my own space. We'll still see each other enough. Besides, if you move in, there's no way you can afford half the mortgage. And you know my parents won't let you stay there without paying your fair share," he shoots back, as if it's the most rational explanation in the world. Ah yes, his condo is, in fact, paid for by his parents. I'm sure they write it off as a business expense, knowing them.

"You could move in with me. Or we could move somewhere else a bit cheaper than your condo," I suggest, hoping anything I say will get through to him.

"No way they'd go for that. You know Mom brought in an interior designer. She'd be crushed if I moved out after all that work," he says with finality.

Naturally, we wouldn't want to upset Victoria, whose assistant couldn't even be bothered to acknowledge our anniversary, let alone her. I contrive a light-hearted tone and fake smile, as much as I can muster. "You're right. It wouldn't make sense for you to leave your condo. We'll see each other enough." I shovel a tasteless forkful of the dessert I haven't even looked at in my mouth, so I don't say another damn word about it.

I'm nearly in a food coma by the time Ada and I finish the meal. Good food can be a balm for the soul, and this meal certainly has been. Ada digs through her purse and puts down some cash as the bill arrives, raising her eyebrows at me, letting me know not to object.

"Thanks for dinner, Ada. And for everything today. It's been a shock, to say the least," I admit sheepishly, worrying my lips while I stare down at my hands clasped in front of me on the table.

She reaches out and gives them a friendly squeeze. I look up, and her eyes catch mine. "Hon, you are exactly who we hoped would accept this job and join this community. We are so happy to have you here. Now, it's not very late, but you must be tuckered out after such a long and unexpected day. Why don't we head home so you can unpack and get ready for your first day tomorrow?"

"Thanks, that sounds like a good idea," I agree with a weary smile, feeling very worn out.

The sun sets as Ada drives us back to her place. The sky is an explosion of orange, pink, and purple, as vibrant as the sunset after a summer storm in this part of the country. A slight shiver runs down my spine as I think about who may be waking up right now to this picturesque view —the *night crowd*, as Ada called them.

We've fallen into a companionable silence in the car, but we reach her place in no time and say goodbye. I run inside to change into some leggings and a shirt better suited to unpacking the rest of my stuff. A cold sweat runs down my back as I step outside. It's growing darker by the minute, so I hurry to the small trailer hitched to my SUV and open it, rushing the bins and boxes inside, making multiple trips. I'm winded and sweaty from running up and down the steps so fast, trying to be as quick as possible. It must be safe if Ada says so... but I just can't help being nervous while I'm out here in the dark by myself.

The crack of a broken twig resonates like a sonic boom in the silence, sounding from the shadows behind some trees at Ada's property line. Icy fear skitters down my spine. The wind picks up in that instant, the swish of leafy branches masking the source. I feel eyes on me, watching me from the darkness, though I can't see anything. In a panic, I grab the last box, slam the trailer door shut, and race inside the carriage house, locking it up behind me.

Panting, I run up the stairs, trying to put it out of my mind now that I'm safe inside. Surrounded by my boxes and bins, I instead focus on where to start unpacking. Truthfully, it's not that much stuff. Clothes. Shoes. Accessories. Some kitchen appliances and utensils. Electronics. Books I can't part with. A box of keepsakes—with everything related to *him* very purposely removed, trashed, or even burned thanks to a few friends thoroughly outraged on my behalf... one of whom has a working fireplace in her apartment. Another of my friends even sold some of the jewelry he gave me to fund my move. I shove the keepsake box in the closet. No need to look through it now to remind me of the friends I miss. And the family I no longer have.

I unpack most of my clothes and shoes, considering what to wear tomorrow for my first day as the new city planner. My wardrobe is small, but my clothes are well taken care of and tailored to fit me—even the inexpensive pieces. I couldn't look anything less than impeccable at my old job... and for the ex and his family. Maybe I can find a good tailor here if I end up buying some new clothes. As much as I loathe the reason I started doing that, it is really nice to have wardrobe pieces that fit as if they're bespoke. Though nowadays everything fits a little looser. Six months of anxiety, depression, and being broke diminished my appetite. But if tonight's dinner is any indication, I'll gain those pounds back right away. I joined the ranks of the Clean Plate Club, thank you very much.

After shoving the empty boxes and bins in a corner to deal with later, I'm thoroughly drained, completely depleted by a day I couldn't have imagined in my wildest dreams. I was just in Atlanta this morning, and now I live in this strange, unexpected world of monsters and magick. And I still have to show up to work tomorrow, like everything is perfectly normal. Of course my dream job had to come with a catch, a *monstrously* large one.

Working with Clancy will be gratifying, but Ben is a completely different story. If Ben could be so dismissive of me in front of Clancy and Ada, what will he be like when they aren't around? He's the scariest monster of them all.

CHAPTER 5
CARA

I pull into the small parking lot behind town hall—toward the back since you never know if people get weird about *their* parking spots. I'm fifteen minutes early, but there are already a few cars, golf carts, and even Vespa-type scooters here. It's such a short drive—so I sit for a moment and think about a route I could take to bike or walk here from Ada's.

Alright, it's showtime. My first day at my new job. I grab my purse and my laptop bag with my personal computer. I imagine Clancy will have one for me, but I brought it just in case. Knowing I will need to go on site visits, I already have a pair of sneakers, an umbrella, and a jacket in my backseat. Not sure I'll need any of it today, but again, better safe than sorry. My kitten heels wouldn't last long walking through the muck of a construction site.

Surprisingly, I may have the newest vehicle in the lot. And my small SUV is a few years old now... enough time to have seen some things. I guess it makes sense people here don't replace their cars often, even if they've found a way to do so online according to Clancy. I should start a list of questions for Clancy and Ada about things I'd probably take for granted that aren't as easy here. There's so much I need to learn about their way of life. It'll be a steep learning curve.

My eyes are glued to the detailed façade of the building as I walk around it, admiring the craftsmanship. Stepping onto the plaza, my gaze shifts down to the center of the business district just beyond it. The bright morning sun shines just above the top of the buildings, cascading everything in an optimistic golden glow. The light beaming through the plaza's live oak tree canopy creates a dappled effect on the concrete and grass. It's a charming vista that I doubt will ever grow old.

While no one is around, I fuss my hands down my pale pink plaid A-line dress, brushing away any wrinkles from sitting in the car. It modestly hits at the knee and the sleeves nearly reach my elbows. Perfectly tailored and professional. My work wardrobe is like my armor—I could march into any office, any client meeting, and slay a proverbial dragon. It projects power and professionalism. Though I hope no actual dragon slaying will be necessary today. As a last step, I quickly smooth my hair, which I've pulled back into the closest approximation of a chignon possible with wavy hair on a humid morning. It's good enough for now. In a burst of confidence, I stride toward the building's heavy wooden double doors to officially begin my first day.

The long, grand entrance hall doesn't disappoint. Tall limestone walls with a geometric pattern lead to a rounded ceiling spanning the length of the rectangular hall. It's decorated with an ornate mural of Whispered Folk—one half oriented around a sun and the other half down the hall oriented around a moon—seeming to depict their historic contributions to the town. It's stunning. Someone had a grand vision and the talent to match. Drifting further down the hall, my feet moving of their own accord, I crane my neck, trying to catch every detail. It won't be a hardship to see this every day.

My eyes stray to a gray gargoyle, wings outstretched, holding a hammer and chisel, looking both frightening and majestic. I squint to focus on the details of the creature. It must be Ben's ancestor. There's certainly a resemblance even beyond their shared... species. The horns, cheekbones, and dark eyes are nearly identical. It ratchets up my concern about him that his family has been here long enough to be an integral part of town history. Maybe he doesn't want a human interloper here infiltrating his hometown. And yet, Ada and Clancy have been so welcoming. It doesn't make sense.

Those thoughts shake loose as I swivel my head, taking in the rest of the hall. Entryways to smaller hallways on both sides seem to lead to offices and conference rooms. In the center of the grand hall, there's an elevator on the left and a wide stairwell with elegant wrought iron railings on the right. At the far end, there's another set of double doors leading outside toward the parking lot. My eyes are drawn up again, staring at the moonlit half of the mural, when I hear, "Miss Bishop, city planner extraordinaire," from a friendly, familiar source... along with a clip-clop of hooves on the marble floor.

"Good morning, Mayor Evermane," I greet him in my most chipper voice.

He huffs a laugh. "Ready for the best job you'll ever have?"

"I believe I am," I answer with an easy smile I didn't know I had in me. It might even be the truth, and that's a stunning prospect.

"Let's head to my office." He gestures toward the hallway he just came from. I walk toward him, but I dawdle, taking one last look around the hall. "Ladies first." His voice gently disrupts me and brings my attention back to him.

"I have been looking forward to this," he tells me with an animated gleam in his eyes as we reach his office—proportioned for a centaur.

"Ada told me your dad was mayor before you. Was much of this his furniture?" I wonder aloud as he navigates the space with ease.

"Ah yes, the Evermane family legacy. Most of it was from my father's tenure. So it worked out well when I took office and could move right in. Our furniture needs are specific, if you couldn't tell. We are not standard sized," he jokes as he knocks a knuckle on his tall antique wooden desk, practically a monster-sized standing desk. His laptop sits on a modern-looking extension that adjusts even higher, closer to his eye level. The ceiling-height stately bookshelves along the interior wall are recognizable from our video interview. He must have positioned himself in front of them. An interesting trick to prevent me from realizing how tall he is. My lips quirk into a small smile just thinking about how far the curtain has been pulled back.

Without paying much attention, I take a seat in a leather, tufted button chair in front of the desk. I don't realize anything is off until I basically have to hop onto it like a tall barstool. My feet dangle with only my toes brushing the ground. I'm not short, so this oversized chair must be made for... someone else. I look up in surprise at Clancy, who is chuckling silently.

"You are certainly welcome to sit there, but you look like Alice in Wonderland in that giant chair," he says, a smile evident in his voice. "No doubt you feel you've fallen down the rabbit hole. I could ring for tea, really complete the experience for you, though honestly, Madge, my assistant, would probably put a hex on me if I tried." He lets out a hearty laugh.

I smack a hand to my forehead and giggle. Obviously, this one is meant for someone like Ben or that ogre fellow I saw yesterday. "We can save the tea party for another day." I hop off the oversized chair and settle into a smaller, me-sized one next to it. Not wanting to waste time, I pull out the pencil and notebook I put in my purse yesterday. I'm a note-taker, and I always try to keep them with me when I'm working. It's a throwback, but I don't care. I never want to forget a detail, and writing helps me commit everything to memory.

"Well, you look ready for business, so let's get started," Clancy begins with a soft clap of his hands, which he then rubs briskly. "As we talked about before, Monstera Bluff currently has around twelve thousand residents, and we've managed to stave off a housing crisis so far. But as a result, we've been expanding the town's footprint, building a new neighborhood along with all of the infrastructure that entails. Luckily, we haven't made too many rushed, clueless decisions that can't be altered or undone by someone better qualified. And that is where you come in." He grins eagerly.

"The town charter was a solid foundation throughout the decades and centuries. Only recently have we needed a more modern sensibility to guide us forward. We've always been a sleepy haven compared to some in other parts of the country and the world. But, much like humans, it seems that our monster brethren are attracted to warmer climates, migrating here in greater numbers. So we're in a bit of a pickle. How do we maintain that small-town feel while we grow? How can we prevent Monstera Bluff from losing what makes it so special? This isn't a problem unique to us, but I want to think we're addressing it the right way by having the willingness as well as the funding to get it right." He looks up in thoughtful contemplation.

"The through line of my best projects has been designing to the human scale. Er, make that monster scale here. Most cities across the country are designed for people in cars rather than for people. It's been this way for decades, nearly a century. And it can be difficult and limiting to try to retrofit human-scale designs into an otherwise pedestrian-hostile environment. So we owe it to ourselves and the next generation to get it right the first time," I agree. Speculating on so many possibilities for improving new and existing infrastructure makes me giddy. We both seem caught up in our respective imaginations.

Clancy fervently nods. "You put into words exactly what I'm thinking. I also want to assure you that you're not alone in this endeavor. Ada and I are always here for perspective and ideas. Ben will also be a great resource for you." My face flushes at the mention of his name. "He is a skilled draftsman and will lead the construction phase of most of your projects. Lean on him at any point."

"I'm sure Ben is too busy to help," I demur, hoping to avoid him as much as possible.

"He will not be too busy. I'll make sure of it." Clancy holds firm.

Despite his good intentions, I doubt he can force Ben into anything, considering how yesterday went. Letting that thought go, refocusing the conversation, I ask, "What about the town council? How will I work with them?"

"The town council will be mostly amenable to your proposals. Their budget approval is required for most projects. You'll have a lot of like-minded allies. That said, it may not always be easy. We have a few recent naysayers who need to be mollified, no matter what we put in front of them. But you will have the backing of everyone who matters most," Clancy explains, trying to sound encouraging.

Better to learn how the sausage is made as soon as possible. "I noticed Monstera Bluff is well-maintained. Clean sidewalks, manicured landscaping, immaculate public spaces. And that's not cheap—it's a lot of resources for a small town. How do you have the funding for big projects along with everything else? The potentially significant town budget and its tiny tax base seem... incompatible," I address with a grimace. The allegation sounds like a stone pitched in a glass house.

He looks amused. "Oh, Cara, you don't think that a magickal little town such as ours wouldn't also use magickal means to supplement the budget?" I must look lost because he backtracks and explains, "Magick can be utilized in so many ways to benefit the town. Personally, I can't wield any magick, but there are plenty of witches and magickal folk living here who can. Ada and her coven, for instance. Their abilities manifest in different ways that are useful to us."

"So the coven works for the town? Ada mentioned they maintain a ward," I note, confused by the concept.

"Not exclusively, no. But we hire them when we need magick for ongoing work like the wards. Our construction companies and other businesses do the same. Mayhap you'd think of them as consultants. Magick can do so much, like move heavy objects and hold them in place, manipulate the size and shape of matter, strengthen foundations and roofs, dry or liquify materials, transform one substance into another. But despite these magickal methods of procuring goods and services, we still have to construct infrastructure and buildings the old-fashioned way... for the most part. The magickal assists just make everything easier and less expensive for us," he clarifies, watching me closely as if to gauge whether any of this information sinks in.

My face must betray my bewilderment because he huffs a laugh as he continues, "I know how impossible this must sound. But ultimately, just do what you do best. Your vision and direction are most important to your job. The town council will consider how to supplement your proposals. And Ben knows all about this too, so he will advise you." My head is still spinning, but I guess I'll learn on the job, then.

He hands a folder full of papers over the desk to me. "I think a good starting point will be to review the Howling Road expansion to the new housing development. Ben's halted work on it. He felt it needed your eyes. Our initial plan was very bare bones. No real considerations beyond just... building a road and everything that accompanies it. Maybe you can work your particular brand of magick on it?" he suggests with a sly wink.

I bark out a self-deprecating laugh. "It's certainly not magick... just a different way of thinking, I suppose?"

He considers me for a moment, then calmly remarks, "But isn't that what magick can be? Swimming against the tide of the world around you, molding it into what you want to see?" That sentiment stuns me into a contemplative silence.

Clancy walks around his desk and gestures to the door, "Let's go to your office and get you set up." I rise from my chair and follow him to an office a couple doors down the hall. "Here you are, madame planner," he proclaims with a silly flourish as he ushers me in.

My eyes light up as I survey the room. It's simple but lovely. On one end sits a large, solid wooden desk with a comfy-looking office chair and two additional chairs in front of the desk for visitors. Bookshelves line the wall behind the desk with some notable urban planning and design texts, along with other titles I've found particularly helpful in recent years. Natural light shines through a large window on the exterior wall. The walls are cream-colored, but the wood throughout the room is dark and rich, contrasting nicely with the neutral color. "I love it!" I exclaim with genuine delight.

Clancy audibly exhales in relief. "Mother Earth, I'm so glad! We want you as happy as a clam at high tide so you'll never leave," he jokes. My smile brightens, and I feel a surprising, bubbling warmth within me. It's novel that he cares so much about my reaction to my office, to get me settled in and comfortable, without actually proving myself first—showing what I can do to bolster him and his office in the eyes of the community. I've never actually been treated with such consideration in a job before. It feels so nice that I could sink into this moment for eternity.

If he notices how affected I am, he doesn't let on. "Your laptop is on your desk, along with files to review this week, like the town charter, a regional map and geographical survey, current operating budget, and recent town projects we've proposed and completed. Send me an email with the modeling and CAD software you'd like me to purchase for you. I'll get that done today. Don't worry about the price tag. After that, focus on the project we discussed. Tear it up, throw it out the window, for all I care. It's barely worth the paper it's printed on," he insists with a self-effacing chuckle.

I try to interrupt to say it can't be that bad, but he anticipates this and stops me with a gesture. "In fact, I've asked Ben to meet with you before lunch to go over the basics of what we need," he informs in an aloof manner, though I can tell he's furtively studying my response.

How can he just toss that bomb into the conversation like it isn't going to incinerate this otherwise refreshingly pleasant experience? My stomach flips, but I do my best to mask the discomfort, nodding as genially as I can muster. He gives me a gratified smile, like he put weight in my reaction to this news. There's no way I'm imagining this unspoken moment between us.

"He will fully support you no matter what direction you decide to take. The project is yours to steer," he enthuses, though I can't share that optimism right now.

After Clancy helps me set up my laptop and office phone, he excuses himself to attend some community meetings. I wander down the hall to introduce myself to Madge, Clancy's assistant, who hadn't arrived yet when I walked by her desk earlier. She must be close to sixty, but I quickly realize it can be hard to tell with Whispered Folk. Learning my monster tutorial of the day, she tells me she's a cervitaur, a word I had never heard before, which is like a deer centaur and much smaller, though she's about my height.

"We're a rare sight nowadays. Most of us aren't very social. Only an Evermane could convince a clan of misanthropes like ours to move here." Madge chuckles.

"Charm must be woven into the Evermane family DNA," I joke.

"You have no idea! My clan has always worked in some capacity with them since we moved here. I continue the tradition by working as Clancy's assistant. I served in the same role for his father when he was in office," she announces proudly.

After talking to her, I head over to the kitchen and coffee nook that Madge told me she keeps stocked. Gloriously, it's devoted to everything caffeine, so I pour some coffee with real cream—the joy!— from the fridge and grab a giant blueberry muffin from a pink bakery box to take back to my office. It is some damn fine coffee and breakfast, indeed.

I spend the rest of the morning reading through the file for the Howling Road expansion project... and it's fine. They took a very basic approach, building an uninspired general purpose four-lane road without consideration for pedestrians or bike traffic. But I'll go out on a limb and assume that Whispered Folk drivers will experience the same pitfalls that allow and even encourage drivers to go too fast, not pay attention, and not properly share the road. I can help reduce the dangers and tragedies that can occur on roads like this.

Before I know it, it's nearly time for Ben to arrive. My hands clutch clammy to my knees as I sit at my desk and gaze at the open doorway. My optimism is dampened by his behavior toward me yesterday. I'm skeptical whether he'll even deign to speak to me today. Insecurities push to the forefront of my mind, forcing me deep into my own head, circling around everything I learned about Ben yesterday. Deliberating the stark contrast of Ada and Clancy's confidence in his character when all I see is coldness.

A sound from the hallway dislodges me from my thoughts, and I belatedly realize it was a soft knocking. Ben occupies most of the doorway—broader-shouldered and taller than I remember—and no less devilish looking. Rather than the creeping discomfort I should feel, a frisson of anticipation travels through me. He's here to talk to me and won't be able to get out of it. This will prove, one way or another, everything I've heard about him. And I'll find out if he reserves this contempt just for me—or if something else made him react rudely to me yesterday. Still in my head, I must take too long to respond because he tentatively steps into my office, angling his shoulders and wings to fit.

"May I come in, Cara?" he prompts in a low and rumbling voice. It's then I notice he's holding a bouquet of daisies.

CHAPTER 6
BEN

"Hi Ben. Um, yes, please come in," Cara scratches out once I've caught her attention.

This morning, I feel especially regretful for how I acted yesterday. It was... too extreme. I need to temper my reaction to her fear. Clancy caught me by surprise with his scheme to bring a human to town. I was mad at his recklessness. But I shouldn't have taken it out on her. Now I'm paying the price for my misdeed. She's already nervous at the sight of me; the wavering half-smile pasted to her face is unconvincing.

She looks stunning today. Her pale dress brings out the rosiness in her cheeks and lips, contrasting beautifully with her dark brown hair and hazel eyes. I should fight the protective instincts she stirs in me. Hopefully, these flowers will be enough of an apology. Daisies for a new beginning. I'll tell her about the project, and then I'll be on my way.

Approaching slowly, I stand in front of her desk. "These are for you," I affirm, hopeful my contrition comes through in my voice. With absolute care, I hold out the vase of flowers to her so she can take them out of my hand without touching me. She remains silent, lips parted in surprise. Her hands reach for the vase, avoiding mine like I suspected, and she brings the delicate blooms to her nose, closing her eyes as she breathes them in.

Placing them on her desk, she traces her fingertips across some petals and down the stems until she finds the small card tied to the bouquet. I wrote a short note, not sure how much to say. *Welcome to your new home. I hope you love it as much as I do. Ben.*

Her eyes gleam with wetness as she reads it. "Thank you, Ben. This is so thoughtful," she finally responds in a thick voice. She's silent again for a dangling moment, only focused on the flowers. But she soon finds herself again, blinking rapidly and gesturing to the chair beside me.

Scarcely louder than a whisper, she offers, "Please have a seat." I squeeze into the undersized chair, barely able to accommodate my tall frame.

A smile pulls at her lips before she meets my gaze again. The sight makes my heart stutter. She smells so heavenly, even from this far away —like a light and refreshing floral perfume—that I have a hard time focusing on anything else.

"I spent time this morning reviewing the road proposal. Would you mind if we discuss it?" she asks, some confidence returning to her voice. If nothing else will be easy between us, I hope this is. I've already seen that her passion for her work makes her shine.

She proceeds to ask me thoughtful questions about daily traffic expectations, other potential developments along the road, the topography of the construction site, and more. I try to be thorough and comprehensive in each response, pointing out noteworthy information in the current proposal, like a land survey and other documentation I've already prepared. For such a rocky start, which I'm full responsibility for, we're having a very engaging discussion.

"We should avoid suburbanizing this development. It needs to be fully integrated into the town through multimodal connectivity—by that I mean, multiple modes of transportation like walking, bicycling, and public transit. That'll need to be a heavy focus as the town expands," she emphasizes.

"I've never been to a suburb, but I have an understanding of why they exist in the human world, and that is not needed here," I agree.

I see the wheels turning in her head as we continue talking. No detail goes unnoticed. Her pencil scrapes the page below it, recording her thoughts. Her teeth sink gently into her lower lip as she concentrates, drawing my eyes to them. The sight makes my body feel hot, and my pants grow tight as I fantasize about those plush lips kissing me, tasting me, her focus redirected to pleasure rather than work. She's pure temptation sitting in front of me, disrupting my train of thought.

In the moment, I decide to make a peace offering, hoping she won't recognize the desperate longing simmering just below my skin. "Cara, despite the first impression I may have given you, I want you to know you have my full support in this work. I hope you will flourish and find fulfillment here."

At first, shock freezes her features, but it melts into a thoughtful expression. "Thank you for saying that. It means a lot coming from you. I feel like an outsider here now, and maybe I always will as a human. I don't want to tell the community how they *should* do things because I admit I don't know the nuances of life in this town yet. But I do know the detrimental urban planning mistakes made in human communities and their consequences to livability and safety. I just want to be able to steer the community away from those as best I can," she explains passionately, her dedication to her profession on display.

"That is what Clancy also hopes to accomplish," I reassure her. "But I also mean in your personal life. That you may consider Monstera Bluff home."

Her face flushes an enticing line from her cheeks down her neck. "I haven't had much of a personal life in a while. But I hope that changes. Everything is so different here. It's hard to see how I fit in."

"I could tell you it will be easy, but those would be empty words. You won't know until you try. It could bring you happiness. And make you a better planner for our town. You can't truly know a place until you've lived there," I counsel.

"Perhaps you're right," she answers quietly. I fear I've struck the wrong chord when she clears her throat and abruptly changes the subject. "I hope you won't mind, but I want to take this project back to the drawing board." She hesitates, worrying her lip. "I apologize if this causes your crew to redo any clearing and excavation. Not that I could ever tell you how to do your job, but maybe give me a week or two, and I promise I'll consider if there's existing work that can be salvaged?"

"No need to design around what's already been done. That's why we stopped work yesterday. Not that I could ever tell *you* how to do your job, but if you need my assistance with anything, I'm happy to provide it," I tell her confidently.

She titters as I good-naturedly throw her words back at her. "Fair enough, I already know I'll need your input to make it successful. I fully trust your guidance."

I'm not sure if she realizes the compliment she's paid me, but it embeds into my soul that she could trust me. Even if she may have just said it to be polite, the words will stay with me. Suddenly bashful, I fidget with my shirt, which feels too constricting right now. She watches the movement of my hands closely, no doubt seeing how inhuman they are. Who knows if Clancy's insistence that I wear a shirt today even matters. It doesn't make me less of a monster, but if it makes it easier for her to sit so close to me, it'll be worth the discomfort.

"Would you want to see the job site? It's just a dirt road right now, but maybe it will help you get started." I wince at my clumsy question, regretting it instantly. She'd obviously rather have Clancy show her the site, spend that extra time with him. But she blindsides me with her shy, tentative smile.

"Really? You'll show me around the site today?" Her voice rises an octave. She sits up straighter, like she's ready to bounce out of her seat.

"Of course, I have my truck and I'll drive us over," I reassure her. "And then we can have lunch after if you don't already have plans?" The words spill from my mouth before I can stop them, like my desire for her has possessed me.

Her smile widens, the most genuine I've seen on her yet. "That sounds like a lovely plan." Mother Earth, she sounds almost excited to go with me.

Cara excuses herself, letting me know she's swapping shoes from her automobile and that she'll tell Clancy we'll be gone for a while. I hope Clancy doesn't say anything suggestive to Cara if he's still stuck on that nonsense about me and her. He'll ask me for every detail later. But this is work. That's all there is to tell.

Uncurling myself from that confining chair, I use these quiet minutes to center myself and restore the "resting stone face" I'm known for, according to Clancy. Pun very much intended by him. My wings extend and stretch while she's still gone, stiff from being shoved behind me in that tiny seat. I listen for her while doing so, mindful that she would be shocked to see me this way. Fire and ashes, I'm acting so foolish. Everything about her mind and body arouses me. I'm coming on too strongly. She deserves space while she adjusts to life here. I'll take a giant step back, even if it pains me. Maybe I can revisit my attraction if it ever seems like it would be welcomed.

My resolve has hardened by the time Cara returns. "Thanks for waiting, I'm ready to go." She sounds a little breathless. I turn around in time to see the shy smile fall from her face. Her eyes narrow ever so slightly before she transforms before my very eyes. She's gone blank, completely neutral in expression and posture. It should be a relief, a mirror of my own actions, showing that we are in accord. And yet, it leaves me hollow.

"Please lead the way," she says politely but impersonally.

She follows me silently to my truck parked just outside. Opening the unlocked passenger door, I help her inside before getting in. As the old truck roars to life, my music blares through the speakers before I can reach to lower the volume.

"Good song," Cara remarks with a quick glance over to me.

"You like Otis Redding?" I ask, genuinely interested.

"Of course. He's one of my favorites," she says like it's a given. Mayhap he is popular in the human world, I'm unsure. I first heard his music at the local record shop. At least it's something other than work we have in common. I leave the music on as we drive away.

She quietly watches the scenery around her. There isn't much to Monstera Bluff, but I doubt she has explored any of it yet. Before I think better of it, I motion toward the grocery store and library on one street. The movie theater, general store, and bank on another. The clinic and post office on the next. Places that will be useful to her.

Her neutral stare follows closely as I point them out. "Thank you. I didn't know that," she voices calmly. Stars above, Clancy and Ada are bungling their so-called welcome committee.

I pull over to a clearing beside the construction site. The crew had only just started leveling a section of the road, the subbase not even added yet. The remaining sections are untouched—just the old, original dirt road that will soon be replaced. Stepping out of the truck, she looks around, seeming to get her bearings. It's a good thing she changed her shoes earlier. The dust has kicked up in the breeze.

"Is this near where Ada lives?" she asks, squinting like it'll help her see through the woods.

"Yes, you're about a half mile as the crow flies," I explain, pointing a clawed finger in the general direction.

"Or you?" she mumbles as her eyes dart from my claw to my tightly folded wings.

"Indeed," I deadpan, trying to hide the quirk of my lips at her joke.

She walks several feet away and begins surveying the site. Cara retrieves her notebook out of her purse and starts writing. She's in her element and I don't want to interrupt.

"The land immediately surrounding the road is undeveloped. Why not build the development closer to downtown?" she questions.

"The woods around here are mainly used by shifters, werewolves, and wolven to run and hunt, so the town will build the development further out. That's why it's called Howling Road," I explain, suspecting this will be quite a surprise for her. Her eyebrows shoot up, breaking through her placid facade.

"You are telling me that they run around here... at any time. Like right now? And so close to where I live?" Her voice turns shrill.

"Yes, but don't be alarmed. They know the difference between you and a rabbit while they hunt." Her jaw drops and she clutches her notebook to her chest. Her head swivels in agitated bursts as she scans the tree line. Seeing nothing, she comes back to herself, briefly shutting her eyes. A sudden calmness washes over her.

"Okay... noted... drivers have to worry about uh *shifters*..." She tests the word carefully like it's strange on her tongue. "As well as wildlife running onto the road." A drawn-out exhale puffing out her cheeks punctuates the end of her statement. I almost grin—no easy feat to get out of me—when she then flips a page in her notebook and takes an actual note about *shifters*. She writes out the word and underlines it.

She asks more questions about our findings in the land survey, still taking copious notes, and inquires about the streets planned in the neighborhood development. My company, Guardian Construction, manages the infrastructure portion, while another construction business in town that specializes in home building and renovation is handling the residences themselves.

"Hmm, it's good you're heading off a housing crisis before it can even begin. Wish the rest of the country took that much initiative," she grumbles. She flips ahead a few pages in the notebook and starts sketching. She draws, stops, erases it, starts again, unsatisfied with her first attempt. She taps her chin with the end of her pencil as she finishes and then meets my curious gaze.

"Here's my initial thought on what we should build." She walks toward me and shows me her notebook.

Her reticence toward me doesn't dim her enthusiasm for her work. She vibrates with the need to share her ideas. "I envision this roadway as a boulevard with safe pedestrian and bike access. To preserve as much woodland as possible, I want a promenade-style pedestrian-only walkway in the raised median of the boulevard with sufficient green space on either side to plant live oaks to grow into a shade canopy. I imagine anyone walking their dog... if you have them here... will also appreciate the green space. I'll need to do more research about the minimum space required for their root systems, so I'll have more exact recommendations for you later."

"We do have dogs here," I confirm, not trying to interrupt.

"Oh, good!" She sounds pleased. "Moving outward, a curb will frame the median. For now, let's run with the standard six-inch curb height. But I want to explore the possibility of twelve inches to create a stronger visual and practical delineation between pedestrians and the roadway"—she taps on each section of her sketch as she explains it—"six-foot protected bike lanes will sit between the median and the single lane of traffic on both sides. The protected bike lanes should be painted solid green to fit with the current accepted standard, with decals affixed to the pavement indicating the direction of one-way travel, moving with the flow of vehicle traffic. Bollards could be built roughly five feet apart —though we can alter that distance if needed—along the outer edge of the bike lane, creating a barrier between it and the vehicle traffic lane. We'll add an extra two feet of space as a buffer between the bollards and the inner edge of the traffic lane. Next, we'll have a standard ten-foot lane for vehicles with a narrow shoulder on the very outer edge of the roadway."

A smile pulls at her lips, caught up in her imagination, as she writes some notes off to the side of her sketch. Her confidence makes her even more radiant.

"This is a good plan. Clancy will agree. He appreciates attention to detail," I advise.

"In the future, I want to propose we build shelters with benches on both ends of the road because there should be a bus service to reduce road congestion. There's no need to push car dependence onto this town. Plus, it seems difficult for residents to purchase vehicles? Am I off base in thinking that?" She looks at me expectantly.

She's sharp as a tack. "Is that your way of telling me my truck is an antique?" I tease blithely, indulging in an opportunity to fluster her. "You're correct. There are inherent difficulties in Whispered Folk interacting with humans to purchase automobiles. Most are purchased used, either by humans we trust or by those of us who are human-passing. And we tend to hang onto them for a long time. There is a top-notch mechanic in town if you ever need one. He keeps these old automobiles running smoothly."

"Interesting, I suspected as much." She distractedly taps her pencil to her chin. "If human trends are adopted here, we'll probably see an increase in e-bikes and scooters since they're cheaper and easier to acquire than a car. The bike lanes should be built to accommodate those as well," she adds, her voice trailing off as she jots down more notes.

It's an interesting idea, though I don't know anything about them. "Those sound like they could be quite useful here."

"Not to get too ahead of ourselves, but once road construction is underway, let's look at the plan for the neighborhood itself. It's important that third places—like parks and green spaces, even a community center—are incorporated into it. And plenty of sidewalks to encourage walkability. Perhaps some traffic calming to ensure it's never difficult to cross the street." She presses her pencil against her mouth as she stares at her notebook again.

I hum in agreement. There's plenty of time to do all of this.

"Could we look at the transitions on either end of the road? I want to get a sense of what the crossings and intersections should look like." Uncertainty flashes across her face, so quickly I could have blinked and missed it. Does she think I won't escort her there? Or does she regret that she'll have to spend additional time with me?

"Of course," I say brusquely. "I will take you wherever you need to go."

She nods. "Thank you. I've waited a long time for a project like this. I want it to be successful."

Well, I certainly don't want her to wait any longer, so we return to my truck to show her the rest of it.

CHAPTER 7
CARA

I'm stunned speechless by the flowers in Ben's hand. This is the last thing I expected to happen. He comes across as a different person—someone completely divorced from who I met yesterday. His features are just as severe, but his cordial expression softens them. Fitting for an office setting, he wears a shirt and pants that fit the description of business casual. But his professional attire can't shield his wildness. The entire picture is messing with my head.

"These are for you." He presents me with a bouquet of daisies in a vase. It's probably the closest thing to an apology I'll receive from him. He certainly doesn't seem like the type to concede much. I wonder why he chose daisies. They're beautiful, though, so maybe he just picked what looked best at the store. I nearly get lost in the sight and scent of them, recalling that it's been a while since I've received flowers. My group of friends, the pragmatic, thoughtful women that they are, always send something like chocolate or cookies. The last time I was given flowers, always red roses, was from Mark over a year ago... well, from Mark's assistant, to be precise.

The attached card nearly makes me break out in a cold sweat. I hate that Mark has taken the joy of flowers away from me. Prepared for another disappointment, I hold my breath.

Welcome to your new home. I hope you love it as much as I do. Ben. Such a simple, heartfelt message... and it's just what I needed today. Tears threaten to spill, but I keep them at bay. I shouldn't get emotional in front of Ben. "Thank you, Ben. This is so thoughtful." I put the lovely daisies near the center of my desk so both Ben and the bouquet are in my field of vision.

Our conversation is constructive, friendly even. He's generous with his knowledge, responding to my recommendation that we completely rework the project like he'd expect nothing less. It's refreshing, if a little jarring, given what I experienced from him yesterday.

I take his words about creating a life here to heart. I hope friendship is possible, another connection to make me feel more at home. My world shrank when I was forced to move away from Chicago. But maybe I can change that here, as crazy as that sounds. I'm horrified that I nearly fainted in fear at the sight of him yesterday. But like Ada says, I've been presented with a new reality, and I need to cut myself slack. Here I am, having a business meeting with a *gargoyle*, a species I didn't know existed a day ago. A different lifetime.

As I'm getting to know the man—gargoyle, I guess—I like who he is, despite our rough introduction yesterday. He's unsurprisingly no-nonsense, but there's a thoughtfulness behind every word. His unwavering attention sits warm inside me, not having experienced this from a man in so long... years, maybe. Mark was too wrapped up in himself to let me speak more than a couple sentences about myself before he redirected the conversation back to him, a trait I've become so aware of that it's now my measure of a man... or monster.

I can barely believe my ears when he invites me to the project site... and then to lunch. My stomach somersaults. It doesn't seem like he would extend such an invitation lightly. He's clearly no social butterfly. I agree without a second thought, not wanting to waste the opportunity to get to know him better.

After I excuse myself to get ready to leave for the job site, I swing by Clancy's office to let him know I'm leaving with Ben for a while. I catch him poring over paperwork, not expecting a visitor. I knock, and he waves me in with a curious expression.

"Ben and I are going to the site and then out to lunch. I'll probably be gone a couple hours," I inform Clancy.

His lips curl into a smirk. "And whose idea was this, if I may ask?"

My face heats at his tone. "Ben offered. But I'll come right back afterward," I assure him, not wanting to make waves on the first day.

Clancy rubs his hands, like he's planning something diabolical. "Oh, did he now? Is that old gargoyle finally spreading his wings?" He cackles at his own pun. I grimace, not quite following his meaning.

"Um, maybe? He seems to be supportive of an overhaul like you mentioned. He suggested I see it for myself so I can get started on the proposal," I reply hesitantly, trying to keep it strictly professional.

Clancy beams. "Well, it seems like you two will have so much to talk about. Don't hurry back. In fact, I insist you take a very long lunch with him. Maybe I'll just see you tomorrow." He flaps his hands, shooing me away before I have a chance to respond. My face flames in embarrassment.

"Thanks... but I'll be back this afternoon," I reiterate, trying to hide my mortification. I leave his office as quickly as possible. While I'm still in earshot, he mutters something to himself along the lines of *hope they really put their heads together to fix that road*. I'm just glad he didn't say it to my face.

That interaction baffles me. They're best friends, so Clancy must be giving me a hard time because of it. It's a strange prospect to entertain anything more than friendship. Everyone here is just so... different from me. Ben is singular, that's for sure. If I do stay here, could I ever be in a relationship with someone who isn't human? I truly don't know... And besides, I've learned my lesson all too well, mixing work and dating. It's a dangerous game I'm unwilling to play again.

I mull over these thoughts as I walk toward my office, but I stop in my tracks by the sight of Ben standing perfectly still, facing the window. He is the vision of an otherworldly statue, almost breathtaking with all his monstrous attributes on display. His curved horns gradually darken to nearly black points, ending at the crown of his head. Striations of his lavender gray skin tone and a darker gray decorate his outspread wings. His tail curls neatly around his feet, the tip looks as though it's been affixed with a spade. He's agile on his feet, yet they seem to be made for him to soar to great heights, perching far above the human world, watching over us. His clothing looks like a costume, playing dress up in the shirt and slacks tailored to accommodate his wings and tail. He doesn't belong in garments so tame.

His wings abruptly close with an audible snap, breaking me out of my trance. "Thanks for waiting. I'm ready to go," I whisper, voice hushed as if I'm standing in a museum in front of a masterpiece.

I wish I could watch him longer, uninterrupted, immersed in those interesting details without his noticing. But we have a job to do. I take a few steps closer, and like in a great work of art, that change in distance shows me a new perspective. Something went wrong while I was gone. That wildness he possessed before seems even more tightly leashed now. His gaze turns hard, indifferent. He's a haughty, impenetrable fortress again—his posture rigid and unyielding. Any cracks through which his personality shined for me are now sealed. It sucks the air out of the room, making me question whether our interaction just minutes ago even happened.

Did I say something to make him angry? Nothing obvious comes to mind. Our discussion had gone so well. Did he overhear Clancy's insinuations? I truly doubt it, and I imagine he's used to Clancy's ribbing anyway. What a painful thought, but it turns out it really is just me. I'm not enough. My fears about him are confirmed. It's a slap in the face, especially now that I've glimpsed the side of him he must only show his friends.

My vision contracts, and with startling clarity, all I can see is Mark. His hot and cold demeanor—the extremes becoming worse every year, never knowing which side of Mark to expect... the fun and caring man I met in grad school or the sneering, deceitful asshole who blew up my life earlier this year. The relationship could be mapped by every loving gesture offset by an act of selfish obliviousness at best, cruel disregard at worst. The scales tipping further out of balance every year, eroding my self-esteem bit by bit. I have to shield myself from Ben's behavior and any consequences it may have on my well-being. It's a pattern in the making that I won't put up with anymore, not even from a work colleague.

It's so easy to build walls around myself again, even if it hurts my heart more than I can express. I carefully construct my own aloof mask, honed from the many years of tiptoeing around and acquiescing to the Hansens, not to mention their snooty, VIP clients like wealthy developers and important city and state politicians we had to impress. I transform into the pristine image of detached professionalism. The ease with which I'm able to slide back into it makes it all the more bitter.

Eight Years Ago

Mark sits on my bed while I dig through my closet for anything remotely professional to add to the clothing pile next to him. I bought a few new outfits to create a formal business wardrobe before my first day working with Mark at Hansen Company, though I could use some more pieces to round it out. Normally, I'd ask a friend for help, but I want to be certain I'll impress my new boss—Mark's mother herself—so I need his expert opinion.

Having worked at coffee shops from high school through grad school, I'm not sad about leaving such a thankless job behind. It's a grind—no pun intended. Not only do long six-hour shifts make my feet ache, but the barista world is getting a little too crazy these days. Latte art is a lofty expectation for someone making just over minimum wage.

My office experience through internships during college and grad school taught me how different working in an office can be from the service industry—and how much that customer service experience can help. I'm looking forward to the stability and routine that comes with a day job. And I'm more than ready to jump headlong into my career. I've been on my own for a while, but now I'll finally be able to take control of my destiny.

"What do you think of this skirt and top?" I twirl for Mark as I model an outfit I picked up on sale earlier this week. Unfortunately, I don't have any savings—and I used what little was left over from my student loan payouts at the beginning of the previous semester to buy these new clothes. I've had to do so much scrimping and saving to make the loan money last until I finally get my first real paycheck.

"Cara, you look good in anything you wear. But Mom can be kind of picky, so she might want you to wear a jacket with that dress. She'll tell you if that's the case," Mark answers with a lopsided grin that turns lascivious as I give him a slow strip tease with a promise of much more. I want to show him in no uncertain terms how grateful I am for taking the time to look through my clothes with me.

I wear my favorite new outfit for my first day of work. Victoria's assistant greets me unenthusiastically when I arrive, but since Victoria isn't in yet, she drops me off at my desk in an empty cubicle. "I'll let you know when Victoria wants to meet with you." She sniffs derisively and turns on her heels back to her own desk.

I flip through an office handbook that I found in a drawer for a little while and then open some files on the computer left for me on the desk. Someone loudly clears their throat near me, and I look up to see the assistant is back, her bored expression unchanged. "Victoria will see you now," she snips at me, her tone bordering on antagonism. It puts me on edge, turning my first day jitters into something sour.

Both Victoria and her husband Paul—Mark's dad and the founder of the company—sit in her office in what appears to be a genuine sign of welcome. "Cara, dear, we're so glad you're finally with us at the firm. We know you'll bring so many fresh ideas to the company. And Mark is ecstatic you're here," Victoria purrs at me.

I paste a wide smile on my face, even if her words remind me that Mark hasn't stopped by to say hello yet. We didn't arrive together, but he should be here already.

"We're looking forward to your perspective on urban planning. You're one of the brightest stars to come out of your program in a long time. We're lucky our son got his hooks into you before any of our competition did!" Paul chimes in merrily, but his sentiment makes me uneasy, like our relationship was some sort of inside job just to poach me. My face freezes while I consider the subtext of their words. After some pleasantries, Paul excuses himself, leaving me and Victoria alone in her office.

"Dear, now that we're alone, I want to have a little girl talk with you.

Mark told me you bought new clothing, but I'm sure you understand that isn't quite enough to represent the Hansen Company brand or to be seen on the arm of our son. From the look of it, you'll need to lose at least twenty pounds so they fit your figure better. We don't want our clients to think we're sloppy, do we? What size are you right now?" she says almost distractedly, as if she isn't annihilating my self-esteem.

"Uh, size twelve," I sputter as I pick up my jaw from the floor. I've never had anyone speak to me quite like this.

My body is curvy, but I don't mind it. I'm a straight size and still able to shop at most stores, even if some barely accommodate my shape, especially in-store. She grabs a pen and notepad, writing something down. She tears off the page, handing it to me. "You need to be a size ten or smaller. I don't care how you do it, but get it done in two months, or you may not find this to be a good long-term *fit* at this office. I want you to shop at these stores or any of similar caliber. I also wrote down the name of a good tailor. Unless your clothing fits flawlessly off the rack, I expect you to have them altered," she demands, her tone so matter-of-fact she could be talking about the weather. If I wasn't holding her damn list of designer brands in my hands, I'd almost think I dreamt it.

The rest of the morning is a blur. An HR person meets with me at some point for new employee onboarding, but I don't breathe a word of anything Victoria said. How can I? It's her company. I wasn't born yesterday. I know HR isn't my friend. They exist to protect the Hansens. The only option I can think of is to talk to Mark.

He finally stops by around lunchtime. I'm still in a daze as he walks up and sits on the edge of my desk. "Hey, where have you been all morning?" I whine in a needy tone that Mark has told me he doesn't like. But I'm feeling too raw to suppress it right now.

"Sorry, babe, lots of meetings this morning. I can't always be around, you know. Want to get lunch?" he asks, not noticing that anything is wrong.

"Sure, I don't meet with anyone until later," I tell him as I grab my purse and stand up. The relief of escaping the office is short-lived when I consider how I should broach the topic of Victoria's ultimatum, the awkwardness bleeding into our conversation leading up to it.

Once we're sitting in a nearby sandwich shop with our food, I blurt out everything, unable to hold it in any longer. "Mark, what am I supposed to do? She made it sound like my job was on the line. I can't be fired from this job!" I moan incredulously, feeling close to hysterics. I shudder at the thought of how getting fired from my first job will put a black mark on the rest of my career. It may derail everything I've worked so hard for.

Mark shrugs like this pressure is no big deal. "I don't think she threatened to fire you. She was just helping you in her own way. You know how she is. Anyway, we all gained a little weight in school," he tries to joke as he pats his flat stomach, kept taut with the help of his personal trainer, as if commiserating, adding, "If she prefers you shop at these stores, just do it. She wants to make sure you click with the firm."

His nonchalance cuts deeper than ever before. "You don't understand, I can't fit into those clothes. Designers like that don't really make clothes in my size. And they're way more expensive than I can afford!" I gasp, whisper-shouting in a feeble attempt to prevent this mortifying conversation from being overheard.

"Use your credit card, I guess. You're smart. You'll figure it out. That's how you got this job in the first place," he remarks without a flicker of sympathy. I can't tell if he's indifferent because he's a man from a rich family and can't relate to how difficult this is for a broke woman, or if he really does agree with his mom that I need to lose weight and dress the part of this nearly impossible standard. I don't push because I don't know if I can stomach the answer.

In the next two months, I do as Victoria asked. After paying for just a few measly items from one of the least expensive stores on the list, I can barely afford food anyway. Victoria notices and compliments me every time I wear a new piece to work—that's to say, she compliments me every time she sees I can fit into another one of her chosen fashion lines—so I know she's keeping tabs. In the meantime, I ingratiate myself with the firm from a work perspective. Putting all my mental energy into my projects, making myself indispensable even if I can't manage to shed the final few pounds.

Finally invited to my first client pitch, I pull out all the stops for this one, working closely with Mark on a project to redesign a busy intersection after a railroad line crossing through it had been decommissioned.

Mark and I are standing toward the back of the conference room, waiting for Victoria to call him up to present our proposal. There's a break in conversation, and I feel someone settle their hand a little too low on my back and squeeze. I startle and realize the hand belongs to one of the clients.

"Sweetheart, it's time for you to bring in our coffee," he breathes heavily into my ear, his tone over-familiar. I freeze, unsure how to respond.

Victoria looks over at me pointedly, and I understand I can't correct him that I'm a junior associate and proposal co-contributor, not an assistant. I grit my teeth in irritation and leave the room to ask someone to help me with a coffee cart. Finally, I have everything I need and return to the room, only to hear Mark presenting my ideas in our proposal without indicating that I had any part of it. Shoving the hurt and betrayal as deep down as I can, I force a carefully impassive expression on my face as I pass around the clients' coffee cups, realizing I haven't made it very far at all.

I should have known better than to believe that Ben wanted to atone for his attitude toward me. He was playacting, manipulating me with flowers and a few compliments to let down my guard. I somehow still failed his test, whatever it was. But I know from experience it's not meant to be passed. I'll never be good enough. Mark and his parents taught me that. I guess man or monster, assholes are assholes.

I'll make sure this visit is quick and then excuse myself from his company. I won't even give him a chance to retract that lunch invitation when the time comes. My head spins and I feel sick thinking about how this will affect my life. If this job doesn't work out, then there's no future for me here. And I'll have to uproot myself again, possibly in a worse position than before. My career is already in tatters, but I won't stay in another unbearable work environment.

The love connection Clancy hinted at will never happen. Period. Just the thought of it sends a horrible shudder through me. I don't need another version of Mark in my life. He was enough of a monster for one lifetime.

Each step towards Ben's truck fills me with dread, like a doomed march. His truck is so old, it's practically vintage. The bench seat is unfortunate, given that I'd love to put as much of a physical barrier between us as possible. What little conversation we make in the truck is clipped, benign, and to the point.

I've had so much professional practice striking the right balance of limited interaction and emotional distance that will still keep the higher-ups happy while I manage to stay relatively sane. God, I forgot how exhausting it is... and how utterly soul-crushing. My friends always likened it to being the help in a period drama. There to serve when you're needed, but otherwise a dispassionate onlooker. Not that this situation is apples to apples. Ben isn't my boss, thank goodness—and Clancy seems like his polar opposite right now—but I hate that I have to do this again.

Surprisingly, Ben isn't subjecting me to the same frosty silence as yesterday, but his manner of speaking is distinctly impersonal, so opposite from the warmth he showed me earlier. He happens to mention a few places in town while I've watched out the window trying to get a lay of the land. But I don't feel like conversing with him beyond that.

As we're too close for comfort in his snug truck, my shoulders stiffen, creeping high enough to cradle my chin. So I try to lower them into a relaxed position to hide how much his disdain affects me. But then it becomes equally hard not to let them slump. Why is it so difficult to look unbothered?

When we exit his truck at the job site, he stands so far away from me, like I smell bad or something. Maybe I do to him. I dread that I will be so reliant upon him for this project. But the faster I get everything I need, the sooner I can be away from him.

The long dirt road, surrounded by dense dark woods, starts at the end of a downtown cross street and runs far enough into the distance I can't see where it leads. Luckily, the road is wide, and there's plenty of space to utilize without cutting into the wooded area. A section was leveled out already, but the rest is unchanged. For the sake of Ben's crew, I'm glad they didn't get very far.

After running through some preliminary questions about the road, I need to learn more about the neighborhood development. "So, Ben, is your company building the entire neighborhood development?" I ask.

"No, Guardian Construction is only responsible for the roads and infrastructure. The initial stage is only partially completed, and there's room to expand a few blocks if needed later on. A home builder is leading that project. Clancy can put you in touch with them," he offers, more than I was expecting.

"Oh, okay, I'll get that from him then. Are those builders also gargoyles?" I ask hesitantly, unsure if it's offensive.

"They're orcs, mostly. But I heard a couple gryphons and shifters joined their crews recently," he tells me, sounding bored, like he's had to explain this one too many times.

Gryphons, shifters, and orcs, oh my. I wish I was brave enough to ask more about them, but I doubt Ben would take kindly to it. So instead, I press, "What kind of housing is being built? Multi-family? Single-family?"

"Both. We will have buildings that will house many families in their own dwellings, along with a mix of homes, both separate and attached, built to suit various sizes of Whispered Folk. Some lots have already been purchased and are being built to suit the owner. Businesses will be opening in the neighborhood next year," he replies.

Relief courses through me. "Good, I'm glad to hear that the plan includes multifamily residences. You sound like a bunch of YIMBYs. I bet we'll have some interesting projects," I muse.

"Yim-bees... I don't understand. Is that a human term?" he asks, confused.

"It means *Yes In My Backyard*. It's a movement in opposition to the *Not In My Backyard* mindset that wants strict residential zoning, often limiting it to single-family dwellings and a restriction or ban on mixed-use zoning *in their backyard*, so to speak, claiming it drives down their property value. And it's true, housing scarcity artificially inflates housing prices. There's so much more to it, but I'll spare you. Restrictions like these became the norm in most cities and exacerbated suburban sprawl, car dependency, and housing shortages. Your town doesn't have these arbitrary rules in place to prevent the construction of affordable and multi-unit housing, so you're planning this development as a YIMBY supporter would," I explain, trying to keep it light and simple.

He looks shocked, almost affronted by the idea of it. "Of course everyone should have a place to live they can afford. Not everyone needs the same style of home. I don't understand why anyone would be against that?"

"You and me both," I remark and leave it at that, not wanting to drag him down with the reality of urban planning in this country.

As much as it pains me, I'll give Ben credit where it's due. He answers every question I throw at him, giving me so much information about the surrounding land, the housing development, the construction site, issues faced by the citizens of Monstera Bluff, and so many other details to consider when designing this project. He isn't completely stonewalling me, and I'm grateful for that... to a point. I'm sure Clancy would be pissed if he withheld this information from me.

We're wrapping up at the construction site now that I've taken a ton of photos at each of the intersections. I brush off my legs and shoes, now dusty from the dirt road. Ben is still allergic to me, so I start walking to his truck and call over my shoulder, "I'm ready to go whenever you are."

The day is hot and sticky though it's mid-October, and I realize how sweaty I've become. I want nothing more than to hide away in my air-conditioned office for the rest of the afternoon. I can't deal with him or anyone else right now. I'm physically and emotionally spent.

Ben strides silently from behind me causing me to startle, heart jumping to my throat, as he opens the passenger door. It's the nearest he's been to me since we got here. His deep, disapproving grimace tells me he's had enough. I wilt under his guarded gaze as I climb into the truck, careful of my skirt. He shuts the door with a heavy thud, the noise surprising me again, and I spring in my seat. My nerves are frayed around him.

He starts the truck, air conditioning whirring to life, as does his music. I can't wait any longer. I need to tell him that I can't go to lunch and make some excuse, no matter how thin it sounds. It saddens me more than it should to break our plan, considering his attitude toward me, but I won't subject myself to an awkward, unwanted meal with him. Despite the professional relationship we'll be forced to maintain, I don't owe him anything beyond that. I've learned my lesson well over the years.

It hurts to know we could have been friends. He dangled that possibility in front of me and cruelly snatched it back. Comparing him to Mark may be too hasty since I only just met Ben. It's unfair, perhaps, on my part, viewing him through my emotional baggage from a painful eight-year relationship. But the fact remains—I must eliminate drama like this from my life as much as possible.

"Ben?" I begin resignedly. Apparently I speak more quietly than intended to because he turns off the music. He glances over at me, mouth still pinched like I'm bothering him. He raises the ridge over his eyes, waiting for me to continue. "Uh, I think I shouldn't waste any time before starting this proposal, so I probably shouldn't go out to lunch today. But thank you for inviting me earlier. Would you please take me back to town hall now?" I request, trying to sound inoffensive.

His flinty expression transforms for an instant—frowning, looking nearly crestfallen—but he blinks it away and returns his gaze out the windshield again. A muscle jumps in his jaw, making his face look strained. He must be annoyed that I beat him to it, taking some control of the situation. Robbing him of another opportunity to make me feel small.

"Of course," he replies coolly as he puts the truck into drive and pulls away.

It's a silent, uncomfortable ride back. It takes only minutes to return to the town hall, but it feels like hours. I'm in my head for most of it, staring out the window. Yet my eyes wander back to him, noticing how tensely he holds himself, his stony gaze straight ahead and body stiffly motionless except for the small movements necessary to drive.

Ben parks in front of the town hall building, and I fling the door open and hop out the moment he comes to a stop, putting some physical distance between us. Before I shut the door, I force my eyes up to him, and he seems reluctant to meet mine.

"Thank you for taking me out there. It was extremely helpful to see it. I'll send you the proposal when it's complete so you can review it and provide feedback." I try to imbue some professionalism into my voice, but it comes out sounding clumsy and stilted.

He gives a curt nod before he says, "Goodbye, Cara."

He waits to drive off until I've walked through the plaza to the front of the building. I watch his truck for a long, unblinking moment. Something crumples deep inside my gut, feeling like I just experienced the end of something that hadn't even started. I inhale shakily, unmoored by the time I spent with him. He's long gone now, his truck out of sight, so I try to regain my composure, smoothing my hair and dress as I walk inside.

I attempt to creep back to my office unnoticed. I'd rather sit quietly at my desk, lose myself in my work, rather than answer any questions about the visit. Just my luck, Clancy notices me immediately and waves me into his office as he's talking on the phone. He's the last person I want to see right now, but I have no choice but to comply.

He has questions in his eyes as he's wrapping up his call. It's obvious he's hurrying to get off the phone, though someone on the other end is not getting the hint. I take a seat in the smaller chair in front of his desk and try not to listen in. I just sit with my thoughts instead, which are more pitiful than they should be.

Finally, he puts the phone down and regards me. "Well, you are back awfully early for someone with a lunch date. So, I take it Ben was being a bastard again?" he announces with obvious censure toward Ben. It takes me by enough surprise that I gasp hard enough to give myself a coughing fit. "That bad, huh?" he jokes with a confiding grin that quickly turns sympathetic.

Getting my breath under control, I nod, unsure what to say. I've always found it best to share as little personal information as possible at the office. So I tell him in the most diplomatic way that comes to mind, "I don't think Ben meant to invite me to lunch, so I opted to come back after the site visit."

Clancy scrubs at his face and then runs his hands through his hair. "Fire and ashes, Ben is his own worst enemy sometimes," he utters in frustration, though I can still sense the underlying affection for his friend.

I smile wanly, wishing I knew Ben a fraction as well as Clancy does, but that'll never be the case. "He was helpful and answered every question I had. I'll be able to start working on the proposal today," I respond as benignly as possible, wanting to steer the conversation away from Ben.

Clancy sees through me. He tilts his head in a speculative manner, assessing me. "No, you aren't getting out of this so easily," he argues in a mock stern voice.

He gallops past the boundary I'm desperately trying to set, pun intended, and I imagine Clancy-approved. I know he's trying to help in his own way, but I still squirm in my seat. He guffaws at my uncomfortable reaction.

"You look as nervous as a cat in a room full of rocking chairs." He heaves a heavy sigh and softens his tone. "As a friend to Ben and I hope to you as well, tell me what exactly happened between the time we talked earlier and now."

I blanch at the thought of recounting everything. This mortifying predicament is careening out of my control. Even if Clancy is being supportive, I don't want this... interpersonal matter... to set the tone of my job here, on day one, no less. I won't be working with him all the time, so what does it matter? My hands start wringing in distress, so I close them into tight fists in my lap to appear more calm while I figure out what to do. Clancy is being pushy, Ben is being an asshole, and I can't win.

Clancy purses his lips and narrows his eyes at me. He presses, "Cara, please understand I'm not judging you. As you may have noticed, we operate differently than what you're used to, and I'm asking for your honesty about what happened. Believe me, Ben does not deserve your loyalty if he did something to make you this upset."

I start to say, "It's fine..."

"It's absolutely not fine!" he cuts me off in a voice that's not angry, but more commanding than I've heard him use. I pause, taken aback, snapping my mouth shut and feeling an uncomfortable pressure in my hands so tightly clasped I'm starting to cut off my circulation. I unwind them and smooth down my skirt before looking up at Clancy again.

"I'm sorry to use my alpha voice on you, but this is important. Now, please go on," he urges, his jovial drawl returning to his voice.

Alpha voice? I've hit my max capacity for surprises today, so I'll unpack that later. I almost groan in defeat that he really expects me to tattle on Ben. He lifts his eyebrows, his expression compelling me to begin. I feel like an emotional punching bag today.

"Um, honestly, I don't know what happened. There isn't much of a story. One minute, I thought we were becoming friendly, and the next, he acted like I was a complete stranger, one he's not too fond of. He was a different person to me this morning—friendly and complimentary. He even gave me flowers. And then, after I talked to you and returned to my office, he became cold and withdrawn again, like a flip of the switch while I was gone. The rest of the day was just awkward. Anyway, there isn't much to complain about. He took me to the job site and gave me all the info I needed. He wasn't hostile or aggressive—he still spoke to me—but he was completely uninterested in my presence. It's disappointing, but I'll get over it. It's not realistic that everyone is going to like me. As long as he doesn't hold up my work, I'll manage," I explain, hoping this is enough detail to assuage his irritation at Ben.

"Oh, he likes you. He just needs to get his tail out of his ass," Clancy huffs.

"Ada told me she was surprised by his rudeness yesterday. I just don't see how being so mercurial means he likes me. He's a grown man, not a child. I don't think there's anything here to dissect that says otherwise," I say regretfully.

He runs his hands through his hair again. "Look, Cara, I'm sorry for his behavior. I thought today would go very differently and that Ben would get out of his own head, out of his own way. He can be blunt and curt, but he's not cruel. As someone who knows him better than probably anyone, I can assure you it has nothing to do with him not liking you. There's something else going on in that thick skull. He's stubborn as a mule, and I can say that with some equine authority in the subject." He snorts horse-like at his joke.

My heart twists at his attempt to reassure me. He wants to salvage this because of their friendship. But I don't know if I could ever trust Ben. He made the conscious decision to treat me like that. Maybe this job is still salvageable, but a personal relationship with Ben isn't.

"Thanks for being kind. I'm going to head to my office now to organize my notes from the visit," I tell him as I stand up from the chair so I don't have to withstand any more scrutiny today. Though I still don't see much in common between Ben and Clancy, both have proven to be utterly exhausting in their own right.

Clancy won't let go of me yet. "Did you still plan to go to lunch?" he blurts out before I can reach the door. It sounds like he's trying to figure out whether he should take me instead.

"No, I'm not hungry. I'm just going to work on the proposal," I answer sedately so I can finally slip away.

"Why don't Ada and I take you to dinner tonight. She's due here soon. We can call it an early day after she and I have our meeting," he offers, perhaps deducing that I wouldn't say no to spending more time with Ada.

"Sure, that sounds nice," I say over my shoulder as I walk out the door.

Seeing the daisies on my desk is like a gut punch. I won't be able to settle until they're gone. I rip the card off and throw it in the waste basket near my desk. Walking into the kitchen, I set the vase on a little table in the corner. Maybe someone else will appreciate them.

It feels like a year has passed since this morning. Sitting at my desk, overwhelmed, I hold my head in my hands, rubbing my temples. A stray tear spills over my lashes. I can't let anyone see me fall apart, have any evidence of it, even if this was an unexpectedly awful day.

I dig my phone out of my purse and open my text conversation with Rose. I didn't talk to her before I fell asleep last night. This situation is so messy and makes me feel like a terrible, two-faced friend. She'd have good advice on how to handle Ben, but I'm too embarrassed to tell her anything of substance right now. Not that I'd even know where to start. *Not only are monsters real, but they love to stir up workplace drama just as much as humans!* Her jokes about the strange things I'd find here were a silly way to lighten the mood so I wouldn't freak out about the move to a small town. But they were *just jokes*. If I were to tell her the truth, she'd think I was delusional, that the strain of the past year finally caused me to snap. She'd lovingly and correctly come get me and force me to seek medical help. So I will have to lie to her.

"Really sorry I didn't call last night. Unpacked and passed out early. Very long day," I write to Rose.

"Figured! Don't apologize! What is the town like? Tell me!!" she sends back immediately.

Trying to stick to the truth as much as I can, as much as feels safe right now, I respond, "Cute downtown. Some nice restaurants! My landlady and boss are both nice. I think I'll get along well with them."

"Yay, I'm so glad! Did you start your job today? How'd it go?" she replies.

"The first day has been interesting... but I'm already working on a project to keep the townies living a car-light lifestyle," I type, hoping this distracts her.

"Just interesting? Good interesting or bad interesting? Did something weird happen?" Dammit, I need to watch what I say. "It's exciting you have a big project already, though. You can show them what you got!" she responds, her usual supportive self.

"Everything's good, just figuring out the lay of the land here! The project will keep me busy. It's a good thing I started now because it needs major help." I try to cover for myself, but the fib feels icky. Like a betrayal.

"Weird question, but did you apply to any other jobs before you got this one? I got a call yesterday from someone saying that I was a reference on your job application and they wanted to confirm your address. But you hadn't said anything about looking at other jobs, and I know you always give me a heads-up. Keep using me as a reference, obvs, but I was just confused. Would that have been your new boss? But then he'd have known where you live, right?" she replies.

Huh. I didn't give Clancy any references. And honestly, he probably wouldn't call up random humans... other than me, I guess. "No, he didn't ask for any. That's so strange someone called you! Maybe it was from when I was leaving Chicago? Did they ask you anything out of the ordinary?" I press, wondering why someone would reach out now.

"Not really. Just whether you were still in the Atlanta area since they were seeking a local candidate. I didn't want to give them too much info, so I said you were still regional. I wasn't about to give them your new address, in case they were sus. Maybe they're just late looking at their resumes. Who knows? I'm just so glad you're out of that job in Atlanta, though. After the accident and the way your workplace treated you... Girl, you deserve a good thing like this, finally! It's your time to shine! I gotta run to a meeting, call me soon!" she sends, followed by a few heart emojis. She's the best cheerleader I could ask for in a best friend.

I shove my phone back in my purse before I break down and tell her everything.

CHAPTER 8
CARA

Later in the afternoon, Ada collects me from my office. Her sympathetic expression gives away that Clancy already filled her in on our conversation. Part of me bristles that he told her, but it probably would have come up anyway during dinner. "Clancy told me we're breaking out of here early to get some food. Is it okay if I join?" she asks, voice soothing, her presence a balm to ease the sting of the day.

"Yeah, let's get out of here," I answer with a genuine smile.

As we walk down the hall, Clancy's waiting for us, his casual posture indicating he's off the clock, shedding the yoke of Mayor Evermane for our outing. "I don't know about you, but I'm as hungry as a horse!" he guffaws with a pat to his firm abs. Ada lets out a sparkling laugh, and I hesitantly giggle, still a little weirded out.

Clancy purses his lips at my reaction, unsatisfied. "Cara, lighten up. What's this body good for if not some horsin' around?" My eyebrows snap up as he reaches back to smack his equine flank.

Ada cracks up, and I can't help but follow suit at this absurdity. Ada nudges me, wisecracking, "Did you know he's also a part-time comedian?"

"Only in your dreams! How dare you besmirch the ancient and honorable Evermane name with that accusation?" He tuts sarcastically.

We walk outside, past the plaza, just a couple blocks to a pub I didn't notice yesterday. The wooden sign hanging above the door reads *The Call of the Wild* with a wolf howling at a full moon. I know now there's meaning behind that... and I feel some trepidation as we enter.

Unsurprisingly, Clancy seems to know everyone here, even affectionately clapping the burly, tattooed, *green* bartender on the arm after some quick, animated conversation. Ada leads me to a high-top table where Clancy will have plenty of room to stand, and we both climb onto tall chairs. A server, human-looking except for her silver eyes, brings menus and water. She asks for our drink order. Unsure of what would even be available, I let Clancy and Ada go first. Clancy orders mead, Ada, white wine. I also pick a white wine—an easy, familiar choice. Carefully sipping water, I gaze around nervously at the other patrons, though I'm much less fearful today.

As we chit-chat, I feel comfortable enough to bring up some nagging questions. "Are there other humans here?"

"Oh, we have maybe a few dozen living here right now. Most are mated to Whispered Folk, which is how they end up here. Funny enough, several of them work at the town hall in the *human relations* department, which a human named, I might add. They help us navigate their world in all sorts of ways, posing as the face of the town when we need it. They're quite busy, which I'm sure comes as no surprise," Clancy explains.

"Is there a support group for humans in monster towns?" I joke, feeling a little loose after a few sips of wine on an empty stomach.

Clancy emits a horsey snort. "Nothing so official!" He turns to Ada. "Fire and ashes, could you imagine what Samuels would think of that? He'd throw a hissy fit!"

Ada's in stitches, slapping her leg, seeming to delight in her imagining of Samuels' reaction. "The council would never hear the end of it!" she wheezes.

This doesn't sound funny to me. "He doesn't like humans?" I ask, wary.

"That's an understatement. But don't worry about him. He's a close-minded old coot and one of only a few here who share that opinion," Ada reassures me as she pats my arm. I hope I can avoid him as long as possible.

"Ada, did you hear about the automobile tires slashed on Atlantic Street last night? The constabulary is looking into it, but whoever did it was sneaky enough to avoid magickal detection. So it had to be someone familiar with magick, or they were told exactly what to do to get away with it," Clancy guesses, looking dubious.

"Yeah, Celeste told me about it. Some pack members' automobiles were damaged," she informs him. They give each other skeptical looks and continue talking about it in low voices, obviously not wanting this information to spread beyond our table.

While Clancy and Ada are occupied, I finally have a chance to peruse the menu. I recognize most of the dishes, deciding on a grilled chicken sandwich since I doubt it'll come with too many surprises. At some point, I'll try Whispered Folk cuisine. When in Rome, I suppose. Our server checks on us soon after. We place our food order, and Clancy asks for another mead. I imagine, with his size, he can hold his liquor way better than most. Though the thought of a tipsy Clancy puts an unbidden smile on my face—he's a little goofy anyway. The smile fades when I wonder if it would make Ben even more silent and sullen. Why am I even thinking about him at all?

"Cara, what is your gut telling you about Howling Road?" Clancy asks, sounding genuinely curious. As I show them my notebook, summarizing my ideas, both of their faces light up. "That's brilliant, Cara!" Clancy exclaims with a clap of his hands.

"So thoughtful. Everyone will love it! It'll be a surefire hit with the council," Ada adds with genuine approval in her gaze.

Hearing their praise buoys my spirit. "I'll probably be able to present something at the next meeting. Tuesday, right?" I offer, hoping I can continue to impress them.

"Introducing her along with her proposal... this is going to be a meeting for the history books," Clancy beams at Ada, whose expression reflects his.

When the food arrives we dig in. Just like at the restaurant last night, the meal is incredible. The chicken is juicy and well-seasoned. The bun is fresh, like it was baked this morning. The tomato and lettuce have the flavor and texture of heirloom varietals. Conversation pauses as we eat, a sure sign everyone is enjoying the meal.

"Do you like it?" Clancy grins, knowing full well I'm happily stuffing my face.

"It's so good!" I enthusiastically exclaim, hand covering my mouth full of food, giggling as he gives me a playful wink while chewing his own bite of food. Swallowing the bite, I ask, "Is all food in Monstera Bluff so amazing? Everything I've eaten here has been delicious!"

"Oh yes, good food is a way of life around here. We won't tolerate anything less," Clancy confirms around big bites of his own meal. "It seems like you're enjoying it too."

"Probably too much!" I say self-deprecatingly, though it's the truth. I'm not skinny, even after my unintended anxiety and depression weight loss plan this year.

"No such thing! How dare you even speak such rubbish?" Clancy gasps in mock horror, making Ada and I crack up.

This sends us into a deep-dive conversation about cuisine and restaurants, and I'm staggered by the number of options here. Clancy wasn't kidding earlier. I reveal that I'm usually an adventurous eater, having grown up with international cuisine in Chicago—so many cheap, family-owned, hole-in-the-wall restaurants nearby. Mexican, Ethiopian, Moroccan, Vietnamese... I love them all. Mid-conversation, the mood shifts as I notice they're both distracted by something out the window.

Clancy frowns and narrows his eyes as he grumbles, "Is that shifty gargoyle lurking around outside? If he takes off before I reach him, I swear I'll clip those wings when he isn't looking." Clancy stomps out the door to the *shifty gargoyle,* whom I have zero interest in seeing right now.

Just when I thought the day was looking up...

Worrying my lips, I stare at Ada, whose attention darts between me and the window—trying to catch a glimpse of what's going on outside. She senses my apprehension and puts a comforting hand on my arm.

"I'd prefer if he didn't join us tonight," I request calmly, trying to perform the delicate dance of letting her know my feelings about Ben without oversharing. I can't risk offending anyone right now since I'm the newcomer in their town, my position here still tenuous.

She gives a pained smile. "Don't mince words on my account. Let that thick-headed male be taken to task." The roll of her eyes gives me the sneaking suspicion she's had her own fair share of experience with *thick-headed males*. There seem to be some universal truths in the human and monster worlds.

Before I can respond, the front door swings open as Clancy marches Ben inside. Ben looks resigned, like he's about to face the hangman's rope. I'd prefer any reaction but that. It hollows out my guts, makes me feel like less than nothing. Ben's slightly outstretched wings remind me of the secret glimpse I caught of them earlier. They must be terrifying and magnificent when fully spread. I wish I didn't care, but it would be incredible to see him in flight.

Perhaps he did try to fly away. I'm sure that pissed off Clancy and bringing him inside... toward me... is quite the punishment for whatever happened out there. I avert my eyes as they walk toward the table, suddenly finding my half-full wine glass on the table much more compelling than it ought to be—making me wish I could drown in the liquid courage it holds. My stomach curdles when I hear Ben's deep, flat timbre right next to me, "Ada. Cara."

We both say hello, though I direct it to my glass, and Ada lets her annoyance with him seep into her tone.

The server pops by to take his order, dispelling some of the tension in the air, causing me to look up at their interaction. "The usual?" she asks, bumping her shoulder to his, like they're old friends. He nods, his face softens for her with a warm smile. A twinge of resentment springs in my chest that she gets a smile from him, and I don't, not anymore, anyway. I wince at my reaction. I'm being completely ridiculous—we don't owe each other anything. It's not my business who he smiles at. Ben's attention returns to the table, his gaze on me for only an instant before it rests on everything but, his expression inscrutable.

Ada pointedly clears her throat. "So Ben, I hear that Cara saved your project?" I can't be certain, but it looks like Ben blushes—or the closest approximation of a blush on gray skin.

He hums in agreement and replies calmly, "Indeed, she quickly came up with a much better plan than I was capable of."

Ada gives Ben a look that could make a grown man wither and die.

"Then it seems like we should all be grateful Cara decided to upend her life to move here, shouldn't we?" Clancy chimes in, stressing each word. "It's almost like she was meant to be here."

The irritated look Clancy gives Ben is laden with some meaning I don't fully understand, though the rest seem to. Ben looks chastened. If they tell him to apologize to me, I might actually die of embarrassment. I do the only thing that seems right in the moment and down the rest of my wine in one painful gulp.

Ada smiles at me encouragingly, asking, "How were you able to come up with something so quickly? Have you designed a road like that before?"

I pause as I look between Ada and Clancy, uncomfortable with the direction of this conversation if they mean to throw it in Ben's face. I wish I could rewind my life five minutes to when I was having fun for the first time in longer than I care to admit.

"Well, I've worked on several projects like this, but in bits and pieces since existing roadways often have some pretty inflexible parameters to work around. I've always thought about what it would be like to put all of that together. So I guess it's a long time coming. Kind of a dream project I always had in the back of my mind," I reply, still feeling self-conscious.

Something in my explanation kindles Clancy's interest. He tilts his head speculatively and asks, "Now, don't get me wrong, I'm so glad you accepted my job offer, and I won't look a gift horse in the mouth." He and Ada snicker at his pun. Remembering the last time I thought about that phrase, right before accepting this job, my stomach sinks. "But if I may ask, why would you choose to work in such a small town over a prestigious firm in Chicago or Atlanta? You'd have known the scale of work in a small town, even as its city planner, is so much different," he observes.

I was hoping to avoid this conversation, at least until they knew me a little better. "Well, I've always wanted to be a city planner. It was my career goal when I was in school. But there's more to it than that. If you really want to know… I'll tell you," I reply, my reluctance evident in my voice.

"Only share what you're comfortable with. Clancy doesn't need to know every detail of your life," Ada interjects, giving him a look. My past weighs on me constantly, affects so much of my life even now. I don't want it to stain their perception of me.

"Only my closest friends know the full extent of why I moved around this year. At the beginning of the year, I applied to firms in big cities across the country. I didn't really care where I moved. There was an opening at a civil engineering firm in Atlanta a lot like the one I was trying to leave in Chicago. Fewer responsibilities with a better title and pay. I was a shoo-in because I was doing work so far above my pay grade for years. So, obviously, I wasn't getting paid fairly for a long time. But that's a story for another day," I sigh. The three of them are staring, hanging on every word.

"If this new job in Atlanta was a step up, what happened?" Clancy spurs me on.

The heaviness of their rapt attention settles into me. "I thought I could rebuild my life… professionally, financially, you name it. My best friend Rose helped me move out there, but when she had to go home, I was totally alone. My colleagues and boss were polite but not friendly. I didn't see it at first, but the office was cliquey and competitive—and as a new hire, it wasn't easy to gain a foothold there. I never felt settled into my job or my life outside of work. I didn't make friends. The city never felt like home." The weight of these memories lifts from me with each one spoken aloud, the relief compounding inside me so quickly that I can't stop the flow after being bottled up for so long.

Ada puts a hand to her heart. "Hon, that sounds lonely. I'm so sorry."

"But there's more," I explain over a hitch in my breath. "I'm always such a careful driver. I grew up in Chicago, taking the bus and train everywhere, so I didn't even have a car until I was in college. When I finally had one—a very old boat of a car I inherited from my grandma—I only drove a couple times a week. It seems contrary to the American experience, but I don't particularly like driving. In Atlanta, there's no choice. There's no getting by without a car. Even though I'm a focused defensive driver, Atlanta's traffic is a nightmare, and so many drivers are reckless. Street racing is a huge issue. I'd read about it in the news, even witnessed it from far away. Well, a few months ago, on the I-85 on my way to a project site, I wasn't so lucky. It was like a dark blur sideswiped me, pushing my car into the traffic barrier on the side of the road."

The flood of memories makes me shaky. And yet, sharing them makes me feel lighter and more like myself than I have in a long time. "Honestly, it could have been so much worse. I didn't have any permanent physical injuries. Some deep bruising and scrapes along the left side of my body, a sprained wrist, a mild concussion. My SUV was in bad shape, but it wasn't totaled. It just... rattled me to my core. I haven't been able to drive along there again. And it's not easy to get around Atlanta without taking highways. It put me in an impossible position," I reveal, my voice thick with emotion. I catch myself cradling my injured wrist, reminded of the pain.

A growl erupts next to me, startling me out of my introspection. "Were they ever caught?" Ben's voice rasps, his eyes glued to mine.

I shake my head no. No one paid the price but me.

"An ambulance took me to the hospital, and after I was looked over by a doctor, I called my boss to let him know what happened and that I'd need PTO to recover. He started acting weird, asking if I was going to file for workman's comp and trying to get me to admit to stopping somewhere after I had left the office—which I didn't. I'm sure he was trying to suss out if they could deny me. It was such a gross, litigious thing to ask me while I was lying in a hospital bed in pain," I say with a bitter bite to my voice.

"Who was there to help you?" Ada frets, looking upset on my behalf.

"No one after I left the hospital. I told my close group of friends what happened, including Rose. She offered to fly out that night. I told her no, but that was stupid of me. I needed her. I just... felt like a burden. She'd just moved me there a few months ago. I couldn't ask her for such a huge favor again on such short notice. The concussion was the worst of my injuries, but it still took me over a month to feel better. By that time, I understood how bad things were at work. Any goodwill I had toward my boss for hiring me evaporated after that conversation.

While I was out, my projects were handed off to colleagues to stick to deadlines. And nobody would give them back when I returned. It was like I was being punished for being injured. I just couldn't do it anymore. Staying at that job. Driving on those dangerous fucking interstates. But most of all, feeling so isolated. I knew the injuries would heal, but the loneliness never would," I confess, a tenuous sense of relief washing over me now that it's out in the open.

I feebly attempt to lighten the mood. "Honestly, Clancy found me at the exact right time. I was mostly back to normal. The bruises and scrapes had faded. My SUV was repaired. I was days away from officially starting my job search to get the hell out of there. I was a little afraid to ask before, but how did you find me?" I ask, raising an eyebrow at Clancy.

"Uh, I was on a deep dive reading urbanism articles online and found your name. So I looked you up to see what you were doing in your career," he says a little woodenly, uncharacteristically tight-lipped. He runs his hand roughly through his hair.

That seems so unlikely, but what other reason could there be. "I can't believe my name is still out there after so many years. I published a few papers in grad school, but there is so much more out there nowadays. I thought everyone forgot about me. Professionally speaking, I basically dropped off the face of the earth while I was stuck at Hansen Company for so long."

I barely finish my thought as a group of unruly, overserved patrons noisily jostle around behind us. I freeze as their booming voices get louder by the second, like they're heading straight for me, sending a shard of icy dread down my spine.

Gulping down a shriek, an arm abruptly wraps around me, tugging me and my chair out of their path... and closer to Ben. Wide-eyed, I stare at the lavender-gray hand grasping, curling protectively around my hip. My attention snaps to Ben's face as he growls ferociously, flashing fangs at the rowdy group behind us.

Sobered by Ben's fierce reaction, a chorus of *sorry* and *we didn't mean nothin' by it* sounds from right behind me—so close I can feel a breeze from their movement. They quickly back away from our table and beeline toward the exit.

"Fucking brownies," Ben grunts as he carefully unwinds his arm from me, but the feel of him lingers there.

It takes all my willpower not to place my own hand over the spot, preserving for a little longer that sense of safety it gave me. He studies me with an unreadable look before glaring at the group, who are finally making their way out the door. Neither of us moves back to our respective places at the table, and now we sit almost intimately close, his body heat mingling with mine.

"Looks like they were three sheets to the wind! You alright, Cara?" Ada exasperates, looking concerned as her eyes flicker between me and Ben.

"Oh, um, I'm fine," I squeak, still recovering.

A faint smile pulls on Clancy's lips, only dropping when he clears his throat and probes, "There wasn't anyone else to help you during your recovery? What about your family?"

Clancy's killing me. Shaking my head, a chagrined laugh escapes me. "Now you're just rubbing salt in the wound," I reply ruefully. Ben watches me now, his eyes narrowing, his lips pressed firm.

Ada makes a face at Clancy. "Don't be afraid to tell him when he puts his hoof in his mouth."

"It's a fair question. Most people have families they can turn to. I don't, though." I sigh, wishing the ground would open up and swallow me right about now so I don't have to spill my guts in front of Ben.

"My mom raised me, though I spent most of my time with my grandparents because she worked long hours. My dad was never in the picture. I guess he left when my mom told him she was pregnant. When I was about fifteen, she started dating a guy she met at one of her jobs. Turns out, she leaned hard into that relationship—the divorced dad and his two young boys, a ready-made family. They got married right away, and I became even more of an afterthought to her at that point, generally ignored by all of them. She was able to cut back her work hours and be the picture-perfect wife and mother to her new family," I explain joylessly, knowing few can relate to that kind of childhood.

"Even your mother ignored you?" Clancy interrupts, sounding shocked.

I shrug. "Yes, when she wasn't yelling at or criticizing me. I was shut out of their family, basically left to fend for myself. My grandma saw what was going on, so she had me move in with her. My grandpa had passed away a couple years earlier. I think she liked the company with me there, anyway. I didn't need to be raised anymore. I was studious. Not a total goody two-shoes, but not wild either. Just a normal teenager. She provided a home when I needed one, and we looked out for each other." I sniffle, choking up at the thought of my grandma. She was the constant throughout my entire childhood. Ben surprises me by handing me a crisply folded bright white handkerchief from his pocket. I give him a small grateful smile as I take it and dab my eyes.

Ada leans across the table to squeeze my hand in a sympathetic gesture. "Is your grandmother still with us?" she asks tenderly.

"No, she isn't. While I was in college, she was diagnosed with an aggressive form of cancer and given only a few weeks to live. I guess I can be thankful she didn't suffer long. Those weeks were a blur. I visited her in the hospital nearly every day, and then she was gone," I recount wanly.

"Sounds like you were lucky to have each other," Ada comforts, her own eyes misty with emotion.

"Cara, you honor us with these stories from your life. Thank you for sharing them. We hope you know we're here for you always, no matter what. Come to any of us with *anything* that troubles you. Lean on our friendship whenever you need," Clancy imparts with such sincerity that tears threaten to spill down my cheeks all over again.

Ada shakes her head fervently, and even Ben minutely nods in hesitant agreement.

"Thanks, that means a lot," I blubber, still feeling vulnerable. Why couldn't I dole out my miserable history piecemeal like a normal person? At least there are a few shameful parts of my past I've kept to myself today.

"I think it's time Cara and I headed out. Why don't I take you to the grocery store to stock up on some things you might need?" she suggests.

I'm sure I look as wrung out as I feel so I'm grateful for her intervention. Clancy pulls some bills out of the leather cross-body bag he wears and puts them on the table.

The sun is setting by the time we leave. The fear of what goes bump in the night swells in my chest again, but it's more manageable today. As we walk toward the door, Ben's hand moves to the small of my back, lingering with a gentle pressure as he ushers me outside. It's a strangely proprietary gesture for someone who otherwise seems not to care very much.

CHAPTER 9
BEN

Sometimes, I curse small-town living. There's no peace to be had. And that's never been truer than when I spot Clancy and Cara situated intimately close at a table as I walk past the corner pub. Fire and ashes, I really should have flown home.

Usually, I do when I'm stuck in the office doing paperwork—the one thing I dislike about owning my business. Stretching out and moving my body in a way that I crave after being cooped up all day indoors, flying will lift me out of any foul mood. But right now, I'm walking the short distance from my office to my truck. The truck I drove this morning, knowing I'd end up taking Cara to the construction site. But of course, after a miserable afternoon thinking way too much about her, second-guessing everything, I run into them like this.

Seeing them together is difficult, especially after putting the necessary space between us today. Everything has changed for me, knowing that someone like Cara is out there, in this town of all places. But she's too human, too sheltered from Whispered Folk, for there to be anything between us. I will never earn her affection, and I don't need to moon over her. Watching how easily she accepts Clancy hits me harder than expected. I rarely envy Clancy—I know his burdens too well—but the handsome, human-looking parts of him put her at ease in a way I never will. I don't know if she's smitten like so many females are, but she gravitates toward him like she could be. And now that I've met Cara, learned more about her, and realized she'll never be mine, I'm not sure I'll find peace here ever again.

Behind me, the pub's door swings open, and I know in my gut it's Clancy, but I don't look back, even at the unmistakable sound of his hooves stomping down the sidewalk toward me.

"I saw you walking by. And I know you saw us too. Join us?" he asks in a deceptively cool tone.

I spin on my heels, grimacing, "Not today."

He crosses his arms, and his voice goes ice cold as he informs me, "I think today might be the last chance you have."

It's astounding that Clancy can be so oblivious. This is one of those occasions when he mistakenly thinks everything comes as easily to others as it does to him. Rubbing the bridge of my nose where a headache is forming, I huff, "I don't think that's a good idea. She didn't want to spend any more time with me today. I'm not going to interrupt you two."

He gives an exasperated laugh, and his eyes fix on me with a flinty gaze. "And I wonder why, Ben? Get your tail out of your ass and apologize to her. Again. I can't believe I even have to say this. You're too old to be so dense."

I shake my head. He doesn't get it, and so we're at an impasse. "Clancy, she's scared of me. Apologize for what? The way I look? What I am?" I reply, trying to keep my voice steady, opening my wings to make my point.

"Unbelievable. You're as dumb as a sack of hammers. No, not for the way you look. For the foolhardy way you're acting. Get your stubborn tail inside. I told them I'd clip your wings if I have to, and I swear to Mother Earth, I'll do it!" Clancy roars at me. He rarely raises his voice, so I know he's angry and isn't going to back down. But what he said shakes something loose in my brain.

"Them?" I ask.

Clancy rolls his eyes and gestures back toward the pub. "Yeah, Cara and Ada. Them."

"So it's not just you and Cara in there?" I attempt to confirm, realizing that the look of warmth and fondness on Cara's face, their close proximity, may not be the cozy date it seemed at first glance.

He looks at me like I've grown a third horn. "Yes, Ada, too. After your performance today, I needed to call in the reinforcements. You really upset Cara, you oaf. She's trying to play it off, but it's clear as day that she's hurt. Now get inside," he orders.

Still, none of this changes the fact that she fears me.

Against my better judgment, I walk toward the pub. Clancy is close behind, like he's afraid I'll fly away. I growl in annoyance as I feel his hand at my back propelling me forward, and he laughs arrogantly at my reaction. As I step through the doorway, Cara looks distressed to see me and then quickly turns away. A few steps inside, Ada flashes a dubious look in my direction. I greet them, but Cara still won't look at me.

The interior is dim, even with the daylight shining through the windows. The dark wood of the long bar, walls, and coffered ceiling absorbs and neutralizes all the light. My cousin is a waitress here, and she takes my drink order. "Hey Benny, good to see you. The usual?" she greets me. I imagine I'm going to be here for a while, so I give her a kindly nod, trying not to take up too much of her time since she looks busy. I settle in, making myself comfortable, even as Ada verbally jabs and pokes at me, as much of a tongue-lashing as I've ever heard from her. I suppose I don't blame her; she doesn't get it either, not having had Cara's fear aimed at her. Not knowing the sting of it. I'm the odd one out in this group, looking as I do. But I play along and let them express their anger. There's no use in trying to refute it.

Mercifully, Ada and Clancy's interest in Cara's background is stronger than their desire to admonish me. And soon enough, they coax some of her history out of her. It upsets me to see her become emotional at times during their incessant questioning, but I may never learn this much about her otherwise. And as Clancy unsubtly mentions that she's supposed to be here, I wonder too what's unfolded in her life that the Seer would have known of her, chosen her above anyone else to bring into our orbit.

Though she does her best to hide it, anguish at the events that drove her from Atlanta is evident in every word, each pause and breath. Her sorrow runs deep. I'm not the most socially adept, but even I can see it. That sparks more concern over the Seer's vision. Clancy and Ada shouldn't be pushing her so hard to open up to them. It could drive her away from us.

Captivated by Cara's words, I almost miss an aggressive group of drunk brownies hurtling toward us, nearly crashing into our table. My instinct roars out. I haul Cara close to me, ready to envelop her in my wings in protection if needed, and snarl at these drunkards who dare to almost touch her. I'm too concentrated on shielding her to savor the moment my arm wraps around her, her hip in my hand. These brownies are a perennial nuisance, and I will not allow their bad behavior to go unchecked. My growl breaks through their revelry, startling them into submission. They heed my warning—at least they're smart enough to do that. They leave, but the damage has been done to Cara's peace, and I was too late to prevent it.

"Fucking brownies," I rage at their timing, how they've compromised this fragile situation. Cara's shoulders are hunched, and the tension in her posture betrays just how scared the disruption made her feel at an already vulnerable moment. I keep her right next to me, remaining vigilant to act quicker should this happen again.

Reluctantly, I release her after checking that she's unharmed, the feel of her lush body, the curve of her hip, branded onto my skin. I'd keep her tucked into my side indefinitely if I had an excuse to, and the feeling heightens after learning how badly her mother failed her. I want to bring her even closer, guard her more steadfastly against anything that would harm or upset her. She gets teary-eyed talking about her beloved grandmother. I know firsthand how special that relationship can be and feel her acute pain at the loss. Belatedly, I realize I put a freshly laundered handkerchief in my pocket this morning, handing it to her while her eyes are especially bright with tears.

Hearing about her family reminds me I should visit mine this weekend. While we don't always see eye to eye, I find great solace in their support and love, considering not all are so lucky. The irony is not lost on me that I see less of them than ever after taking over the family business. But my father set us up well when he retired a few years ago, and now we have nearly too many projects lined up. Not only that, but my younger brother has also been away for several years, so I feel additional pressure to be there for my parents in his absence.

Ada announces that she and Cara are leaving, and I'm glad she's cutting off Clancy, who seems not to realize Cara looks beyond fatigued, her eyes rimmed red from weariness. He would keep going until she fell out of her seat in exhaustion. She hasn't yet realized she should tell Clancy to knock it off. I'll have to find a way to explain to her she doesn't need to cater to his every whim, even if he is her boss. She's too kind and acquiescent to stand a chance against his busybody tendencies.

Escorting Cara to the door, Clancy shoots me a meaningful look, gesturing toward where he intercepted me earlier. I nod my understanding before we say our goodbyes and part with Cara and Ada, who head in the opposite direction. "That was good work, Ben. Though you should learn to communicate beyond grunts and growls." His chastising words are offset by a satisfied grin. "Those brownies... Mother Earth, I couldn't have dreamt it better."

I roll my eyes that he could even entertain such a notion. "You're lucky I was next to her. Were you going to let her get barreled into by those drunks? Ashes, she would have run away from here and never looked back," I chide, my disbelief in his recklessness growing.

"It's a good thing she had you here to protect her, isn't it? Aren't you glad I suggested you come in?" he asks too innocently, mischief twinkling in his eyes. I grunt in defiance, trying not to let on that he's right.

Regardless, tonight opened my eyes to so many ways she could be pushed away without us even realizing it. "I won't be there all the time to keep her out of harm's way. You still don't get it. She'll always turn to you or Ada. Not me. Make sure you keep her safe, too, Clancy. She's too important," I argue, trying to get him to understand.

As we reach my truck, Clancy claps a hand on my shoulder. "I hear what you're saying. Of course I'm going to do everything I can to make sure she's happy and safe." He pauses, running his hand through his hair. "That's why I humbly ask you to heed my advice when I say that you need to find a new way with her," he pleads with me earnestly.

"Alright, I'll think about it," I promise him. And I do, until the wee hours of the morning, unable to fall asleep, wondering just how complicated this situation with Cara will become.

The next day at work passes quickly, mired in switching gears, getting crews assigned to smaller backburner projects we originally booked to start at later dates. Another day spent indoors doing paperwork and managing clients makes me irritable. And with no plans in the evening, I finally have time to lose myself in flight, soundlessly and wordlessly soaring above the town toward the Atlantic coastline. Stretching my wings and letting them guide me in the moment.

It's getting dark earlier these days, so I'm able to travel outside the bounds of our ward, unconcerned about being spotted. I fly until the coast is barely a blur in the distance. My vision is good, if not better, in the dark, so I track a thunderstorm rolling through, gathering strength over the ocean. I can't help but fly along its dark, churning edge, feeling the electrical charge in the air. Witnessing the pure, unadulterated power of nature is hypnotic and meditative in a way that puts my mind at ease. As the storm stalks closer to shore, I return home just in time to hear its rain patter at my windows.

I tell myself not to think about Cara over the weekend, but that's easier said than done. Saturday morning, I fly to my parents' house, picking up a box of my mother's favorite pastries from the bakery on the way. Knocking on their front door, I'm greeted by her looking more than a little rumpled, wrapped in her robe. "Good morning, sweetheart!" she addresses me more cheerfully than usual in her singsong voice.

"Good morning, Maman," I greet her as I enclose her in a hug, pressing a kiss to the top of her head.

"Hey, son! Good timing, just put the coffee on!" my father calls out from the kitchen. I don't doubt the 'good timing' part. Any earlier, and I'm sure I would have interrupted them...

Since my father retired, he's kept busy with projects around their house, the kind that never actually got finished while he was running the business. Today, the downstairs bathroom looks like its own construction site. Guess he can't keep away from those for too long. Even as he's gotten older, he's as strong as ever, but with a thicker band around the middle now that he's stepped away from daily manual labor. I can tell my mother likes his belly because she always absentmindedly rubs it as they sit draped all over each other like teenagers in love. Retirement has put a spark back in their relationship. Maybe they consider this their second, indefinite honeymoon.

My mother is a wolf shifter, part of the local pack, though my brother and I don't share any of those traits with her. Even though, as a rule, Whispered Folk pairings greatly favor one set of genetics over another if they have children, there was no question my brother and I would be gargoyles. The magickal origins of my kind ensure it.

In medieval France, gargoyles were animated from the ubiquitous stone statues into flesh and bone by powerful warlocks and witches at the behest of the few who were aware of such potent, powerful magick and could afford it. We became the guardians of their riches, mayhap also of the secrets they wished to keep hidden away. We were never meant to be given full life from our stone origins, just mindless, deadly soldiers who could be transformed back and forth as needed.

Such powerful magick tends to go awry—twisting in strange, unexpected directions, taking on a life of its own—sometimes in the truest sense possible. We became our own kind, fully unshackled from our magickal creators, so much more than the mindless guard dogs they created us to be. And yet, that magick has made us different from most Whispered Folk in very distinct ways. We are attracted to naturally evolved species; their life essence is necessary to balance our magick-borne origin. And for whatever reason, we're mostly male, though I've heard some female gargoyles now exist.

Our ancestors were solemn, serious, and protective. Like me. Yet, my father and brother both inherited the gift of gab, a lightness certainly not originating from our gargoyle side. Their gregarious natures are likely inherited from the mothers and grandmothers in our long family lineage. But that's not supposed to happen, so we've been told at least. Maybe the magick within us is changing again, even now, and we shouldn't make the mistake of assuming we fully understand it. Our makers never even expected us to have sentience and free will, let alone pursue relationships and be able to reproduce as our own kind.

Certainly, an unreserved personality helps my little brother Lucas thrive in the human world, letting him blend in better than I ever could. My brother is much younger, ten years my junior, still in his twenties. While in New York City, he finished his architecture degree and now works at a big architectural firm to gain experience before moving back to a Whispered Folk community. My parents worry about him and his safety around humans, but he seems like he's in his element, enjoying his time there. How he can wear such a hefty glamor for so long every day, up close and personal with humans, I have no idea. Then again, he also prefers working in an office rather than outdoors with his hands, something else I don't get.

"Are those what I think they are?" my mother coos at the pink box in my hands, her silver eyes lighting up as she clasps her hands in front of her heart. I open the lid to show her the pains au chocolat inside. "And I didn't think this morning could get any better!" she gushes, then takes the box from me and heads into the kitchen, ignoring my burning cheeks as she all but confirms my suspicions about their early morning activities. Ashes, she can be shameless sometimes.

My father pulls three sets of mugs and plates from the cabinet and places them on the kitchen table. "So, I hear we have a new human in town and you've already met her." My father grins at me, wasting no time trying to confirm what he's heard from the small-town rumor mill. Any whiff of someone new to town, especially a human, will set tongues wagging. There goes my attempt not to think about Cara.

I give him a flustered look as I reply, "You hear, Père?"

"Your old Père may be retired, but I'm not living under a rock." He chuckles.

My mother shakes her head as she teases, "You know Père and his friends. They gossip like a bunch of old hens."

My father balks, like he can't believe she would say such a thing, and then playfully growls, "Old hens, she calls us. More like a bunch of wise old crows!" He winks at me as he pulls her to him, giving her an affectionate squeeze and a kiss on the cheek.

I smile at their antics as I sit at the table, but I'm dreading this conversation. My father pours the coffee as my mother plates the pains au chocolat. I'm in the hot seat, so to speak. There's no point in denying I've met Cara.

"You heard correctly. Cara is a human, and Clancy hired her to be our city planner. She started on Thursday. We're working together on the Howling Road expansion project," I verify, hoping that will be the end of it, knowing it won't.

"Well, even though you have not had luck finding a mate here yet, don't get discouraged. You know there are Whispered Folk here mated to humans. It happens sometimes. Mayhap if you think she's pretty and you get along..." my mother trails off knowingly.

I can see that same glint in her eyes that Clancy gets when he talks to me about Cara, the unsubtle scheming. I don't like how presumptuous it is that they think she'd want to be anything more than a work colleague.

Measuring my words, I refute her gently, "She will be an asset to the town, even though she's a human. She's very sharp, with good experience, and is well suited for the job. She's new to us, Whispered Folk, so it may take time until she's comfortable here. But Clancy has taken her under his wing to get her settled. He wants the job to work out so she'll stay here long term. As for her personal life, I don't believe she's mated or attached. And I'm not sure my thoughts on her attractiveness matter for the job." I sound defensive, but I don't want to give my mother false hope.

"Under his wing? Shouldn't you be doing that, son?" My parents laugh at my father's joke, and a calculating look passes between them.

"That part where I said she's brand new to Whispered Folk? It means I absolutely should be doing no such thing. My appearance is unpalatable, too monstrous. It's already upset her," I reply, giving them no quarter in this.

"Sweetheart, Clancy isn't human. How does she act around him?" My mother's earnest question can't hide her crystal-clear motives.

"They seem to get along well. But you know how easy that is for Clancy," I retort flippantly, weighted heavily by a history of having similar conversations with them many times over the years.

It's long been a point of contention between my parents and me that I wasn't as social as him, dated barely a fraction as much as Clancy —who, by any measure, dates far too much. By choosing to measure me against him, they're refusing to see me for who I am, especially after so many years of hearing it.

"Well, I think you're not giving her enough credit, especially if she hasn't run away screaming yet. She can't be a shrinking violet for long around here!" she surmises, like it's a given.

I disagree. I can't remember anyone arriving here without knowing the true nature of the community. But there's no use arguing with her on this point. "She's only been here a few days, Maman. It's going to take her longer than that for her to feel safe around most Whispered Folk," I reason with her.

"Maybe Clancy has his eyes on her? Is that why he hired her? He needs to settle down soon now that he's the mayor," she suggests with faux innocence, the sharp look in her eyes betraying her tone.

"No," I nearly snarl. "That is not why he hired her, and that is not going to happen!"

A smile spreads across her face, and I know I've been baited and caught. "My my! It seems you feel very strongly about that. But what if someone else asks her out first, and you lose your chance? Clancy dates so many females, he will give you pointers on how to win her over," she declares, as if the matter is settled.

"Don't fret, son! Females find gargoyles very attractive. We are very good and attentive mates," my father adds confidently as he smiles at my mother. She takes his hand and appreciatively hums her agreement.

They're lost in a loving gaze for a moment before my mother clears her throat, returning her attention to me. "You should bring some pastries to her. I know these are very popular with humans."

Mother Earth, these two lovebirds are ridiculous lately. I can take a hint, so I shove the pain au chocolat from my plate into my mouth and start to get up. I slurp down my coffee in a few quick gulps before I tell them, "I'm not going to just show up at her home. But you're right that humans do love these as much as we do. Thank you for reminding me. I had better head out. It was good to spend time with you this morning."

"Benny, you don't have to leave so soon," she protests weakly, and I can see them ogling each other in a way that makes me want to scour my eyeballs. I'm happy they're deliriously in love after all these years, but they're still my parents, and I don't want to witness the lusty side of their relationship. They'll be quite wrapped up in each other the instant I'm gone.

We say our goodbyes, and I'm in the air again, my mind never straying far from Cara as I soar over the town, maybe a little too close to her carriage house than is wise or necessary. It concerns me that my parents already knew about her, probably having heard much more than they let on. And if even my parents see her as an object of fascination, worthy of gossip, then so many others will, too. It's not as if she's the only human here. But the others came here with their mates they met elsewhere. Not many Whispered Folk can spend enough time in the human world to meet, connect, and fall in love with a human, so the number of humans here remains relatively low. Most are mated to shifters and witches who can move among humans more freely. But she's come here on her own, a first for us in Monstera Bluff.

Clancy isn't hiding her—and shouldn't be. She's already started her job inside the town hall. But she's not just any new resident, and the community will soon realize it. He has done a lot for Cara, providing her with a job and a place to live—no small things. But he doesn't seem to have any other plan for her at this point other than to hope it all works out. There's a gnawing, twisting feeling in my gut that something's amiss, something Clancy and Ada don't see. The Seer wouldn't have been shown a foreboding potential future for Cara unless there was a real threat to her. Clancy's instincts to rush headlong into bringing her here may have left us unprepared, and I worry about the consequences... and about Cara.

CHAPTER 10

CARA

By Friday afternoon, I'm dying for a low-key weekend—time to process everything I've learned in the last few days. Not to mention my eyes feel crossed from looking at my computer for so many hours. I can't possibly consume any more caffeine, yet I'm about to drop —the worst combination of wired and tired. I pour so much mental energy into the proposal that I have little else to give, especially after such an utterly surreal few days. It's also the perfect opportunity to hide, as embarrassed as that makes me feel. I'm still so nervous to go anywhere on my own, even though I know it's fine... probably.

Plus, I promised my friends we'd have a video chat now that I've had a couple days to settle in. And Rose reminded me I need to give her a call beforehand to talk—just the two of us. We love our group of friends —five of us total—but we're each other's ride-or-die. I've been putting off calling her all week, and I can't keep it up any longer since we all happened to be free for the chat on Saturday night.

Ada and Clancy haven't outright banned me from talking to anyone about my life in Monstera Bluff, but I couldn't live with myself if something bad were to happen in this community because of something I said. It's like a precious little parallel universe—that admittedly freaks me out, though a little less every day. It's almost too much responsibility for me. Like I'm leading the whole town on a walk across a tightrope with no safety net—the risk is all too real. My plan with my friends is to stick to the basics and leave out, well, everything juicy and weird that I so wish I could tell them. *Yes, Rose, the lizard people are my new neighbors!*

Carrying my work laptop and a huge pile of reports and town documents as I walk out to my SUV, I decide I have enough courage to stop by the grocery store Ada took me to last night. Though I bought plenty of groceries, I was kidding myself to think just one bottle of wine was sufficient for this weekend—especially with girls' night tomorrow. I'll have to limit myself to keep me on my toes during the call, but I know I'll feel like a terrible friend afterward and want to drown my sorrows after we hang up.

My confidence falters when I enter the store. I avoid eye contact with anyone—just pick up a polished wooden basket and head straight to the liquor aisle. It's by no means a big selection, but it's enough. Interestingly, some of it looks... locally sourced... though a lot of it is standard, human-made bottles of alcohol. I grab a red and a white wine and then wander to the checkout line. Ada told me yesterday that the baskets are enchanted to remain unweighted even if they're full of groceries, making it so easy to carry around while shopping. They even sell bags to take home with the same magick. It's incredible. The basket in my hand feels as light as a feather while I wait until it's my turn to check out. The counter doesn't have a conveyor belt, but it's modeled after a normal grocery store. Down to the sweet treats and other tempting items on display, so easy to pick up while you're waiting. I give in and pick up a bag of freshly baked cookies, scanning for an ingredient list to make sure it's not something unexpected and unappetizing.

Without warning, I feel a painful tug on my hair. Startled, I gasp and whirl around, finding myself inches away from the cute, gray, wolfy face of a toddler in the arms of a distracted human-looking woman in line behind me. He looks like the child I thought was a dog before Ada told me about monsters. A lock of my long, wavy hair is seized in his tiny, furry fist, pulling it uncomfortably tight. He giggles while snarling in a way that would be adorable if he didn't give my hair another abrupt yank. An elongated "ow" escapes my lips as I rush to clasp the hair taut to prevent it from pulling at my scalp.

The woman holding him immediately whips her head around to face me and looks mortified as she realizes what the boy is doing. It's definitely the woman from the other day. "Max, please give this nice lady back her hair," she coaxes the young child to loosen his hold. "Remember how Daddy and I taught you to make 'soft fingers'? Use your soft fingers around others, please," she gently admonishes.

My eyes dart between her and the child. The sharp little claws on his small paw-like hands retract, and my hair falls free. Some of it to the floor.

Her round, otherworldly silver eyes look genuinely contrite as she explains, "I swear, I don't get a moment's peace with this one. I'm so sorry he got hold of you. He's stronger than he looks. And he loves pulling on hair, jewelry, you name it. My hair used to be almost as long as yours, but that didn't last long after I had him!" She huffs a rueful laugh as she smooths her thick, blonde, chin-length hair behind her ear.

I grin at her and Max, who's now staring at the bag of cookies in my hand, clenching his furry little paw hands like he wants me to give them to him. "No harm done. He seems very curious." I chuckle as his gaze moves continuously between me, his mom, and the cookies.

He growls a babyish sounding "Mama gimme!"

"Oh, that he is. He takes after his father in almost every way. I'll have my work cut out for me as he gets older, won't I?" she coos at her son, bouncing him on her hip while taking his little outstretched hand in hers so it's less nerve-rackingly close to my hair.

"How old is he?" I ask, a safe topic about babies.

"He's only two, but wolven grow quickly, so he looks older than he is. Nothing will be safe from his little grabby hands for a while yet," she jokes as she presses a kiss between the fuzzy ears atop his head. Wolven... Ben mentioned them to me at the job site.

"Anyway, sorry I'm being rude, I don't think we've met before. I'm Val. Are you new here?" she asks, her gaze inquisitive but warm.

"Nice to meet you. I'm Cara. I just moved here this week," I answer.

"Welcome, then! This is a great community. I hope you'll like it. What brings you here?" she asks enthusiastically.

"A job at town hall. I didn't know anything about this place before I got here, but I think it'll grow on me," I respond without thinking.

I mentally kick myself right away, realizing that may sound odd. It may not be advisable to advertise my situation to a near stranger, even if she seems perfectly nice. Hopefully, she chalks up my response to general awkwardness, which, to be fair, is also true.

The line in front of me moves, and I put my bottles and the cookies —which I still haven't confirmed are something I'll be able to eat—onto the counter. Thankfully, the cashier takes my credit card, even though most people here use cash it seems. It's something to keep in mind. The total is remarkably cheap. Hopefully the wine will be a lot better than its *three buck chuck* price tag.

As I step away from the counter, I turn back to Val and give her and Max a small wave and a smile. "It was good to meet you. I hope to run into you both again soon." I find that I really do mean that, which is relieving in its own way—maybe I'm feeling more settled here.

Max starts squirming in Val's hold, and she puts him down, unsuccessfully trying to take his hand. He bounds straight toward me, upright on his furry legs. The backward canine-like joint shows below the bottom of his shorts leading down to his bare furry little feet. His claws scrabble on the floor as he takes off. I freeze, unsure of what to expect, while Val lunges for him too late. When he reaches me, only several feet away, he hugs his furry little arms around my exposed leg below my skirt, sniffs me, and licks the skin on my kneecap. He then turns back around to his mom so nonchalantly, lifting his arms to be picked up again, that I can't help the bewildered giggle bubbling out of me. "Max must really hope so, too!" She guffaws, sounding both exasperated and amused by her son's antics.

"Bye-bye!" Max tells me in his raspy voice, but his focus drifts to his mom before I can respond. "Mama, where are the cookies?" Val quickly waves goodbye to me as Max turns his attention to the person in line behind them, reaching for their basket. That child seems like an adorable handful.

I'm still smiling at that unexpectedly sweet interaction when I get home. I open a bottle of red since the temperature has dropped quite a bit and it seems like a storm is going to roll through. I text Rose to ask her if she's free to talk. She calls immediately.

"I've been waiting all week to talk to you! Stop holding out on me... I was beginning to think you fell into a black hole. Tell me everything!" Her voice bursts into my ear, wasting no time.

I laugh uncomfortably. "Where to begin... This place is not quite what I thought it would be," I remark, trying to sound innocuous.

"Oh? How so?" concern unmistakable in her voice. I take a long, slow breath and consider how to describe my experiences without coming off like a crazy person.

"I figured this would be a sleepy little backwater town where I could melt into the scenery and live quietly for a while. But I don't know if I'll fit in here. And why stay if that's the case?" I admit, honestly.

"Cara, did something happen to make you feel that way?" she presses, sounding genuinely distressed.

"No, I'm probably just spiraling. Almost everyone has been nice so far. I'm just so happy to hear your voice. I miss you." I sniffle as I try not to cry. Everything I've bottled up this week is seeping out now that I'm talking to my best friend, the closest person I have to family.

"Aw, I miss you too. It's only been a couple days since you arrived. You've only ever lived in big cities before. It'll take time to adjust to a small town. New places are lonely—everyone already has their friends and routines, but you'll find yours soon, too. Believe me, when I moved to Chicago it took a minute to feel like home. Don't write everything off yet. You sounded so positive about your job and your boss yesterday. That's a good sign!" she encourages.

Swallowing the lump in my throat, I try not to get emotional. "Yeah, that's going well. I don't think I mentioned it, but I have my own office, not just a cubicle. It's unbelievable—it all feels very official and grown up. I'm already making progress with my first project. There's not much red tape here, just surviving town council approval, so I think it'll get off the ground really quickly."

"No red tape! That sounds like a dream!" she squeals into the phone. "You wouldn't even believe the funding issues I'm dealing with right now. There's no budget for anything. I'm literally at a standstill with every one of my projects. Ugh, sorry, didn't mean to blow out your eardrum. Or make this about me. I'm just very glad for you and obviously a little jealous."

We share a laugh. I'm not sure why I was so nervous to talk to her. "I don't mind at all. All this job talk feels like the older, simpler times I miss," I lament.

"Oh god, my griping about my job frustrations does feel like old times, doesn't it?" she whines self-consciously. "And I still haven't done anything about it. Talk about being stuck in a rut. Let's table the job talk and focus on how close you are to the ocean. Are there any beaches in town? And when are you going?"

"Rose, I'm sorry, I didn't mean it like that. I just like talking about something other than my messed-up life. And you only bitch about the job because you care so much. Don't feel bad about that," I apologize, feeling like a jerk.

"I know, but sometimes I need the wake-up call because nothing has changed in years. Transit funding will never improve," she admits regretfully.

"But you really don't want that change forced on you like it was on me. You'll move on when you're ready," I offer reassurance. Rose truly has no reason to feel bad—her complaints are absolutely warranted. Her expertise is in public transportation, and there isn't a glut of transit agencies or advocacy groups that can offer her the kind of hands-on job she wants.

"Well, thanks for that, but I still want to know about the beach situation. It's only October, and it's already so cold here," she pouts.

With everything else going on, I hadn't even thought about how I'm probably only a few miles from the ocean. "Gosh, I bet it's close. I'll have to find out. I don't know my way around that well yet," I ponder, distractedly thinking I should ask Ada about it this weekend.

"Well, you should go tomorrow and send me pictures. Walk barefoot in the sand and forget about everything except how amazing it feels. I wouldn't need therapy if I had that for more than a few months in the summer on the lake. Just be glad you don't have to deal with Chicago winters anymore," she utters dramatically, and we both giggle.

I agree half-heartedly, but I'd take a lifetime of Chicago winter if it meant things had turned out differently. If Mark hadn't betrayed me. If

I had never signed that insane non-compete agreement. If I didn't let him railroad my career after grad school. If I never met him in the first place. So many *ifs*. I would love to feel in control of the trajectory of my life again.

I promise her I'll ask around about any nearby beaches, and this prompts her to ask about everyone I've met so far. Initially I panic, feeling unprepared—how much do I say? But then I recite in my head that *monsters are people too... Talk about them like you would anyone else.* I start by describing Ada, her generosity and bright spirit. How I think we'll end up being good friends. And Clancy's laid-back but confident nature—that he can even be a bit of a clown in an endearing way. Ben is harder to pin down. He's closed off on a personal level and unpredictably mercurial. An actual friendship between us seems unlikely, yet he's so close with Clancy and Ada. He's knowledgeable and supportive of the work I'm doing, but working with him won't be pleasant. Ultimately, I realize that it's not hard to talk about all of them without revealing their non-human nature.

Rose is unusually quiet on her end. It makes me realize I've been rambling on about those three. I finally pipe down and wait for her to respond. She breathes loudly into the line, then finally remarks, "You seem really focused on Ben. Do you think you might like him? I only ask because he reminds me too much of Mark, even down to the family business part, and it worries me that you'll get involved with another narcissist. You're too people-pleasing for your own good, and guys like Mark will keep taking advantage of that. You don't need to bend over backward for people to like you. Don't forget how you did everything for Mark and his horrid, evil family, and they still treated you worse than dog shit. Don't fall back into that pattern."

Her words sucker punch me, and I fumble to respond, "I think Ben only barely tolerates me, so it would be stupid of me to have feelings for him." That's a non-answer if I've ever given one, and I'm not sure why I say it like that. Though she's right, I shouldn't knowingly put myself in that position again—Mark left me too broken, and I still haven't fully healed. Regardless, Ben's not even human; there's no possibility of anything between us. Still, these comparisons between them won't leave my head.

Rose scoffs. "Well, he's an idiot if he only barely tolerates a gorgeous, smart, amazing woman who's obviously better at urban planning than he is, because he was about to botch a very expensive road project at the taxpayers' expense! He needs to get his overinflated ego checked." She could say a lot more about this particular male archetype who features so prominently in both our dating and work histories, so I'm glad she lets it rest there.

Eventually the conversation winds down and I start yawning. Unable to keep the bone-deep exhaustion out of my voice, we say goodbye until tomorrow night's chat. Sitting on the living room couch with the glass of wine I barely touched during the call, I try to remember everything I said and if I slipped up and revealed anything unusual. I'm not equipped to lead a double life, but I think it went as well as it could have. I stare out the window at the rain, now coming down in sheets. It's calming, so I listen to it while sipping the remainder of my wine until I can't keep my eyes open and then finally drag myself to bed.

Eight Months Ago

Walking into the office early, I'm greeted by stares and whispers from everyone already there. I'm not exactly popular here since I generally keep to myself. I'm always slammed with work. Anyway, Victoria and Mark show no favoritism toward me, so there isn't social currency to be gained by being my friend. But this is unsettling.

I get to my desk and check my email. At the top of my inbox, there's a company-wide email from Victoria that Mark and the firm are mentioned in the style pages of the Tribune. I've been so busy juggling projects recently that I can't keep up with the news. I barely have time or energy to read anything at all, so I never would have seen this article otherwise.

Clicking into the link, I'm shocked to see a photo splashed across the page of Mark... holding hands with another woman. She's stunning, like a model. They look... right for each other... and clearly in love. I feel myself start to throw up and grab the wastebasket under my desk, quietly retching bile from my empty stomach. I grab a tissue to wipe tears from my eyes and saliva from my mouth while still staring at the photo. The caption underneath reads, "Mark Hansen, Senior Vice President of the Hansen Company, and Olivia Manning, daughter of Congressman Lorne Manning and his Principal Fundraiser, attended last night's Chicago Historical Society Gala. The newly engaged couple met at a campaign fundraiser for the Congressman last year but have kept their relationship under wraps until recently."

And that's when I see the ring. An enormous diamond engagement ring on her finger, which she unsubtly angled toward the camera. How could he have hidden an entire relationship from me? And now I'm forced to read about it in a fucking newspaper? We've been together for eight fucking years. Why not just break up with me instead of cheating and humiliating me so publicly? Oh my god, was he having sex with both of us for an entire year? Were there others before her? The pain building in my chest starts to overwhelm me. I want to scream and never stop. But I can't. I'm in the office and I need to remain dignified. I start to hyperventilate, and my vision tunnels—I'm going to pass out.

It suddenly occurs to me... they all know. Everyone in the office saw the article already, and they all knew he was cheating when I walked in. And not only that, but he's also engaged to the other woman. He's going to marry her. And not me. Never was going to be me. Apparently the last eight years of my life have been one big lie. I don't understand what I did to deserve this. I love him, and I thought he loved me. Our relationship just had its own timeline since he had so much on his plate. I did everything he asked of me. How am I not enough?

Shoving myself out of my chair, I stumble away from my desk, not looking at anyone, focusing on each step in front of me to get out of the office as quickly as possible while trying to keep the blurring of my peripheral vision at bay. Without knowing where I'm going, I find myself in the elevator. The door opens in the downstairs lobby, and on wobbly legs, I force myself out, holding onto the wall for support. No one is around except a dark silhouette in the corner with eyes that seem wrong. The figure balloons until he reaches the ceiling, his shadow spilling outward, saturating everything in its path like pitch black ink. He shouldn't be here. I don't want him to see me.

I stagger to a restroom down the hall and lock the door. Now that I'm finally all alone, I collapse, falling to the floor on my knees with my head in my hands, weeping uncontrollably.

Waking with a start, sweaty and nauseous at the memory, I realize something wasn't right in my dream. There shouldn't have been anyone in the lobby. As far as I remember, it was blessedly empty that morning. No one stood in a corner that day watching me with unnatural yellow eyes. That memory is already traumatic enough. It's disturbing that my subconscious found a way to twist it even further.

I crawl out of bed and walk to the kitchen for a glass of water to dilute the wine now curdling in my stomach. I'm almost afraid to go back to sleep, but looking at the clock, it's too early to get up. Riffling through the stack of documents I brought home from work, I pull out town council meeting minutes related to some recently completed construction. Surely this will put me to sleep again. I settle back into bed and begin reading. The storm must have passed earlier because the night is remarkably quiet until the wind starts whistling through the trees. I wouldn't have even noticed, except it almost sounds melodic, intentional.

The next morning, the documents are still in a messy stack next to me in bed while I lay there trying to fully wake up. Even the dreamless sleep afterward wasn't enough to shake off the uneasy feeling that nightmare gave me. It still clings to me. A knock at the front door makes me jump, providing the adrenaline boost I need to finally get out of bed. Ada's bright smile almost blinds me as I open the door, not ready for it. She looks perfectly coiffed while I'm in pajamas with bedhead and a greasy face.

"Good morning. What can I do for you?" I rasp, my voice still thick with sleep.

"Mother Earth, you look like you were cozy as a bug in a rug in bed! Sorry to swing by so early, but I wanted to ask you to join me for a walk to the bakery this morning for some coffee and breakfast?" she asks optimistically.

It seems like she won't let me stay in my shell, and I appreciate that. "Sure, it sounds like a nice way to start the day," I answer, and we agree to meet outside in half an hour.

I brush my teeth and quickly hop in the shower. Luckily, I washed my hair yesterday, so dry shampoo and smoothing cream are enough to make it presentable. With a few swipes of pale blush, black mascara, and lip gloss, I look nearly ready for public consumption. Donning a simple, stretchy, cotton short-sleeved dress and some vintage-looking sneakers, I step outside to see Ada getting up from her porch swing.

We stroll down the road toward downtown. She points out nearby houses and tells me how old they are and who lives there, acquainting me with the neighborhood. We reach the bakery before I know it. A familiar hue of pink covers the door, and the sign above it reads "Pearl-house Pastries." But those aren't what draw my eyes.

I audibly gasp as I see a tall, gray figure holding a pink box swiftly exit the building. It's Ben, I have no doubt. He spreads and beats his long, leathery wings, and it looks like he's climbing an invisible escalator to the sky as he lifts off, his long tail trailing behind, reminding me of a dragon—or at least, my idea of one. I'm struck dumb by the gracefulness and athleticism of his body in flight, and my steps falter to a stop since I'm unable to look away. His wings are so much larger than I realized when fully extended. I feel a curl of warmth low in my belly, making my face heat up in embarrassment. Hopefully Ada doesn't notice my reaction.

She pauses next to me and smiles at me once I've come back to my senses. "It's a small town. You can't help but run into everyone all the time." She snickers but then clarifies with a shrug, "Had he seen us, he'd have stopped and said hello. Looks like he had somewhere to be." I highly doubt he'd willingly come talk to me, but I keep my mouth shut to not spoil the moment.

A bell on the door rings pleasantly as we step inside. The temperature is warm and cozy as several ovens are fired up, baking decadently rich pastries. The interior concept is open so customers can see, hear, and, most importantly, smell everything being made. Many of the pastries look French—croissants, kouign-amann, and eclairs, but there are fruit-filled buns and other items I've never seen before. The pink theme extends to the interior only in light touches.

Stacks of pink boxes sit near the register, but the majority of the shop's large interior is exposed wood or painted white. Only the chairs at the dozen or so small tables inside are that unique shade of pink.

Ada and I drool over the display case as we stand in line. Squeezing my belly fat, I admit wryly, "I could get used to breakfast like this—I think Madge brought some to the office on Thursday—but I better walk off the calories to work from now on."

"And it will be entirely worth it, walk or not," she agrees, sounding amused. Ada points out Whispered Folk cuisine that she's sure I'll enjoy, and I choose a sweetmeat fritter-looking pastry. Her recommendation is spot on. It's delicious and pairs well with coffee.

We sit at a table and her expression turns serious. I'm about to break out in a cold sweat, so I question her, "Was there something you wanted to talk to me about?"

Her mirthless chuckle warns me I'm not going to like it. "Well yes, but I don't want to worry you overmuch since there isn't anything for you to do about it. Clancy and I anticipate that there will be some disagreement about your appointment with one of our town council members, Ralston Samuels. He's a warlock and not part of my coven—I want to make that clear. His views over time have become increasingly radical, against both humans and some types of Whispered Folk he incorrectly deems inferior to himself. He's calculating about how he presents himself in public, so many here don't grasp the depth of his prejudice, but what he lets on is still quite alarming. Like me, he comes from an old family but uses that name and history to leverage power and strongarm others into doing his bidding."

"He's that anti-human guy you mentioned the other night? The one that would freak out over a human meetup group?" I confirm apprehensively.

"He is. We don't know if he knows about you yet, but we gather he will very soon. Your presence at town hall won't have gone unnoticed. But Clancy, Ben, myself, and others will take care of this, so do not let him fool you into believing you're unwanted or undeserving. Any scene he makes will reflect poorly on him, not you. If he or his cronies ever try to harass you while we're not around, get yourself out of the situation or go somewhere very public and squeeze hard on this amulet, which will alert us right away," she explains, handing me the magickal equivalent of a panic button from her purse.

It appears to be a small but weighty locket. Feeling the gravity of her words, I agree immediately, though I try not to let on how unsettling this is, especially if there's no real solution in place other than avoiding him and pressing a button.

"But it's not all doom and gloom around here! You'll probably see members of my coven come over to the house more frequently in the next couple of weeks to get ready for Samhain, which we always hold as a festival for the whole town. The coven performs our rituals first, and then the community joins. We think most non-witches like it because there's food and a big bonfire. Music too! You'll have to come!" she announces eagerly, giddily gesturing her hands.

Her enthusiasm is infectious. "I've never heard of *saw-wen*, but it sounds like a blast. When is it?"

"It's on October thirty-first when the veil between the realms of the living and the dead is thinnest. The coven gives offerings, performs rituals and spells, and then we all feast and party! It'll be a good chance for you to meet more of the town, too!" she says fervently, her hands demonstrating the thinness of the veil that night—making it look quite thin.

I blink rapidly, bemused, because that would mean Halloween isn't just about costumes and candy, after all. Frankly, I wish I could go back to the blissful ignorance of not knowing otherwise.

Ada fills me in on festival planning, and it's clear she'll have her hands full until then. Hopefully, we'll still have time for outings like this. We clean up our table as we get up to leave. Walking outside, the image of Ben taking flight flashes in my mind. Who were those pastries for? I rub my forehead forcefully, trying to push him out of my brain. It's almost shameful that Rose called me out so correctly—Ben has indeed been living there rent-free since I met him.

For my own peace of mind, I should fully disengage from him beyond our required professional interaction. I try not to dwell on him while we walk around. So instead, I tell Ada about my friends from back home, including Rose, and that we all have a video call tonight. It reminds me to ask her about nearby beaches—Rose will bring it up again. Ada gushes about all the great spots nearby and how there are canoes and kayaks available to anyone along the beaches and through the brackish inlet waterways that connect to the ocean. I know my friends will flip out about so many aspects of Monstera Bluff—I'll have plenty to share, even without the monster part. I better not paint too pretty a picture, though, or they'll plan a visit soon.

CHAPTER 11

BEN

The dreaded night unavoidably arrives, and I'm on edge as I enter the town council meeting hall. Clancy has been aggravatingly unbothered the last few days, ratcheting up my own anxiety about a Ralston Samuels confrontation. Samuels hasn't raised a ruckus yet, but his silence worries me even more. He wormed his way into influence in recent years, and he'll leverage that against her. He already wields much of his political power to undercut Clancy's plans, reputation, administration... you name it. I'm caught up in that by proxy, as he usually opposes my company's contracts with the town. He and the other two warlocks recently elected as council members gleefully wreak havoc on what has traditionally been a cooperative governing body. It makes these town council meetings abnormally tense.

The one thing I'm not concerned about is Cara's new plan for the road project. It's remarkably well-considered and written. She emailed it to me first thing this morning for my review in case I had any changes to recommend before her presentation tonight. I adjusted some of the budget numbers and made some recommendations on the graphics she created in her modeling software, but that's it. It's going to retroactively make everything Clancy and I slapped together look amateur. I would be embarrassed for myself if I wasn't so glad she took over.

Cara sits by herself in an empty row toward the back of the room, her posture rigid. As if sensing my arrival, her gaze meets mine when I walk in. Her flustered expression reveals her battling thoughts—wary it's me, yet relieved to see a familiar face. Ada and Clancy have already found their spots on the raised dais at the front of the room. Clancy, with his formidable centaur body and that Evermane brand of tenacity, is positioned behind a carved wooden lectern, looking like the leader he was born to be, ready to preside over the meeting. He nods a greeting to me, a smile curling at the edge of his lips as he watches me take a seat next to Cara.

"Hi," she exhales breathily. Her posture sags a little in relief.

I'm affected as well, but in a way she'd never feel comfortable with. I lean toward her to quietly wish her luck. Before I'm able to, her delectable scent washes over me, like sweet and refreshing jasmine on a warm spring afternoon—reminding me of the vines that grow around my childhood home. I first noticed it that day in her office. It's an inopportune time for my cock to stir and thicken in response, my infatuation with her making itself evident. I fight my instinct to shelter her in my arms, comfort her with kisses and soothing words until she falls apart in my embrace. I'm attracted to her in such a visceral way, it overwhelms me. I inhale a long breath of the air around her, knowing it should be my last, before I discreetly whisper, "You have nothing to fear tonight. I'll be with you during your presentation. Direct the questions you're unsure of to me. I'll back you up."

She grips the binder in her lap a little tighter and mutely nods her head, her hair shaking out more of that lovely scent. She nervously eyes the dais, where most of the council members have already arrived, and chews on her bottom lip. "Ada told me about that councilman she's worried about. That he won't like me because I'm human. She told me he'll probably make a scene or try to intimidate me," she divulges in a hushed tone.

"Samuels. I won't let him get near you," I growl, unable to hold it back. Unfortunately, I know that's not entirely true. I can't be everywhere at once.

Her voice falters. "She gave me a magick necklace just in case. Is he... here yet? I don't know what he looks like."

Ada already told me about the amulet—it was a good idea not to leave anything to chance when it concerns this sanctimonious, arrogant male. Fire and ashes, if living among monsters hasn't made Cara run away yet, this asshole's behavior still might.

Samuels and his two council cronies are still conspicuously absent, so I inform her, "The three you need to be aware of aren't here yet. You'll know which of those pricks is Samuels. The other two fawn over him sickeningly, like they're under a compulsion spell, but we know they aren't, making it that much worse."

Her jaw drops as she digests that information, and she quavers, "Can someone really do that to another person?"

I sigh, wishing I had kept my big mouth shut. Stars above, I feel bad for adding to her grief—her nervous energy was already potent enough before I spilled that tidbit of uncomfortable truth. "Some magick wielders can, if they are powerful enough to conquer someone's free will, but it's rare. And not always used for nefarious purposes. Samuels' magick is strong, but if he was capable of anything close to that ability, he hasn't demonstrated it yet." I try to gently assuage that tinge of fear in her eyes. Her expression softens and I'm glad to offer her some relief.

Commotion from outside the door interrupts us. "Is it..." Cara utters almost inaudibly as she slinks low into her seat.

Sadly, it is. Always one for a grand entrance, Ralston Samuels— aging, cadaverous, and wildly jealous of anyone with power or influence he doesn't possess—swaggers down the center row toward Clancy, flanked by his two toadies, Dalton Atticus and Norman Weatherby, both power-hungry warlocks with half a brain between them. Somehow, they made it onto town council, and we've been paying for it ever since.

"Clancy, you have much to answer to," Samuels booms over the din of the mostly full room. The trio aren't taking their seats but instead stand at the front with a dominating presence.

"Gentlemen, you've finally decided to show up. You know that late entrances are only fashionable at parties, not at government assemblies," Clancy drawls, unconcerned by their peacocking display.

"Now see here, boy, I have it on good authority you've brought a human here under our noses," he sneers as he turns around to face the room. "You dare threaten the safety of our community? And you didn't think we would notice? This is a dereliction of leadership! She's parading herself around the building like she belongs here. Taking a shiny new town hall job that should have gone to one of our own. You may be mayor, but your power is still limited. You still have to answer to the *people*." As if this dog and pony show is of any benefit to the people.

"Come now, Councilman Samuels. You know very well humans are welcome in this community and several do live here peacefully without any of these so-called 'safety issues' you're quick to accuse them of. In fact, she's not the only human in this room right now, so I suggest you conclude this speech you obviously practiced in the mirror this morning and take your seats. *Now*," Clancy orders, his voice laced with alpha authority. He won't put up with anti-human sentiment, especially since they, too, are part of the *people* here in town Samuels pretends to be concerned about, even if they are small in number. By now, the audience, as well as the seated council members, are whispering and looking uneasy at the trio's gratuitous power play.

Samuels' belligerence is undeterred. Scanning the crowd with his beady eyes, his voice rises to a fever pitch, "Where is she? This human who doesn't belong here with no connection to the Whispered Folk. Show yourself, so we know who to hunt down when trouble comes knocking at our door." Derision drips with every word, and for an instant, the room is stunned to silence. The only noise is the shifting of seats as the crowd looks around anxiously.

Clancy is about to shut him down, that is, until another council member, a naga named Viran, who normally can barely keep his eyes open during these meetings, has clearly heard enough and pipes up, "Stand down, Samuels. You will not make a mockery of this meeting or make this town look anything but welcoming. It is beneath you, and beneath your office, to stand here and try to persecute our newest resident with no evidence behind it. Sit down and shut your trap so we can start the meeting already."

Clancy chuckles darkly. "Well said, Councilman. I think we're all in agreement this behavior will not be tolerated. Get. To. Your. Seats. Now."

Samuels sputters, but his ego won't let him admit any wrongdoing.

"Fine. If you think starting the meeting on time is more important than addressing our town's safety and security, I guess I'll just take my seat. Mark my words and be sure to put this in the meeting minutes: this human's arrival is a stain on our community! There's already been an increase in crime and vandalism since she arrived. In a week, she's already compromising our town. Humans and their malicious ways will infiltrate us before we know it. We'll be watching her!" His two sycophants grumble their agreement and glare at the audience, mayhap seeking out Cara as they follow toward the dais and sit down.

During this outburst, Cara curls into herself further, trying to avoid discovery. She looks up at me in dismay, tears shimmering in her eyes. I'm seething, bristling with rage that he'd dare spread such lies about her. My stony facade is about to crack as a surge of protectiveness urges me to wrap my wings around her, shield her from this slimy male's threats. As if they can sense it, Ada and Clancy both make eye contact with me, signaling that I should defend her if the need arises. I incline my head, showing the sharp teeth I often keep hidden, ready to give in to that primal instinct to guard at all costs. I can barely pay attention to the proceedings in front of me, with my undivided focus on her safety as the meeting finally starts.

The Seer's warning about Cara screams through my consciousness. Samuels is a threat. There must be more to this than anti-human bluster and an opportunistic political gambit against Clancy. Though I'm not sure it's wholly welcome, I try to lend her some comfort, wrapping an arm around her shoulders and lightly rubbing her shoulder in a soothing motion. At first, she freezes, going stiff under me, but then relaxes, leaning into me slightly, letting me know the touch is welcome.

"Well, we're off like a herd of turtles. Maybe if we can stick to the agenda without further interruption, we'll get home before the sun comes up," Clancy scolds, side-eyeing Samuels as he gets the room in order. For a time, the meeting is predictably boring with a long list of business to get through. A welcome reprieve for Cara to compose herself before her presentation. Samuels' accusations have forced it into a public declaration that she is the so-called dangerous human Clancy smuggled in, and I don't want Samuels to put too big of a target on her back for those idiots who do support him.

"Next, we'll hear a proposal from Kiernan Lykander, director of the Parks Department, for replacement playground equipment to be installed in the Howling Woods Canopy Park," Clancy announces.

A tall dark brown wolven in his tan and olive green park ranger uniform confidently walks forward to give a presentation on the enhancements proposed to the vertically oriented park and how it will benefit the community's children. He's held his position for a few years and is already a strong advocate for making sure all Whispered Folk children have places to play.

Kiernan is about to field questions from the audience when Norman Weatherby interrupts him. "So you're asking us to put good money into a place only the animals, I mean *shifters*, will use? What about children who don't like traipsing a mile through the woods to get to a park? It's in the middle of nowhere! We might as well call your sad excuse for an agency the *pack department,* considering how you're funneling all its funds," he disparages.

Celeste Longclaw, another council member and an elder in the Wolf Pack, obviously takes issue. "That's the point of this park, Weatherby. The canopy playground can only exist because it's connected to the tall pine trees in the woods. There's also plenty of equipment at ground level that every child can utilize regardless of their abilities. The park is for flying folk, shifters, any child who likes to play outdoors, not just the Wolf Pack. You'd know as well as I do if you'd have bothered to read his proposal that some of the funding is going toward maintaining the walking path to get there. Not every child in this town prefers a pristine, boring swing set over play equipment meant to teach them to fly and climb and run. You're sounding a little addled, Norman, calling our children *animals*. You could use a bit of the fresh air out there to clear your head."

Kiernan looks unfazed by Norman Weatherby's outburst, probably having anticipated an issue from one of the warlocks. He nods in acknowledgment at Celeste and addresses the audience again. "Councilwoman Longclaw's explanation is correct. This park is situated where it is because its unique construction can't be replicated outside of the woods. That said, I'd be happy to take any questions about the new equipment and the updated park design." Luckily, the warlocks sit out the rest of the discussion.

The revised Howling Road proposal is next on the docket. Clancy looks over at both of us, silently letting us know he's going to introduce the topic. I give Cara's shoulder a quick squeeze in response. She blinks up at me with a fleeting smile.

"I'll go up there with you. Make your presentation as planned. Not even Samuels can argue against the changes you've made," I whisper.

She rolls her eyes. "No, but I'm sure he'll try."

My lips quirk at this small show of confidence in herself, even in the face of everything she's borne tonight. We stand, and all eyes in the room turn to us. I glare at Ralston Samuels, daring him to make more of a scene than he already has.

Clancy clears his throat, bringing some of the attention back to him, and begins, "Our next item on the agenda is a revision of the Howling Road construction proposal. And I'd also like to introduce our new city planner, Cara Bishop, who is leading this project. She is working under my office, and she brings impressive experience and education in urban planning and a sorely needed fresh perspective to help guide our town as it grows. I'm more than happy to hand over the reins to her." He chuckles at his pun. "Please join me in welcoming Ms. Bishop to the town and her new role."

A fair amount of applause greets us as we reach the front of the room, as if most of the attendees and council—with obvious exceptions —don't mind how or why she's here. It's the reception I hoped for.

Standing off to the side, I keep Samuels in my sightline while I watch Cara. She shuffles to the front, eyes cast downward, looking strained. Clancy already sent the revised proposal to the board, so he knows it'll win the majority vote of the eight council members—his vote decides a tie if needed—but this presentation is for the community's benefit. It's not lost on anyone that this is not just a presentation of the revised proposal, but also of herself and her philosophies.

She's overly quiet as she begins, "Good evening, everyone. I'm Cara Bishop, the new city planner of Monstera Bluff." A pause lingers until she stutters, "Wha-what I l-love about a town like ours is how deeply we care about our community members, and we…"—a cough in the audience startles her, interrupting her speech. She glances at Clancy, who gives her an encouraging smile before she continues—"we see the benefit of good urban design to continually improve our quality of life. I grew up in a very big city, so big it felt like the well-being of its people was an afterthought. The city lost itself after so many decades of poor urban design that focused so heavily on putting more cars on the road. Even as a kid who regularly rode the bus or a train, before I ever had the words for it, I understood that the fabric and livability of a city is crushed under the weight of car dependency."

Taking a long breath, she wrings her hands nervously in front of her. Her gaze skitters across the room before landing somewhere above the crowd. "Over the years in my career in Chicago, I did my best to chip away at it, working on projects to improve bike and pedestrian safety. I even designed the addition of new bike lanes to a downtown neighborhood to combat over-congestion on the roads and provide safer routes for commuters who choose not to drive. Yet these are nearly always small-scale patches to a much deeper problem, a band-aid placed over a gaping wound."

She looks over at me for an instant, just long enough for me to catch her eye and nod. She smooths her hands down her skirt, fidgeting a little, but presses on, her voice louder, blunter, "Now, you may wonder why I'm telling you all of this as I present a road construction project"—some laughter sounds from the audience, and luckily it seems to bolster her confidence—"I went into this project with the interest of the community, its livability, in mind. Your town is expanding, which requires more housing and roads, a bigger overall footprint. Yet, your quality of life should not suffer as a result. You should be able to walk, bike, or drive safely no matter where you live, no matter where you want to go. You should always feel connected to the rest of the town and its citizens. As the town grows, I hope to help guide you through it so that five, ten, twenty years from now, even though the town will be bigger, it won't feel that way. The beautiful, unique characteristics that make Monstera Bluff such an attractive place to live will remain intact. That the everyday lives of citizens will continue to improve."

Her breath hitches audibly as she concludes her introduction and gestures for Clancy to start a slideshow. Utilizing key points and design mockups on her slides, she concisely summarizes her new plan and how it differs from the previous one. What she hopes to accomplish and accommodate with these changes. She receives questions about the budget and timeline, so I step in to provide more detail. Overall, her presentation is a success. No one objects to the changes. But as expected, Samuels can't hold his tongue for long.

He starts huffing in faux self-righteous anger about the plan. His false bravado may convince some, but I hope most can see through it. "How dare we just sit here and roll over for *her*, a human. We don't need her for this. She's going to make us live like humans do. It's obvious that she and the mayor are in cahoots, trying to take over the town using bike lanes as their cover story. Nothing is stopping her from exposing us to humans. It's unacceptable that this council so blindly accepts the risk. You're going to have the blood of Whispered Folk on your hands if you fall into their trap!" he snarls disdainfully, sounding even more unhinged than earlier. He must think this is the chink in Clancy's political armor that can be exploited—a way to rile up his supporters.

A diminutive figure stands up in the audience. It's Darla Rallis. Even though she's a Seer, who are just as renowned for their wisdom and insight as they are their gifts of seeing the future, she's still youthful, though her eyes betray her old soul. At a young age, she's already a very powerful, respected witch. Unfortunately, this power has a tradeoff—it dampens her emotions, helping her see and guide without judgment. Her visions show the good, the bad, and everything in between.

The room hushes, including Samuels. Fire burn it to ashes, Cara is going to find out about the Seer's vision. I know Clancy hasn't told her yet. He should have anticipated this was going to happen. Maybe this was his plan. But Cara's going to hit her breaking point. This is too much for her to bear in a single evening.

"Cara Bishop. I saw her. I told Clancy to bring her here. He did this with my blessing. She's supposed to be here, at this junction in her life, this moment of history in our town. If she's made welcome, can make a home here, I see a brightness. If not, I do not know what will happen, but there is a darkness, a shadow behind it," she states sedately—her usual demeanor. All eyes are on her, including Cara's, now blown wide in shock.

Clancy smiles warmly at Darla, and there's a glint of victory in his eyes as he acknowledges her, "Thank you, Darla, I appreciate you jumping in to explain that. Yes, Darla told me to seek her out, but it is her education and experience, as well as her open and altruistic spirit, that truly makes her the right fit for our community. Whether she is Whispered Folk or human doesn't matter. She's the best for the job in my eyes, and I hope in yours as well. Her arrival here doesn't herald the opening of the floodgates for all humans to move here or learn about us. We will remain hidden from the human world. But mayhap it reminds us that humans who understand the nature of our community and accept us can coexist with Whispered Folk. And indeed, there are currently dozens of humans living and thriving here who are valued long-time members of the community, and this will always be the case. Now, back to business. I motion to vote on this updated proposal. All in favor?"

Unsurprisingly, it isn't unanimous. The trio votes against it, but the motion passes with the rest of the council in favor, and they issue the amended permit to proceed with work. Thankfully, Cara is spared any more public speaking. We return to our seats together, and I'm determined to keep her close for both our comfort. She squeezes her hands in her lap, her face frozen in a stunned expression. It seems like she'd prefer to be left alone, so I hold myself back. Now that Samuels knows who she is, he's staring daggers at her the entire time. His obsession is disturbing.

As the meeting adjourns and everyone begins filing out, an elderly male with kind eyes, another human in town, approaches Cara. "Hello, young lady. It's good to meet you. I'm Walt, that other human in the room." He laughs at his callback. "Welcome to town, and if you ever want to talk about being a human in a monster town or what it's like to be mated to one, I'm happy to share any wisdom I've gained."

She stares silently, her mouth hanging open in surprise. With a slight sway of her head she comes back to herself and holds out her hand to shake his. "Nice to meet you, Walt, I'm Cara. Um, mated? What do you mean?" she dazedly wonders.

"Mated, like married in human terms, though it means so much more than that. True life partners. Acton is my mate. He's why I moved here decades ago. I was a park ranger and I had no idea about Whispered Folk until I happened upon him one day at my park in Appalachia. He's a dryad, like a forest nymph, and at the time, he was living there, so it seems we really were destined to meet," he explains while waving toward his mate, a male half-covered in moss and vines, who is engaged in his own conversation near the door.

"That sounds romantic," Cara utters, her tone sincere.

"I'll tell you all about it sometime," he offers cheerfully, "I'll give you my number and we can meet for coffee." They exchange numbers, and he says goodbye to both of us and excuses himself to return to his mate.

With her phone and her binder in hand, Cara looks a little lost now that the maelstrom of the meeting is over, unsure of what to do. A few others from town hall walk over to offer their support. Luckily, Clancy and Ada soon join us, both grinning from ear to ear.

Ada brings her in for a hug, "Moon and stars, you did spectacularly well tonight, hon. I'm so proud of you," she exclaims as she squeezes Cara. "You are so brave, and we're sorry you had to face that bigoted vitriol."

After Ada releases her, Clancy puts a hand on her shoulder with a grim smile. "I want to thank you, Cara. We've asked too much of you already. I promise this abuse won't continue. Ada and I are meeting with the rest of the council right now on how to censure those three, get ahead of their antics as best as we can."

Cara's face looks drawn, her smile strained, eyes lacking their normal sparkle, like every ounce of her energy was depleted by Samuels' viciousness and the long slog of the meeting. "Um, thanks, I appreciate it. I still have the necklace, and I'll use it if I ever need to. See you tomorrow morning," she responds, sounding overwhelmed, retrieving the small amulet from her pocket.

Clancy reminds her, "It's a town hall tradition that those of us who attend only work the afternoon following these meetings. I'll see you in the office after lunch."

Clancy and Ada say goodbye, and Cara and I are left standing there alone. She's fidgeting, her eyes looking hunted, stuck in a loop, scanning the room endlessly, that amulet still clutched tight in her hand like she's ready to use it. Before I can think better of it, I blurt out, "Do you want to grab a drink? I thought... you may not want to be alone right now."

She looks caught off guard, and her eyebrows snap up. "Um, are you sure you want to?" she stumbles through her words.

"I am sure," I say, my voice resolute.

"Alright. I could use a drink," she acquiesces, still sounding dubious.

Maybe I can talk to her and put some of her fears to rest. Though I wouldn't blame her if this experience inextricably sours her view of Whispered Folk. It shed a damning light on us.

"Where would you feel most comfortable?" I offer.

"That place we went to the other night is fine. Call of the Wild. Do you think those council members will be there?" she asks, shrill anxiety creeping into her question.

"No, that's exactly where we should go if we don't want to run into them. They wouldn't be seen at a pack-owned establishment," I assure her.

"Oh, pack-owned..." she repeats, whispering absently to herself.

After dropping off her presentation materials at her desk, we walk together, mostly in step, from town hall down the well-lit sidewalk to the pub. She's quiet, lost in thought, with concern still etched on her face. She offers an apology for needing to decompress on our walk over, and I insist there's nothing to explain. It was a rough night. I want to console her, but I don't give in to the urge to take her hand in mine or wrap a protective wing around her. It would be so easy for me to do so, especially after putting my arm around her earlier. With her eyes on the sidewalk in front of her, I gently guide her by the elbow toward the door she's too distracted to notice. She looks up in surprise but gives me a small, unfeigned smile as we head inside the pub.

It's uncommonly quiet, even for a late Tuesday night. A few tables are occupied in the shadowed corners. There's only one patron at the bar, an older wolf shifter I recognize from Maman's pack, sitting by himself on one side, not looking to be social. We take a seat at the other side of the bar. The space will be dark to her human eyes. At this hour, there are only a few low-burning candles on the bar and tables offering their light, but I can see Cara perfectly. The usual late-night patrons prefer it this way.

She looks like a weight lifted off her shoulders the moment she takes off her suit jacket, hanging it on the back of her bar stool, and sits down. The bartender greets us, and without skipping a beat, she orders, "Bourbon. Neat, please."

"Make that two," I say.

The bartender, an orc named Halvor who prefers to go by Hal, sets glass tumblers in front of us and pours generously. He must notice she's human because he also reaches below the bar and grabs another small tea-light candle, lighting it with the snap of his claws. The additional light doesn't cut through the dark much, but at least Cara will be able to see her drink. I nod my appreciation as he steps away.

She holds up her glass, and I clink mine to hers as we lock eyes. "Cheers," we say in unison. Her eyelids flutter closed as she takes a large sip, setting it down with her gaze on the bartender. She subtly nods her head toward him, murmuring, "I thought you said this was a *pack-owned* bar? Is he a werewolf and a jolly green giant?"

I almost spit out my mouthful of bourbon at her unexpected remark. I swallow it roughly before I embarrass myself. Smirking at her observation, I answer, "No, he's just an orc. Most of the staff here are weres, shifters, or wolven in the pack, but not all of them. He's here because he's very good at his job. And he can work nights around the full moon when a lot of the pack are... otherwise engaged."

She nods and affirms, "The full moon. That makes sense, I guess."

We return to a companionable silence for a few minutes, occasionally taking sips. Earlier, Cara looked very buttoned up and professional in her suit. Now, with her jacket off, she appears sultry and stunning. Although not showing much skin, the silky short-sleeved top is smooth and shiny, perfectly hugging the generous roundness of her breasts. The top of her skirt highlights the dip of her waist, the swell of her stomach, the thickness of her thighs. Her long hair is pulled up into a twist, showing off her long, delicate neck. I try not to ogle, but I can't help watching her out of the corner of my eye, admiring her luscious form.

Her mere presence is arousing, jasmine sweetness and warmth, making my body burn for her.

She sighs, deeply and drawn out, and breaks her silence. "Why did you ask me out tonight?"

"I... wanted you to know you aren't alone, especially since Ada and Clancy couldn't be with you right now. You need time to let off steam," I confess, though it's not the full story. I don't want to add to her stress.

"Oh... that's very thoughtful, thank you," she replies distractedly, returning her focus to her drink.

"It shows your strength that you were able to stand up and make a case for yourself and the project after enduring such abuse from those cretins. They're wrong about everything, Cara. And everyone knows it," I reassure her.

She abruptly turns to me, her brows furrowed. "I've dealt with difficult people, difficult men especially, in my career. But having those insults and threats hurled directly at me by a complete stranger felt different. At least they're upfront with their hatred of me. I'll give them that. Of all the things to be judged for, being human was not one I ever expected to deal with." She takes a slow sip. "If he was questioning my qualifications for the job, I could address that. But if he doesn't want humans to be in this town, there's nothing I can do to change his mind. And he'll continue to take it out on me." Her voice hitches, clearly wanting to say more, but swallowing the rest of her words.

"He's a weasel, plain and simple. The town is on your side. Most of the council is too. Try not to let him upset you over much. He's using you as a scapegoat to undercut Clancy. It's not personal, but I know he makes it feel that way," I urge, but I'm too vexed to sound comforting.

She shakes her head, voice trembling, "But he's right, I don't belong here. This town wasn't made for me. The opposite, in fact. To get away from humans."

I could strangle the warlock for putting these doubts in her head. "Cara, you belong here just as much as anyone else. I'm not proud of it, but I also questioned Clancy's decision to hire a human. I was wrong, and I realized that very quickly once I understood your experience would be good for the town. Please trust that others who aren't sure yet will come to the same conclusion," I admit, full of self-loathing that I ever assumed the worst of her.

She crosses her arms over her midsection, folding into herself. She darts her gaze away, looking down with a pensive expression on her face. She murmurs, her voice barely audible, "Is that why you don't like me? Because I'm human?"

CHAPTER 12
CARA

Ben sits next to me, obscured in shadow. It's so dark that it feels like a confessional booth, just the two of us. And now I've stupidly bared my soul and made things unbearably awkward. I didn't even mean to say it out loud, that accusation that makes him sound no better than that councilman. Tears swarm my vision. I shouldn't have agreed to this drink. He was compelled to babysit me because Clancy and Ada were busy. The way he put his arm around me earlier made me feel so safe. It was selfless of him, that show of solidarity, even if he isn't particularly fond of *me*. And now I put him on the spot. I'm pathetic.

He doesn't say anything for an unnervingly long stretch. I can't bring myself to look at him. I'm so embarrassed. "I..." his low voice trails off before picking up again, "I do like you, although yes, I have apprehensions because you're a human. Because I'm... so different from you, I won't get too close."

His words are bruising. "I'm not sure that I see your point. I get along with Clancy and Ada well, and Clancy is half-horse! It's okay not to like me, to not want to be my friend. I don't know why I put you on the spot like that. I'm being emotional, and I apologize. You don't need to justify anything. We're just colleagues. It's fine," I lie, attempting to sound convincing, though if I were a stronger person, it would be the truth of the matter.

He grunts, sounding exasperated. "I can't be that kind of friend to you, Cara. I'm sorry." There's a flatness to his voice that I haven't heard since that horrible day with him last week.

I could cry at how unkind he sounds. So I take a long sip of bourbon to buy myself a moment to think. "Alright. Friendship is off the table," I remark tartly.

There's not much else to say. Still holding my glass, I down the rest of my bourbon in one large gulp, relishing the burn trailing down my throat. It gives me the jolt that I need to get out of here. This was a mistake. All of it. I'm tired, so deep in my bones. In my soul. All of these feelings brewing inside me boil over with reckless abandon. I don't care anymore.

"I don't want to justify my existence here. There seem to be other humans who live peaceful, fulfilling lives in town, but for some reason, I'm singled out among them. By you, by Samuels and those other council members. I feel duped in how I was brought here. Some lady who I don't know told Clancy to hire me, and everyone thought that was perfectly reasonable. It makes no sense. Don't get me wrong, I'm grateful to have been given this opportunity and Clancy seems fully in support of me. But if I will always be treated badly or differently because I'm human, I can't stay. I've learned through some very bad experiences that a job is just that and nothing more. I can't compromise myself any further just to stay in one, even if it's the one I've always dreamed of. This has been the wake-up call I've needed, so thanks for that." I raise my empty glass to him in a mock salute. At least Ben has the decency to look remorseful.

The alcohol has loosened my tongue, so I press on with my rant. "Funny enough, I told my best friend I don't know if I'll fit in here. And, of course, I didn't mention anything about... well, you know." I gesture at our surroundings as I babble on. "She took it to mean I was having a hard time as a *big city gal in a small town*, and I let her believe that. It'll be an easy way to spin things when I move on. Maybe that's for the best. This doesn't seem to be the place I need right now. I just want to be able to live quietly and work somewhere I'm allowed to do my job and flourish without being the town pariah who requires a fucking panic button. I'm giving Clancy my notice in the morning," I reveal. I can't take back these words now. And I don't want to.

Ben makes a choked noise, sputtering, "What? Cara, you can't leave. I'm sorry you had to learn about the Seer in that way. Clancy should have explained it to you. Darla's visions aren't always straightforward, but she wouldn't have seen you if you weren't meant to be here. Besides, Clancy would never have hired someone unqualified for the position, human or Whispered Folk, regardless of Darla. You're even more than we could have hoped for. It's clear Darla was right about you. And do not believe a word out of Samuels' mouth. He is the town pariah, a constant pest, not you. He sows discord for his own gain. None of this is on you to fix. Clancy and the council will take care of it now that he's gone too far."

The absolute nerve of Ben to try to talk me out of leaving. It fuels my indignation. "It's for the best. My presence is causing a town rift. I'm not worth it, to be frank. There are plenty of people out there with my skill set. He can hire someone else who is less objectionable to the town. It's probably a good thing we aren't friends since I'll be gone soon," I snark at him.

"I don't want you to leave. Please consider staying," he pleads solemnly.

"*You* don't want me to leave? But you don't want to be friends, either? What am I missing here?" I hiss more quietly as the realization hits that other people are probably listening to us.

He scrubs a hand over his face, lacking his usual haughty composure. "I often find social situations difficult, so I usually keep to myself. But I find that I'm especially at a loss around you. Mayhap I went about our interactions the wrong way," he admits ruefully.

Uncertain what he's getting at, I silently wait for him to continue, not caring if it's making him uncomfortable. He exhales loudly, exasperatedly, and I notice his hands clench into fists and spread back open, still tense, where he rests them on the bar.

"I can't be friends with you because I will develop an attachment. Honestly, I already have. That doesn't happen very often, and I've never felt this degree of attraction to someone, so I cannot pretend I don't feel it. You are so new to Whispered Folk that you will not feel the same about me, maybe ever. I look fearsome to you, and I understand why. I'm not blaming you. Just stating the truth. It is better for us both if I keep my distance outside of work," he divulges, sounding resigned.

I'm struck speechless. His hot and cold act was to protect his heart? From me, of all people? I'm nothing special. I'm pretty enough, I suppose, but not gorgeous. Even now, at my lowest weight since my teens, my body is still too thick to fit societal beauty standards. My career has been derailed, I basically live paycheck to paycheck, and I have no support system outside of my small group of friends who live halfway across the country. I've been in crisis mode since I found out about Mark's cheating, and I'm still spiraling if tonight is any indication. I have nothing to offer anyone besides being very good at my job, but that seems to have become more of a curse than a blessing. Rose would slap me upside the head if she knew my thoughts, but sadly, it's all true.

Whatever image of me built up in his head isn't real. The irony is not lost on me that he believes something similar about himself. Other than the fact that he's a gargoyle, some mythical monster I thought was just a decoration on old churches—and that's very strange to me, I can't deny it—he's a successful business owner who has a close-knit family and is best friends with the mayor. If we were to compare notes, I'm clearly the loser misfit in this situation.

He looks dispirited, and I realize I've been in my own head this entire time, staring at nothing, as if there's a great void in front of me.

"Cara, you've had a very difficult day. This is part of the reason why I initially didn't support Clancy bringing you here. He should have been upfront about the nature of our community and let you decide if the job was worth it since the complications of living here affect you the most. Clancy barrels through his grand plans sometimes without considering the consequences. And Samuels' reaction is one of them— he's a master manipulator. It's how such an annoying little worm has gained a position of power in town. Believe me, you're just the latest excuse to stir the pot and cause trouble for Clancy. Please stay, you deserve better than Samuels' treatment... my treatment... of you," he beseeches.

I twist toward him in my seat to fully look at him in the flickering candlelight. While I can't see the fine details of his features, the shape of his strong square jaw and prominent brow stand out. His tall height, sturdy and muscular build, and even the austere facial features could be handsome if he were human. They are handsome, in fact, striking in their own way. I shouldn't pretend to deny it. Yet, the faintly illuminated outline of his tucked-back wings and the horns that sweep from his forehead across the top of his head highlight his otherness. It's a contrast that's hard to reconcile. His dark eyes glint in the low light, enough that I can see them more clearly than anything else. They search mine, waiting for my reaction, but I still hesitate, trying to wrap my mind around what he's telling me.

He closes his eyes and turns away from me slightly. It's the most vulnerable I've seen him.

"Forget I said anything. It's unfair to you. Just one more thing to deal with on top of everything else," he murmurs, voice laced with regret. Looking down at the glass he's barely touched, he adds, "It's been a long night already. Mayhap we should call it."

Part of me agrees with him, but I know that if the night ends on this note, the rift between us will be permanent. It's now or never, this chance to lay it all bare, to learn what's going on inside his head.

He signals to the bartender.

"Wait," I blurt too loudly, so much for trying to be discreet. "This is just a lot to take in at once. I'm glad you told me... about all of it," I explain more quietly.

The bartender walks over and asks, "Another drink?"

Knowing Ben is going to push me away, I answer before he can, "Two more, please." The bartender pours more bourbon into our glasses and resumes his spot near the other side of the bar, giving us plenty of space again.

"Cara..." he warns.

"Ben," I challenge, determined to get him to listen.

This moment with Ben feels like a crossroads; what happens tonight will impact my future. But what would that be in this town full of absurd impossibilities? Nothing feels real except my emotions. It would make more sense if this were a dream—or a psychotic break—that I awaken from one day.

Am I only lovable in a fairy tale? I'm not sure what dating Ben would look like. Dating anyone here, for that matter. If we're compatible physically and emotionally in that way. If that's something I'd even be into—being with someone human-*ish*. Dating, in general, has seemed so unpalatable in the wake of Mark's infidelity. I don't know how I'll ever trust a man again. But I could be doomed to be alone forever if I stay here. I've been caught up in so many other unfamiliar aspects of living here, I haven't put nearly enough thought into whether I'd be okay with that.

"I don't want to forget what you said. It's just... this year has been awful. There's a lot I haven't told anyone here, not even Ada. It messed me up, to put it simply. I'm not the same person I used to be. I'm not sure if I have anything to offer romantically anymore," I confess, my eyes stinging at the truth of it.

"Cara, what happened? You can tell me anything. It will stay between us," he pledges in his graveled, hushed tone.

A peal of self-deprecating laughter escapes me. "This is going to sound unbelievable, but it's true. Every pathetic second of it."

As I recount in embarrassing detail my sordid history with Mark, a sense of shame fills me that I could have been so naïve. That I let myself be treated terribly for so long. Maybe Ben will understand that trusting part of me is gone forever. I'm too cynical now.

There's a hollowness deep inside me after such a profound betrayal. It's hidden away, locked up tight like an empty room that I'm too poor to heat in winter. Opening up that empty drafty space where safety and security should live is a luxury I can't afford. So now I operate without it. Incomplete. Smaller on the inside. But I survive.

Nursing my drink, I circle back to a thought that kept me going through each hardship. When life beats me down the hardest, I have to find a way through, no matter what it takes. Right now, I don't know whether the way through keeps me here or leads me elsewhere.

Ben's attention on me hasn't flagged this entire time. Taking another spicy vanilla sip of bourbon, I regard him over the lip of the glass before I continue, "In a way, this place is an escape from reality.

Everyone who caused the most pain can't reach me here unless I let them. I've essentially disappeared from their world."

He nods in agreement. "A tabula rasa, you can start fresh. It makes sense that the Seer saw you."

"Yes, but I'll always carry those experiences with me. I'm nobody, Ben. Sure, I have a sob story. That doesn't make me worthy of some magical intervention," I reason.

His voice turns reflective. "I'm not so sure. It seems like you needed a break from the human world right when we needed you. There's a touch of fate in that. And like you said, mayhap you can leave those troubling elements behind."

I protest, "It hasn't shielded me from everything. I've never dealt with outright threats before."

"Our world is far from perfect, as you've seen firsthand. Please know, despite what happened tonight, you are safe here. I'd never let anything happen to you." The moment feels heavy, like this is some type of binding promise to me.

"Thank you, that means a lot." I smile shyly. It looks like his whole body relaxes.

Ben takes a long swig of his bourbon and sets the glass down, staring at it for a moment. He starts to say something but falters, like he's changed his mind. I lean closer, my curiosity piqued.

When he finally speaks, he sounds tentative, almost apologetic, "Can I ask you more about Mark?"

"Of course," I respond automatically.

"Does he still hold a place in your heart?" he seeks earnestly.

I can't hide the look of revulsion on my face and declare, in all honesty, "No, never again. He disgusts me, and I'll never get over how much I hate him for ruining my life. Finding out he was cheating on me, getting engaged to someone else while still dating me, puts all the other cruel and controlling things he did to me into perspective. I was heartbroken, of course. I loved him, but now I'm just so angry. He used me for eight long years. I see that now. With absolutely no remorse, either. It obliterated my ability to trust others. At any point, I can be dropped and discarded and forced to leave. I don't know if I'll ever feel secure anywhere or with anyone ever again."

"Cara...I'm so sorry this happened to you." His sorrowful voice makes me want to comfort *him*. I quickly squeeze his large hand resting on the bar. His skin is warm and textured, rutty but not rough against mine, reminding me of how scared I was to shake his hand last week.

"Thank you for saying that. And I apologize that this is the version of me that you're getting," I say wanly, trying not to sound too bitter.

"Don't apologize for who you are or what you have survived. You have overcome so much. You should never have been mistreated, and you aren't any lesser because of it," he rasps.

His attempt to console me is sweet. "You sound like my best friend, Rose. She tries to tell me the same thing."

"She must be a smart female and a good friend."

"She is. But I've said too much. I didn't mean to dump everything on you like this was some therapy session." I laugh mirthlessly. "If we're being honest with each other, when you asked me here tonight... I considered saying no, but I'm glad I didn't. Things between us are awkward. And I understand why that is now. But witnessing your friendships with Clancy and Ada made me sad that, for some reason, I wasn't worthy of it, too."

"Cara, that's not the case..." he cuts in.

"I know there's more to it. But it's how I felt. Our situation is complicated, but I don't want us to ignore each other. I'm just not sure how to go about this while respecting your wishes."

"Mayhap it shows my lack of maturity. Or inexperience with females. I should not have caused you distress. I was trying to avoid it, though I fumbled that completely," he relents. "I hope that knowing how I feel doesn't... influence you in any way."

"I'm grateful to hear that, thank you. God, I'm sorry this is so weird. I'm so weird sometimes," I moan, covering my face with my hands.

"No more than me," he huffs.

"You mentioned emotional maturity. How old are you, if you don't mind me asking? I honestly can't tell with anyone here," I squint my eyes as if that would help me see him better, but his face is still mostly nebulous in the dark room.

"I'm thirty-eight and so is Clancy. We have been close since we were both young. Our kinds age at more or less the same rate as humans. Our life expectancy is similar to a long human lifespan, so not much differ-ent. If you ever met my baby brother, you would know I look my age," he jokes.

I crack a wide smile and find myself giggling. "You could tell me you're twenty-nine, and I'd never know the difference."

"After next year, I'll be forever thirty-nine, how about that? When you meet my father, you'll see how I'll age eventually. Though he still looks good for an old man," he offers in good humor.

Meet his father? Like, meet his family? He'd want me to after all of this, even if it turns out I can't return his feelings?

"Ada told me you're a gargoyle. Is your entire family made up of gargoyles?" I ask, curious to know more about him, not squandering this new-found receptiveness toward me.

"On the male side, yes. My father and brother are gargoyles. My mother is a wolf shifter in the local pack."

I can't hide my shock. "Your mother is a werewolf?"

He guffaws as he corrects me, "No, a shifter, not a werewolf. They're related but not the same. Wolven, werewolves, and wolf shifters each have a different relationship with the moon. And before you ask, no, I'm not any of those things. I'm just a gargoyle." I can hear the smile in his voice, even though I still can't see it in the low light.

"But... why aren't you, if your mom is?" I can't help but sound confused.

"Now I have a story for you. If you want to hear it?" he teases.

"Obviously!" I exclaim, intrigued.

He turns more fully towards me in his seat and tells me about how gargoyles were created from stone statues to guard the rich and power-ful. Unable to contain myself, I interrupt, "Can you turn to stone?"

He doesn't sound offended, but I can tell I've struck a nerve. "No. I wouldn't want to anyway. When my ancestors were transformed back into stone, they essentially ceased to exist, only to come alive again to deal with the next threat. Probably the earliest, most rudimentary gargoyles had no self-awareness. Loyal, vicious, airborne, they were the most perfectly lethal soldiers of the time."

Ben pauses, as if for effect, but in actuality he reaches to take a sip of his drink. Still, he weaves a compelling tale, and I'm hanging on every word.

"Eventually, the elites who held dominion over us couldn't turn us back to stone. The magick that animated us had changed. A generation of gargoyles came alive with full consciousness and individuality. Truly flesh and bone like any other creature, though from magick and not natural evolution. Those who created us probably accepted payment without admitting this likelihood to the buyers. Even so long ago, magick wielders would have known the risk—that magick so powerful is unstable. And soon enough, gargoyles were easily able to break away from their creators and captors. Some remained in Europe, but many came to America, Canada, and elsewhere during the time of French colonial expansion," he recounts.

"Your ancestors came here that early?" I ask.

"Yes, an ancestor, my many times over great grandfather, settled in Louisiana. I'm not sure what my family name was before that, if there even was one, but he was the first Garde-Pierre, or *stone guard*, that my family knows of. Over a century ago, my great-grandfather moved here," he explains.

"Ada mentioned that your family has only been here a few generations when she was telling me about her family founding Monstera Bluff," I remark, putting the pieces together in my brain.

"Ah yes, compared to the Mayweathers, we are still newcomers," he quips.

"Ben, you're made of magick! I can't believe real gargoyles existed right under people's noses," I gush.

He grins playfully. "And we still do! Though I understand what you're saying. I think those who saw us at the time were not long for this world. So that could be why our existence other than as decorative stone statues wasn't well known."

"When I first saw you, I thought you were a demon or a devil. That sounds terrible, I'm sorry. But I had no idea what to think." I grimace, embarrassed.

He chuckles darkly. "That explains why you were so fearful when we met. I'm not offended. Gargoyles were designed to look like infernal creatures, ironically enough, since we often guarded cathedrals and other grand religious buildings."

"That's kind of you to say. It's one of the many things I've struggled with in my first week here. I hope you won't hold it against me," I acknowledge, feeling humbled.

"Think no more of it," he responds sincerely.

"So, how does this relate to your mom being a shifter and not a gargoyle?" I remind him.

"Historically, all gargoyles were male. So we sought out mates from other species, including humans and Whispered Folk. The children of these pairings have always been gargoyles. The theory is that we are attracted to the life force of evolved species to balance out that unstable magick within us. But gargoyles are bound to change, and we already have. There are a few known female gargoyles alive now, the first of our kind. Justifiably, their families are very protective of their privacy, so not much is known about them. However, their very existence proves we continue to evolve," he reveals, sounding introspective.

"That's unbelievable, Ben! Is it scary that your species could change at any time? You're not... set in stone? Oh god, I sound like Clancy, I've spent too much time with him!" I groan.

"He'd probably give you a raise if he heard you say that. Nothing would make him prouder." I crack up, laughter cutting through the quiet in the dark pub. "But to answer your question, I see it as a good thing. So far, it has been beneficial to us. I imagine it will continue that way," he muses.

We finish the last of the bourbon in our glasses, and I can't contain a huge, full-body yawn. It must be past midnight at this point. "Alright, we really are calling it a night now. Are you able to drive?" Ben ensures.

"I think so, I'm tired, but I'll be fine. My car is back at town hall, though," I tell him.

"I'll walk you there," he volunteers as he stands up and pulls money out of his wallet, putting the bills on the bar.

Taking my jacket off the back of my barstool, he holds it out for me. The intimacy of it makes me bashful as I slip my arms through it. My face feels warm. He waves goodbye to the bartender as we leave. His hand brushes the small of my back as we walk out the door, the feather-light touch enough to make me shiver.

Outside, under the bright, nearly full moon, I can see him much more clearly. He looks down at me and asks, "Are you cold?"

Although the temperature is not what caused me to shiver, I realize that I am. Mid-October in the deep south is still warm during the day, but overnight temperatures have started to get chilly already.

"A little, but it's just a short walk," I answer, trying not to be a bother.

He doesn't seem satisfied with my response. "I could..." he stammers, "put my wing around you to help block the breeze?"

Oh. I've felt his body warmth before, and he runs hot. I'm sure it would feel nice right now, but it's a dangerous gesture to accept. Too intimate for this friendship still on a precipice. And yet, his hopeful expression captivates me. "Sure..." I relent, trying to sound unaffected.

A corner of his mouth quirks up just slightly, revealing a hint of sharp fang. I shudder again, and he must believe I'm positively freezing because he steps forward and unfurls his wings, wrapping them around me like a cozy cocoon.

I gasp in surprise and find myself leaning into his body, which is a veritable furnace covered in sinewy muscle. His hands cup my shoulders and stroke down the back of my arms to my elbows, sliding up and down slowly. His dark, earnest eyes study me, lingering on every part of my face in reverence.

"Is this better?" he rasps low into my ear, his breath tickling, as he leans his face close to mine. Words stick in my throat. I nod, causing his cheek or perhaps his lips to skim my ear with the movement. It shoots a torrent of arousal to my core, making me deliciously overheated and overwhelmed. "You smell so good, like home," he murmurs, husky and hot. The blatant desire in his voice makes me needy for more, and I tilt my head to give him better access.

My hands reach up to the hard plane of his chest, anchoring myself while I'm utterly surrounded by him. His thick muscles, crafted from manual labor, flex underneath his crisp dress shirt as I rub and explore. "Cara..." he groans, pulling me even closer as his hands find my hips.

Our bodies melt into each other, and my breath catches as I notice his heavy, hard length pressed against my abdomen. It suddenly feels like we're wearing too many clothes. We're both burning up beneath each other's touch, and I want to feel his skin against mine. He wraps his arms around me, holding me tightly, almost lifting me up, as he bends down to nuzzle my cheek and neck. A whimper escapes me as his lips, and a hint of teeth, brush right below my ear. He growls, sounding satisfied at my reaction, the vibration against my skin heightening my pleasure.

As he nibbles his way down my neck, the pub door swings open loudly as other patrons leave, startling us both. The moment abruptly feels too real, too alarming, and my arousal is doused by panic. Both of us come to our senses at the same time. He releases me and takes a step back while lowering his wings. His expression turns guilty, and I have a hard time meeting his eyes, feeling so embarrassed with myself.

"Ashes, I don't know what came over me, I apologize," he offers, sounding contrite.

Me neither, to be honest, I did not expect to react to him like that. "I think we both got swept up in it. I don't mean to lead you on. We should probably go," I mutter, exhaustion settling in.

We walk wordlessly toward the town hall parking lot. The streets aren't busy, but it's livelier after midnight than I'd expect—with more businesses open, too. I guess the night-dwelling population is pretty active. After a couple blocks, the cold seeps through my jacket again. I sneak a glance at Ben, noticing his furrowed brow and distracted gaze. I can't begin to understand what happened, how things turned heated between us so quickly, but he looks like he's beating himself up about it. I know he's attracted to me, so he doesn't regret it. Maybe he worries that I do, but he shouldn't. I was a very willing participant. I felt sexy and desired in his arms. It was unbearably intimate to feel the undeniable proof that I turned him on. It's powerful to know someone wants you like that. But I'm not ready to repeat it yet, no matter how good it felt in the moment. There's too much else to consider right now. I'm not even sure if I'm going to stay.

Hating this renewed awkwardness hanging in the air between us, I interrupt the silence, extending an olive branch. "You can still put a wing around me while we walk if you want."

His eyes fly to mine, brows raising in surprise. "Is that something *you* still want?" he asks, sounding doubtful.

"I think so. I'm just not ready for anything more," I admit self-consciously.

His lips tug up into a genuine grin, and I return it in kind. He gently places the wing behind my shoulders and back, curling it slightly around my outside arm. Since he's so much taller than me, I feel completely surrounded by it. I'm instantly much warmer, like I'm wearing a heated leather cloak. He stands next to me, but there's still some space between us since his wings are so long. With my interior arm, so as not to disturb where I'm tucked in, I reach across myself to lightly smooth my fingers along his wing. It feels like textured leather. I trace over bone or cartilage along the edges and as well as the valley of skin between.

He wiggles his wing where I've been studying him. "Oh!" I cry out, giggling, "Sorry, it's just so fascinating."

He grunts in agreement, "That's what all of you earthbound keep telling me."

"Earthbound? That's rude. And who are all these other earthbound people admiring your wings?" I ask with a flash of jealousy I didn't anticipate.

He hums and shrugs his shoulders. I can feel the movement in the wing.

"A gentlemale never tells," he teases.

I laugh incredulously and he smirks in response. Oh my god, I believe we're flirting.

"And here I thought I was special, getting to use your wing as a coat," I quip, lacking self-control.

"You are, Cara. I don't loan it out to just anyone," he reassures, taking my hand that's next to his and bringing it to his lips for a kiss.

He lowers it and lets go, walking on like nothing of the sort happened. I keep pace, still tucked beside him, but I'm struck speechless. From the charmingly smug look on his face, Ben knows it. Holy smokes, this guy knows all the right buttons to push.

We approach my SUV in the parking lot behind town hall. It reminds me of the end of a date, even though it assuredly wasn't, despite the... heated embrace... and flirtatiousness at the end. Right? Ben lifts his wing away from me and tucks it back behind him with the other one. His gaze burns into mine as we face each other beside my driver's door. I worry my lips as a wave of bashfulness washes over me. He patiently waits for me to speak first, and I hope that means he's letting me set the tone for how we end the night.

"I'm glad we hashed everything out, and I mean it when I say I will understand if you keep your distance from me. Especially because I don't know if I can give you what you're looking for right now." I sigh, full of regret.

"But what if that whole idea of staying away was a stupid mistake, a misguided attempt at chivalry? I want to spend time with you. However you'll let me," he professes.

My stomach somersaults at his tender words. "I'd like that too," I say in relief.

"May I bring you flowers again tomorrow?" he asks tenderly.

I'm sure if I told him no, he'd respect my wishes. It would be the wiser course of action, but I can't bring myself to do it. It just seems so nice for a change, so caring.

"Only if you'll still talk to me afterward," I quip good-naturedly, thinking back to that first time.

He takes my gentle ribbing in stride. "I promise I'll never stop talking to you again."

Since I'm not sure a hug would stay innocent, I put out my hand to shake. It seems inadequate, but it would feel wrong to leave without offering any gesture like this. Like he did that first day we met, Ben grasps my hand gently, holding it for slightly too long. Except now, he slowly opens my hand and brings it up to his mouth, pressing a tender kiss to my palm and then to the inside of my wrist. This time, the sight of my hand in his much larger, monstrous one sparks a different kind of nervousness. I haven't felt butterflies in a long time, but they're unmistakable.

"Goodnight, Cara. Sleep tight," he bids as he steps back for me to get into the SUV.

I feel breathless as I fumble for my keys to unlock it. As soon as I get in and start it, he leaps into the air and takes off, circling once overhead and then flying away. It's an exhilarating sight.

The drive home is fast, and I'm exhausted as I step into the carriage house. After chugging a glass of water, I quickly shed my clothes, scrub the makeup off my face, and fall into bed. Sleep hits me almost immediately. Everything that happened with Ben takes a bit of the sting out of the scary outburst at the town hall meeting. But it's not enough to stop a vivid nightmare from taking hold.

I'm suddenly in a courtroom, a defendant on trial, and the judge orders me to take the stand. Ralston Samuels steps forward to cross-examine me. He yells relentlessly, spittle flying in my face as I sit on the stand.

"Why are you here, human? Why haven't you left yet? You don't want to know what we do to your kind here. You're not long for this world..."

I have no time to answer, my tongue a useless lead weight in my mouth. I can't defend myself from the questions and accusations hurled at me.

The courtroom is packed. Everyone in town is watching my worth and integrity being reduced to nothing by Councilman Samuels. I try to find Ada, Clancy, Ben, anyone, but I don't recognize a soul. Everyone is hazy, indistinct. My eyes won't focus on anyone, just the undulating mass growing angrier by the minute.

On and on it goes, each attack worse than the last. "We'll hunt you and skin you alive, human! You never should have stepped foot here. No one can save you now. No one even wants you, you fatherless whore."

I search the room for a lifeline, calling out for anyone to help me, yet no one is willing to stand up to Ralston Samuels and the mob backing him up. A swell of noise rises from the crowd of onlookers, a mix of chatter and chanting turning into shrieks and shouts. My eardrums threaten to burst. From a bench at the back of the room, a shadowy figure emerges, standing tall above everyone else, with glowing yellow eyes boring into mine. Suddenly, the room dims except for his sinister, unblinking yellow stare. He's been following me, looking for a way in, and now he finally caught me. He won't let me escape this time.

CHAPTER 13
CARA

I walk into my office promptly at noon with a sandwich and coffee from Midnight Mystic. Clancy doesn't seem like a stickler, but he told me to arrive after lunch, and I don't want to rock the boat. Something changed in me since last week. Last night even. I'm not afraid of being around Whispered Folk, with the obvious exception of Ralston Samuels and his cronies. But I have a panic button in my pocket for that. It seems monumental, in a way. I guess Ada's immersion technique works.

True to Ben's word, there's a bouquet of daisies tied with a ribbon on my desk. The beautiful arrangement of fragrant red and white blooms makes my desk smell heavenly. Beside it sits a pink box from the pastry shop. Inside are six macarons in a rainbow of colors. He probably didn't get to take the morning off, making me feel bad I kept him out so late... except I'm certain he doesn't mind. It changed everything between us. This is quite a romantic gesture.

Since no one is watching, I melodramatically flop into my desk chair, throwing back my head and groaning at all the decisions I need to make. I can't fall for someone's potential. I've been burned by it before. But Ben seems different somehow. Rose is going to flip out when I tell her he and I... what? Made out? No, just had a hot and heavy embrace. I can already hear the squeal she'll let out, followed by some good-natured *I told you so's* and much-needed reality checks about not falling into old patterns. Oh no, what happens when she wants to see a photo of him? Or she tries to look him up online? This is uncharted territory.

First things first, I check my work email because it's bound to be a shitshow. Sure enough, I received dozens of emails this morning. Quite a few are from town hall employees I've never met who work overnight. This detail blows my mind, though it's obviously unfair to block a segment of the population from working for the town because they're nocturnal. Some people introduced themselves and congratulated me after the meeting ended, but it's nice for others to reach out by email, too.

It's no surprise I've received an invite to an informal meeting in Clancy's office with some council members this afternoon. Too bad I can't officially meet them under better circumstances. Last night hung a black cloud over my new role. First, though, I need to talk to Clancy alone. He needs to tell me the truth about that woman who supposedly saw me in a vision. Whatever that means. Mentally preparing myself, I resolve not to let Clancy smooth-talk his way out of it. There's no reason to hide anything from me at this point.

I knock on the open door of his office, and Clancy looks up from his computer and motions for me to come in. "Well, if it isn't our preeminent urbanist. I just want to tell you again how well your presentation went. Everyone... well, almost everyone... was quite impressed. We did have a few village idiots in attendance," he conspicuously clears his throat and rolls his eyes.

"Thanks, Clancy. It was difficult to tell, considering everything that happened. Um, one thing I did want to bring up is that woman who said she saw me? What is that about? And I assume you didn't actually find me on the internet like you said?" I push, careful not to sound too accusatory. He is my boss, after all.

His expression turns satisfyingly contrite. "Ah yes, the cat's outta the bag, but it seems there was no other way. I'd have spilled eventually, but I didn't want to spook you too much, considering the surprise of a lifetime you had when you got here." He chuckles.

"Well, I've had enough of those for a couple lifetimes now. Frankly,

I'm getting used to it. So, to be clear, that woman had a vision about me?" I prompt again.

"Our Seer, Darla Rallis, is quite the boon to our community. She has a rare gift. Generations can pass without a powerful seer. She isn't just some fortune teller with a crystal ball. I took a chance and asked her who I should hire for this job. I knew it was an important decision for the town, and I wanted all the help I could get. When she sees, it's like she's deep in a daydream that takes time to snap out of it. Lo and behold, it happened that day. She saw that I should hire Cara Bishop of Chicago. Her words are worth their weight in gold. She told me you need to be made to feel welcome here, so that's one of many reasons why I'm taking Ralston Samuels and his goon squad so seriously. He isn't going to stand in the way of you being here. You can take my word on that," he affirms in uncharacteristic seriousness.

"Ben told me something similar last night. How did you know it was me, of all people?" I ponder aloud.

"I looked you up online," he responds cheekily.

At least he had given me a half-truth the other night. "It just took me by surprise. I thought I got this job based on merit, not by some divine intervention," I lament.

"I understand it looks like that but think of it this way: you had to have the experience you did for Darla to have seen you. She simply pointed me in the right direction. You qualified yourself for the job," he reassures with unfeigned support. "There's that saying, *you need the sand in the oyster to make the pearl*. Samuels is that sand—the annoying grains of it you find in every nook and cranny after visiting the beach, but I digress. We'll get through this and come out all the better for it."

I can't help my watery smile. "That's a nice thing to say, thank you."

"Well, Cara, you can thank me by telling me why Ben brought you another bouquet of flowers this morning," he tries to bargain, grinning devilishly.

I bark out a laugh. "What did *he* say about it?" I respond, trying to sidestep any discussion of Ben.

"Absolutely nothing! He said I should mind my own business for a change. I told him everything in town is my business. He suggested that I get a hobby, so I reminded him that gossiping is probably the most popular hobby in this town. And then he told me to get a life, so I pointed out that life is not worth living without a little gossip. You see where this is going. Needless to say, I didn't get anything out of him," he animatedly complains.

"They were just a nice gesture. Not much to tell," I deflect demurely, hoping my cheeks aren't too pink.

"I don't buy that for a second. So tight-lipped and no fun at all. Moon and stars, you two were clearly made for each other." He harrumphs in feigned indignation, smiling the entire time.

Ada taps lightly on the door. Her timing couldn't be more perfect. "Am I interrupting anything?" she asks breezily, unaware that she's sparing me from Clancy's third degree.

"Nothing we can't pick up later." He smirks mischievously in my direction, letting me know I'm not off the hook just yet. His insistence that I spill the tea would be annoying, except I know he's doing it out of concern and love for Ben, not actual gossip-mongering. He's getting a kick out of pretending otherwise.

Four council members arrive with Ada, and we sit around the conference table in the office. Everyone is here, minus the three obvious exceptions. Clancy shuts the door and introduces everyone to me. I remember Viran, a man who looked half snake with a long green tail. He spoke up at the meeting, but I was too distracted to register much about the other council members. Everyone seems friendly and, more importantly, on the same page.

"How many females thanked you for *helping* them with their proposals, Clancy? Four? I think that's a new record. Marieke didn't look so happy listening to those other females sing your praises, though I doubt she'll have much time to stew about it getting the salon doors open," Viran ribs, his banter jovial.

"Someone should tell her to take a dip in the ocean and cool off," Ada teases.

"If looks could kill, she'd have sent Uta to the healer. But I would have acted as her werewolf shield because I can't wait for her noodle bar to open. She told me the other day about her apprenticeship in Japan. Her menu is going to be stellar!" Celeste exclaims.

"Quit beating a dead horse, Viran," Clancy jokes to a couple of answering *boos*. "To her credit, Uta barely mentioned me. I just happened to let her know that Gregor was retiring and closing his locksmith shop, not even thinking she'd want the space because it's so long and narrow. Nope, turns out she wants to install a long bar counter for her customers to sit at. I did make her promise she'd have a table or two in the back with enough space for me since these hindquarters were not meant to fit a bar stool." He punctuates it with a slap to his haunches.

"I'm sure you did, Clancy. You'll just be going there for the noodles." Viran guffaws.

"Wasn't the place broken into over the weekend? I heard there was a bit of damage, but no leads on who did it," Ada mentions sympathetically.

Celeste sighs. "The irony of breaking into an old locksmith shop. It needed one of those magickal alarms like the ones you sell at your shop, Ada. But Samuels wasn't totally wrong last night. There's been an uptick in vandalism and other incidents this past week that have the constabulary stumped. The timing of it is highly suspect. Not that we think you're terrorizing the town, Cara, despite what ole doom and gloom says." Her eyes roll so hard that her entire head moves with the momentum.

"It sounds like he's angling for your job, Clancy. I wouldn't put it past him. *Humans are running amok, and the streets are unsafe.* It sets up an anti-human platform nicely for the next election," Viran observes.

The playful side of Clancy is gone, replaced by the steadfast leader who wants to guide his community to a better future. "You're shrewd as always, Viran. As we discussed last night, we're all in agreement that Samuels, Atticus, and Weatherby won't be content to rest on their laurels after last night's performance. It's not a question of whether they'll pull another stunt. It's a matter of when. We've been too tolerant of their antics in the past, and it's only escalated since they made it onto this governing body."

"They're already treating council meetings like they're the only judges of who in this town is worthy enough. And it obviously isn't the pack," Celeste cuts in bitingly.

"We know those three have always openly disdained non-magickal Whispered Folk, those of us they deem lesser kinds, and now, as elected members of the council, they have an official channel to denigrate us in very public ways. And yet, Samuels can also position himself as the savior against *human interference*. This new anti-human sentiment is a self-righteous mask for his deep-seated bigotry. An easy bogeyman to rile up fear and hate in Whispered Folk, especially in those of us who haven't interacted much with humans. Conveniently, that's the segment of our population who shouldn't otherwise care for him. It's just more cruel manipulation," Clancy speaks impassionedly.

"And so he can what? Cut off all interaction with the human world? Kick out the humans who live here? It makes no sense. Like it or not, this is the world we live in," Viran snaps.

"The humans who live among us bring great value to Monstera Bluff. Through their vocational expertise, their love for their mates, their friendship to all of us, they are a boon to our community. We need to be more diligent in protecting them from any attacks or repercussions. Our contacts are already reporting that the three have begun asking everyone to be on the lookout for suspicious human activity loudly and publicly around town. Ada and I will coordinate with the chief constable to make sure our constabulary is aware and ready to intervene when necessary. That said, our contacts also stressed that most of our citizens who heard them didn't seem swayed, mostly brushing them off. Still, we can't underreact because any talk like this could embolden someone to hostility against the humans living here," Clancy concludes as the group chatters in agreement with his statements.

Celeste chimes in, "The wolf pack has never understood how those three got elected and in such quick succession. There's never been a question those bigoted warlocks can't stand us, so it wasn't through our support. It's no secret they bad mouth our businesses and block proposals that help our pack. Clearly, they've been up to something this whole time, planning for some endgame. Cara, we're so sorry they're using you to stir up trouble in town. You have the full force of the pack behind you. Several of the humans here are mated to pack members, and we count them among our own. Even if that weren't the case, we would never stand by discrimination against any of our neighbors." Her heartfelt words release some of the anxiety welling in my chest, and I let her know how grateful I am.

The group agrees to maintain eyes on the three councilmen. Ada also gives me a more thorough explanation of my panic button amulet, letting me know that it puts a temporary protection spell on me when activated and sends an SOS to quite a few more people than I previously thought, including everyone currently in the room.

We adjourn and Ada follows me to my office. "I bet you thought life in a small town would be so much more boring than this! Now you have witches and werewolves looking after you," she jests, and we both giggle —some much-needed stress relief after that meeting.

"I've definitely never had such an army behind me before," I banter back, trying to sound lighthearted.

"Oh, hon, you're worth all the fuss. And we want you to stick around for a very long time," she insists sweetly.

Planning for the Samhain festival is in full swing, so she tells me about strengthening the ward she put around the property since she won't be home as often.

"Go out and explore. Have fun. Get to know the town. Don't let this hold you back. I'm always a phone call or text away. And speaking of, you should reach out to Walt. He told me you exchanged numbers. He's a dear old friend, basically family. He'd love nothing more than to talk your ear off about how to navigate life...and love... as a human among monsters," she giggles melodically, "He's an expert!"

Her enthusiasm makes me smile. "I was planning on it! I want to know more about how he met his... mate. I'm not quite sure what he meant by that, though."

"Oh, I think you will one day," she remarks knowingly.

The afternoon winds down, and I finally have time to text Ben to thank him for the gifts on my desk. I eat another macaron as my phone lights up with his call. It's like a jolt of caffeine to the system. I'm suddenly wide awake and jittery.

"Hi Ben," I answer too eagerly.

"Cara, I've been wanting to hear your voice all day," he purrs, low and indulgent. My breath hitches, and I know he can hear it through the line.

"I'm glad you called," I manage to reply, sounding winded.

"Would you have dinner with me tonight? I thought we could have a picnic at the beach. There's a perfect spot on one of the rivers where we can watch the sunset," he asks. The naked longing in his voice delights me.

My stomach flips. This is undeniably a date. I don't know if I can risk it. There's so much at stake if we don't work out, if he turns on me. He could make my job unbearable, turn Clancy against me, ruin my career. Mark was sweet and thoughtful, a perfect gentleman when we started dating. And that ended in total disaster. What if I'm not seeing Ben for who he is? He already showed me that he can be callous. If someone shows you who they are, believe them.

And I don't know if I'm truly attracted to him. I've been so emotionally fragile that I could just be responding to his overtures without having real feelings for him. He's built like a human man... but with more. I'm not sure I can deal with that. And what is this *mate* situation I keep hearing about? It's unwise to think about commitment and permanence when I probably shouldn't be involved with a guy at all.

And yet, it occurs to me that perhaps I should try. He appeals to me like no man has in a long time. Not since the early days of my relationship with Mark. Still, I don't owe it to Ben, even though he seems to be courting me now. But maybe I owe it to myself to see if this can go anywhere. To see if I can finally move on from the bad experiences of my past and feel a semblance of happiness again. This town is fighting so hard for me; I should do the same for myself.

"That sounds wonderful," I accept, heart full of the possibility of something new.

"I'll pick you up at six," he confirms, with a smile in his voice.

After ending the call with a flurry of sweetly awkward assurances we're both looking forward to it, I immediately remember to text Rose.

"I'm going to the beach with a friend tonight! I'll send some pics!" She's going to be jealous.

I feel as light as a cloud as I head home to freshen up after work. A picnic sounds so special and intimate. He had to have prepared for it before he called. There wasn't enough time otherwise if he was at work. A fluttering affection blooms in my chest, thinking about how he organized it even though he wasn't sure I'd say yes. It makes me even more sure of my decision to go. As I step out of my SUV at the carriage house, the breeze picks up, whistling a discordant tune through the trees. It sounds just like the storm last week, but when I look up, the sky is clear. Are these woods making the sound? It's unsettling, so I hurry inside and slam the door as quickly as possible.

Never having gone on a picnic date to the beach, I'm unsure what to wear. Fashion is probably the last thing on Ben's mind. Thinking about what is both cute and comfortable, I choose a stretchy cotton short-sleeved dress that brings out the green in my hazel eyes and dig out a pair of flip-flops from a box of shoes I haven't unpacked yet. I consider grabbing a light sweater in case it gets cool, but then my memory shifts back to last night and the feel of his wings around me. I forgo the sweater.

Like clockwork, a vehicle turns into the driveway at six. I run down the stairs and open the door to Ben stepping out of his old truck. He's wearing a short-sleeved shirt and jeans. I marvel at the custom tailoring on his clothing to accommodate his wings and tail. They fit him like a glove, hugging his musculature. A wave of insecurity hits me, making me second guess my own rather plain outfit, wondering whether it's flattering enough. But his eyes drink me in with blatant appreciation, making me wonder why I doubted myself.

"You look stunning," he says while his eyes roam over me.

"Thanks, so do you," I return the compliment with a demure smile, a blush rising in my cheeks.

A sharp-toothed wolfish grin splits his face. With his hand at the small of my back, he walks with me to the passenger side and holds open the door, shutting it gently once I've settled inside. A wicker picnic basket sits on a folded dark blanket in the center of the bench seat. It couldn't be more perfect for the occasion.

He drives a short distance to the ocean. We park in a worn area of grass, and he leads me along a path through the dunes. I kick my flip-flops off the moment we step onto the sand. I grab them in one hand and then reach for him with the other. Lacing my fingers through his, I find a comfortable grip for both of us. It feels right, despite the differences in our hands, how his engulfs mine so completely. Desire thrums through me even with this innocent physical connection. Our breakthrough last night opened a floodgate between us, his mere presence stirring a need within me. We stroll near the water so I can dip my toes in. The temperature is colder than I expected, but it helps cool my over-heated body. Taking my phone out of my purse, I snap a couple photos of the water and quickly send one to Rose.

We reach a curve on the beach where the mouth of an inlet river meets the ocean. We follow the bend and the river snakes around a bit, providing a perfectly carved view through the trees to where the sun will set in the west, opposite the Atlantic Ocean behind us. It's already golden hour, and the sun shines a cozy orange-yellow glow over every-thing. Ben finds us a level spot and spreads the large blanket down, setting the basket on one end. I carefully sit down, trying not to get my sand-covered feet on the blanket before brushing them off. He does the same, reaching into the basket and pulling out a rolled-up Turkish towel. "For your feet," he mentions as he hands it to me. It works like a charm, brushing the sand off my feet without sticking to the towel. I hand it back to him and he does the same before setting it aside.

As he takes everything out of the basket, he tells me his family visited the beach all the time growing up. "My brother and I even learned to fly here as young boys. My father decided this was the best spot since crashing into the water or sand would provide a little more cushion. I remember my mother cheering me on from the beach while my father flew by my side for the first time, teaching me how to lift myself higher and soar through the air. Landing was the trickier part, and I ended up wiping out more than a few times. I have even clearer memories of watching my brother since he's so much younger than me. I was a teenager at that point. My mother and I watched together as my father taught him like he did for me a decade earlier," he remembers. The sternness seems to melt away from his face as he talks about it, like the memories thaw him from the inside out.

"Do you think you'll teach your own kids here someday?" I wonder aloud before realizing what I've said. My cheeks heat in embarrassment. I have no filter around him.

"I wasn't certain that was in the cards for me, but I won't lie and say it hasn't crossed my mind lately. Especially thinking about who I would be having them with," he answers suggestively.

My face is fully flushed now, but I can't help the smile tugging at my lips. He takes my hand nearest him and brings it to his mouth, brushing the lightest kiss to it. I want so much for him to lean in and take me in his arms and kiss me for real, but it seems he's going to make me wait.

"Right now, though, I'm thinking mostly about what I'm going to be feeding my beautiful date. I've brought spicy chicken hand pies, fruit, cheese, and some white wine," he explains, as he turns his attention to the food containers he'd been setting out for us, "I hope this sounds good to you?"

"Ben, that sounds like the perfect dinner. Thank you for bringing all of this," I coo, truly excited to try everything. He opens the bottle of wine and pours each of us a glass. "Should we make a toast?" I suggest.

"May I teach you one that Whispered Folk often say?" he muses.

"I would love that," I agree enthusiastically as we clink our glasses together.

He recites, "May the moon and stars above bless us in hearth, home, and love."

I'm not sure if eye contact is important when Whispered Folk toast like it is to a lot of humans, but I figure I should do it nonetheless.

I repeat his words as our eyes lock, "May the moon and stars above bless us in hearth, home, and love." We both take a sip, and our gazes find each other again.

"We have many toasts and sayings, but I've always liked this one the best," he admits. "And I hope that Mother Earth in all her glory also finds it in her heart to grant it to us."

I've looked at Ben with new eyes since last night, but I can tell this is a side to him he usually keeps to himself. He seems sentimental and romantic. I hope I helped to bring it out. And I hope it never goes away.

We take our plates and dig into the food. Everything tastes delicious. The hand pies are flakey, the chicken inside flavorful with a little heat. The fruit is a mix of apple slices and berries. He brought two types of cheese, a sharp cheddar and a rich and creamy triple creme. All of it pairs perfectly with the wine. Well done, Ben. I feel spoiled by this and the macarons from earlier.

Mercifully, we talk about light topics as we eat, namely food and the best meals we've ever had.

"On special occasions, my grandmother on my father's side would make boeuf bourguignon. I always asked her to make it for my birthday. No one's was as good as hers," Ben remembers fondly. "I have the recipe, but I can't recreate it quite the same."

"I know what you mean. My grandma made the best Thanksgiving dinner. It's always been the best food I've ever tasted in my life. I remember all the dishes, but she must have had her own special flourishes she added to the recipes because I haven't had a Thanksgiving meal like it since she passed," I recall, those holiday feasts still vivid in my mind.

"What is your favorite food?" he asks around a large bite of a hand pie.

"Probably authentic tacos. I miss my favorite cheap taco place in Chicago, but there were so many great spots for them across the city," I reminisce. "What about yours?"

"I prefer simple French fare, maybe not one dish in particular, but that style of cuisine in general. I think it's hereditary because my father and grandfather would say the same. Luckily, I can find that here in Monstera Bluff most of the time. Good food is plentiful here. Mayhap you'll be able to find a close approximation to your tacos one day," he reflects thoughtfully.

As we finish eating, the sun sits low and large on the horizon. Golden hour turns into a vivid pink and orange sunset. He moves the plates and containers back into the basket and we adjust so that I'm leaning against his shoulder, his arm around me, with my legs tucked to the side. We sit in companionable silence and admire the sunset with its vibrant colors streaking across the sky. But I'm distracted by his hand gently gripping my hip, his fingers digging in ever so slightly.

Ben has taken a lot of initiative, and so I'm emboldened to do the same. I move my arm beside him, which had been supporting my weight, and put my hand on his thigh, well above his knee. It forces me to lean on him even more, so I'm gingerly draped over him.

In response, his hand on my hip squeezes, and he draws me flush against his side. I intended to initiate a kiss, but now I'm feeling inexplicably bashful. From the corner of my eye, I see Ben looking down at me. He draws his hand up to my chin and gently angles my face toward his. Those midnight blue eyes burn into mine, within them a lingering echo of uncertainty, pleading for permission to kiss me.

I close the gap between us and press my lips to his. They're smooth and strong, powerful like the rest of him. His fingers frame my face, holding me to him as he deepens the kiss. His tongue sweeps along my bottom lip, and I open my mouth to let him in. Our tongues meet and dance back and forth between our mouths. We taste like the wine we drank, adding to the intoxicating thrill of this intimate act. He pulls away for an instant only to nip at my lips, seductively scraping a fang along my bottom lip as he sucks on it.

My arms move around his neck, resting on his broad shoulders. He returns to kissing me deeply, our tongues caressing, angling our mouths in a way that melds us together. I rub my hands along the back of his neck and head, and that light texture on his skin is addictive to touch. It's probably a remnant of the stone his ancestors came from. Regardless, I can't stop caressing him. He feels that good under my hands. He groans hungrily into my mouth, letting me know how much he enjoys my touch, and the vibration of it sends tingles into my body. His hands begin to move as well, skimming along my waist and hips, along my outer thigh, but it's not enough. I want his hands all over my aching body. It's driving me wild.

I'm so turned on that I squeeze my thighs together for any pressure it'll provide. My core is on fire, arousal coursing through my veins. He must feel me squirm in need because he scoops me up by the ass cheeks and hauls me astride his lap, molding me to him. Straddling his big body forces me wide open. My thick thighs bracket his hips, and my legs wrap around him. My breasts crush against his chest, providing some pressured relief. I feel the outline of his arousal below my core, and the fly of his jeans nestles along my seam, covered only by my panties. I can easily rub my clit against him. His hands finally venture higher, sliding along the edges of my breasts. I whimper into his mouth, the combined effect of the friction against my pussy and his hands on my breasts winding me higher. He rolls and pinches my nipples over my dress and I mewl against him.

"That feels so good!" I cry out as he releases my lips to kiss and lick down my neck.

He tweaks my nipples more forcefully, and I begin to rock myself against his hard bulge, warm and swollen in his pants.

"Cara, take your pleasure on me," Ben shudders as he scrapes his teeth along my neck.

Grinding myself on his dick, I settle into a rhythm that has me arching into him again and again. I can't help but whine and keen as I get closer to orgasm. He moves his mouth to my breast and sucks hard on one of my nipples over my dress, still tugging at the other one with his fingers. His other hand takes a firm grip on my hip to guide my core harder and faster against him as he cants underneath me. Focusing on the delicious increase in friction against my clit, I dig my nails into his skin as the burst of heat explodes low in my belly, making me cry out in pleasure. My body feels blissfully languid as I sprawl against him, panting hard as I come down from my high.

Reality hits, and I can't believe I was so wanton and sexual on a public beach. Anyone could have seen us!

I hide my face in Ben's neck in embarrassment and whisper, "I hope I didn't put on a show."

He bursts into laughter and moves his hands to cup my jaw, making me look at him again. His eyes are ablaze, full of both lust and affection. "Don't worry, it was a private performance," he reassures me. His lips crush mine in a scorching kiss, and his harsh moan sounds almost like a growl. His naked desire for me reignites my fervor, so I greedily press my body into his again. He strokes his hands from my face down my sides and reaches under my dress to take hold of my thighs. He pushes himself up to kneeling, holding me up and against him. I squeal in surprise and tighten my arms and legs around him as he gently lowers me backward until I softly land on the blanket.

Still kneeling, he hovers over me, looking enormous, his broad shoulders and chest and outstretched wings blotting out the darkening sky above me. His size is intimidating but also unbelievably erotic. While his eyes drink me in splayed out below him, we're no longer connected and I can't stand it.

I reach for him, whining, "Ben, I need more of you."

He chuckles darkly, and lowers himself over me, resting his arms on either side of my head, completely consuming my view.

"You're the sexiest sight I've ever seen. Your pleasure is so beautiful to watch," he rumbles from above me.

I moan, getting even more turned on by his words, and hug my thighs around his waist, pulling him down onto me. His kiss-swollen lips are too enticing, so I nip and tease at them.

"Hmm, I think it's time for dessert. Can I taste you, Cara?" he purrs.

"Please, Ben. Anything!" I beg.

Ben's grin is feral. He pushes himself down my body, kissing and kneading all the way. His hands dip under my dress and brush along my inner thighs. After pushing my dress up, he hooks his thumbs around the waistband of my panties and tugs them down my legs and over my ankles. Once they're off, his shoulders press my thighs apart and hold them in place. He's at eye-level with my fully open pussy, nothing hidden from view. His hot breath skates across my core as he stares at it up close.

"Such a pretty pink, delicious-looking color. And already glistening for me. I'm going to devour every drop of you," he groans.

He parts my labia with the pads of his fingers, careful to keep his claws away from my delicate skin. He darts his tongue out to lap at my clit. "Oh Ben, oh my god, that feels incredible," I cry out. This spurs him on, and his tongue delves between my pussy lips, licking and slurping up and down my slit, then zeroing in on my overstimulated clit, making me squirm and thrust beneath him.

His tongue pushes into my opening, feeling so hot and firm inside me. I feel myself clench and pulse around him as another orgasm builds. He rubs my clit with the pad of his finger and I whimper at the sensations. "You make such pretty little sounds. Play with yourself while I eat you up," he growls, and then immediately thrusts into me again.

I pinch my nipples while he continues working his tongue inside me and drawing circles around my clit with his finger.

"I'm so close! Keep going!" I wail in ecstasy.

I feel something snake between my thighs, and soon, there's a new sensation inside me. It's firm and fleshy, but in a different way. I raise my head in alarm.

He kisses along my inner thighs and rasps, "I'm dipping my tail into your pussy, testing how soft and open I've made you." I moan and drop my head back onto the blanket.

He slowly pumps the spade of his tail further into my channel, and I cry out when he hits a sensitive spot deep inside. Then, he keeps rubbing against it. His hands move to grip my thighs, while his skilled tongue zeroes in on my clit again, laving and sucking on it. I thrust my hips to increase friction and grab hold of his horns to press his face harder against me. I scream out my pleasure as my pussy contracts and squeezes his tail inside me, releasing a flood of liquid. Using his horns, I weakly shove his face away from my overly sensitive clit, and he greedily laps up the wetness I've leaked out of my opening.

"You taste as good as I imagined." He grunts as he sucks my juices from his tail.

He pushes himself up and lays beside me. I rest my head on his shoulder, still boneless and euphoric.

I smile sleepily as I stare deeply into his eyes and tell him, "We have to come back here more often." He barks out laughter and kisses the top of my head affectionately.

We lay wrapped in each other's arms until the last of the light fades. I offer to take him into my mouth, make him feel as good as he made me, especially since he brought me to orgasm twice. He gently turns me down, saying that this was very pleasurable for him as well. It makes me melt even more for him.

After it's fully dark for a while, we decide it's time to leave. Our picnic supplies take only a few minutes to pack away. We walk back to Ben's truck using the flashlights on our phones to light the path. He drops me off at home. As we say goodnight, he pulls me into a deep, tongue-tangling kiss, threading his fingers through my hair, leaving me breathless. He waits until I've gone inside and locked the door before driving away.

When I'm inside, I head straight to the bathroom and study myself in the mirror. My reflection looks rumpled and well-used. My hair is wild, and most of my makeup has been wiped away. I'm glad it was dark by the end of our date, so he didn't see me so bedraggled. Even though I'm exhausted, I take a quick shower to wash the sand and stickiness from me. I can't believe that so quickly I went from kissing to dry humping to being eaten out by a guy I thought hated me just a couple of days ago. Time stopped during the date. Everything could have taken place within a matter of a few minutes or hours. The reality is somewhere in between. But the most striking memory about the date is how insatiable we are for each other. We could have kept going all night long.

I'm in bed and nearly asleep when my phone buzzes with a text message. I check it, thinking it could be Ben. It's an unknown number, never a good sign.

"I was so worried when you disappeared, but I wanted you to know I've found you again. Seems life hasn't worked out for you since you've left Chicago. Your job is here waiting for you when you're ready to come back."

What the hell does that mean? Other than my friends, there's nothing for me there. This couldn't possibly be Mark, could it? No way, he's probably already married to his model-gorgeous fiancée, living his high society life, doing what his mommy and daddy tell him. I'm sure he hasn't thought about me since I last talked to him over eight months ago. Certainly, he wasn't thinking about me when he was stringing me along for so many years, hooking up with her behind my back, and then, after only knowing her a year, handing her everything I ever wanted from him on a silver platter.

He can't be so delusional that he thinks I'd return to that god-awful place after everything that went down, right? And to find me here? Does that mean in Monstera Bluff? I haven't updated anything online about moving. I've only told my closest friends about Monstera Bluff—and even they know the bare minimum. The town is supposed to be a secret, hidden in plain sight. This has to be a sick prank, trying to scare me. Plenty of people have my phone number, though most connected to him and his family are blocked and long deleted. Probably why they're hiding their number. My stress level spikes. I couldn't get this at a worse time, right as I'm trying to go to sleep after my first time being intimate with Ben. I don't need Mark hanging over my head any longer.

Fully awake again, I decide to make some herbal tea and grab my laptop to watch a mindless show to wind down. As I step out of bed, I catch a glimpse of the dark woods out the window. Glowing yellow flashes from somewhere behind the trees, unmistakable with no other light sources around. I blink and it's gone. It was too small and still to be a flashlight. It looked like light reflecting off an animal's eyes. Yet, there's nothing it could have reflected. It's pitch black out there. I turn on my bedside lamp and scrub my eyes. Clearly, I'm overtired and not thinking straight. I make my tea, open my laptop, and don't think any more of it.

Eight Months Ago

Feeling raw and rung out, I can't cry anymore. My tears have run dry, so there's nowhere for my misery to go. It'll rot my insides, shrivel me into a husk. My heart feels like it died after learning about Mark's infidelity this morning, and my body is just now catching up. Somehow, I managed to make it home and call Rose. She promises to come over the instant she can sneak out of work.

"I don't want you to get in trouble." My voice grates.

"Cara, trains won't stop running just because I skip out early!" she soothes.

"There's no guarantee, you know how they are," I answer, trying to get her to see reason.

"Fair enough! And I'm proud of you for making a joke even when you're feeling like this. I'll be over in about an hour. And I'm just so, so sorry he's done this to you. He's such a bastard. You don't deserve any of this," she consoles me.

That's sweet, but I've never felt more pathetic in my life. The pain is even sharper than when my grandparents died. With them, at least I knew they truly loved me and did all they could for me. I'll miss them forever. But this betrayal cuts deeper than I thought possible. It was so cruel and senseless. I have nowhere to go if I quit my job unless I want to start over. Whether in a completely new city or in a completely different profession, it's the biggest reason I haven't left already. The non-compete I signed kept me trapped, but at least I was trapped with Mark. I will never be able to face him and his horrible parents every day. It's too insulting. My entire adult life has been built on lies and I'm completely fucked.

The phone rings, and I don't even look who it is because I figure it's Rose again or one of our other close friends to whom she's no doubt spread the word. She called this an *all hands on deck* situation. "Hello?" I scratch out, rough and croaky.

"You're not at work today. Are you sick or something? You're supposed to call in. How haven't you figured that out by now," goads the last voice I want to hear.

"How could you, Mark? I did everything you asked for. Changed my lifestyle. Worked my ass off for you and the firm. And then you cheat on me? Get engaged to someone else? Fuck you, I'm done. With all of it," I shout. I'm on the verge of hyperventilating.

"God, you're always so emotional. I was going to talk to you at work today and let you know about her, but you weren't there. I never told you we were going to get married, so I'm not sure why you assumed we would. That's on you, Cara. You've always gotten so intense about everything. Don't blame me for that," he responds defensively.

"'Are you serious?! You were going to talk to me at work? Tell me you're breaking up with me and you're marrying your mistress instead of me while we're at work? Unbelievable. What's wrong with you? Of course I thought we'd get married someday. We've been dating since we were in grad school. You could have just broken up with me if you didn't want to be with me anymore!" I rage at him.

"Listen to yourself, Cara. That's exactly what I'm doing right now. Sorry I didn't break up with you on your preferred timeline, when it's more convenient for you," he scolds, and I can hear his eyes rolling in his voice.

He's psychotic, completely deranged, to think that I'm somehow the unreasonable one in this situation. That my expectations were absurd, thinking we'd eventually get married. I won't even ask why he chose her over me. I already know I can't compete. It's no contest. That captioned photo of them is burned in my brain forever. Deep down, I'm not at all surprised he'd justify it like this. He'd always been self-absorbed, barely considering the feelings of those around him, and I excused it because he had a lot on his shoulders with the firm, managing clients as well as projects. For what he lacks in civil engineering and design skills, he excels in C-suite material. His ego grew in tandem with his job title.

"My timeline? You've been cheating on me for a year with her! What the fuck? You've lied to me this whole time. You could've given me an STD. You are such a piece of shit, Mark. I'm never talking to you again," I scream.

Before I hang up, he interjects, "Stop with the dramatics. It wasn't serious with her until recently. Mom's been pushing for me to propose to her since it'll raise the profile of the firm, so it's not like I knew I was going to marry her this whole time. I thought you understood how this type of relationship works with someone like me. I was never going to marry you. Besides, it's not like we have to stop seeing each other. Clearly you love fucking me. I can barely keep you off my dick. Even she doesn't fuck me as much as you do. We just have to be a little more discreet about it so as to not upset the missus. And if you have an STD, it's not from her, so get over it."

My jaw drops. I can't believe any of this. He just revealed so much to me in his narcissistic little rant and probably doesn't even realize it. Before he can say another word, I hang up and block his number. It's not like I need it for anything. I don't even have a toothbrush at his place since he always made me take everything home. There's nothing shared between us except eight lousy years down the drain and not a single thing to show for it.

CHAPTER 14

BEN

After dropping off Cara, I arrive home feeling a sense of peace and rightness, something I haven't experienced in a long time. Tonight with her was... everything I could have hoped for. She's so responsive to my words and touch. They set her alight. I've never been as affectionate or vocal with females in the past. I like that I can give myself to her in a way I've never given anyone else. This part of me is hers, and hers alone. She inspires it. There's electricity between us like I never thought possible. I won't be able to stay away from her now. She is my mate. I know this with every fiber of my being. I may have known it all along but couldn't stomach the thought of her rejecting me. So I did it first. How unbelievably stupid and shortsighted of me.

I didn't think I'd ever find a female who could be my mate. Certainly never thought she'd be human. I've already reached thirty-eight years, and while not all that old in the span of a life, certainly many have settled down by that age. My parents were so much younger than me when they fell in love. It made me think it wasn't in the cards for me. I've probably encountered every eligible female in this town, and I knew my mate wasn't among them if she even existed at all.

That's not to say I've gone without physical affection. I've had casual partners in the past, though much more discreetly than most, especially Clancy. He probably thinks I've remained celibate my entire life. Well, that's not completely true. He knows of some of my past experiences, but not many. I never felt the need to flaunt it the way he does. He loves the thrill of the chase and when females fawn and fuss over him as well as share his bed. He craves that attention with every new female in his life—and there have been many.

I cared that my past partners had a good time, that we were both satisfied with our experience together. But I've never felt more than a fleeting sexual interest or attraction to any of them. I know it was true for them, too. That's why I felt comfortable engaging in it. Simply an occasional itch to be scratched until I found the female who would be my mate.

With Cara, it's already so much more. We've only begun our exploration of each other, and it's by far the best experience of my life. Everything is heightened because of my deep affection for her. She drives me completely wild. I already know I love her, but I will grow to love her more with each day we are together. She is everything I've ever wanted.

It's not that late. I took Cara home before nine. There's no way I'll be able to sleep anytime soon. I need to proceed wisely with Cara, make her feel safe and loved so she'll accept my offer of matehood. Humans' expectations are different than Whispered Folk's. And I don't want to mess up again. Despite Clancy's extensive history with females, I know he's never been with a human. And it occurs to me that my brother Lucas might have romantic advice for me. He isn't mated, but he's lived among humans for several years. And most importantly, he won't tell our parents about the conversation. I'm not trying to hide her. I just don't want to overwhelm her. Both Maman and Père will be overjoyed, and lovingly... though annoyingly... insert themselves into our relationship immediately. A big reason I have never been open about companionship.

The phone barely rings. "Big brother, what are you doing still awake? Don't you have some dirt to move around early in the morning?" he quips.

Laughter spills out of me. "Always. A big stretch of it this time, and I wouldn't have it any other way. How is life going? Maman thinks you aren't spreading your wings enough. But I reminded her that you fly awfully high to reach the top of those skyscrapers."

He snickers. "Of course it's our dear earthbound Maman who worries about such things. I'll be sure to tell her that I fly nearly every night right over the heads of unsuspecting New Yorkers. My invisibility pendant works just as well as my glamor. The coven here is powerful."

I hum in agreement, knowing how true that is. There's a decent-sized Whispered Folk population there who can integrate themselves into the city because of it. It's how he's able to live and work there without detection.

"So, why are you really calling this late? I know it's not just to catch up and pass along Maman's worries. You sound like you're in a good mood," he notices, sounding amused and curious.

"I didn't realize I was so easy to read," I joke.

"Well, maybe not to most, but I can see right through you," he brags with a smile in his voice.

"You have me there, little brother. I called because I need your advice... about human females," I explain tentatively.

Lucas cackles and crows, and I can hear that he's pulled the phone away from his face while he gets it out of his system. "Ben, this positively made my night. I'm so happy you need my advice about this. Is there a particular human female you have in mind?" he replies, composing himself.

"Yes, and I want her to be my mate. Her name is Cara, and she's only been in town for a week. Clancy hired her as a city planner. We went on a date tonight," I say giddily.

"Home already? Well, I guess taking it slow is one approach. Probably the best way to go with a human anyway," he muses.

"That was my instinct, but what do you think I should do to have the best chance with her?" I question.

"Well, it seems she's already attracted to you if she agreed to go on a date. And she knows what you are, which is essential. I must still be very careful when dating a human female. I keep it very casual because I do not want to maintain such a fundamental lie to a partner I care for greatly. Though there are plenty of young witches in the coven, who seem to like the winged look." He chuckles.

"Cara also seems to like it now. Though she was scared at first. It took several meetings until she came around," I confide.

"That is what we are all afraid of, no? She hadn't seen many Whispered Folk before?" he deduces, hitting the nail on the head.

"Indeed, Clancy brought her here under false pretenses. She didn't know anything about us," I confirm.

There's a brief pause on his end of the line. I'm sure he's in disbelief, much like I was. "That rascal Clancy wouldn't do such a thing, would he? Ah, but if she is a pretty female, all bets are off with him. I can't believe he got away with it. Did he have designs on her?" Lucas ponders.

"No, he is not going to even look at her like that!" I growl.

"What was I to think? You know how Clancy is around females. He's the resident paramour, all good looks and charm. He may have sound advice for you, though. If he knows she's yours, he won't interfere. He'll do all he can to help you," Lucas offers.

"Clancy didn't seem to want to pursue her. And that is wise since she works for him. When we first met, I thought mayhap she had feelings for him, but that wasn't the case. He has pushed me toward her this entire time. But he doesn't know about human relationships, and I don't want to give him too many details about us yet. Our relationship is too new, and I don't want to embarrass her by talking about her private life with him," I clarify.

"Ah, that makes sense. It's good of you to be sensitive to that. Humans like to take their time when deciding on a mate. They take years to do so instead of weeks or even days like we do. Our hearts make our decisions for us. Humans are too stuck in their heads. You may scare her off if she feels smothered by talk of mates, so tread lightly on that topic for now. Focus on romance and courtship. And be sure to spend a lot of quality time with her outside of the bedroom," he counsels.

"Lucas, you're a good brother, thank you. I'm taking your advice to heart. Even Clancy could learn a thing or two from you," I voice my appreciation. "Your future mate will be lucky to have such a thoughtful male."

He laughs self-effacingly. "I don't know about any future mate. But Clancy doesn't want to learn these lessons or else he'd be in danger of actually acquiring one himself. But you're welcome, I'm glad I could help. I won't say anything to Maman and Père, but they'll hear about it soon enough when you're seen together around town. Consider letting them know she is a friend you spend time with. It could keep them off your back if any gossip reaches them."

We hang up not too long after. He's given me much to think on. Convincing her to choose me as her mate will not be an easy task.

The next morning, I awaken early, just like my brother joked. Late mornings aren't a luxury I can afford in the construction industry except on occasional weekends. I hope Cara is the same. I can imagine us on Saturday morning strolls around town, having coffee and pastries, or going to the beach to watch the sunrise over the ocean. I should find out what she likes to do in her spare time. I will make sure she can do that here. Now is the time to put my brother's guidance into action. I send her a text message asking her to lunch at Midnight Mystic. She replies immediately saying that she'd love to.

Biding my time until I see her, the next few hours are spent in my office talking to clients and reassigning a team to break ground on Howling Road. The office remains mostly unchanged from the days my father ran it, right down to its open-door policy with my crew.

"Hey boss, happy to get back to the site tomorrow. We're thinking about one of those new houses. It's a good incentive to keep the job moving along," jokes Orson, a long-time crew member I used to work alongside every day as a younger male. The bear shifter is one of my best employees and a team lead.

"Oh? Are you and Halia looking for a little more space now that you have a little one on the way?" I ask, knowing they've been talking about it since they mated.

Tove, another member of the crew and a good friend of Orson, must hear us talking. They pop their head in, chortling, "Yep! Halia's convinced they'll be a family of bears, and she'll be the odd one out! They'll need a lot of space to run around."

"She doesn't know that. It's too soon to tell. Besides, I wouldn't mind at all if we had a house full of little sylvans, antlers sprouting from their cute baby foreheads. Either way, we'll be closer to the woods, and she'll be happier for it." He grins in that goofy way he always does when he talks about his mate.

"Well, it's a good thing we didn't get held up too long! We've got a lot of road to build before Halia's due date. No pressure or anything!" Tove claps their large green hand on Orson's shoulder as they walk out. "See ya tomorrow, Ben!"

I have a good group working for me, and I'm putting my best team together for this project. It'll be satisfying to see the progress. I hope Cara will be as impressed as Halia undoubtedly will be.

I wish I could speed up time to see Cara sooner. Alas, not even our coven could achieve that kind of magick. Unexpectedly, I receive a message from Clancy and the owner of the residential construction company overseeing the housing development that two of the structures were damaged overnight in a fire. It had to be arson, but what was the point? And why now? Clancy said the constabulary is considering increasing surveillance of the area off-hours, and I let them know we'll also keep an eye out for anything unusual. It concerns me that someone could sabotage our project as well.

Arriving at Midnight Mystic before Cara, I sit at a table in the corner where we can talk without interruption. The door chimes, and Cara sweeps inside, her curved figure accentuated by a flattering fitted sweater and knee-length skirt. She always looks elegant, and it makes me want to take her to a secluded spot to dishevel her in the most gratifying way. But I remember my brother's words, and I will abide by them. Her shy, radiant smile when she sees me floods the room with even more light. I join her at the counter to buy her lunch. Unsure of how much public affection she would like, I take her hand, kiss it, and hold it in mine until we sit at our table. This contact may provide fodder for gossip, but it is innocent enough, and I don't want her to question my feelings for her.

She turns to me, looking achingly beautiful, her eyes sparkling as she speaks. "You didn't have to buy my lunch, Ben, but thank you. I've been looking forward to this since you reached out this morning."

"The pleasure was all mine. You were all I could think about. I would do this every day if you let me," I profess.

Her lips curve into a smile as she leans in tantalizingly close. Her delicate jasmine scent imbues the air, mesmerizing me. "And it would be my pleasure to return the favor just as often," she purrs impishly. Suddenly, I'm very aware we aren't just talking about lunch, and nothing could make me happier.

I draw her in for a kiss and growl, "I'll keep that in mind for our next date."

"At first, I thought you were the most mystifying man, keeping your distance from me. But I understand you better, Ben. You were trying to take care of me then, too, in your own way. But I'm so glad we realized it wasn't what either of us wanted. It's been such a long time since anyone has taken care of me that I forgot how nice it is. Anyway, this is my long-winded way of saying thank you for everything. It makes me feel special," she divulges, sounding so sweet and earnest.

"This is the least you deserve. I should be doing more. So much more that you forget that horrible male who made you feel unworthy," I insist fervently.

A laugh bubbles up from somewhere deep inside her. "Guys like you give fairy tales a good name. I'm not sure what else you think you can be doing, but this is just right..."

A server delivers our sandwiches to the table, disrupting Cara's thoughts. We begin eating, but I try not to let it keep us from our conversation. It's imperative that I learn more so that I can keep being a good mate to her, even if she doesn't recognize me as such yet. "Do you miss anything from your life before you moved here?" I inquire.

"Well, my friends, of course. I'm not sure when I'll be able to see them again. It'll be impossible to bring them here." She sighs, looking pensive. "My life turned out to be so boring, so sad. For the last few years, I worked endlessly. I didn't have a life beyond sixty or more hours of work a week, going to the gym sometimes, occasional dates with Mark, and squeezing in quality time with my friends as much as possible. Before life became so hectic, I loved my yoga classes and walking through Chicago's incredible museums. I do miss those a lot. Even when I barely had enough money for groceries, I had a membership to the Art Institute. I would go there every week, finding something new and unexpected each time."

Her expression turns wistful. I want to hear more, so I prompt, "What about when you were young?"

"I used to love art classes as a kid, especially painting. But there wasn't much money for extras like that when I was growing up, so I didn't continue with it when I got older. Spending so much time at the Art Institute made up for that in a way. I've always wanted to garden, too. My grandma had one in the backyard of this old three-flat she and my grandpa lived in when I was young. She let me help her plant seeds in the spring, and I'd water them all summer. It felt so special to eat a tomato or pepper straight from the garden. She was so generous, letting me eat all her hard work! It was my dream to live somewhere with enough green space for one. That never happened, either. I guess you can't miss something you never really started."

Cara's sweet, floral scent already inspired me to plant jasmine around my own house, reminding me of the carefree springtime of my childhood. My mouth twitches slowly into an affectionate smile, having just figured out our next date. She will love it.

"Saturday morning, you should come over to my house and help me with a project," I suggest, purposely evasive. "Wear something comfortable that can be easily washed."

I'll be sure to have the supplies needed for her, like gloves and tools. Mayhap she'll remember some of the skills she learned from her grandmother.

Clasping her hands to her chest, she gushes, "Are you keeping it a secret? I can't wait to find out what we're doing." She inclines her head toward me and worries her lip. "What about you? What do you like to do?"

I ponder her question. We're a lot alike in that our work has taken over too much of our lives. "I had more free time before I took over the company from my father. When I was a younger male, I worked on the crews to gain experience as a builder. Gradually, I started helping my father, learning how to manage the business. It took up a lot of my time to do both. I still work with my crews when we're stretched with projects or short-handed, but I spend far too much time in the office doing operational work I don't care for as much. As a gargoyle, I fly every day, usually along the shore and over the ocean. The sunrises and sunsets are especially beautiful from that view. That's when I usually go. Clancy and I spend a couple nights a week together, even now when we are both much busier. I used to spend time with my younger brother before he left for New York, inventing silly competitive games, wreaking havoc around the house, according to our mother. I also like art, mostly drawing. It helped me when I learned architectural drafting. My brother is also very skilled at it, much better than me now that he works as an architect in New York City. I listen to a lot of human-made music and watch their movies. I probably sound very boring to you," I confess, sheepish that my life lacks excitement.

"No, you sound perfect," she swoons. "How did your family get into the construction business?"

"Well, it is a common vocation for gargoyles. We are often builders and architects, as well as security and law enforcement. It seems very cliche, but it is what we drift toward. Since our ancestors were first made of stone, we seem to have an affinity for it. It doesn't speak to us in a literal sense, but we have a knack for knowing just how to use each slab, like a gut feeling. It's why many structures here are made of stone. My great-grandfather and grandfather built much of the downtown. We've taught ourselves how to use wood and brick and concrete, but stone is still our preferred construction material," I relate.

"You are a wonder! You can do so much!" she raves, her eyes lighting up in surprise.

"I am a very typical gargoyle. But I'm glad you think I'm more," I say lightheartedly.

"Have you had many girlfriends? Were you ever married... um, mated?" Cara questions hesitantly. "You seemed to know that waitress at the pub last week. Is she a friend?" She glances at me curiously through lowered lashes.

I chuckle low and husky—I believe my sweet mate is jealous. "I do know that waitress... She's a cousin on my mother's side," I tease, drawing out my response, gratified to see the relief in her expression afterward. "She's part of the wolf pack here. You'll be able to tell who they are from the light of the moon in their eyes, a silver cast that is unique to them."

"Oh, she seemed to know you well by the way she interacted with you. And you're very skilled at certain... activities. So I thought maybe... Well, I'm being silly," she stammers, barking out a contagious laugh that I can't help but echo.

"You have no reason to be unsure about other females in my life. There have not been many, and they are long in my past. There is no one I want but you," I reassure her wounded heart, hoping to spare her any unnecessary insecurity.

She gives me a goofy grin, biting her plump lower lip. I'm about to lean in to kiss her again when I'm interrupted by the trilling of Ada's voice. "Cara and Ben! So good to see you two together having lunch. I was just stopping in for some coffee on my way to the shop."

Cara blushes prettily under Ada's knowing gaze. "We were just finishing up. Why don't we walk out together?" Cara offers.

We get up from the table, following Ada outside. Ada tells us about some of her preparations for Samhain. Local restaurants and even some amateur cooks will have booths with food and beverages. Taurus Farm grew a crop of large turnips to be carved into lanterns. The wolf pack is providing wood for the giant bonfire. Members of the coven will have a station to help community members create altars and memorials for their deceased loved ones and provide enchantments on them. There are even some limited opportunities to commune with the dead, though, Ada assures Cara, whose eyes grow impossibly wide at that revelation, that it is not scary at all.

As we stand on the sidewalk talking, a brownie jogs by, shoving flyers into the hands of everyone on the street. Brownies are an annoying bunch full of mischief, so I crumple the piece of garbage in my fist.

Cara reads hers with a panicked look in her eyes. "Oh my god, what is this? Is it about me?" she frets, face turning ashen.

She hands me the flyer that reads, *Close our wards and keep humans out! They are a danger to our community! Your family's lives are at stake! The mayor's new human whore is a spy sent here to end our way of life. It's no coincidence crime and vandalism have increased since her arrival. Don't trust her or any human apologists!* I feel my own rage pooling as I smooth out the flyer forced on me. It's full of the same vicious lies and insinuations meant to fan the flames of hate.

Ada looks at the paper and swears. "Fire burn it to ashes! How dare that spineless bastard pass out hateful material like this. Samuels is mistaken if he thinks we'll turn a blind eye to it. We need to meet with Clancy and the constabulary right away."

I will end Ralston Samuels for this. No one threatens my mate. I must be snarling because both Ada and Cara reflexively tense.

"He's going to answer to *me*," I vow, my gaze meeting Cara's.

"He's going to answer to *all* of us," Ada clarifies, trying to mollify me. Ada pulls out her phone and calls Clancy, filling him in on the situation.

Clancy's angry voice booms through her phone, "Meet me at my office in an hour. I'm setting up an emergency meeting."

Stony silence descends on our group as we hurry to town hall. A few other council members, constabulary, and town hall officials are already in Clancy's office. Most everyone has gathered when Ralston Samuels himself shows up.

"What's the meaning of interrupting everyone's day? We have better things to do than be at your beck and call," Samuels complains boorishly.

Clancy seethes, barely containing his fury. It nearly matches mine. "How dare you make direct threats against members of the community. We know these flyers are yours. And this is your one and only warning before you are expelled from the community. I don't care who you are or what position you hold. You are a paranoid bigot who is resorting to blatant lies to push your agenda," Clancy denounces him. "You are not above the law. This will not go unpunished."

Samuels points a skeletal finger at Clancy. "Don't kid yourself that you have a shred of evidence tying this back to me. Plenty of good citizens are rightfully upset that a human showed up here unannounced. It's not my fault if they choose to warn their neighbors about her," Samuels rakes his eyes up and down Cara's form with malice. "If she smells like a whore, looks like a whore, then she's probably a lying human whore."

I bellow my wrath. Clancy and a wolven constable near me hold me back from attacking him.

"She is no such thing, you misogynistic piece of shit. Get out of my sight before I let Ben tear you limb from limb. And don't worry, we'll have our proof it was you. You'll answer for your crime," Clancy warns in a deceptively calm voice while his eyes glare with feral intensity.

Samuels shrugs carelessly and jeers, "I wouldn't be so sure. Call off your pathetic guard dog. What will people think when they learn their human-loving mayor threatened his biggest political rival with violence and criminal prosecution? This is just getting started."

CHAPTER 15
CARA

I'm in a state of shock as Ralston Samuels cruelly dresses me down in Clancy's office. I freeze, with no voice to defend myself, no reaction whatsoever. But it turns out I don't need it. Clancy and Ben do it for me. Ben transforms into a savage predator, ready to strike down his opponent. I can see why his kind was so coveted and feared. Samuels wouldn't have stood a chance against him. Clancy slings his words and authority like well-honed weapons. Samuels finally leaves, parading out of the room like a haughty prince sniveling at his subjects.

Ben rushes to my side, wrapping a steadying arm around my waist and gently patting my cheek. "Moon and stars, Cara, are you alright? Say something," he worries.

Dizzy and frantic, I fall into his chest and cry, fat tears falling down my cheeks. "It's hard to breathe," I finally mumble into his shirt, my short breaths coming fast.

Ben whispers sweet and soothing words as he rubs my back, trying to reassure me I'm safe.

"I'm taking her to the clinic," he growls to the room and sweeps me up into his arms. I press myself close, not wanting to face the world. When we're outside, he unfurls his wings. I'm surprised by the force of the wind they create as he flaps them. I feel a swooping sensation, but I hold my eyes closed, not wanting to know if we're flying in the air. I hold tight to him, crushingly so, as a kernel of worry he'll drop me pops into my stuttering brain.

We stop abruptly, the slight impact jostling me in his arms. He angles our bodies through a doorway, where a female voice greets us. I don't want to look at whoever it is, just curl further into Ben. He explains I was in a state of shock and wants a healer to look me over. Doesn't he mean a doctor?

Ben carries me into another room and lays me down on a table, staying by my side and holding one of my hands. Without the comfort of being in his arms, I force myself to awareness, looking around the room. Standard medical equipment I'd expect to see in a doctor's office, like gloves, bandages, cotton swabs, thermometers, stethoscopes, microscopes, among other things, sit on a desk. Yet the presence of other, stranger items makes me apprehensive, like a mortar and pestle, some kind of diffuser, a basket of stones, and a fancy chemistry set like the one in Ada's shop sitting amongst the medical supplies. A golden liquid is boiling, being distilled from one glass to another in the chemistry set like my arrival interrupted someone's work. Shelves of beakers and bottles full of colorful liquid, some of which look alive and swirling and others viscous and disgusting, line one of the walls.

"Where are we, Ben? Is this a hospital?" I croak. My throat feels thick and parched.

He looks down at me, and with his free hand, he gently brushes aside some hair stuck to my tear-stained face. "Of sorts," he replies. "It's our healers' clinic. I want to make sure you're okay."

Before I can ask more questions, a human-looking woman with spiky black hair knocks on the doorframe and enters the room, a gentle smile on her face. "Good afternoon. I'm Thea, and I'll be treating you today, Cara. Thank you, Ben, for bringing her in," she remarks warmly as her dark brown eyes swiftly survey me. "May I touch you while I examine you?"

My gaze skitters to Ben, who squeezes my hand affectionately and gives me a slight nod. "Um, sure, go ahead," I answer with a nervous breath.

Concentration is written on her face as she slowly moves her hands along my entire body, hovering over most of it but touching me on my abdomen, upper chest, neck, and head. Her hands seem unusually warm as they pass over my skin. She grabs the stethoscope from her desk and listens to my heart. Even now, it's beating so fast I can feel it pound in my chest as I lay here.

Finishing her exam, she takes a step back and her tranquil expression returns. "You've had a panic attack. Nothing to worry about. But I want you to drink a calming tonic to still your mind and lower your heart rate. You will feel better very quickly but be quite lethargic since you're not used to this dose, so take it easy for the rest of the day," Thea declares, then swivels toward the shelves of liquids. She selects a large jar of light blue liquid, opens it at her desk, then pours a few ounces into an empty vial and hands it to me. "You're free to go after you drink this," she instructs.

Looking at it makes me want to gag. It seems unnatural. My throat closes at the mere thought of drinking it. Seeming to understand my dilemma, Ben rubs my arm as he leans in and whispers, "It doesn't taste bad. It's a very common remedy here. I'm going to get my truck. I'll be right back in a couple minutes. Try to finish it by the time I return."

I nod, trying to be cooperative but still feeling uneasy. The healer walks out of the room after Ben, leaving me on my own. I sniff the vial, but the liquid doesn't have a scent. I slowly tip it to my lips, taking the tiniest sip possible. It lands fruity and slightly fizzy on my tongue. It's not horrible, but it's certainly not tasty. Like a medicine flavored for children, it doesn't fully mask whatever is in this concoction. I'm still sipping on it when Ben comes back. It's already taking effect, my limbs feel languid and my head is heavy. He tips the last of the drink into my mouth, making sure I swallow all of it, then picks me up and carries me to his truck.

I barely realize we've made it to the carriage house when he asks me for my keys. I blink a few times, and I'm sitting on the bed, Ben removing my shoes. He picks up some pajamas from the end of my bed and helps me change into them. It distantly occurs to me that he's seeing most of my body while I change, but I can't find it in me to care. He tucks me under the covers, promising me he'll be down the hall until I wake up.

Tugging at his sleeve before he goes, I muster up my remaining awareness. It seems important that he should know. "Mark may have reached out to me last night. I'm not sure because it was a blocked number," I quaver, quickly depleting my energy. He hands me my phone to unlock, and I show him the text message.

He rumbles in alarm, "This can't be a coincidence."

I'd ask him what he means, but my eyelids are far too heavy, and I feel myself drifting off.

It's dark outside my window when I wake up from a deep, dreamless sleep. Still groggy, I walk to the bathroom and clean up a bit, washing off my makeup, fixing my hair. Down the hall, Ben is fast asleep on the couch as promised.

I approach him quietly, laying a soft hand on his shoulder, whispering, "Ben?"

His eyes open, instantly alert. "Cara, you're awake. How are you feeling?" he asks, sitting up while looking me over.

"I'm better, feeling more like myself. Thank you for taking me to the doctor. I'm sorry I reacted so badly," I apologize, self-conscious about taking up Ben's time.

"No, Cara. Don't even think such a thing. Of course you were upset. I'm so sorry he's finding new ways to attack you. You don't deserve to be insulted and slandered," he assures, sounding regretful.

"Would you sleep next to me? I don't want to be alone right now." I sigh, hoping I don't sound needy.

"Of course, I would do anything for you," he promises.

He follows me into my bedroom. I slip under the covers, making sure there's plenty of room for him. Still wearing his outfit from earlier, he climbs in next to me.

"You can get more comfortable if you don't want to sleep in those clothes," I offer.

He pauses, seeming to make up his mind, and stands up to get undressed. It's fascinating how he removes his shirt around his wings. Two seams I hadn't noticed run down the back from each wing slit to the bottom of the shirt. He pulls them apart so the back panel of his shirt that rests between his wings is freed. Then, he simply pulls it over his head by the back of the collar. He also takes off his jeans, so he's standing in just a pair of black boxer briefs.

I can't help but ogle him, so broad and muscular. I saw him shirtless the first day we met, but I'd been too nervous to admire him. He catches me looking and gives me a sinful smirk as he joins me in the bed.

"You need rest, Cara. Close your eyes, and I'll be here when you wake," he purrs in my ear as he wraps an arm around me and pulls my back against his chest. The warmth of his body instantly comforts me, and in no time, I'm falling back asleep.

My cell phone rings, startling me out of a dream. I must have moved around in my sleep because when I open my eyes, I'm facing Ben, one of my legs shoved between his. It's light out already. We must have slept through the night. He reaches over me to grab my phone from the nightstand. Clancy's name lights up the phone.

"Would you answer?" I ask, wishing I could put off real life for just a little longer.

He nods. "I'll talk to him, but I'm going to put him on speaker so you can hear."

"Clancy, it's Ben. I'm with Cara at her place," he states simply.

"Ah, good. I need to speak with you both. Cara, stay with Ada today. She said you can help her with tasks for the Samhain festival. She'll call you in a little bit. Ben, there were some shop break-ins downtown last night. Nothing that can't be cleaned up, but I thought you should be aware. Let your crews know to be careful and to keep an eye out for any signs of sabotage," Clancy cautions.

"Thanks, Clancy. I'll call you after I talk to them," Ben replies.

Once the call ends, Ben's body language softens, and he lies next to me again, gazing at me with a concerned expression. He wraps his arms around me, rubbing circles on my back.

"Do you want me to stay with you today?" he whispers, restoring the intimacy interrupted by Clancy's call.

I move my hands to cup his face and pepper soft kisses to his lips and cheeks. He continues to hold me, affectionately but chastely, accepting my affection without asking for more. His tenderness cascades over me, bringing me peace.

I lay my head on his shoulder as I respond softly, "You should make sure everything is alright at work. I'll be fine with Ada. I don't want to be scared and hide."

He hugs me tighter, kissing my forehead. "You'll be safe with her today, but I suspect Samuels will keep trying to intimidate you into leaving. We won't let him pull a stunt like that again. Clancy is working on censuring him, mayhap even getting him kicked off the town council. The constabulary is keeping an eye out so his unhinged behavior doesn't escalate or spread. But stick by Ada today to be extra cautious," he murmurs comfortingly.

I nod, soaking in the warmth of his body, tempted to declare I change my mind and want him to stay in bed with me all day. But I shouldn't keep him. He has responsibilities, a business to run. I have a date with him tomorrow morning, assuming nothing terrible happens today. I'll see him again then. Marshaling all my willpower, I propose he checks on everything at work. I'll be fine with waiting here for Ada's call. Ben grumbles affectionately and reluctantly leaves, but not before kissing me thoroughly, making sure my thoughts won't stray far from him today.

Ada calls, and we plan to drive together to open her shop. I'm upset that I can't go about my day like normal, but I understand why they want to keep me close. The prospect of encountering Ralston Samuels or anyone connected to him really worries me. Mob mentality is dangerous, and he's trying to stir it up.

Ada waves me over when I step outside. "Good morning! I hope Ben took good care of you last night," she coos, laughing at the shocked look on my face. "I don't mean like *that*. He was just so worried. His protective gargoyle instincts kicked in."

"He was really kind to help me so much," I reply truthfully. We get into her Wagoneer, and she studies me, narrowing her eyes.

"You should talk to Walt today. I think you should hear what he has to say about living here and being mated to a Whispered Folk. There's something between you and Ben. Frankly, I'm glad he pulled that stick out of his ass and acted on it. Gargoyles are natural protectors, like I was saying. I'm sure this whole predicament with Samuels sped things along, but he'd have gotten there eventually," Ada speculates.

Considering what's happened, that makes sense. The town council meeting changed everything between us. I'm not glad this harassment is happening, but at least it has a silver lining.

I nod in agreement. "You're probably right. I'll text Walt right now."

By the time we reach Ada's shop, Walt and I have made plans to meet there and talk over lunch. I sit in a plush chair by the window and make calls for Ada, confirming details from the food and merchandise vendors, noting any changes to her list. Her shop assistant, Sunny, comes in while I'm on the phone, setting a latte and a cinnamon roll on the table next to me.

"Councilman Samuels is rotten to the core. He's mean to anyone he thinks can't benefit him. I'm sorry you're dealing with this," Sunny laments, looking heartbroken for me.

I respond with a wan smile. "Thanks, Sunny. I appreciate your support. Most everyone has been so kind about it."

The shop door opens, and a young woman with long dark hair and olive skin glides in. She's the one who spoke up about me in the town council, the psychic named Darla. Sunny excuses herself, stepping away to greet her.

Darla's gaze sweeps the room and finds me. "I thought you may be here today. I heard about what happened," she launches into abruptly. I stare at her mutely, alarmed by bluntness. "I should introduce myself, as our knowledge of one another may be one-sided. I'm Darla Rallis, a witch in the local coven."

It's hard to feel comfortable around her when I still feel raw about her involvement in bringing me here. "Nice to meet you, Darla. I'm Cara... but I guess you already know that," I reply awkwardly.

She smirks, though not unkindly. "I do know that, but I don't know anything else about you, just that the pieces have fallen into place to bring you into the fold, into our community when otherwise it would have been impossible. Mayhap we need you. Mayhap you need us. Probably a little of both. I truly don't know the future. I rarely get a full glimpse when I See. But I just know I'm glad you're here, there is a rightness to it I can still feel."

Bristling under the weight of her words, I try to joke to ease the tension. "I guess I didn't need to try so hard in my job interview."

She nods, a smile hovering at the edge of her lips. "You did exactly as you should have. I doubt you would have done differently had you known it was a sure bet. Don't worry too much about my part in it. There's no point. Easier said than done, I know. Maybe consider it permission to live your best life, whatever that may look like to you. Your employment is only one part of it, though many consider their trade their purpose in life. Your contentment, your satisfaction, is also of great importance. Don't overlook it now that you're here."

I bark an incredulous laugh. "So you're telling me don't worry, be happy?"

She nods appreciatively, "Yes, I suppose I am."

Before I can dig any further, her phone rings and she apologizes that she has to take the call, leaving the shop. Throughout the rest of the morning, other coven members stopping in to help with the Samhain festival echo sentiments like Sunny and Darla's. Ada's shop stays busy, acting as their operational hub. I don't mind helping out this morning, especially if she's keeping me caffeinated and fed. Time flies as I go through her task list.

When Walt and Acton step into the shop a while later, Ada glides over and greets them each with a fond kiss on the cheek. "It's so good to see you both! Acton, I'm not sure you've met Cara yet, she is new here, staying in my carriage house. Walt, thank you so much for offering your valuable wisdom to her!" Ada lilts, her eyes shining affectionately on them both.

Acton, a man of moss, bark, and vines—so otherworldly with dazzling green eyes and a boyish face—holds out a verdant hand. I shake it, the lush and feathery texture feels pleasant on my skin.

His voice wispy like rustling leaves, he greets me, "Cara, it is a pleasure. Your bright spirit chases away the shadows to light the way forward. We shall do everything we can to stop the force seeking to extinguish it."

Walt reverently pats Acton's shoulder and regards my awed expression with humor, "My poetic mate wants to welcome you and let you know that this nasty business with Samuels is personal to him, too. Now, let's have some lunch and chat human to human."

Ada leads Acton to the other end of the shop, already deep in a discussion of their own. Walt and I take a seat in the front window where I'd been stationed all morning, and he lays out a spread of paper-wrapped sandwiches and small containers of salads from a paper bag he carried in.

"My arrival in Monstera Bluff looked different than yours. Acton and I were newly mated, madly in love, and wanted to create a life together openly. And that life was possible here in a monster town. I came here with eyes newly opened to this world, but at least I was already aware. I was a young man then, in my prime, longing for a life of adventure and natural wonder. That's why I became a park ranger, but ultimately, I found everything I was looking for in Acton. It was an easy choice to leave the familiarity of the human world for him. I'd do it all again in a heartbeat," he recounts nostalgically.

Even though he had a heads-up about Whispered Folk, it couldn't have been easy. "Did you feel nervous here even though you knew about Whispered Folk? How did you eventually fit in?" I wonder, hoping it can shed light on my situation.

He chuckles self-deprecatingly. "I was probably a little too enthusiastic, bordering on annoying, when I first got here. Honestly, I couldn't believe someone like Acton would come into my life, making me one of the few privileged humans let in on this whopper of a secret, I was in hog heaven. I talked everyone's ear off, wanting to learn more about them and their kind. Ada's parents were some of the first true friends we made here, though. They were so welcoming, helping us get settled. Humans in town were even fewer in number back then. Her parents had experience in the human world, so it was thanks to them that we settled in so quickly. Acton and I have known Ada her entire life. We've tried to be bonus uncles to her, especially after her parents passed."

"She had mentioned they passed. I'm sorry for the loss of your friends," I sympathize.

"Thank you. It was some years ago now, but their loss is still felt by everyone. They'd be so proud of Ada. I make sure to remind her of that all the time. I'm sure she's sick of hearing it from me by now," he admits with humor.

His self-effacing attitude is endearing, so I assure him, "I'm sure she still appreciates it after all this time. How did her parents help you when you arrived?"

"They did quite a bit, to be honest. Acton knew of this town, and they offered to help us get settled into an apartment and found us jobs fitting our interests. I ran the parks department for a long time, retiring several years back to let the new generation take charge. I'm an old man now, and though he doesn't look it, Acton is an even older man," he reveals, fondness in his tone.

Looking between the youthful Acton and the aging gray-haired Walt, still strong and trim for his age, but getting up there in years, I feel an acute pang of sorrow at the obvious implication. "How old is Acton?" I ask, tears burning in my eyes.

"Ah, he's well over a hundred and fifty now and will probably live another hundred years after I'm gone," he responds, very matter-of-fact. The breath is pulled from my lungs at this fundamentally sad mismatch. Yet Walt seems very accepting of it.

"Did you know that... when you decided to be his mate?" I falter, unsure how to address it respectfully.

He smiles, though there's a hint of sadness in his eyes as he explains, "I did. He was already a hundred years old when I met him. So I've always known my mate will live a long life, far longer than mine. He will have another human lifetime after I'm gone. I hope he outlives me by even more. I felt guilty about it when I was younger. That our time together would be a blip in his very long life. But he promised me that every minute, every hour, every day we spend together makes all the years we'll be apart worth it. And I believe him. We've made the most of it by loving each other so completely that the fire in his heart will burn even after I'm gone. It will warm him for the time he walks this realm without me."

A tear rolls down my cheek as I try to keep composed. Their story tugs hard at my heart. He reaches out to squeeze my hand and consoles, "Don't let this upset you, I'm still here by Acton's side. We've had the most amazing time together, and I have plenty of years left in me, decades, hopefully. I just wanted to share this with you to help you understand the immensity of mates' feelings toward each other. Acton knew all of this when he asked me to be his mate. He never considered otherwise. It's a commitment for life and beyond that. If you find a mate here, it will be the same. They will be yours in heart, body, and soul. It's not a magickal bond or anything, but perhaps an example of dedication in its purest form. I think we humans tend to overcomplicate it. Let unimportant details and desires get in the way. But we should take a page out of their book because Acton's love has been the single most important thing in my life."

I give him a weepy nod. It has an undeniable appeal, especially after my own experience of being tossed aside by someone I thought I'd spend the rest of my life with. "How did you know you wanted to be Acton's mate?" I blubber, still overcome with emotion.

"I think I knew right away. He was the most enchanting person I'd ever encountered, and not just because he's part forest." Walt chuckles softly, turning inward for a moment. "I couldn't imagine a life without him even minutes after I first encountered him. We met in secret for a while at the park, but it wasn't enough for either of us. That's when Acton suggested we come here."

"I've met someone, but I don't know if we could be mates. It's such a leap of faith that I'm not sure I have it in me to take. I'm trying, but it's hard." I sigh.

His expression turns empathetic, and he muses, "Think of it like love at first sight, something the movies would tell you is the highest form of romance. But that doesn't mean it isn't scary seeing your future take shape in front of you, especially in a way you never expected. Your heart will decide for you, not your head."

I huff a laugh. "It definitely wasn't love at first sight."

"Well, the second, third, or even fourth sight doesn't lie either," he teases.

Acton and Ada seem to be discussing Ralston Samuels and the other warlocks. "Is Acton worried for you with this anti-human, anti-*me* poster being distributed?" I fret.

"He's refusing to leave my side, which I can't say I mind. But I'm not that concerned for myself. I have a lot of friends. I've lived here most of my life. The community knows me. In all these years, I've learned the real monsters aren't the ones you can outwardly see but the ones who hold hate and prejudice deep inside where it festers into something dangerous. Councilman Samuels and his warlock buddies look more human than most around here, and yet they chill me to the bone," he replies, his tone sobering.

"So what is the difference between warlocks and what Ada is? I'm struggling to understand the nuance," I probe, trying to make better sense of the situation.

"Warlocks are a bunch of self-important misanthropes, in my opinion. They probably have their own understanding of the differences, but from what I've seen, it boils down to valuing a coven or not. Covens help channel all the members' power to help each other. They work together to make their collective magick more stable, less likely to fail. Many magick wielders, each contributing smaller amounts of magick, creates a better outcome than fewer magick wielders contributing a lot. The ward around our town wouldn't be possible without the coven, for example, since nearly all of them contribute to it. The tradeoff is that covens restrict how much magick witches wield in their individual pursuits to be sure they can always support each other," he interprets.

"Why would they have to restrict magick at all? Can't they just use all the magick they want?" I question.

"Magick isn't limitless. Sort of like your body's energy or endurance. You can train to run a marathon, but even then, you can't run one every day for the rest of your life. And when you do cross that finish line, you're put a fork in me done. It's a finite resource and constantly needs to be replenished through rest. Warlocks essentially don't want to share any of their magick. They seek to empower themselves as much as possible, often recklessly. It's admittedly more lucrative. They can cast more spells and make more potions every day, but it's also dangerous. Magick can be hard to control, but those guys think they know better than everyone else," Walt opines, clearly having given this a lot of thought.

"So, if warlocks are a bunch of loners, why are these three working together?" I press.

"It's not unheard of for warlocks to have loose alliances, but Samuels, Atticus, and Weatherby are taking it to another level. They've been egging each other on for years now. I'm not surprised they're stooping to this now." He scoffs.

"I guess I was one human too many for them," I observe sarcastically.

"Believe me, they'd be happy to toss out half the town if they had their way." He snorts. "Besides those three, I trust everyone on the council and Clancy, too. They'll figure it out."

As Walt and I talk more about his life here, he doesn't ask who I'm seeing. He probably already knows. Ben and I have been affectionate in public together. It wouldn't be hard to figure out at this point. Walt shares more stories about him and Acton, how it took a while to get used to Acton's eating habits—or lack thereof—and living together in general with someone very inhuman. It makes me appreciate everything Ben and I have in common, including our lifespans and taste in food. It gives me a lot to think about, *the shape of the future,* as Walt puts it.

Ada wraps up her day at the shop soon after Walt and Acton leave. I text Rose to see if she's free to talk tonight. And I confirm with Ben that we're still on for tomorrow morning. He asks if I feel comfortable at home by myself tonight, and I respond that I'll be fine. I appreciate how thoughtful he is. He was so careful with me last night and this morning. I can tell it's a genuine offer, not just a ploy to sleep in my bed. We'll get there soon enough, I'm sure.

Letting Ada know I'm going to stay in this evening, we do some uneventful grocery shopping on our way home. I buy everything I need to make chicken noodle soup. I'm slowly getting my fridge and shelves stocked, making the carriage house feel like a real home.

Rose lets me know she's a *boring old maid with no Friday night plans,* so I call her while I make dinner. She fills me in on the situationship drama going on with one of our friends. And I make a mental note to text our friend something supportive later. Hearing about my friends' bad dates feels comfortingly normal, like I'm not halfway across the country from them and separated by a magickal barrier. But it also makes me feel sad that these amazing women put up with some truly ludicrous bullshit from mediocre guys—and occasional gals, too. If they ever found out about the concept of mates, I have a feeling they'd plan a one-way road trip here.

I'm unsurprised when Rose uses that as a segue to bring up Ben. "How's Mark version two-point-zero treating you this week?" she asks dismissively. It irks me that she's using that tone to talk about him, but I haven't updated her yet, so I can't hold it against her.

"About that..." I begin.

"Cara! No!" she interrupts, knowing me too well.

I laugh nervously as I tell her, "Yeah, he did like me after all. He was just trying to give me space because I'm new, but it came off as really dismissive."

"That sounds emotionally stunted. Are you sure about him? Has he tried to turn it around on you? Pressure you?" she voices concern.

"I mean, he should have gone about it differently, but I understand where he was coming from. We've talked about it, and he's genuinely remorseful," I clarify.

"Just promise me you'll be careful. Even if he says he's sorry. You can forgive, but you don't have to forget. But now you have to spill everything. Have you gone out yet? Have you kissed? I need to live vicariously through you," she teases.

"You'll be happy to hear our first real date was at the beach two nights ago to watch the sunset. That's when I took the photo I sent you. And tomorrow morning, I'm going to his house for a secret activity he has planned. I have no idea what it is yet. He's a very good kisser, better than Mark," I divulge.

"If he's a good kisser, I bet he's good at other things too." She cackles.

"Oh, he's very good at that, too." I laugh in embarrassment.

"Cara! How dare you hold out on me!" she scolds mockingly.

We fall into a fit of giggles. She suggests I make him give me head every night to make up for the bad first impression. I already know I won't even have to ask for that, but I keep that detail to myself.

"So, I'll accept that he isn't another Mark, but what is he like now that he stopped being a frigid little bitch?" she snarks, making us both crack up.

I tell an edited version of his story about his family and business, plying me with flowers and food. "He's kind and thoughtful in ways I wasn't expecting to be treated ever again. I just didn't think I would find someone like that. I'm used to being... expendable. But he seems like he's all in. And I want to trust that, but it seems too good to be true," I ramble, working out my feelings as the words leave my mouth. "A relationship with him would have challenges, though. I'm not saying it'll be easy or perfect. But right now, the positives probably outweigh the negatives. But I still can't tell if that's the honest truth or if my judgment is clouded by infatuation. Am I focusing too much on his potential instead of who he really is? I went down that path with Mark and I can't do it again."

My dear friend sighs deeply through the phone. "Cara, you're spiraling. I'm sorry I brought up Mark, comparing them to each other. Your mom and then Mark really did a number on you. But it's clear now Ben is different. I shouldn't have said it. I was being a jerk. As much as Mark taught you how to look for red flags and take them seriously, you do need to give a new relationship a chance, especially with a good guy who deserves you. Take it one date at a time. Don't worry so much about the future just yet. It's not like he's going to ask you to marry him tomorrow, right?"

"Uh, probably not," I answer truthfully.

"*Probably* not!" She howls in laughter. "Then you might have found the most anti-Mark guy out there."

Not too long after, I feign exhaustion and end our call. I am tired, though. That's not a lie. The mental gymnastics needed to talk about Ben takes a toll. But even if Rose doesn't know the whole truth about me and Ben, she does have some good points. I need to relax a little, enjoy our dates without analyzing them to death. The chicken noodle soup is the perfect comfort food to settle me into a quiet night. As I mindlessly watch a show on my laptop, my phone buzzes.

"You're wasting your talent in that redneck town. Don't you want to do work that really matters?" Unknown number again. I was hoping this sick prank would be a one-off, but apparently not. I can't entertain the notion that it really is Mark. It's too fucked up to think about.

The threats, mysterious texts, uncertainty about Ben, guilt about my friends. My mind races while I lay in bed, but eventually I fall asleep. It's still dark when I'm woken up by whistling, a deranged song sounding all around me. Like it followed me out of my nightmare. I can't remember much else about what I dreamed, except something was pursuing me, nebulous and enigmatic. Only occasional glimpses of its yellow eyes let me know it's close by. But that song is still in my ears, vaguely threatening, the notes not quite right. Even now, it raises the hair on the back of my neck. The wind picks up outside, sounding through the trees, sounding similar to that strange whistle. I must have heard it while I was asleep.

Six Months Ago

I park my car in front of a nondescript newer apartment building. After checking the address on the front of the building, I see that my GPS is correct. It's my new home. I sigh, turning to Rose in the passenger seat next to me. "I guess we're finally here."

She attempts an encouraging smile, but it looks forced, more sad than anything. "You know, we can turn around and head back, drive overnight and be back at my apartment by tomorrow morning. You don't need to leave Chicago if you truly don't want to. We can figure out something else for you. You can stay with me until then, rent-free. However long it takes," she pleads. "You can call this new job, tell them you've reconsidered. No harm, no foul."

I wish I could do that. She has no idea of the depth of my desire to stay. But I can't. I have to move away to have a career. Mark took everything from me, and this is the only path forward. I've already drained my meager savings in the last couple of months since I quit my job at Hansen Company. Breaking my lease and signing a new one proved to be unbelievably expensive. But I couldn't stomach the thought of stepping foot in that office again. I left that day I found out about Mark and never came back. I didn't even pick up the stuff from my desk, not that any of it had any value. Even at my most naïve, I wouldn't have left anything sentimental there. A receptionist I was friendly with mailed me my diploma she must have snagged before it was tossed out with the rest of my stuff. One kindness amidst the shitstorm my life has become.

Rose helps me unpack my SUV and the rented trailer behind me. I gave up my furniture when I was packing up my old apartment, sold and donated as much as possible. So nothing is too heavy for us to lift by ourselves. Once the boxes and bins are in, Rose assesses the place with a skeptical eye. I was lucky enough to find a furnished apartment, though obviously it was meant for temporary stays. It looks like a hotel, transitional and impersonal.

"Once you've settled into your new job, you'll be able to get a more permanent place. There seem to be cute neighborhoods here, lots to do. It'll take time, but you'll make it your home," she encourages. "I know you never thought you'd move out of Chicago. And I wish you didn't have to. But you can start over here. You found this new job so quickly. You didn't give up. I'm so proud of you. If you do ever need to move in with me, that offer stands indefinitely. Tomorrow. Five years from now. Doesn't matter. Maybe you can take some risks, figure out something new in life, a different line of work. I'm always here to support you, even if we aren't a train ride away anymore."

The thought is tempting. Her beautiful apartment, with its peaceful flower garden that blooms in the late spring and summer, is a slice of heaven, to be honest. But I can't take advantage of her, even if she would never see it that way. She's the most generous person I know. I'm so lucky she's my best friend.

"Thank you, Rose. That means so much to me. I promise I'm going to make it work here. I just can't go back. The thought of running into Mark makes me sick. I can't let him take even more from me," I blubber, my eyes burning with tears.

"He'll never take me away, that's for sure. I hope that asshole rots in hell for how he's treated you. I hope he finally sees what he lost and regrets it for the rest of his miserable, shitty life," she declares, her voice fervent and angry.

"That isn't going to happen, but I wish it would too." I huff a sad laugh.

Tired after the long drive and unpacking my stuff, we order delivery and open a bottle of wine. It leads to reminiscing about all the fun we've had together. Laying out at Montrose beach in the summer, happy hours spent at the brewery in her neighborhood, long walks along the lakeshore on Saturday mornings, near-weekly get-togethers with our friends at Rose's place. It's true; you don't know what you've got till it's gone. Well, deep down, I always knew our friendship was special.

The night ends earlier than I hoped, but we're exhausted and planning on getting up early to explore the city tomorrow. Neither of us has ever even been to Atlanta before. Lying in bed in this dark, unfamiliar bedroom, staring up at the ceiling, it's like a nightmare I can't wake up from. If Rose wasn't next to me, I'd feel even more lost, more hopeless. I can't stand the thought of her flying home in a couple days. I'll have to face reality.

I'll never tell her, but I picked myself up as much for her as it was for me. I don't want her to keep worrying about me, so I found a way to rebuild some semblance of a life. If there's something I know how to do, it's showing up for work and doing my job. On repeat, indefinitely. That's what I'll do here. Hopefully, it's enough to convince her I'm doing better. Maybe I'll be able to convince myself someday.

♡ ♡ ♡ ♡ ♡

When I wake to my alarm in the morning, I'm still tired. I slept poorly after the nightmare. But the excitement of spending the morning with Ben propels me out of bed to shower, shave, wash my hair, and apply light makeup. I take time to pick my outfit for the mystery date and choose a pair of cropped wide-leg jeans that I can move in and a black fitted V-neck t-shirt. It'll be versatile enough for whatever he has in store.

Since I don't know where he lives, he offered to pick me up bright and early at nine in the morning. Tires crunch on the driveway right on time. I rush downstairs as he steps out of his truck, feeling the grin split my face when I see him. Racing to him as he opens his arms, he folds them around me as I rise on my tiptoes to kiss him. Our lips open and tongues meet as I hold his face in my hands, crushing myself to him. His hands rub along my back, venturing down to cup my backside, pinning us together.

He kisses along my jaw, murmuring low, "I want to do this every morning."

"Me too," I breathe.

We finally disentangle and he helps me into his truck. A telltale pink box on the seat and two coffees in the cupholders greet me.

"We'll have breakfast before we start our project today," he teases, enjoying the fact I still don't know his plans.

There are no clues in the car, so I'm antsy by the time we reach his house minutes later. He lives only a few blocks away. I had no idea. I'm unsurprised his house has a limestone façade—a tall, narrow, rectangular two-story with a full-sized front porch on each level. Both porches are symmetrically spaced, with a door on the right side and two large windows on the left. The decorative wrought-iron railing in front of the porches and the dressed arched windows make the house look like it belongs in New Orleans rather than coastal Georgia.

He notices me studying it and remarks, "My great-grandfather built it when he moved here, and my grandparents lived in it until they passed several years ago."

"It's stunning, Ben. It has so much character," I exclaim.

"I think so too. My great-grandfather wanted to bring a piece of home with him."

We step through the front door on the right side of the porch into a long foyer with a staircase along the right wall leading upstairs. The ceilings are tall, but that's unsurprising considering Ben's height. We enter the living room to the left of the foyer and follow through to the dining room, separated by a cased opening. A narrower doorway on the other side of the dining room leads to a large eat-in kitchen at the back of the house, which also has an entrance at the back end of the foyer. It isn't a huge house, but each room is spacious. The interior details aren't over-done. It has the right amount of beautiful touches to make it charming but not maximalist. There's unpainted wood trim everywhere, including an ornate wooden fireplace surround that looks hand-carved, providing a contrast to the light-colored walls. Tall windows with thick, decorative casings line the entire house. Plaster medallions on every ceiling. A few pieces of artwork hang from picture rail molding on the walls. His furniture looks comfortable and oversized but doesn't crowd the space.

We sit at his kitchen table as he serves breakfast. "I wasn't sure what you'd like," he admits as he unpacks half a dozen assorted croissants and rolls from the box. He pulls a bowl of chopped-up fruit from his refrigerator along with a pitcher of orange juice. It's the coziest breakfast.

"It seems like everyone's home here belongs in Architectural Digest," I joke while admiring the white kitchen with beautiful gray stone counters.

Ben laughs. "Well, I do come from a family of builders. I guess Whispered Folk have always taken what they like best from human culture and suited it to their own purposes. Why build something ugly?"

As we savor our coffee and breakfast, he tells me more about the house and some memories of it from his childhood. "I'd run or fly over here all the time to play when I was little, probably several times a week. Mémé, my grandmother, always baked cookies for me. For my brother, too, once he was old enough to eat them. There'd always be a fresh plate on the counter and a pitcher of lemonade. She was a skilled baker, though I didn't realize that until I was a teenager and began to appreciate food beyond cookies. Pépé, my grandfather, always praised her baking and cooking. He was always so pleased she learned French recipes for him," he reminisces.

"Did she teach you and your brother how to bake?" I ask.

He smiles, caught up in some memory. "She did, though I wish I remembered more. I can still bake a galette and roast a chicken, the basics, like she taught me. I haven't even changed much about the kitchen since she passed. Just replaced a couple appliances. Most of her utensils and dishes are still here in good shape."

I run a finger along the plate in front of me, wondering if it was hers. "What about your grandfather? Were you close as well?"

"Very close. One of my favorite memories of him was on the coldest nights each winter. He'd sit with me in front of the fireplace and tell me about gargoyles and our history. I don't believe the season had any sort of significance to the stories, but it became my favorite time of year, a much-loved tradition. Pépé was quite the storyteller. He had a way of making his tales come to life. They seemed so exciting to me as a young boy. He passed away just a few years ago at a very old age. My apartment at the time was small, but I wasn't sure if I wanted to move in here. Seemed like too much space with too many sad reminders of Mémé and Pépé. But after a few months of caring for the empty house, I realized it was easier to move in. It turned out to be a lot more comforting to be here than I thought possible," he recalls.

"They sound loving. I wish I could have met them," I reply wistfully, lacing my fingers in his.

"I do, too, my belle," he answers, the endearment making me blush.

Ben clears our dishes after we've finished eating. "So, what did you have in mind for us this morning? I have no idea what kind of project would even need to be done!" I wonder aloud.

He chuckles. "I was thinking of planting some jasmine around the house. My mother has always grown it along the front of my parents' house, and the scent permeates many of my childhood memories. When I met you, your fragrance was so reminiscent. It brings me peace and calm. I want to surround myself with it even more."

"I smell like jasmine?" I ask in disbelief.

"You do, sweet and sultry," he rumbles into my hand as he brings it to his mouth to kiss.

We head outside to a neatly organized bundle of seedlings, tools, gloves, and towels. "I was thinking I'll grow it along the porch railing, so we can sit outside here in the spring and enjoy it while it blooms," he suggests, watching my reaction.

My heart skips a beat. He's thinking of us in the future. "I can't wait," I respond with a huge grin.

Kneeling on large towels to prevent grass stains, we dig a row of holes in the empty flower bed in front of the porch, placing a young jasmine vine in each. We even out the soil and then water them. "There's a magickal plant growth mixture I'll buy from our garden shop that will ensure the vines grow nicely this first year," Ben explains, "Small white blossoms will cover the railing."

As we finish planting, he suggests we look at the backyard. "My grandmother had a vegetable patch at some point, but I don't remember too much about it. There wouldn't be anything to salvage anyway. You could use this space to start a new one if that's something you wanted to finally try," he offers, his voice careful like he doesn't want to spook me.

Rapidly blinking back the tears prickling at my eyes, I answer with a wavering smile. "That is so thoughtful, I think I will. If you really don't mind, that is. But how did you know? That I want a garden?"

"Cara, I could tell how much your grandmother's garden meant to you when you told me about it. Sharing this space with you to explore a new hobby would bring me the greatest joy," he professes, the longing in his voice laid bare.

Holding his muddy hand in mine, we walk around the space he suggests, and it will work well as a garden plot. I'll have to research what I can grow in this climate. Even though I'm sure there are magickal concoctions that would allow me to grow anything, the joy is in the work itself, so I want to keep it as natural as possible.

"Is there anything you want me to grow?" I ask, considering he's letting me do this in his yard, he should pick some of the bounty.

"Hmm, okra and cucumbers? I like to make pickles with them," he chooses.

"Excellent idea! I don't think my grandma had okra, so I'll have to do my research on it," I effuse, giddy at the possibilities. His face lights up, like my enthusiasm has delighted him. And that makes me even more excited to get started.

Since we've finished outside, we head back into the house to wash our hands and freshen up. "Do you want to use the bathroom upstairs?" Ben asks, looking mostly innocent.

I can't help but giggle, letting him lead the way. We enter his bedroom, situated at the front of the house. The porch on the second level is identical to the one below. A narrow set of French doors with leaded glass leads out to it.

"Maybe the jasmine vines will grow all the way up here," I muse as I look out the glass.

"We'll open the window and let its scent envelop us while we make love," he suggests, eyes darkening as he gazes down at me.

Before he can take that thought any further, I brush a kiss against his jaw and head into the adjoining bathroom to wash the dirt from my hands and arms. He joins me at the sink and does the same, handing me a fluffy towel after I've rinsed off.

I tug at the bottom of his t-shirt, which has a couple smudges, and purr, "Looks like you'll need to change out of this."

He obliges, undoing the seams below his wings and pulling it over his head. His warm body smells a little salty and musky, a heady mix. I rub my hands across his gray shoulders and down his chest, pausing to rub my thumbs over his slightly darker nipples. He groans deeply and his arousal fuels mine. I move lower, splaying my hands over his strong abdomen. He doesn't have the defined six-pack abs of a bodybuilder, but he has thick, visible muscle carved from physical labor. It's even sexier than something gained from a gym.

Slowly, I run my fingers under the waistband of his jeans, teasing back and forth before circling my arms around his waist. Through my lashes, I look up at him, inviting him to make the next move.

"Cara, let me make love to you," he croons as he cups my cheeks in his hands.

"Yes, Ben," I answer breathily, and he leans down for a soft kiss, slowly opening me up to him.

Soon, the kiss turns debauched, his tongue thrusting in my mouth, no doubt mimicking what he'll be doing to me soon. I moan in anticipation, the tension coiling tight inside me. His hands tug my t-shirt over my head, breaking our kiss temporarily, and then he reaches behind my back to unlatch my bra. I slide it down my arms, tossing it to the floor next to my shirt. My bare breasts press against his chest, and the skin-to-skin contact feels incredible. I want to rub myself against him. He reaches between us, cupping my breasts in his hands, his fingers brushing across the peaks.

"Your nipples are hard for me, Cara. Are you turned on knowing that I'm going to fuck you so deeply it will feel like your first time again? And I'll keep doing it until you forget any other male has had you before," he growls, his expression gone feral.

His words drive me wild. My panties feel wet against me. "Yes, Ben, I need you!" I beg.

He picks me up, carries me out of the bathroom, and lays me on his giant bed. He unbuttons my pants, and I lift my hips so he can pull them off me. He moves my knees apart, baring my panty-covered pussy.

"You're soaked, Cara. You've ruined your pretty panties. Is your body getting ready for me?" he teases.

"So ready!" I wail, needy for his touch. He peels them from me, and I tremble as the air hits my exposed pussy.

"My cock is ready for you too, Cara. I'm going to show you how fat and swollen you make it," he grunts as he undoes his jeans and shoves them off along with his boxer briefs.

Like I suspected, his groin is hairless like the rest of him, and it makes his cock and testicles look huge. His cock has a row of ridges along the top, right where it will feel exquisite rubbing inside of me. Unlike the rest of him, its tip has a pink hue. It's blunt with a long deep slit, already dripping with semen. His hard length is probably eight or nine inches, and its thickness sends a shiver down my spine. He'll have to warm me up to take him. It would be an uncomfortable fit without foreplay.

"I want to touch you, Ben," I whine.

He chuckles husky and low. "Soon enough. First, I'm going to make you come on my tongue and tail so you're nice and soft and open to take me to the hilt."

He climbs onto the bed between my legs and pulls my knees wide over his shoulders, burying his face into my curls, licking up and down my slit. His hands snake upwards along my sides and finally reach my breasts, rolling my nipples between his fingers. I squirm under the dual sensation, mewling as he licks my clit.

"I love how responsive you are, so needy for me," he whispers into my pussy as he sucks on my labia.

"Give me your tail, Ben. I need to feel it," I moan.

He hums deeply in approval, sending delicious vibrations throughout my pussy. "I thought you'd never ask."

The instant it rubs against my opening, I jolt. I'm so wound up it nearly sends me over the edge. His mouth focuses on my clit again, circling his tongue around it as he begins to pump shallow strokes into my channel.

"More!" I wail, thrashing my head on the mattress and grabbing onto his horns.

"My greedy girl," he hums again, vibrating directly into my clit.

At that moment, he plunges his tail even deeper, sliding it in the channel behind my clit. I see white behind my eyelids as my orgasm crashes over me. I moan loudly as he continues to coax it out of me, thrusting through the pulses in my pussy, prolonging the sensations.

He slows and stops his attention on my clit just in time before it gets too intense. He pulls his tail from me with an embarrassing squelch.

"So warm and wet for me," he rumbles into my inner thigh, kissing and licking my skin. He moves my legs off his shoulders and pulls himself up my body.

I wrap my legs around his waist so that the hot, hard length of him rests on my core. I'd only need to angle my hips up slightly, and he'd be notched into my pussy. His midnight blue eyes bore into mine.

"Cara, this is all I've ever dreamed of, finding someone like you and making her mine. You'll be so full of my cock that you'll feel empty without it. You'll be so full of my seed that it'll never stop dripping out of you," he growls, wild and dominating. Pleasure flows through every inch of my body at his words.

"I'm on birth control, Ben. I need to feel you come inside me," I purr.

He flashes his wolfish grin. "So am I. I'm going to fill you up so full, Cara. Over and over again."

I moan, closing my eyes. His dirty words alone could bring me to orgasm.

He sucks and licks down my neck and moves to my breasts, gently biting each nipple with his sharp teeth and then easing the flash of pain by licking them. After lavishing each one with plenty of attention, he holds himself up with one arm so he's hovering over me. His eyes devour my bared body—the large pink nipples on my breasts, soft stomach, and plump thighs. He strokes his cock as his eyes focus again on my spread-open pussy, using his bubbling pre-come as lube. Just the sight of his swollen, dripping cock makes me wetter, my body getting ready to take him. He taps the blunt, leaking head against my clit, sending sharp tingles of pleasure through my body. I writhe from the sensation, and he rubs the head up and down my slit, then circles my clit and presses against it.

He repeats his ministrations, mingling our fluids until I'm gasping. "Ben, I need you inside me. I feel so empty."

His cock sliding along my pussy feels so good, but it's not nearly enough. He slots the flat head right at my entrance, so much thicker than the end of his tail, stretching the ring of muscle. He sinks into me, pushing a little further with each thrust, teasing me open. He's so thick that I feel every ridge and vein against my inner walls, including that extra ribbing and that deliciously unique texture of his skin dragging inside me. The extra friction makes me pant and whine. He feels huge, going so slow and stretching me wide. Nothing this big has ever been inside me before. He was right. It is like the first time all over again. Sex has never been like this. I'm already seeing stars with each thrust, and by the time he's fully seated within me, I'm about to peak.

"Don't stop, you feel so fucking good. I'm so full. Keep going," I whimper, barely coherent.

He grabs my hips and slams into me, his cock hitting a spot so deep I've never felt anything like it. His claw tips bite ever so slightly into my skin, ratcheting the sensation in my body even higher.

I cry out as I buck and arch underneath him, meeting every hard thrust, "Ben, yes, that's it!"

My moans are continuous and uncontrollable, letting him know I'm so close. He hammers into me, hitting that unplumbed spot again and again until pleasure explodes in my body. His thrusts are so deep that I clamp down hard enough on his entire length that he has to push through the tight squeeze. I've never orgasmed so hard in my life.

"Your pussy fluttering around me feels so good. Do you like being impaled on my cock?" he coaxes, punctuating his question with an especially deep spearing inside of me during the aftershocks of my orgasm.

"So good, oh my god," I ramble unintelligibly, still so aroused, every thrust winding me up again. His cock thickens impossibly more, and he drills and grunts his pleasure, his movement turning erratic. Hot ropes of semen splash deep inside me, heating and filling me even further. The sensation sends me over the edge again, a smaller orgasm flashes through me, and I hold Ben's big, warm body to me as tightly as I can.

I'm out of breath. Ben is panting equally hard in my ear as I feel him soften and pull out of me, shifting his weight off me as he rolls to my side. "That was incredible, Cara. You belong in my bed," he croons as he cups my cheek in his hand and kisses me deeply. I taste a little of myself on him, which is strange but also incredibly intimate.

"If you're offering up orgasms, who am I to say no," I tease, peppering his cheek and neck with kisses.

"They're always on offer, but only to you," he growls into my ear, lightly nipping the lobe.

"Only to you, too." I sigh, loving this flirtatious side of him.

Laying my head down again, I study his face up close. I haven't had much opportunity to do so in the daylight. With my fingertip, I trace along his strong jaw, his pointed ear, his temple, his horns. His eyes close blissfully as I caress his face, learning him, accepting him. I brush along his lips, and he playfully bites at my finger, sucking into his mouth and swirling his tongue around it.

Giggling, I shift my body, throwing my leg over his hips. It causes wetness to seep out of me, and I squeal in embarrassment as it dribbles onto the bed. "I'll be right back," he purrs, pulling my face toward him for a brief kiss.

He rolls out of bed and steps into the bathroom. The water runs, and soon he returns with a warm, wet towel and carefully wipes off me and the spot on the bed. He rustles around in the bathroom afterward, probably cleaning himself off, and returns to lie down next to me.

Curiosity gets the better of me, so I ask, "You said you were also on birth control?"

He grins, pulling me closer so our bodies are pressed together. "Yes, our healers have a birth control potion. And then another to reverse it when desired. Nearly every adult here takes it," he explains.

My mouth gapes at how convenient that sounds. "Wow, I think I need to switch to that."

He grins at my shocked expression. "We're fine with my dose, but certainly it doesn't hurt if you want to take it instead of what you use now."

"This would be such a game changer in the human world, so much easier for women," I rhapsodize.

"Magick can be very useful," he agrees.

As I continue to explore him, my hands roam over his arms, shoulders, wings, and down to his butt. I squeeze a cheek. It's much firmer than mine, more muscle than fat. "I've been wanting to do that for a while. You're so hot." I snicker as I lazily gaze into his eyes.

He presses his forehead to mine and hums, "You can touch me anywhere you want." He nuzzles my face, rubbing his nose on mine.

"Can I touch you here?" I venture, moving my hand along his waist toward his cock.

"Absolutely," he grunts as my hand brushes his semi-hard cock.

I rub my thumb along the ribbing and ask, "What are these for?"

He chuckles indulgently. "I think you know what they're for."

"I guess I do…" I tease, taking his thick cock more firmly in my hand, pumping up and down the length.

"A little gift to help our species along, I believe," he hisses, hips bucking as I quicken my speed. "Did I not give you enough orgasms, my belle? Are you eager for me again?"

"I think it's your turn this time." I smile into his mouth as I begin kissing down his brawny body.

He rolls onto his back, adjusts his wings so they lie comfortably underneath him, and puts his hands behind his head. "Your mouth on me is such a gift, Cara. I'll never know anything sweeter," he murmurs, husky and hot.

I suck on his nipples and then lick down his abdomen. Positioning myself to kneel between his legs, I rub his thighs and cradle his swollen balls, which in my naughty imagination are full to bursting with seed for me. As I gently cup and tug on them, his cock twitches to life, sputtering a pearly bead of pre-come out of his blunt pink tip. I feel like I've won a prize, bringing him back to life from his refractory period so quickly.

I carefully scrape my fingernails along the skin of his sac and then up and down his shaft. He draws in a sharp breath and sticky, wet pre-come leaks down its swollen head.

Finally bringing him into my mouth, I revel in his taste, a salty mineral flavor oozing on my tongue.

"Suck on the tip, use your hands to pump me," Ben directs in a hoarse voice, his eyes rolling back in his head as I follow his instructions.

His cock is too wide to take more than a few inches into my mouth comfortably, but I suck and swirl my tongue around it while I squeeze up and down the base with my hands. Wanting to sustain the act a while longer, I lick up and down the vein on the underside of his shaft, making his cock jump and stir.

"Mother Earth, that's so good, my belle. Let your hungry tongue learn the length of me," he growls. "Watch me while you take me in your mouth, how you make me come undone."

His stormy gaze is on me as I lick and suck along his balls and shaft, lapping up his leaking pre-come. He looks like he could eat me alive, but I've beat him to it. His cock starts to twitch and spurt, and I can tell he's tantalizingly close to his peak. Bringing him between my lips again, his cock bobs hard against my tongue, wild and alive. I pump my hands, building a rhythm with my mouth. My eyes still never leave his as he shouts through his shuddery orgasm, and hot, syrupy come surges into my mouth. I swallow over and over, trying not to waste a drop.

As he softens, I release him with a wet pop, and his spent cock falls against his thigh. He reaches for me, and I climb to lay over his sturdy body, hard planes pressed against my softness.

"I'll never forget the sight of your lips around me for as long as I live, Cara," he promises, kissing me long and hard.

A warmth blazes in my chest at the rightness of this moment in his arms. Laying my head on his chest, the resonant thump of his heartbeat and the vibrating bass of his voice sound like the most calming music. As we talk about everything and nothing, he rubs soothing circles on my back, surreptitiously kissing the top of my head. We could happily spend the afternoon in bed, but our growling stomachs force us to finally get up.

We get dressed, freshen up, and head down to the kitchen, devouring the leftover pastries on the table. "Let's walk and get lunch," Ben suggests. "Maybe we can also visit the garden store to buy seeds for your garden."

I beam at this thoughtful man. "I like that idea," I answer, wrapping my arms around his waist and leaning up for a kiss.

"We aren't going to get very far if we keep this up," he hums into my lips. I giggle as we pull away from each other. He's right. We'd probably end up in a compromising position with me on the countertop... an idea to file away for later.

CHAPTER 16
CARA

The midday sun is warm as we walk hand in hand away from his house. Ben and I can't stop grinning at each other as we talk about where to go to lunch. I suggest somewhere with shaded outdoor seating, and he says he knows just the place.

Not wanting to ruin the amazing date we've had, I haven't brought up the second text message supposedly from Mark. But it feels wrong to keep it from Ben any longer, especially since he was concerned about the first one. When I show it to him as we walk down the sidewalk, his brow furrows. He takes my phone and stares at the two mysterious messages.

He grunts in distaste. "I told Clancy about the first one. His concern is their pushy and vaguely threatening tone that mayhap Mark found something about us. The coven doesn't believe that's the case... yet. He also talked to Wyck to make sure something about us hasn't popped up online. We've been lucky so far, but we can never be too careful," he explains, still preoccupied with the messages like he's trying to decode them.

He takes out his own phone, snapping a photo of my screen. After handing my phone back, he sends a flurry of text messages, responses buzzing almost instantly. "Alright, Clancy and the council are up to date now, and they're having Wyck scour online as best he can to figure out if there's any kind of information leak. Mark seems to just be human, so he shouldn't have any way to find out about us," he says, sounding frustrated.

"Who is Wyck again... Wait, did you check up on Mark?" I ask, belatedly realizing what he meant.

"Wyck is our resident tech and software whiz. He's a young male troll, the one who bumped into you at Midnight Mystic on your first day. A good male, just young and awkward, better with computers than people," he responds, pausing with a sigh. "Cara, of course I investigated that horrible toad who treated you so poorly and drove you away from your home. There is no reality in which I would not have done so. He is too pompous for his own good. It was unbelievably easy to dig into his life and find out what he's been up to. I apologize for not telling you sooner. I didn't betray your confidence and reveal any details about your history with him. But I did ask Wyck to help me look into him and report those results to me and Clancy."

I'm stunned to hear this, but I guess it isn't surprising he'd be proactive about it. It's smart of him, to be fair. The thought of Mark finding out about Monstera Bluff and the Whispered Folk makes my skin crawl. He needs to stay in my past. If I can't escape him here, then I won't be safe anywhere.

"I understand. Just don't tell me anything about him. I don't want to hear it," I insist, sounding a little petulant. I turn away from him as a fresh wave of grief hits me.

He looks somber as he takes my hand, tugging it to get me to look at him again. "I won't tell you anything except this, his firm has been named in some breach of contract lawsuits very recently and as a result lost several lucrative state contracts. You were more important to the firm than he realized. Or their behavior toward you had a cascade effect in the office," he discloses.

"I didn't have many friends there. They wouldn't have cared that I left," I retort.

"I wouldn't be so sure. The way they treated you would not sit well with most. It was deeply malicious on a personal and professional level, to the extent that it quite possibly destroyed their reputation with the rest of their staff. I imagine their engineers were not subject to the same legal agreement that you were? There would be nothing to compel them to stay working in an environment full of sabotage and deceit where they could be the next target," he reasons.

I exhale shakily, considering his words. Others in the office were painfully aware of my situation and didn't agree with it. I hesitate to make assumptions about people I wasn't exactly popular with. Still, it makes sense they'd look out for their own careers if they recognized how dysfunctional the office became.

"I doubt anyone staged a walkout on my behalf. But I don't know what happened to the projects I was working on. I guess if several others left in quick succession after me, it would put them in a serious bind. It wasn't a huge office. Mark wasn't an exceptionally talented engineer himself. He wouldn't be able to pick up the slack on his own. If he misrepresented the firm to new clients to secure contracts and then delivered some faulty assessments or designs, it could lead to lawsuits. There's a lot of opportunity for error," I ponder aloud.

"Indeed, something went very wrong for the firm after you left. I bring this up because if those messages are from Mark, it could be a sign of desperation on his part. And he obviously cannot be trusted. It is something we need to take seriously, especially since he claims to be keeping tabs on you," Ben insists, sounding concerned. Hearing this stirs up a tangle of emotions, none of them good.

"Thanks for looking into this, Ben. I'm worried about what he'll do. I'll tell you as soon as he contacts me again," I promise.

He releases my hand to cradle my face, and my eyes lock onto his fierce gaze. "Your well-being is my number one priority, Cara. He won't get to you here. I'll make sure of it," he pledges.

I know it's the truth. Rising on tiptoes, I circle my arms around his neck and pull his mouth to mine. In a tellingly protective gesture, he wraps both his arms and wings around me in return, covering me in my new favorite safety blanket.

My cheeks are flushed when I finally break the kiss and whisper, "Thank you, Ben. Now let's forget about that asshole and have ourselves a nice afternoon."

As planned, we visit the garden store, and I end up talking to a bovine-looking woman—a female minotaur and the owner of the store,

Ben fills me in after—about suggestions for a beginner's vegetable garden in this climate. She seems pleasantly surprised that I want to grow everything the old-fashioned way, and she assures me they have plenty of seeds, fertilizer, and other supplies with varying levels of magick from which I could choose. Ben buys one of the magickal growth solutions for the jasmine we planted earlier. He told me he'll use it the next time I come over. I can't wait to see how the magick will work.

Walking along the main street, store windows and light poles display posters for the Samhain Festival next week. They advertise *food, games, fortune-telling, a bonfire, and magickal delights for the whole family to enjoy* after sunset.

Ben notices me studying the poster and remarks, "Magickal abilities are stronger that night when the veil between worlds is so thin. The coven performs spells and rituals to honor our dead and ask them to bless the coming year. Some of the witches' magickal displays after the rituals are impressive. It's quite the show. Would you like to go with me?"

"Yes, I would love to! I haven't really seen magick other than a little at Ada's shop. It sounds like fun," I marvel, so excited to witness these *magickal delights.*

"I've seen several films with your human Halloween in them. We don't dress in costumes like you do. The coven will have special robes to honor the day, but otherwise, people dress as they usually do. Sometimes there is mask-making for children, though some adults wear them too," Ben points out thoughtfully.

"I was just about to ask that! Are you sure you're not a mind reader this close to Samhain?" I jest.

"The only use I'd have for it would be to tease out your most hidden desires," he murmurs suggestively, sending a trembling down to my core.

Ben and I end up at a busy cafe for a late lunch, but we're able to get a table outside like we'd hoped. It's a great day for dining al fresco. The trellised patio offers plenty of shade. A lanky man with purple skin and long white hair plays guitar in the large outdoor dining area. We're waiting to order food when the musician begins to whistle a melody while he plays. Suddenly, my vision narrows, and I'm surrounded by that familiar discordant tune from my nightmare, the sound of the wind blowing through the woods. I look up to see a spectral pair of glowing yellow eyes staring at me from a shadowy face. I know I've seen them before. So many times now. I'm shaken from the vision. Actually shaken. Ben's hand on my shoulder snaps me out of my trance.

"Cara, you were frozen for a minute," Ben worries over me. "Are you feeling alright?"

"I... don't know. I experienced something like déjà vu. But I'm not sure if I just imagined it or not," I confess, weirded out. The musician's song sounds nothing like the melody I just heard. And there is no yellow-eyed shadow man now. There probably never was.

I look at Ben, still perplexed. His brow knits, observing my reaction, and he pushes, "Imagined? Fire and ashes, did you see something?"

"Yellow eyes. And I heard a song, not this one. But I've heard it a few times now... I think," I say, struggling to recollect the details.

His eyes go wide in shock, and then understanding dawns as he mutters, "It's no accident Mark knows where you are. Something may have followed you here."

The rest of our lunch is quieter than usual. I'm not feeling very talkative after finding out this recurring presence in my dreams I'm only starting to piece together could be something sinister. None of it feels real, which makes me hope that Ben is overreacting. He asks me to tell him everything I can remember. Somehow, I forgot most of it until just now. The music must have conjured a memory.

Ben's uneasy gaze meets mine. He takes my hand, bringing it to his mouth for a slow, comforting kiss. "I don't want to alarm you, but there are ill-natured magickal entities in the world we call Malefic Folk. None that live here. Our ward protects us from humans as well as their kind. They are not allowed here under any circumstances. The fae are mayhap the most dangerous. They're more spirit than corporeal, and it seems to have corrupted them—they have no morals or honor. Their magick allows them to manipulate the veil in ways that most magickal Whispered Folk cannot, making them especially powerful in dark ways. I worry that one has set its sight on you," he reveals.

"What should I do?" I fret. This has escalated far beyond what I believed possible.

"I don't want to pressure you, but mayhap I should stay overnight with you for now to make sure nothing happens. You're vulnerable in your sleep if it's accessing your dreams. It probably can't harm you in them, but I'm not sure. I need to talk to the coven about this. They will know more about the capabilities of the fae. Spending these nights together will just be sleep if you wish it. I am not going to take advantage of the situation. I want you, Cara, so much. But not under duress," he stresses in genuine concern.

Ben and I have already jumped into bed, but it's true this would rush our relationship, applying extra pressure to our blossoming relationship. But it doesn't sound like he's exaggerating. It's written plain on his face he isn't taking it lightly.

"Alright, we should do that. Thank you for offering," I agree, feeling a modicum of security that he will be watching over me.

"Cara, thank you for putting your trust in me. It is not misplaced," he replies, sounding unquestionably relieved.

He calls Clancy and fills him in. Clancy asks that I update him and Ben on any new dreams or sightings I have. His phone begins buzzing the moment he hangs up. He shows me the messages, and I help him respond to questions about the dreams and the potential sighting out my window. I hadn't connected the dots at all. But Ben's right that it can't be a coincidence.

For the rest of the day, Ben touches me one way or another. Holding my hand or a simple touch on my arm or lower back. It's probably a comfort to him as much as it is to me. He helps me pack a bag to bring over to his place for the night. Though he offers to trade-off between nights if it makes me more comfortable, I agree to stay the weekend at his house.

We spend a relaxing evening watching a movie and cuddling on the couch. I'm exhausted after being so stressed out about an evil entity infiltrating my dreams. It makes me scared to fall asleep that night.

When I tell Ben about my fear as we climb under the covers, he tries to soothe me, "I'll be right next to you, my belle. If I notice you're having a nightmare, I'll wake you up. But the fae won't be able to hurt you in my bed."

At some point during the night, I dream about Mark. We're at Hansen Company. I have my own office, a hugely welcome change from the cubicle I occupied for so many years. I'm working at my computer when Mark knocks on the open door. Looking up, I beckon him inside. He shuts the door behind him, closing the blinds on the strip of window next to the doorframe.

"What can I do for you, Mark?" I ask, unsure which project he'd need an update on.

"You know what I want," he leers, his eyes now bright yellow orbs. He unbuckles his belt and unzips his pants. The gold wedding band on his finger glints in the lamplight from my desk.

"This is wrong, Mark. We can't," I answer in shock, an icy streak shooting down my spine.

"You really don't think I gave you this office for any other reason, do you, Cara? I know you're not that naïve." He smirks.

Paralyzed with fear, I can't move... until I feel myself falling. Falling into nothing, traveling further away from those haunting yellow eyes, growing smaller in the distance but never blinking out.

I would have fallen forever, but I'm awoken by the buzz of a message on my phone on the nightstand. "Cara, you're making a huge mistake ignoring me. I can make your life easy or hard, your choice."

Ben's still asleep when I turn over in bed and look at him, his stern features smoothed over and relaxed. I'm so grateful for him at that moment that I can't stop tears from falling down my cheeks. As if sensing my mood, he reaches out to me in his sleep, tucking me closer to him. The ache in my chest dulls, and I fall into dreamless sleep.

♡　♡　♡　♡　♡

Clancy comes over to Ben's house the next evening to play card games and listen to records, claiming he's so bored because everyone's busy getting ready for Samhain later next week. Personally, I think he misses Ben and wants to spend time with us as a couple. He's over the moon now that we've gotten together after the initial hiccup.

Perusing Ben's small record collection, it's mostly soul and blues, with some New Orleans jazz and more recent rock albums mixed in. I pull out a few to place next to the record player to play tonight. I ask Ben where he got them, and he tells me he purchased them from the record store in town... run by a vampire.

"He's an interesting male, very knowledgeable about music. He spent a lot of time in Chicago. You'd probably have a lot to talk about!" Clancy enthuses.

"He's a vampire?" I gulp, realizing this is who goes bump in the night, and I'm going to have to rethink going outside after dark.

"He is. I see that look in your eyes. Don't fear him. He only takes from willing hosts or the blood bank. Ben, you should take her there to pick out a few new records," Clancy tries to reassure me. I blink up at him and drop the subject. It's too weird for me right now.

Spending more time talking than playing our game, Clancy broaches the subject of the fae in my dreams. I've already told them about the latest dream and text message. "The coven says it can't physically hurt you unless it's near you. But that's the frightening thing about fae. They can wield their magick from afar, unlike most other magickal Whispered Folk. Fae are chaotic evil incarnate with power to match. They dreamwalk, entering your mind while you sleep, learning about you, manipulating you. It's probably why you had that dream about Mark," he adds regretfully. "It had to have been disturbing."

"Is there anything I can do to stop it?" I fret, feeling violated this thing is trying to learn things about me in my dreams. Ben senses my distress and takes my hand.

"No, but the coven is constantly checking the wards, reinforcing them so the fae can't enter without them knowing. They're also tracking whose travel amulets are passing through the wards. Unfortunately, Samhain preparations have limited their time to do more research for us. The warlocks' harassment, Mark's messages, and this fae interference, it's all so much Cara. I wonder if I should have brought you here," Clancy says remorsefully.

Ben snarls low and meaningful, "She would have to deal with Mark and the fae regardless of whether she was here. But now we can watch over her. Samuels and his cronies can be dealt with. Mark and the fae are the bigger problem."

Clancy nods. "You're right. It is just hard to make sense of the fae. Is Mark sending them after Cara? The cost of doing business with a fae is higher than most are willing to pay. Samuels could possibly have something the fae wants. But he's here, already able to spin Cara's arrival and these random crimes as a public 'I told you so' thrown in my face. A human like Mark would have very little to offer and shouldn't even know about their existence. Still, we can't rule anything out."

"Both Mark and the warlocks want me to leave here, and their threats are getting worse. I don't know what to think anymore," I remark, feeling defeated.

"We'll figure it out, Cara. Once Samhain is over, the coven will have more time for it. There are still many resources at their disposal. They won't rest until it's solved," Clancy insists confidently.

Ben's phone rings at that moment, causing all of us to jump in our seats. We burst out laughing, needing to cut through the intensity of the moment. Ben reaches for his phone, showing us it's Lucas, his brother. Clancy gestures he should pick up.

"Ben! Where've you been, big brother? You missed our weekly call, and I thought maybe you flew too close to the sun. Or perhaps a certain human female hasn't left your bed." Lucas chuckles. We can all hear the baritone of his voice from the phone at Ben's ear.

Ben rolls his eyes, setting the phone on the table and turning on the speaker. "Lucas, little brother. That human female is right here next to me, as is Clancy." He snorts.

"Well, you could have told me. What am I to think when all I get are some vague excuses that you're too busy for me. Hello Clancy. Hello Cara. I'm sorry, my big brother will only pick up his phone when he's with company. Clancy, I'm glad your meddling worked. Ben deserves a good female by his side," Lucas teases. I blush that Lucas knows who I am. I guess they've talked about me.

"Well, good to hear your voice, Lucas. It's been too long. I take full credit for these two getting together." Clancy snickers as Ben sends him a withering look. "Though Ben is not lying when he says things have been *livelier* than usual around here. But we can talk about that another time. How's New York treating you these days?"

Lucas talks about his job at an architectural firm. Much of it sounds familiar to me. He's enrolled in continuing education courses and learning new design software tools, some of which I've used in the past. It's clear he's taking advantage of all the training opportunities he can. Makes sense if his time there is limited.

"Ben could use a partner at the office. He'd love more time to pour cement and frame outbuildings again. Whatever it is that builders do." Clancy laughs. Ben just looks thoughtful about it.

"Ben can have all the fun he wants with that. I'll keep his seat warm at the office." Lucas laughs.

"Oh, is that you telling us you're coming back soon?" Clancy pesters.

"Not quite yet, I'm still a young male in his prime in a city full of beautiful females. Besides, I probably have the best commute of any New Yorker. Nothing beats soaring between the skyscrapers while the city below is stuck in traffic," he muses.

♡ ♡ ♡ ♡ ♡

At the office the next day, Monday, Clancy goes into full mother hen mode, checking on me constantly and asking his assistant Madge to do the same. Between them, I barely have any time to get work done. Clancy and Ben decide to alternate taking me to lunch throughout the week, since Ben is so busy getting the Howling Road project off the ground. It feels like being babysat, but I'm touched by their care, so I don't complain.

Naturally, I can't have a peaceful morning. During one of the few moments I have to myself, drinking my morning coffee, my phone buzzes on my desk. Picking it up, that same unknown number shows up, which sinks my stomach the moment I see it.

"There's so much I'll give you when you come back. An office. A raise. A promotion. You won't even have to beg for it anymore."

"Son of a bitch," I grumble, unsure if I'm directing it to the situation, to him, probably both. I screenshot the message and send it off, as usual. It sparks the memory of that gross dream I had the other night, one I'd much rather forget.

Clancy's at my door almost immediately, checking on me. A dark look passes over his face.

"He's still at it, I see. Are you alright? Do you need anything?" he solicits.

"I'm fine. Just annoyed." I try to shrug it off.

"Well, let's get out of the office soon. I have an idea for lunch." He grins.

It's a particularly beautiful day, so Clancy suggests we take our lunch to a nearby park to eat. I sit at a bench as he stands, looming over me with his large horse body. I'm used to it now, though I don't love having to crane my neck to look at him.

He grins cheekily. "Can I sit, or do you want to keep using me as a sunshade?"

I chuckle around my bite of food. "I don't care. You should do whatever's comfortable. I'm just minding my own business down here eating my lunch."

He guffaws as he bends his back legs underneath him, followed by his front legs. He's still tall. Even in this position, his human torso is higher up than mine, but it's much easier to converse with him now.

"The things I do for you. You've reduced your boss, the *mayor*, to being a receptacle of leaves and dirt without my groom broom handy to wipe it off. The indignity of it," he teases.

"Groom broom!" I cry out in hysterics.

"You have no idea the lengths I go to in keeping up this handsome coat," he gripes overdramatically.

"I'm sure you love every second of it, knowing how many compliments you get," I tease.

He loudly harrumphs, though it comes out more like a horsey whinny, which sends me into a fit of giggles again. We take a few more bites of lunch before he asks about Ben, which I know he's been dying to do since we got together.

"How is it going, playing house with Ben? I suspect you didn't think you'd have a live-in boy toy so quickly after moving here," he asks point blank, golden eyebrow arched inquisitively.

It cracks me up, the thought of Ben, who so earnestly wears his heart on his sleeve, as a boy toy. "Ben likes looking after me. I'm still getting used to it. I haven't lived with someone since I had a roommate in grad school, and that was obviously a very different experience. I've certainly never lived with a boyfriend before. It's good, easier than I thought it would be. But we haven't truly moved in together, we're just staying the night with each other, so I guess I haven't thought about it too much," I consider.

"That's Ben for you. Yes, gargoyles are known for their protective streak, but Ben takes care of those he loves most. And that's most certainly you, Cara," he confides without artifice.

"He does care a lot about me. I feel the same," I admit.

"Are you calling him your boyfriend? Such a cute human concept," Clancy remarks, a smile in his voice.

"I guess he is my boyfriend," I reflect, mulling over the implications.

That conversation sticks with me throughout the week as our sleep-overs have continued. His hunger for me shows no sign of waning. Our sexual chemistry is off the charts, though since he's been watching over me, he acts more tender and reverent toward me. Everything about him feels right.

Still weighing Clancy's words a couple nights later, I find the courage to ask, "Ben, what are we?"

Ben looks amused, a patient smile on his face as we lay together in my bed. He responds, "What would you like us to be?" I wish he would tell me what he thinks we are, but he already insisted he isn't going to pressure me for anything.

"I think you're my boyfriend," I decide.

"Then I'm your boyfriend," he confirms with a kiss.

"Are you sure that's what you want? I know that's not customary here," I question, feeling like I'm forcing him into a role he might disagree with. Whispered Folk go from zero to sixty in their love life, it seems, from casual dating to mates with nothing in between.

He slides me closer to him so that I'm soaking in the warmth of his broad body. His expression is unguarded as we look at each other. "I don't care about what's customary. And neither should you. It's not up to others' standards to decide how we should be together. This is it for me, Cara. I love you with my entire being, and that will never change. We can label it any way you want to," he declares, his midnight-colored eyes searching mine.

My breath is frozen in my chest. He *loves* me? Deep down, I already knew, but hearing the words out loud makes it undeniably real. I'm too shocked to speak, so I try to express my feelings through my touch rather than my words. I skim my hands over his chest to his face, running them along his horns and down the back of his neck to the base of his wings. I want to touch him everywhere, but first, I need to feel him inside of me.

Nudging him onto his back, I climb over him, straddling his sturdy hips. I take his rapidly swelling cock in my hand, pumping it a few times until pre-come oozes out of his slit, lubricating it. I rub it along my spread-open pussy, using it to stimulate my clit. He's leaking so much pre-come it's already dripping down to coat my opening. I can't wait any longer to put him inside me. I position myself over him and sink down slowly. It feels like I'm clenching tighter each time I rock on top of him until it's a squeeze to get him all the way inside of me. He breathes my name on his lips when I'm filled completely and he bumps my cervix.

We both groan as I bounce on his lap, placing my hands on his abdomen for leverage. The tug of his cock in and out of my pussy creates a pleasurable heat that spreads throughout my body. Ben's jaw is slack, his sharp teeth on display, as his eyes dart between my blissed-out face and the jiggle of my breasts and soft stomach with the motion. I raise myself until just the tip of his cock remains inside me and then bottom out again, pressing him as deep inside me as he can go. Rocking and bouncing on him, I keep his fat cock inside me where it belongs.

My desire for him is coiled so tightly that my orgasm is already close. Ben uses his fingertip to draw circles around my clit, releasing the pressure in my core created by the slide of his thick cock. I wail his name as his hips cant upward. His cock jolts and flexes inside me, flooding my channel with his release, prolonging my orgasm. He growls seductively, flipping me onto my back and driving his still hard cock into me until we're too exhausted to continue.

♡　♡　♡　♡　♡

The next morning, Ben reminds me it's Samhain and he'll pick me up from work in the afternoon. Samhain is a much bigger deal than I thought. Town hall feels like a party atmosphere when I arrive. The morning is more socializing than work. It's fun to have an excuse to get out of my small corner of the building. Someone set up a table with food like apple tarts and pumpkin bread, which pairs very nicely with my coffee.

By lunchtime, town hall is a ghost town, just a few of us left in our offices. Luckily, Ben texts he's on his way and that he has a pre-festival date planned for us. Waving goodbye to Clancy, I notice Ada is sitting there too, looking just slightly less perfectly coiffed than normal—the only indication she's likely stressed out. I tell them Ben and I will see them later at the festival. They both call out their goodbyes, but immediately jump back into whatever they're discussing as I walk away.

Ben brings me back to his house, and I can't hide how excited I am about our date. I change out of my work clothes into a flowy linen-blend maxi dress. He's in his kitchen warming up food when I come downstairs. The whole house smells like autumn. "What is that?" I ask, sidling up beside him to sneak a peek.

"Spiced parsnip, potato, and apple soup for Samhain. There's also rosemary-roasted chicken and a loaf of fresh bread with butter. We can sip on apple brandy as well. Let's have a picnic in the front yard and watch the jasmine grow. The plant growth solution may work even better than usual today," he suggests enthusiastically.

"I was hoping you would use it soon! Such a good idea to wait until today." I beam.

We head outside and with our picnic spread out and ready to eat, Ben takes the glass bottle of solution and pours a bit onto each young seedling we transplanted. He stoppers the bottle and sets it aside. He joins me on the blanket as we dig into our food. At first, nothing happens. I look over at Ben and he seems unconcerned.

Smiling at me, he explains, "It'll begin in the roots first. We just can't see it yet."

Soon enough, the vines spring to life, reaching for the wrought-iron railing around his front porch. They twist and curl their way around the decorative ironwork. The end result looks like it's taken years to grow. His home seems even more charming this way, the green vines adding warmth to the austere colors of the stone and wrought iron.

"It's not done yet, my belle. This is why I waited until today," Ben reveals right as the finale begins. Even though they're out of season, flowers bud and bloom into little white stars, wafting us with the sweet, delicate scent of jasmine. We bask in it for the rest of the afternoon from our spot on the blanket.

By nightfall, the light of the giant Samhain bonfire can be seen all the way from Ben's house, shining like a beacon. Casting an orange glow across the darkened sky, it signals the start of the festival. We walk toward it, and the closer we get, the higher it seems to rise. The flame licks upward, dancing in the sky. The occasional shower of sparks rains down on townspeople milling around. Several witches chant and sing, probably a continuation of their ritual earlier, their voices nearly drowned out by the bonfire's roar.

We walk around the lines of booths, where merchandise and trinkets are being sold, much of it magickal. There are so many tables set up with games and crafts for anyone's participation. It's nearly too much to take in. We continue onto a turnip lantern carving station. Ben and I request one, and the volunteer hands us the tools we need to core and carve it.

"This reminds me of a jack-o-lantern!" I exclaim happily as we get to work coring out the inside and then designing the face. Since even a giant turnip is nowhere near as big as a pumpkin, the face we come up with is simple.

"This is the best part," Ben mentions as he sets the turnip in a twine holder. The volunteer returns to us, and with a few words, a light glows to life inside the turnip and its face smiles and blinks at us.

"Oh my god!" I screech in shock.

Ben laughs heartily at my reaction. "It's just magick, it's not alive! Would you like to hold our lantern, or should I?" he croaks while still shaking in laughter.

"You can," I squeak, still a little freaked out.

Ben leads me over to a handwashing station that looks like a flowing fountain. "Hold your hands in the water. They'll be completely clean and dry when you remove them," Ben instructs. I do so, and he's right. They feel so clean.

"Should we get some dinner?" I suggest.

"Yes, the food options are always so good," he remarks enthusiastically.

We both end up choosing a smoked pulled pork plate with fried potatoes and stewed apples, washing it down with cold apple cider. We walk past a candied apple vendor, and immediately, I gravitate toward it to buy one for later. I guess I have simple tastes at heart if I want one of these more than any of the jewelry or baubles we looked at earlier. Ben insists on paying for whatever I want, which is a very loving gesture.

Moving on, I pull him to a table to make offerings to the dead. "Is it appropriate for me to make one for my grandparents?" I ask him, unsure of the context of the offerings.

"I believe so. You can write a message to them in the afterlife. It is more likely they'll receive it tonight because of how thin the veil is between our worlds," he explains.

The volunteer comes over to us and asks what we'd like to leave for the dead, mentioning it can be a simple message or an item like a trinket or coin—anything that can fit inside an apple.

Both Ben and I decide on messages to our grandparents. We each take our small slip of paper and consider our words. I keep mine simple, writing, *I love you, Grandma and Grandpa. I miss you every day. Life hasn't been the same without you, but I found a place where I think I'll find happiness. I wanted you to know in case you worry about me. Until we meet again. Love, Cara.*

Ben doesn't try to read mine, and I appreciate the privacy. As instructed, we each tightly roll up our message and slide into a narrow hole already carved into an apple. We speak the names of our grandparents to our apples and hand them over to the volunteer. The volunteer speaks something else I can't hear to each apple and tosses them into a magickal purple flame behind him. The apples evaporate on contact, leaving only a small puff of smoke.

I'm dazed as we walk away, the possibility my grandparents may receive that message weighing on my heart. Ben pulls me away from the crowd, looking at me with concern.

"What's wrong, my belle? Are you upset?"

"Not exactly. I just can't believe I sent a message to my grandparents that might get to them, wherever they are. They've been dead for years, Ben. It's unreal that this is even possible. I've wished I could talk to them, do something like this for so long. The fact that it may have just happened is overwhelming," I cry in a mess of emotions.

He wraps his arms around me, and we stand there for a long while, holding each other. "Do you want to watch some of the magick shows? It may help you feel better," he whispers softly into my ear.

"Take me to the *magickal delights*, Ben," I answer, sniffling, recalling the posters around town.

We walk past the bonfire again, as grand and imposing as it was earlier. Our turnip lantern lights up the dark street as we head away from it. We turn a corner, and we're met with the glow of bright swirling lights in every color of the rainbow, accompanied by a low beat of live music played by a group of Whispered Folk musicians. Children dance and play together, the lights swirling around and between them, even forming figures that are moving along to the music with them. The more the kids dance, the brighter and faster the lights become. Some of the parents and adults join in, having as much fun as they are. We edge closer to the dance floor, and the lights start to swirl around us—green, pink, blue, yellow. We sway to the music, mesmerized by each other and the light show looping around us. Giggling as one of the dancing forms tries to cut in to dance with me, we decide to move on to the next show.

We don't get far when Clancy trots toward us, waving for our attention. "Ben, Cara, so glad I found you. I don't know what's gotten into people tonight, but windows were smashed all along Magnolia Street, including at your office. The head constable wants you to check if anything was taken," he informs us, looking dismayed.

"Of course, we'll head over right now to look." Ben sighs, looking at me regretfully.

"Oh Ben, I'm so sorry this happened," I lament, but he waves it away.

"No, I'm sorry to cut short this night with you," he apologizes.

We walk with Clancy toward his office. Shattered glass is every-where, shards scattered inside the vandalized businesses and all the way down the street. It's truly a mess.

Ada finds us. "What a rotten thing to happen tonight, right when everyone was so busy at the festival," she decries. "Why don't I take you home while they deal with this, Cara. I parked my automobile just a couple blocks over."

I hesitate, unsure what to do, but Ben agrees, "That's a good idea. I'll come over when I'm done here, if that's alright?"

"Of course, I hope the damage isn't too bad," I console, sad that his night has been ruined. Ada and I walk to her Wagoneer, both of us stressed and quiet.

Ada finally breaks the silence. "What did you think of the festival? Is it anything like you imagined?"

"It was unbelievable. I've never experienced anything like it. I can't wait for next year's," I answer honestly.

When we arrive at Ada's, she stays in the car as she drops me off. "I'm going to head back for now to make sure everything is under control, but I'll be home in a couple hours. Text me if you need anything!"

Exhaustion hits me hard when I step inside my carriage house. It's later than I usually stay up. Plus, I've been sleeping so poorly lately, worried about the recurring nightmares. They're still hard to recall once I'm awake, but they seem more frequent, more invasive the last few days. Those yellow eyes are seared into my brain, though, like a bogeyman always watching. I should probably stay up and wait for Ben, but I have no idea how long he'll be dealing with the vandalism at his office. He'll come over when he's done, so I leave the door unlocked for him. Getting into bed feels like such relief. I'll fall asleep in no time.

The nightmare finds me again like I feared, but now it feels real for a change, like a waking dream, and I know I'll remember every moment of it afterward. I'm trapped in the dark, and the only thing I can perceive is that damn whistling. There's no light, no sense of body or place. I'm part of the darkness itself and all that exists is this malevolent, creepy tune. It goes on and on, lulling me further away from myself, the essence of me. It's my entire world now and nothing can penetrate it or make it stop. It will continue until the end of time.

I wake up in a sweaty panic to a man's face above me. I shriek in terror, shocked not only by his presence, but also his unnatural appearance. It's so wrong-looking. His skin is stretched too thin and torn in some places and falls too loose and wrinkled in others. It's like the skull beneath it is misshapen and broken. Still, something about him looks familiar... and it dawns on me—this is Mark's face. Like I've never seen it before. This thing... is wearing Mark's face. Solid, glowing yellow eyes peer down at me from his face, shining brightly in the otherwise dark room. Their depths are like a whirlpool, constantly moving and swirling, simultaneously hypnotizing and repulsive, fueled by pure evil. This is Mark, but it's not him. This is something far worse.

Not-Mark's smile opens into a disturbingly wide grin full of cracked teeth, lips pulled too tight over his gums. It's a horrific caricature of the man I once loved. He's lying on top of me, his face inches from mine, pinning me down with his hands and body. I can feel his nails digging into my wrists where he holds them. His cruel expression doesn't waver as I struggle to move, still screaming, but he's too strong for me. I can't get leverage while my body is prone beneath him. He stares at me in disgusting amusement as I struggle and cry out for help. I'm no match for him, and he leisurely lets out a haunting, mocking cackle at my failing attempt to get away. A long, dark, inhuman tongue uncurls lasciviously from his mouth, and he starts exploring my face and neck with its abrasive and gummy texture while I wear myself out, struggling with all of my strength, growing tired and defeated. The tongue feels like the flat edge of a knife, the promise of violence close and very real.

"Hello, my little bird. Are you surprised to finally see me? Do you like this new body? I wore it just for you. Thought maybe it would bring you comfort in your final moments," he taunts, laughing uproariously at my fear and disgust.

"Help! Ben! Ada! Help!" I scream at the top of my lungs while I push against him as hard as I can.

"You're all alone, little bird. No one is coming. You loved to fly away, so this body asked me to be your bird catcher. I've been watching you since you got here, but I couldn't help but make myself known to you while I was nearby, biding my time and waiting for the perfect moment to make a move. You've been so much fun to play with." He sounds like a stalker, his tone laced with malevolence and obsession.

"Who are you? Why are you here?" I spit out at him as I crack my knees into him to no effect.

"No one you know, dear little bird, but you seem to know my face, yes? You made some people very upset. It looks like you've been causing all sorts of trouble in both the human and the magickal worlds, now haven't you? Hmm, such a feisty one to cause so much trouble every-where she goes. I can see why. You almost look lovely enough to eat, though unlucky for you, I don't fuck humans. Just kill them, sorry to say," the terrifying stranger jeers, and I shriek as loud as I can and grapple against his hold again with renewed energy.

"Keep fighting, little bird. Your suffering is like an aphrodisiac. This body has had you. I can feel it. It still wanted you when I took it. Who knows what all he had planned for you? But he was never going to get very far. I was made a much better offer by a vindictive little warlock to make your exit from here a little more... permanent. So much chaos. I love to be in the middle of it. And I can't wait to cause so much more once you're gone. It'll be so fun to get rid of you just like I did this human I'm wearing. His end was so swift that I think I'm going to draw yours out a little. I'll enjoy it even more," he mocks.

"You killed Mark?" I screech, horrified at the thought, and yet the evidence is in front of me.

He giggles gleefully. "Oh yes, he was paying so much money to track you down, but then you flew away to build a new nest where no human will ever find you. That's when I got involved. I can find anyone in their dreams. He was so impatient, kept pestering me about your location. So I told him but didn't mention he wouldn't be able to get in. Oh, that drove him wild. I delighted in killing him when he became too demand-ing. He wanted to come back here to seduce you away, you know, by force if necessary. The desires and whims of humans are so pitiful. He thought he had control over me, holding human money over my head like it meant anything to me. He didn't even realize the deal he made with me wasn't for money. I took great pleasure in showing him just how little he and his money matter. He was a gnat buzzing in my ear, and I ended him just as easily."

I can't let this abomination kill me. I can't die now that I've just found myself again. When I've found Ben who loves me, and I love him just as much. He erupts in that bizarre laughter again and rubs that disgusting oversized tongue up and down my cheek over the tracks of my tears.

He finally pulls his tongue away and hisses into my ear, "Your fear tastes so delicious."

I scream even louder and try to headbutt him. He easily evades me and lazily drawls, "All your chirping and squawking won't help, little bird. No one can hear your last moments but me. And it's music to my ears."

He sneers down at me, giving me one last lick as he says, "Now be a good girl and stay here while the world around you burns, won't you, my naughty little bird?"

He chants, breathy and ragged, in a language I've never heard before as he moves off me. I'm clamped down to the bed the moment he does before I can get away. He calmly whistles that familiar trill, the disturbing tune that's haunted my dreams for weeks, the sound slowly fading as he disappears down the hall and out the door. I try to sit up, but I'm completely stuck. It feels like dozens of hands have pinned me down everywhere, including my head and face. The harder I push against them, the more searing pain shoots through my body, like claws gripping me and ripping into my flesh. The sting doesn't fade, and I feel warmth trickle down my skin, so whatever is holding me here is real enough to hurt me, not an illusion. The only thing I can move freely is my eyes, but I can't even move my head to get a look at what holds me down.

There's smoke somewhere nearby, the smell getting stronger by the second. Is the carriage house on fire? Am I going to burn alive? I struggle even though it hurts, but I can't move these things gripping me at all. I'm just tearing my skin. I'd be willing to cut myself to ribbons to get out of here, but I'm pushing and pulling with all my strength and getting nowhere, just growing so tired by the effort and the pain. I scream and shriek for help. I don't want to die, because if I do, I have a feeling I'll be stuck in that nightmare forever.

CHAPTER 17

BEN

The bashed-in windows along the street are perplexing. Nothing in my office was stolen or even touched. I suspect that's true for the rest of the street. The constabulary doesn't know who did it, but they are already questioning the other business owners in case they have any leads as well as following up on some likely suspects. Unfortunately, there are known mischief-makers who may have taken it too far this time. Clancy and Ada are trying to get in touch with everyone else affected by the vandalism, but it's been difficult because nearly everyone is at the festival.

Rejoining Clancy on the street, I let him know that there's no damage beyond the broken glass. Our grim expressions match. This all seems so senseless. "Something is rotten in the state of Denmark." Clancy snorts.

"This is extreme, even for our more devilry-minded brethren," I observe. "Like it's designed to take our attention away from Samhain, taint the festival somehow."

Clancy agrees. "You're right. So many of us are here, like we've been lured away." It dawns on both of us—much of the town is left to fend for itself... including Cara.

"Fire burn it to ashes! How could we have been so blind? Call Ada.

Tell her to meet me at her house. I'm flying over there now. I'm not wasting another minute," I declare as I take off in flight.

Before I'm out of earshot, Clancy bellows out to me frantically, "Ada's already on her way. Her wards were set off a few moments ago."

I circle overhead, flying silently in the dark sky, high enough I'd be difficult to see from the ground. The nearer I soar to it, something feels off in the area around Cara's apartment. The carriage house is covered by the same wards and spells that protect the rest of Ada's property, but there's something different, out of place. I'm only a little attuned to magick, so if I feel it, it must be extremely potent. Landing in the driveway, both the main house and the carriage house look fine, but that's when I smell it. There's smoke somewhere, like a distant campfire. Right as I begin to explore around the grounds, Ada's automobile rips down the road, screeching into the driveway.

Leaving the headlights on, she jumps out and screams, "Something's still here! Check on Cara!"

Running to the carriage house, I smack into a hard barrier, right in the face, giving me a bloody nose and probably worse. I fly overhead, but it's no use getting through. It's like a bubble around the entire building that I'm able to land, jump, and scratch on, but to no effect. As I investigate, a ghostly chorus of voices echoes through the night. Startled, I fly toward Ada behind the carriage house, where she faces off against a dark figure whose bright yellow eyes match Cara's description. A human body lies nearby, a male. Relief courses through me that it isn't Cara. As Ada dodges and blocks spells slung by the fae, a trail of at least a dozen spirits follows her, stretching and compressing like an accordion. Their hollow voices sing and shriek out their own spells and incantations, lending their magick to Ada's fight. As she runs forward, I'm able to see these spirits in better definition. Right behind her are her parents. I'd recognize them anywhere, even though it's been years since their deaths.

I don't want her to lose concentration, but she needs to know about the carriage house. Whatever is going on beneath that spell may be gruesome and deadly. There's no time to lose if Cara stands a chance.

"There's a barrier around the carriage house! Help me get past it!" I call out, gaining the attention of some of the spirits.

Their ghastly, unearthly cries repulse me, even though I know they're on our side, casting spells to remove the barrier. The realm of the dead isn't meant to be seen or heard so openly by the living, and this phantasmic display proves it. Samhain has turned the veil on its head, though. Mayhap it's the only reason we have a fighting chance to save Cara and subdue the fae.

The carriage house remains quiet and unchanged for far too long. I'm losing hope that I'll find Cara alive with each passing second. But then, suddenly, the smell of smoke intensifies until it nearly chokes me, and to my terror, the calm view of the house dissolves to show flames spreading rapidly across the front of the building. I fly through the nearest window, glass shattering around me, catching on my wings and arms.

"Cara! Cara, where are you?" I yell repeatedly as I duck around flames that are beginning to spread through the building. I don't see her in the living area, so I make my way back to her bedroom, looking in every spot she could possibly be. I hear noise, but it's hard to tell with the sound of the fire blazing at my back. I check the couch, where it's beginning to smolder as the room around it is turning into a fiery furnace. She isn't there or around the dining table. I move back toward her bedroom area. The fire hasn't reached there yet, but it's moving fast.

Finally, I hear her whimper as I reach her bedroom doorway. She's lying prostrate on the bed, and I want to run to get her out of here as fast as I can, but I need to understand what I'm dealing with. The scene before me becomes more horrifying the closer I get. Some foul magick has been cast here. The air is concentrated with it, sticky and uncomfortable like walking through spider webs, the closer I get to Cara's bed.

Beastly hands with claws even deadlier than mine have sprung from some hellish realm through her bed to hold her down. They're clutching every part of her body—arms, legs, torso, and even her beautiful face, where her eyes bug out at me in sheer terror, confirming she's still alive. The tips of the claws have already dug deep, gouging her skin. Many of the slashes are bleeding profusely from her fight to get loose.

She cries and screams a muffled "Ben! Help me!" from underneath a hand pressed tightly across her mouth and chin, holding down her head, blood oozing down her cheek where the clawed hand ripped into her delicate skin.

I snarl out my rage that anyone would dare injure her. This image of her in so much pain and terror will haunt me for the rest of my days. Though my ancestors were vicious fighters accustomed to gore and bloodshed, I am not. I use that gargoyle cunning and strength to create and construct. I've never seen this kind of violence before or dealt with it in such a visceral way. The malignant scene sickens me, but there's a primal instinct that still dwells within me, giving me the nerve to do what I must, to use those gifts to save my mate.

The hands are grotesque fleshy manifestations that I'll have to wrench away from her. Luckily, they don't seem to do much else than grip around her, though with monstrous, magickally-enforced strength. With all my might, I grab a bloody finger from the hand on her face and pull it backward with a nauseating crunch that I can both hear and feel. It's bent at an unnatural angle, clearly broken, and luckily stays that way. There's no telling what this profane magick will do—if it will heal itself or even try to grab onto me along with her if I get too close. I wish she didn't have to hear this cracking and snapping of bone and sinew that goes on endlessly as I remove each hand from her, but there's nothing I can do but free her as fast as possible. Cara whimpers at each sound, no doubt scaring and disgusting her further, even if it's a relief to be free of them.

As I lever back the wrist on the hand that was covering her face, she starts sobbing, "Ben, how did you know? How did you find me? There was a man in my room with yellow eyes. It was Mark! But it wasn't! He did this to me. He's trying to kill me. It was him whistling at me all this time. He was toying with me. Oh my god, Ben, I thought I was going to die."

"I'm getting you out of here, my belle. Try to stay still for me," I say as I quickly press my lips to her mouth, to her forehead, some of the only places on her body not streaked with blood. It is as much a comfort to me as it is to her. And then I get back to work with renewed determination.

I try my best to pull each hand away without raking the claws even further against her marred skin. She cries out every time I fail, a new red line blooming across her pale skin. Each gash I cause is another bone-deep scar on my soul. But I need to work faster. The smoke is getting worse. It's harder to breathe by the minute, and there's already a haze in the room thick enough to make it tough for me to see as I move across her body to free her. She would never have been able to break free on her own. And most Whispered Folk wouldn't be able to help her either. My strength barely matches this abomination's. I can only snap one or two fingers at a time using all my brawn and with significant effort each time. I barely got to her in time to have any chance to free her. And I know in my soul I wouldn't leave here even if I had been too late. If I couldn't free her in time, I'd have stayed by her side until the very end, the fire taking us both, because I know without a doubt I can't live without her.

Cara starts to cough uncontrollably, wheezing through each breath. Time is running out. The fire rushes toward us in the hallway. I can hear its roar growing dangerously close. I messily pull away the rest of the hands from the last leg, her flesh torn by some of the hands there isn't time to fully free her from. We have to go right now or we'll both succumb to smoke inhalation. She screams as I pull her off the bed, her body limp and bleeding. She's barely clinging to consciousness, and I worry she's losing too much blood.

I kick a foot through the bedroom window, pushing out the biggest glass shards to the ground below. My foot is injured and bleeding, but I don't feel it. Safely cradled in my arms, I tuck Cara into me and push through the window, jagged edges scratching at my arms and shoulders as I squeeze through. We take flight, and I look behind me one last time, thick dark smoke billowing in our wake. Ada and her spirit protectors continue their onslaught against the fae. They're too focused on the fight to even notice as I fly Cara as far from the scene as I can. Coven members drive and run through the property, no doubt Clancy having sounded the alarm. Some are using their magick to douse the flames in the carriage house. But most are running to Ada's defense.

I want to kiss Cara's beautiful face so badly, but I don't dare do anything to slow my flight to the healers' clinic. Her injuries seem life-threatening. The healers need to see her immediately lest she bleeds out from these deep wounds. Mother Earth in all her glory, I was close to losing her. I still am, she isn't out of the woods yet. I'm covered in both of our red, slippery blood. Sharp pain threads through my body as my adrenaline wanes, letting me know the extent to which I'm also injured. But I hold onto her even tighter and fly faster than I ever have before. The Samhain bonfire still burns, lighting my path to the town center. I descend too quickly in front of the clinic, skinning my damaged feet along the sidewalk to stop myself.

Bursting through the door, I yell for help as our healers scramble to put her on a gurney and take her into the surgery. A nurse insists on looking over my wounds, but I refuse until Cara is stabilized. My entire body is throbbing. I can feel more blood seep out of my cuts with every heartbeat. I accept some towels and begin the arduous task of wiping Cara's and my blood from myself, checking the cuts I can reach for bits of glass. My wounds are numerous, so the blood pools on my skin again as quickly as I can wipe it away.

One of the healers calls out from the back, "Get the gargoyle in here!" I jump up, the pain in my body increases tenfold, and hobble into the surgery where Cara is being worked on.

The healer glares at me, snapping, "Get in that bed! Stay put so we can fix you, too. And stop bleeding everywhere!" When he turns back to Cara, I rumble a protest but do what I'm told. I'm starting to feel woozy from blood loss, so I shouldn't fight it any longer.

The healers move fast around Cara, focusing on the nastiest cuts first. Her skin knits back together a healthy pink where they've already begun their work. Thankfully, she's unconscious for this. Her mind needs to heal as much as her body. Luckily, the healers have ways to help with that, too. One of them droppers a potion into her mouth.

Another healer who's just begun cutting through my clothing to get to my wounds notices and remarks, "For her blood loss. Speeds up the development of blood cells. She'll be right as rain soon."

I nod my thanks and lie back as she tends to me.

"Do you want me to put you under?" she asks softly, her gentleness in diametric opposition to her colleague.

"No, I want to be with her when she wakes up." I grunt through my teeth as she pulls too hard on my bloody, aching wing. Luckily, I'm thoroughly numb soon thereafter, especially as they set my broken nose, and they begin healing the rest of me much the same as they are Cara.

A healer tells me to get some sleep because Cara will be out until the morning if not longer. But I simply can't. I need to see with my own two eyes that she's alive and breathing. That this fae isn't coming back to take her from me. Mayhap only a few hours have passed since we arrived, but I guard her like the precious treasure she is. I won't stop until she's safe.

It's still the middle of the night, and there's a great commotion at the front of the clinic. Before I get up to see what's happening, Maman and Père burst into the room, crowding my bedside.

"My Benny, we came as soon as we heard! I thought we were too late," wails my mother. I lift my arms to her, and she holds me tight, crying into my shoulder.

"Son, I'm so glad to see you healing. I don't know everything that happened, but you are such a brave male to save your mate from a powerful fae. You make your old Père proud." My father chokes up as he hugs both of us, wrapping us in his long, leathery wings.

When my mother's tears subside, they release me and help me sit up in bed. I'm still very sore, even with the numbing salve and the magick to heal the burns, scrapes, gashes, and chunks missing from my skin. They're a patchwork of pink on gray right now, but they'll disappear in time. My mother eyes the other bed in the room where Cara sleeps peacefully, modestly covered in a blanket.

"Is she your mate?" my mother wonders aloud.

"Yes, this is Cara Bishop. She's endured so much the last few weeks. Tonight must have been so terrifying for her. When she feels up to it, I will be happy to introduce you. But I fear it may take some time yet. Her injuries were more severe than mine," I explain mindfully, knowing how much they want to meet her and how worried they must be for the both of us. Cara will love them, but there is no need to rush anything because her recovery is the top priority.

"I flew straight here after freeing Cara and escaping the fire, but what is the news since then? I haven't heard anything," I ask wearily.

I'm afraid of what may have happened after I left the scene. Père sits on the edge of the bed and Maman climbs onto his lap. They both look exhausted now that they know I'm safe.

"We were at Samhain when there was talk of burglaries and then a house catching fire during the festival. Many of the witches were called away, so that made everyone nervous. We went home after that, but then Clancy called to tell us that you and your mate were injured in the fire and that you were here in the clinic. He said that it was caused by a fae, but it's been trapped in a magickally sealed cell for questioning and punishment. Ada suffered some injuries from the fae, but no one else was hurt," my father recounts, tears in his eyes.

"Ada fought so hard. I'd never seen anything like it." I sigh, rubbing my hand down my face, along my broken nose. "It could have been so much worse. Maman and Père, I love you both so much. Thank you for coming to us. You should go home and sleep if you can. I'll call you when we are discharged. Since Cara has lost her home, she will probably move in with me. Please call before you come over for the time being. She may be fragile for a time." I break it gently to them.

My mother's eyes shine with tears as she agrees, "Oh sweetheart, of course. She will be so happy to have you as her mate."

After my parents leave, I stare at Cara for endless hours, waiting for her to wake up. The healers come in and check over her periodically, telling me everything is healing well. I've almost lost my battle to sleep when I hear a sharp gasp. I spring to my feet to get to her bedside, pain streaking through me with every step.

"Cara, my belle, how are you feeling?" I whisper, looking deep into her beautiful hazel eyes, trying to hold back my tears of relief.

"Oh Ben, you saved me," she mewls as she starts to cry. I kiss her forehead, gently brushing her hair out of her face.

"Of course I saved you. I love you. I'm so sorry I let that happen to you. I should never have had you go home by yourself. It's my fault you almost died," I admit, guilt eating me up inside.

"Ben, I love you so much. So much. I thought I was going to die and never have a chance to tell you. I was so scared I would lose you as soon as I found you," she sobs, breaking my heart that she knew her end was so close.

"You're telling me now, my belle. And you make me the happiest male alive to hear it," I console.

"Ben, what he did isn't your fault. He told me he was watching me and waiting for any opportunity to kill me. You didn't do anything wrong. He would have found me no matter what," she insists, her hands framing my face, making me listen to her.

"But I failed you. I should have known better. If I had realized I left you to the mercy of that fae even… a minute later, I don't know what would have happened," I confess, weeping, looking away in shame as tears stream down my face.

"No, Ben, don't think of it like that. So many things could have happened, but they didn't. You figured it out in time. You saved me. We're here together because of you. We have the rest of our lives together starting now." She smiles through her tears.

"Oh Cara, my mate, I will love you forever. I will never stop proving that to you," I cry into her hair as I carefully pull her into my arms.

She looks up at me, kissing and caressing my lips and cheeks, and whispers, "We'll never stop proving it to each other."

We lay together in her bed for a long time. The healers come in but don't say anything about it, accepting that it would be useless to tell mates to go back to their respective sick beds. They inform her of the type of healing they provided, fixing internal and external wounds, including a significant amount of damage to her lungs from the smoke, and fighting the blood loss she experienced. They also encouraged her to keep taking her calming tonic to help prevent lasting mental trauma from the event and to help her sleep better to speed up healing. Her external cuts and gashes have already begun to knit back together and, within a couple weeks, will be unnoticeable. Apologetically, they ask that she stay for one more night for observation before they let her go home to be sure her organ functions and oxygen level remain normal. She calmly listens to the healers, assuring them she will do all they ask.

The healers leave, and a nurse comes in to bring us breakfast. We're both surprisingly hungry. Our carefree dinner at Samhain seems so long ago. As we finish up, Cara takes a long look at herself. Her injured body must be difficult to accept, even if it's temporary. The intense pain of it will still be fresh in her mind. Her pale skin is crisscrossed in pink puffy lines where her cuts are healing.

"I look like an albino tiger," she whines, poking one of the wounds and wincing at the lingering ache.

"The most brave and beautiful albino tiger." I chuckle.

"We're matching," she observes as she more tenderly brushes a finger across a near-identical set of deep grooves scratched into my arm.

"That we are," I agree, catching her wandering hand and placing a kiss on it.

We both take calming tonics and sleep the day away. We're woken up for an evening meal, and the healers confirm we are both recovering as expected.

As we finish eating, Clancy knocks on the door, looking more peaked and pinched than I've ever seen him in his entire life. "Mother Earth, I've never been so happy to see a sight," he greets us, seemingly dead on his feet.

"Clancy, rest if you need to. You look almost worse than us!" Cara chimes in, shocked at his haggard appearance.

"I thought I may have lost you both. I've never been so scared in my life. And now Ada is injured, too. She'll be okay, but... I'm so sorry to have dragged you into this mess, Cara. I almost killed my best friend and his mate. I will never forgive myself," he utters, genuinely remorseful.

"You two need to stop raking yourselves over the coals for this!" Cara commands, pointing a finger at both of us. "You're both exactly alike trying to take the blame. It's not your fault! You've both done everything in your power to help me!"

"If I hadn't brought you here..." he tries to interject, but she cuts him off.

"No! Blame Mark. That fae. The situation is their fault. And neither of yours." She stands firm, brooking no argument.

"She will not let it go, Clancy. Best to give in to this demand from my mate," I contend, giving his arm an affectionate squeeze.

He scrubs his weary face, combing his fingers through messy hair, acquiescing, "You're right, as always, Cara. I just regret all that's transpired under my watch. I should have known better."

"What happened after I left with Cara?" I ask Clancy. "My father filled me in a little, but he was missing a lot of details."

"I've spent the entire night and day trying to figure that out." He sighs, his expression bleak. "But this is what we've determined. Some teenage brownies were paid a handsome fee to break all the windows along the block where your office is located. As soon as we caught them, they confessed remorsefully to all the vandalism that's happened recently, realizing they'd gone too far. If you guessed it was Samuels who paid them to do it, you're right. The young males felt like they couldn't tell him no because of his position in town. Samuels and the warlocks left town after the fae was captured, so they had to be connected to the fae's attempt to murder Cara. The fae isn't talking much, but we know the fae was connected to Mark by a private investigator who was tracking Cara in Atlanta. A wallet and two phones were found on Mark's body. From those, we found out he kept tabs on you, Cara. He even had photos of your workplace and home. When you became untraceable, I guess Mark shelled out enough cash to entice the investigator to get a fae to dreamwalk and find her. The amount must have been staggering," Clancy recounts.

"Was the investigator Whispered Folk?" I interrupt.

Clancy nods. "Had to be, though passing for human. We still don't believe Mark knew about the Whispered Folk, even after interacting with the fae."

Cara looks ashen as she mentions, "The fae was wearing Mark's body. He wasn't pretending to be Mark, but he was inside his body and using it."

Sounding disgusted, Clancy explains, "The fae are incorporeal and shapeshifting in this realm, taking any form that suits them best—plant, animal, shadow, human, Whispered Folk. This one probably took on a male human-like form to best suit their needs, making deals with Mark and Samuels. And conveniently, that form would scare you the most in your dreams. Fae powers are strong and corrupting. Killing and inhabiting bodies is one of many gruesome things fae can do. From what I understand, it's been a long time since leaders of the Whispered Folk have dealt with a fae threat so directly. And now that we have this one in our custody, leadership will have to figure out what to do with it. They'll be here next week."

Stress is etched on Clancy's face. No doubt there will be a lot of arguments and frustration ahead. "Where are the warlocks?" I remind him.

"They're long gone," he remarks. "Probably left when they realized Ada and her ward defeated the fae. It was likely too late to apprehend them here in town, even if we knew they had anything to do with it at the time. We think the fae approached Samuels rather than the other way around, if you can believe that. Cara, your courtroom nightmare that featured Samuels must have led the fae to him. The fae must have figured out he'd be easy to manipulate to get through the wards. Even if the fae sought him out to get to you, I still don't have the faintest clue why Samuels would agree to it. He had to know a deal with a fae is never worth the trouble. It always comes with a high personal cost. Fae are notorious for this. But fire and ashes, he went for it anyway."

"Is that how the fae got through the wards? Did Samuels let it in?" I ask, shocked.

"Yes, it's the only way the fae could have gotten through. The coven and constabulary are still investigating. But they think he gave the fae someone's amulet to cross freely. It's a true betrayal to our town," Clancy mourns.

Cara looks dismayed, asking, "How is Ada doing? I can't believe she took on that horrible thing and won."

"Physically, she is fine now. But the fight drained her magick, and she was hit with a fae spell that prevented it from returning. It'll take time to counteract the spell, if it's even possible. She may never fully recover her abilities. Only time will tell," Clancy laments.

"She was not alone that night," I add. "Her parents' spirits were there along with many others. They passed through the veil to help her."

Clancy nods, disbelief in his expression. "She did not realize that would happen either, but she would have been defeated quickly by the fae without them. There are centuries of unbroken ancestral magick woven into her land. She thinks the spirits were generations of her ancestors whose magick still strengthens the protective ward around her home. Being so close to midnight on Samhain, the breach in the ward must have summoned them to the land to defend it. Seeing her parents has added to her grief. I believe she is taking that the hardest at this point."

"Poor Ada, I can't imagine how that would feel." Cara exhales raggedly, tearing up.

"She is tougher than she looks, but I should go check on her before it gets too late. I'll be helping her sort out the fire damage to the carriage house. The structure is beyond saving. Cara, I'll let you know if we can salvage your belongings. We haven't even had a chance to look yet," Clancy discloses, sounding apologetic.

"Thanks, Clancy. That's very kind of you. If there's anything worth saving, please drop it off at Ben's house. I think he may have just gained a permanent roommate," she teases through her tears, smiling at me affectionately.

"I believe I have room for that," I purr, kissing the palm of my sweet mate's hand.

The next morning, we're allowed to go home. Cara looks better today, more rested than she's been in the last few weeks, if nothing else. The dark circles under her eyes have nearly vanished. The calming tonics should continue to help with that. The palpable relief on her face when she steps through my front door gouges at my heart. She's been through so much. I wish she would have moved in with me under happier circumstances, but I'll do everything I can to make that up to her. Luckily, she has some clothes at my place that she brought here earlier in the week, so she can change out of the robe provided to her at the clinic. We curl up on the couch and watch movies until we can't keep our eyes open. We sleep most of the day away, only waking up to a call from Maman letting me know she left dinner for us on the front porch.

While Cara rests after dinner, I check in with Clancy, who doesn't have any updates on the whereabouts of the warlocks, except that they're likely hiding out in the human world. He believes they will be widely broadcast as wanted fugitives by the time the assembly of Whispered Folk leadership arrives next week. Clancy asks me to tell Cara he's giving her a few weeks off, likely more, to recover and decompress. He and the remaining town council members will be very busy in the coming weeks with the fallout. Nearly everything else has been put on pause.

After I end my call with Clancy, I reach out to my crews to make sure they know I'll be back next week. My father generously stepped up to oversee the cleanup of the office and crew reassignments in the aftermath.

When I call Maman to let her know how much we both enjoyed the food, she confides in me, laughing, "Your father is loving every second of being back there. If I didn't know better, I'd think he regrets retirement. The real reason is that all the business owners have been checking in on each other. You'd think there was a big block party every day. He forgets the office isn't a social club."

Placing those calls saps my energy completely. Now that those responsibilities are squared away, I attend to Cara, who is lightly snoring, sprawled out on the couch. I pick her up, carry her upstairs, and put her to bed. I watch her peaceful slumber for as long as my eyes stay open. But the healing potions we brought home are too strong and soon I'm succumbing to sleep as well.

The next thing I register, Cara presses against me, wearing only a sultry smile. She must have woken up a while ago because she looks freshly showered and bright-eyed. I nudge her onto her back and lay on top of her, between her legs, using my wings to cage her in.

She wraps her legs around my waist, pulling my core to hers. "Ben, I missed being alone with you," she coos as she cups my face in her hands. "I think I've figured something out about you."

"What would that be, my belle?" I wonder.

"Your love languages. Acts of service. And dirty talk. I want both of those right now, please," she teases through lowered lashes.

"Servicing my sexy mate with dirty talk. Your wish is my command," I growl, hungry for this beautiful female under me.

I kiss her deeply, tongues meeting. I'll never get enough of her taste. Her scent. Her touch. I've missed this as much as she has. And I'm so relieved she feels well enough to initiate lovemaking.

"Cara, do you feel how swollen and straining my cock is? It's already leaking seed onto your hungry pussy," I groan as I drag my shaft along her wet slit, bumping the head to her clit.

"Yes! I feel it," she mewls.

Kissing down her beautiful, ample body, I plump her round breasts with my hands and suckle her nipples. Flushed with desire, she moans her pleasure, arching into me.

"Your body is so soft and pliant, ready to be fucked by your mate," I declare, making her squirm even more beneath me.

Dipping a fingertip into the wetness of her silky pink walls, I swirl it around her clit, making her hips buck under my touch.

"Play with yourself, my belle. Show me how aroused you are at the thought of being stuffed full of me," I command.

She pinches her nipples as I continue rubbing her clit. Her moans rise in crescendo as I slide the spade of my tail deeply into her tight channel, hitting that spot that always sets her alight. Her pussy clamps rhythmically around me in orgasm.

"That's it, my needy girl. You're ready for my fat cock now," I rumble low as I kiss back up her body.

"Yes, yes, so ready, Ben! I need you inside me," she wails.

Gritting my teeth, I notch the head of my cock to the entrance of her pussy. "I can already feel your empty pussy kissing my cock. I think she missed me," I tease.

Before she has time to react, I thrust deep, making Cara cry out and dig her nails into my back, her head rolling around her pillow in ecstasy. Her tight channel grips me so hard that heat licks through my entire body as I move within her.

"Use your pussy to squeeze out my seed. I have so much for you," I growl darkly into her ear as I lift her up by the butt cheeks, anchoring her to me, and changing the angle I'm penetrating her so she feels me more deeply. My testicles slap into her backside with each thrust. She keens at this new angle and tries to undulate to meet my movement, but I'm in control, setting the pace. I watch as my cock pistons in and out of her channel. Her cream mixed with my pre-come coats my shaft. I can see it every time I pull out. "You're such a good girl, taking all of me, that I have a little treat for you," I offer her wickedly.

The spade of my tail snakes behind her and rubs along her back pucker, massaging the ring of muscle, aided by her wetness still coating it. It's a hint at what's possible if she wants to explore another day.

"Ben!" she exclaims, her pussy clutching me tighter, pulling me in deeper.

"You like that? There's so much fun we can have with it," I promise huskily.

I grunt and strain the closer she gets to her next orgasm, her channel growing tighter. I clench my inner muscles to keep myself from spilling in her too soon. My seed already boils within me, ready to spill over deep inside of her. I won't last much longer.

"I'm already leaking into your hungry pussy. She's already filling with my seed. That's how badly I want you full and dripping of me," I pant, pressing my pelvis more firmly against her clit, rubbing it with each stroke.

In no time, she's falling apart around me, moaning my name. "That's it, my mate. Pull all my seed from me. Get it nice and deep inside you," I bellow as her channel pulses around me, unyielding in its grip, begging for my come. My cock jerks hard inside her as my seed surges through it, spurting into her silky depths.

Her body lays languid beneath me, and I start to move off her. "No, don't," she stops me. "I like the feeling of you plugging me up. You came so much inside me."

"Good girl, keeping it where it belongs. I couldn't have dreamed of a better mate. I love you so much." I hum as I nuzzle her temple. My wings still surround us, binding us together as one.

"I love you too, my mate." She sighs, a smile in her voice. "And thank you for following the brief."

CHAPTER 18

BEN

Nearly every seat in this large town hall meeting room is taken by leaders of the Whispered Folk and investigators from around the continent, mayhap even further afield. I was summoned to answer questions about Samhain night, though I refused to bring Cara, even though she was asked here as well. Clancy and Ada agreed we should keep her as far from this as possible. The fae is captured, contained, and no longer a threat to her. She needs peace to heal.

Two phones were found on Mark's body outside the carriage house —his personal phone and a burner. They helped fill in so many gaps about how Mark could even cross paths with a fae. It's surprising he lived as long as he did while in its presence. The private investigator in Chicago who connected Mark to them disappeared, mayhap realizing the grave lapse in judgment they had setting a fae's sights on a haven town. Fire and ashes, they will be severely punished when caught.

Despite the evidence available to them, investigators question me about Cara's and my experience and any clues the fae left for us. I reiterate the information we already gave the constabulary. Sick of answering questions, I turn it around on the group in front of me.

"What are you doing to find the warlock fugitives? Ralston Samuels is not only guilty of bringing a fae into our town but also doing so with the intent to murder my mate. Atticus and Weatherby are his accomplices in attempted murder and should be treated as such," I snarl, fury slipping through my stony façade.

A powerful coven leader from New York City, Niven Whitehall, is heading up the search for the warlocks. He watches me patiently, undaunted by my anger, though understanding of it.

"We alerted all haven towns and outposts of their crimes in case they turn up to start a new life. However, it seems unlikely, knowing the great risk of being caught. We believe they'll remain in the human world for now. Plenty of Whispered Folk live among humans. Still, we worry that these three will pose a unique security threat in multiple ways. They may inadvertently expose themselves to humans as none of them have lived outside of Monstera Bluff. Also, they may seek to directly harm the town again. Thus, we consider our top priority to apprehend them as soon as possible. They've committed atrocious crimes already and are capable of more."

When I told Cara weeks ago that only an extremely powerful magick wielder could compel someone to speak or act against their will, Niven Whitehall was the one I had in mind. Though he isn't exercising it today, it always makes me wary when in his presence. He investigates serious crimes among the Whispered Folk and uses his power to compel the truth from suspects and criminals. He is an honorable male, and we are lucky to have his assistance, though his abilities make many uncomfortable. It seems like a lonely life, even if he has found an important purpose.

A group of head constables representing the largest haven towns sit along the side of the room. One of them stands up, declaring, "It'll require all of us to step up our efforts protecting our towns. Hunting them may be difficult, but we will be ready. If this warlock was willing to deal with a fae, there isn't much he wouldn't do."

Monstera Bluff's town leaders in attendance look pleased by their responses, so I feel more assured the urgency they express is genuine. Clancy took a step back from the investigation since the initial aftermath, leaving it to more experienced hands. His focus is now on restoring calm in our community.

He pipes up, his voice stormy, "Has anything been found in Ralston

Samuels' home that indicates what he sought to gain from the fae? And what price he agreed to pay beyond entry through the wards?"

Niven looks grim, explaining in his gruff voice, "There wasn't much in his home or office. We strongly believe it was an impulsive decision on Ralston Samuels' part when the fae approached him in a dream. He would have recognized the dreamwalker as a fae and, in full awareness, struck a deal to let the fae into town in exchange for political power. But this power would undoubtedly come with costly favors owed to the fae at the great expense of your town and your people."

"He paid a group of teenage brownies to vandalize the town on repeated occasions during a three-week period. Those teenagers eagerly wanted out from under his thumb. He used their riotous natures against them while leveraging his power to convince them to keep upping the ante. He began doing this before encountering the fae with the intention of destabilizing the town after the arrival of the human Cara Bishop to stir up anti-human sentiment," Clancy acknowledges. "We can all surmise this was to create false pressure on my office and to force her to leave. But to jump from vandalism to murder is extreme."

Niven nods in agreement. "Yes, mayhap that was part of the desperation. The original plan wasn't working. Her connection to Benoit Garde-Pierre created difficulties, as did the other friendships she formed. We must also consider that the fae skillfully exerted influence over him, using his delusions of grandeur against him to persuade him to violence. The fae does not care how many lives are lost. This bargain with Ralston Samuels was an easy victory, he could kill a human and then gain easy access to the governing body of your town."

The thought does not sit well with the room, murmurs erupting about the fae's motivation and what could have happened if it succeeded. There would be no limit to what Samuels could have given the fae if he became mayor, consolidating power, and then shaping the town into some mockery of itself. Relief courses through me that we were able to stop him, but it's bittersweet. The townsfolk are still troubled that one of our own invited in the fae. Confidence in our safety has waned. There are calls to strengthen our wards and change the magick behind our travel amulets since no one considered this hazard.

When the meeting adjourns for the day, Clancy motions for me to join him in his office. "It is enough responsibility to run one town. I do not envy the task these investigators face to maintain security across all our communities," he drawls, sounding worn out.

"Let's get a drink. I need to unwind before heading home to Cara. I don't want the stench of this day on me when I return to my sweet mate," my voice scratches out, strained from the long interview. My hands scrub my face, trying to shed some stress.

"Your injuries are looking good, Ben. But I'm glad everyone in the room saw the severity before they fully faded. Helped tell your story for you," he points out as he looks me over as we walk outside in the sunlight. I nod in agreement. The thought crossed my mind as well.

We walk to Call of the Wild, where the familiar smell of old wood and good food puts me at ease. Halvor steps out from behind the bar and pulls me into an unexpected bear hug.

"Your cousin told us what happened. So glad you and your mate made it out of the fire. It's on the house tonight. Give our best to your mate," he announces, voice stirring with emotion.

"Thanks, Hal. Appreciate your kindness." He claps me on the shoulder before heading back behind the bar.

"I'm not sure when you'll pay for a drink again in this town," Clancy observes in good humor. "You and Cara both."

I huff a laugh as my cousin delivers a round of mead. She encircles me in a quick hug and stretches to peck my cheek.

"Your parents are coming over this weekend since Lucas is in town, but your Maman reminded me you and your mate won't be there. I hope you'll both recover soon. We'd love to spend time with you when you're well," she says, full of sympathy.

"We'll be there next time," I promise her. She moves on to her other tables, but not before she beams a genuine smile at me and winks playfully at Clancy.

Clancy and I take long fortifying drinks. It's been a trying day. Clancy eyes me, and I know he has something on his mind.

He pauses like he's unsure about it. "While you were recuperating, I talked to the coven and they made sure that no blowback will reach us —and, more importantly, Cara—when the human authorities investigate Mark Hansen. His remains and his phones have been... taken care of. And let's say that any paper trail leading back to her has been... lost. Not that human police would be able to find her here. I will tell you more if you truly want to know, but I reckon you don't," he assures me.

"No, it is better I don't hear it. I will only tell her she has nothing to worry about. She has a soft heart that needs protecting," I confirm. My belle needs to rest, relax, and be made love to. She doesn't need any other distractions right now.

"Darla apologized to me the other day." Clancy runs his hands through his hair as he sighs. "She believes her vision laid the foundation for this to happen. I told her that's hogwash. Something else was bound to rile up those old warlocks. Or something worse could have happened to Cara. Still, she was disappointed in herself because she didn't see any of this happening. Couldn't warn us further."

I nod in understanding. "Darla shouldn't blame herself. My mate is correct that the only ones to blame are Mark, the fae, and the warlocks. Blaming ourselves will do no good. We just need to make sure they're brought to justice. Hopefully, Darla can help with that. I'm sure she's already doing all she can."

"She's working with the investigators to aid them in finding the warlocks. Hopefully they don't try to poach her away from us," Clancy jests.

"Fire and ashes, what do you think the fae really wanted? You are the strategist here. Why did it do this?" I question, puzzled over why my sweet, strong mate was caught in the middle.

Clancy's eyes darken as he considers their motives. "The fae was lucky enough to find two males both warped and narcissistic enough to fall for its schemes. Cara is special. Mother Earth, not that I need to tell you that. Mark squandered her, pushed her away, and then regretted it. Through his new mate, Mark was about to be politically connected, right? He probably sold out a lot of people in his life so the fae would find Cara and get her back."

"But didn't the private investigator just hire the fae to dreamwalk?" I interject.

"Yes, but what is some money to a fae when it can gain something more valuable? That Whispered Folk private investigator connecting them should have known better. Mark was an easy target," Clancy surmises.

"Cara's involvement was incidental, which makes me angrier. She was a convenient excuse to strike bargains with those dishonorable males," I seethe.

"It was," he confirms grimly. "Samuels' drive for power must have looked even more enticing to the fae, so he played them both. Whatever vision the fae presented Samuels, mayhap positioning him like a king, drove him to insanity with his quest for power."

"Samuels always cared for power more than the town," I concur.

"And that bastard really does hate humans, so she was an easy target to fixate on as his first step in securing the fae's vision of power," he adds.

"What would fae do with political influence?" I wonder.

"The tricky thing about the fae is that we know so little about them. Why they're even here at all. But if it saw the opportunity to be a shadow ruler of our town, it could sow the seeds of chaos at a greater level. Destabilize life for the Whispered Folk here and elsewhere. Maybe expose us. They could have a vendetta against us. Or they could be doing this for their own sick amusement," he theorizes, holding his chin in his hand and looking pensive.

His reasons sound close to the truth. I'm glad Clancy is a kind-hearted leader. Otherwise, he'd be quite a formidable adversary.

Another round of mead later, and we both feel lighter. Kiernan Lykander stops by our table. He's a distant relative on my mother's side and a friend of Clancy's. I don't think he and Cara had an opportunity to meet, but they both work in town hall, and he was at the council meeting to witness the harassment toward her.

"Can't say I'll miss those three warlocks. They were always causing trouble, but I'm sorry you and your mate were caught up in it. Those flyers Samuels spread to drum up hate against humans were some of the most despicable things I've ever seen. I can't believe he grew up here and turned out like that. Something was not right about him," Kiernan observes, shaking his head in disgust.

"Indeed, Kier, he was backing the wrong horse." Clancy snorts. "It was completely irrational. We have always had humans in our town.

They are good mates, good friends and neighbors. Not only is Cara working to improve our community, but she happens to be my best friend's mate. I'll never hire anyone better than her!" We laugh at Clancy's levity, but his point is true.

"My mentor Walt is human. I wouldn't be the wolven I am today without his guidance, both as a park ranger and as an upstanding male. He saw the potential in me when I was just a young pup, knew I had the passion and skill to care for our land. I wouldn't have even recognized it in myself without him," Kiernan argues fervently, "Plus, I see how well humans fit into our pack. One day, I hope to be lucky enough to find one of my own." He turns over his fur-covered hands and arms, looking down at them in earnest and frowns. "Ah, but mayhap that is easier said than done."

I clasp his arm, still slightly outstretched, shaking it gently to get his attention. "Kier, I never thought it would happen for me, either, that I would find a mate at all, let alone a human as smart, brave, and beautiful as her. And yet Cara proved me wrong. Don't give up hope. We don't know what our futures hold," I encourage him. If Cara and I could find each other, there is hope for anyone.

"You're right, Ben, anything could happen. Wish your mate well for me. I hope to see her around town hall again soon," he offers sincerely before taking his leave to sit at the bar to talk to Hal.

When Clancy and I try to settle our tab, we're waved away good-naturedly. He still puts a few dollars on the table as we head outside. It was good to spend this time with Clancy, and we promise to meet again soon. I look up to the sky, ready to take flight. The sun is already setting, the deep colors painting a pretty picture on my flight home. But the most beautiful sight I'll behold tonight is my mate waiting for me with open arms.

EPILOGUE
CARA

Clancy and the town council had to regroup after the Samhain night attack, dealing with security issues across the entire Whispered Folk world, so a lot of non-essential town hall projects have been put on hold. Clancy reasons I should take it as an opportunity to recuperate fully. Turns out I get to take an entire month off work, fully paid. It's the longest break I've had since high school. Even after my accident in Atlanta, I took less than two weeks until I was back in the office. And my recovery from those injuries was a lot slower. The magickal healing has been astonishing. I'm completely physically recovered in around ten days. Even the worst of my physical scars disappear. Nightmares about what the fae did to me, seeing Mark's grotesque face above me, still find me in my sleep. But less often with each passing week. They don't feel invasive like they did when the fae dreamwalked. Just normal, run-of-the-mill nightmares, which I can deal with. The calming tonic prescribed by the healer surely helps.

Mark's death was full of complex emotions for me. I rightfully hate him, and I cannot fathom the purpose of his plan to find me—seduce me into being his mistress and work for him again?—but he still didn't deserve to be murdered. He was obnoxiously arrogant, especially in the last few years. I'm sure because of it, he was easily tricked into a dangerous bargain by that fae. He thought his money and local prestige made him untouchable. Obviously, he got himself in over his head. He made that choice, so I don't harbor any guilt about his death.

Rose calls me right after the story breaks in local Chicago news. "Cara, I have to tell you something about Mark. It transcends the spirit of the information diet we agreed on. It's just too important. Mark is missing! Like, an actual missing persons case! I'm sorry to break the no-update rule. But this is beyond insane!" she blurts out.

I couldn't be sure what the news would say about it, so I don't have to feign much surprise when I react. "Oh my god, missing? What are the police saying?"

She texts me an article link while she tells me what she knows. "Investigators have no solid leads. His parents said he's been out of town on business a lot lately, but they don't know what could have happened," she explains.

"I wonder if they know more than they're letting on. They're so focused on appearances, I have no idea if they'd spill everything they knew if it brings to light anything bad about them," I speculate.

"Girl, that's Victoria in a nutshell. She was always a complete ghoul. I'm sure she's just waiting for him to come back from some bender. Who knows, maybe he was into something way worse than just being a cheating sleaze," she theorizes.

"He probably was," I agree, wishing I could tell her the extent of it.

Talking to her in the days following the attack helps my emotional recovery. It isn't easy to hide what happened. She notices I sound off.

"Is everything going okay with your job? With Ben? You sound kind of worn out," she fishes hesitantly.

"Both are good. Really good. I have some news for you about both of those things. So... I'm moving in with Ben," I announce.

"What!" Rose squeals. "So soon? Is that a good idea?"

Spinning my story to something resembling the truth, I answer, "Well, there was a... structural issue with my apartment, and I can't live there anymore. It's not the landlord's fault. She's been great, and we're still good friends. She feels genuinely awful about it. Ben has a beautiful old house, and it just makes sense that I move in with him. Why bother trying to find a new place when I'm spending so much of my time over there anyway? He's already given me space in the closet, my own dresser drawers. So yeah, it's good. I feel completely at home there. He's been so happy about it, too. I can't even begin to describe it."

Rose cackles. "Cara, you just managed to lock down a good guy in weeks. Weeks! When that asshole Mark dragged his feet for eight years and then turned out to be a total lying asshat. Who is now missing. That's neither here nor there, but obviously, the grass was *not* greener for him after he blew up your relationship. I think I need to leave the city to find something like what you now have. Guys here do not want to commit. And it's so difficult meeting anyone worthwhile in person, even worse on an app."

"I've thought about this too... And to clarify, not your string of crappy dates and hook-ups." I laugh, hoping I don't give her the wrong idea. "But I think this town could really use a bus system. It'll be a lot of work, I won't sugarcoat it. It'll require planning traffic studies, scheduling interviews and meetings for public input, determining budget and staffing needs, researching and completing purchasing orders, setting the routes and schedules, all from the ground up. But it could be done by someone with the right type of experience and aptitude. And if the town council goes for it, I'm going to recommend you lead it. Insist on it, in fact."

Rose is quiet on her end, and I'm about to ask her if she's still there when she finally responds. "Cara, that's such an amazing thing to do for me. Thank you. I know there's no guarantee they'll go for it. But if they do, I'm all theirs," she blubbers, emotion heavy in her voice. After all the support she's given me, this is the least I can do. I'll make sure the town council will be too dazzled by my proposal to ever consider turning it down.

Out of morbid curiosity, I check the Tribune headlines periodically. Mark's missing persons case is ongoing, and there is a lot of speculation as to what happened. Deal with the mob gone wrong. A fast and hard fall into drug use. A rip current pulled him too far into the lake. And so on. Nothing to do with monsters or fae or me, thank goodness. Mark's too-beautiful, politically connected fiancée seemed to have a short period of mourning his disappearance, but she's already moved on to the next too-handsome, too-rich businessman. I guess it's lucky for her she probably wasn't all that in love with him.

My friends back in Chicago like to say things about him like, "Karma is a bitch." If only they knew how crazy the real story is. But I'll never tell them.

A week after Samhain, I feel ready to meet Ben's parents. My in-laws, I suppose, now that I've accepted that we're mates. Even his brother from New York will be there. Honestly, it was silly of me to try to pretend he was just my boyfriend when there was really no question about his permanence in my life. That lasted approximately a day. After the attack, when I finally had the courage to tell Ben I loved him, it was a certainty I couldn't deny any longer. Listening to Walt describe his relationship with Acton during our lunch date that week before, I knew in my heart that Ben and I were the same. I was just too stuck in my head about it to call it that.

His parents invite us over for an afternoon cookout after Ben lets them know we're finally up for it. Well, when I'm up for it, Ben is too kind to frame it to them like I was the one holding off. But it feels like the right time now, especially while his brother is in town. Ben is excited to see him. I've noticed they talk on the phone at least once a week and text all the time. His brother was beside himself with worry when their parents told him about the attack. He insisted on coming home as soon as possible. It warms my heart how close they are. I'm really looking forward to going to his parents' place, but I do have some jitters.

"Are you sure we don't need to bring anything?" I repeat to Ben, nervous about first impressions, not wanting to be rude.

"No, my belle, Maman specifically said they have everything handled," he reassures me.

"Okay, sorry, I just want them to like me," I fret.

"Cara, they already love you. It is a done deal," he soothes.

Luckily, most of my clothes were saved from the fire. Everything in my bedroom was salvageable, including my purse and computer. One of the witches in the coven removed any smoky smell and ashy remnants from the items. I tried to get her to explain how it works, and she described it as the magick zeroes in on the smoke particles based on their high carbon level and pulls them from the fabric. It seemed very science-like to me, to be honest. Something that could be bottled and sold. So that means today I get to wear one of my favorite outfits: a navy blue wrap dress made of sturdy cotton with a nice structure and my tan strappy sandals. I know the family gathering isn't dressy, but I still want to look nice.

When we walk up to the house, only two blocks from ours, his parents and brother spill out the front door like they were watching for us to arrive. It's adorable and puts me at ease that they're probably just as nervously excited as I am. Ben is a spitting image of his brother and dad. They're like a time progression of the same person. Ben and his brother embrace, putting their foreheads together momentarily in a loving gesture. His mom envelops me in a huge hug, quite the feat considering her very small stature. I tower over her, so she must be five foot two tops. She looks like a human, except her silver eyes signifying she's a wolf shifter. Her very tall mate is still nearly the same height as Ben, around six foot eight. The difference between them is endearing.

"Cara, we've been so excited to meet you! Welcome to the family! We knew Ben's mate was out there somewhere. We're so happy you two finally found each other," she exclaims ardently, her face beaming with joy.

"This is my brother Lucas, my mother Lillian, and my father Nicolas," Ben introduces.

"You should call us Père and Maman if you wish, Cara. You're our daughter now. We want you to feel like you're a member of the Garde-Pierre family," Nicolas offers. My eyes brim with tears, and I give them a watery smile.

"Père! You're overwhelming her!" Lucas goads lightly.

"No!" I clarify. "Not in a bad way. I haven't had a family in a long time. I'm just so happy to be accepted into yours."

"You say that now, but you're already Maman and Père's new favorite person. The daughter they never had. Get ready for family over-load," Lucas jokes with a fond smile.

"I think I like the sound of that," I insist, squeezing Maman's hand.

The cookout is relaxing. We sit on their back patio while Père grills steak and sweet corn. Maman and Lucas share stories about Ben growing up. Ben blushes through each one but doesn't try to stop them. It seems he knows better. The stories would probably get even more embarrassing if he did.

"When he was a young boy, about seven or eight, poor Benny's wings were really starting to grow, and he was so clumsy with them. That's right around the time gargoyles learn to fly. At Clancy's birthday party, he and Clancy were roughhousing, and Ben knocked over the birthday cake with one of his wings! He was so sorry about it that he cried. Clancy told Ben, 'It's just cake! Who cares about cake when there are presents!' It was so precious. They were the best of friends even then," Maman recounts.

"Ben was not always so precious! After I finally learned to fly, Ben convinced me to dive bomb into the ocean with him for fun, except half the time he'd mess with me, and grab my foot or tail so I belly flopped instead." Lucas laughs uproariously at the memories, Ben joining in.

"Benny, you didn't! I never knew that!" Maman sounds affronted.

"It didn't take long before he couldn't catch me anymore. Then I got my payback." Lucas grins wickedly.

"He'd scoop up some poor fish minding its own business and smacks me with the slimy thing while I was his own personal hang glider pulling him to shore. Then he'd cause me to fall in and make me swim back on my own!" Ben chuckles. Their sibling rivalry, if you'd call it that, sounds good-natured and silly. They seem to have enjoyed growing up together. It's no wonder they're such good friends now.

Père looks over his shoulder at us as he flips the steaks. "Don't forget when young Ben kept tripping over his tail!" he chortles. Maman laughs so hard she bends forward with tears in her eyes.

"Oh yes, he'd get so tangled up in himself. All feet, wings, and tail for quite a few years. Even tripped himself down the stairs on his rear end a couple times," she recalls.

"Don't worry, son. We all went through that awkward stage," he calls out cheerfully as he returns his attention to the grill.

"I'm well past that awkward stage now." Ben turns to me with a devilish grin. "Are you ready for a little flying lesson?"

"What... me?" I stammer. My eyebrows practically lift to my hairline.

"Of course! It's a perk of having a gargoyle mate," he says with humor in his eyes, holding his hand out for me to take.

His family whoops encouragingly as I look at them in surprise. Biting my lip in uncertainty, I finally reach for him. He pulls me to my feet, and we walk hand in hand to the middle of the yard. He stands in front of me, and I look up at him wide-eyed. Even though he's flown with me twice before, I wasn't in a state to remember. The prospect of doing so now feels equally scary and exciting. My breath comes in quick, ragged bursts from the adrenaline rushing through me.

"Trust me, my belle," Ben soothes as he hoists me up with one arm under my backside. He folds his other arm around my back, pressing my chest to his. Instinctively, I tightly wrap my legs around his waist and hug my arms around his neck, holding on for dear life.

"Don't let go of me!" I whisper breathlessly in his ear.

"Never," he promises as he makes his final adjustments.

His wings stretch to their full span behind him and start beating powerfully, creating a small windstorm around us. With a seemingly small leap upward, he sets us airborne, lifting us steadily higher. I yelp at the initial sensation. A knot forms in my stomach like when I've ridden rollercoasters. I resist the urge to shut my eyes, instead focusing on how we've already reached the top of the tall live oak trees that line the neighborhood. We're still upright and he turns us so I can see over his shoulder the small figures of his family far below us, waving and cheering us on. Lucas takes flight as well, perching on the roof of the house to watch us go.

"I'm going to tip us forward a bit so you're on your back. You won't fall. Keep ahold of me with your legs. If you feel up for it, go ahead and let go with your arms," he instructs.

I nod my understanding against him. Slowly he eases me backward so we're less upright. I gulp down a nauseous feeling, trying to breathe through it. In this position, he speeds up, flying us far away from the house. The motion feels surprisingly smooth. He can glide great distances, only beating his impressively long wings when he needs to gain speed or elevation.

"Where are we going?" I squeak, tightening my stranglehold on him.

"To where it all began," he tells me.

He glides over downtown, swooping low and then gently climbing again as we maneuver over town hall. It's a wild perspective to see it all from high above as well as upside down. I shriek as he gently rolls us so I'm on top for an instant. The new view is incredible as we head toward the coastline. Once we're over water, I loosen my grip ever so slightly to test how it feels. Ben still has a vicelike grip on me, making me confident enough to let go of his neck completely. I stretch my arms in the air and lean my neck and shoulders backward a little more, granting me an almost panoramic view of the coast. He roars with laughter as I hoot and holler while dancing my arms around.

"I knew you'd be a natural," he smirks, looking proud.

"I didn't!" I beam as our eyes meet.

He leans in for a brief kiss before steering us back to his parents' house. We arrive only a few minutes after the steaks are ready. My stomach growls as we join his family at the table. Who knew flying could work up such an appetite?

The rest of the day continues like that. Warm, friendly, welcoming. Before it gets dark, Ben and Lucas fly around, showing off their advanced aerial tricks, looking like something they've practiced together for years.

Ada was dealing with a lot in the weeks following that awful night. She's been so busy with the town council while recovering from her injuries and cleaning up the remnants of the carriage house. We spoke on the phone a bit, but it wasn't until a couple weeks into our recovery that she stopped by Ben's house to talk in depth about everything that happened. She promised me she was doing alright, all things considered, but I'm not sure I believed her.

We're finally able to meet for lunch, and she asked Walt to come with us. Other than a brief call to wish me a speedy recovery, I haven't spoken with him at length since we were at Ada's shop. It's been an eventful time since then, so there will be a lot to catch up on. We meet at

Roaring Wood, which seems to be Ada's favorite spot. When I walk up to them in front of the restaurant, Walt greets me like an old friend, bringing me so much joy.

After we step inside and get seated at our table, Walt immediately turns to Ada, noting with some contempt, "So the big fella is back. And still staying with you?"

Ada nods and remarks, "Helping me a bit. But he's overstayed his welcome." She looks forlorn.

Walt explains to me, "Ada's ex-mate Norrell has returned for now—probably until they get that fae to crack. He lives in Canada at a Whispered Folk outpost. He's a clan leader there, so he was asked to join that safety council being held here for Whispered Folk leadership to address the fae attack."

"Ex-mate? Oh, you mentioned you were divorced when we first met," I remember.

"As good as. We're nothing to each other now," she confirms with a wan smile. "But don't let that worry you about mates in general. What happened to me was quite unusual, to say the least."

"Is this the first time you've seen him since he moved back to Canada?" Walt treads lightly.

"Yes. Ashes, it's been about fifteen years since he walked out. Not long after my parents died. I wish I could have gone the rest of my life without seeing him again." Ada exhales shakily.

"Is that true, though? Maybe this will give you the chance to finally close that chapter for good. No more 'what-ifs'. And allow you to open your heart to someone new who will appreciate you like you deserve," Walt consoles.

"Mayhap you're right, Walt. I don't know him anymore. He isn't the same male he used to be. The male I fell in love with no longer exists, so there's no reason to hold onto what once was. To waste any more years on it," she agrees.

Ada is subdued for the rest of lunch, her vivaciousness tamped down, but we all still have a nice time. I fill them in with everything about Ben, being mates and moving in together. They're both so visibly happy for me.

Toward the end of lunch, she admits she had an ulterior motive for our meeting today.

"Walt, I want you to consider running for one of the three vacant town council seats. Now, I know you like to keep your mind sharp, keep yourself busy and active. So I think this will be a perfect fit. Besides, you go to all the meetings anyway, so Mother Earth, you may as well cast a vote on things," Ada appeals.

Walt chuckles. "I'm an old man now! What's an old human got to offer the town council?"

"You are young at heart. And you're not *that* old anyway. At least consider it, please?" she encourages.

"I suppose I'll take it into consideration. You're right, I do go to more meetings than most," he concedes, looking thoughtful.

"I have a weird question for you both. My friends are clamoring for a photo of me and Ben. And I'm not sure what to do. Should I just... photoshop a random internet stranger with me? I don't know how to produce something believable to keep up the pretense," I ponder.

"Wyck, our tech whiz, created an app exactly for this! It places a very realistic-looking filter on Whispered Folk's faces to make them appear human. It does a great job creating unique faces based on their existing features. He's even working on one for video right now. That'll be so helpful for Whispered Folk who can't pass for human. There's a download link on the town's website. He's such a talented young male, doing so much work to help us navigate the human world a little easier. From what he tells me, the photo app is helping to train and perfect his more sophisticated live video tool. So the more you use it, the more it helps him," Ada effuses, sounding very proud of his accomplishments.

"I don't post photos anywhere, but it sure is fun to play with! Acton would have turned heads as a human. Already does as a dryad, though," Walt adds, a dreamy look on his face.

When I get home from lunch, I download the app and convince Ben to do a quick photoshoot. The app makes him resemble a bald, buff Christopher Meloni. Ben doesn't get the reference, but it sends me into hysterics. I can't wait to send it to my friends. They'll be jealous.

When I finally return to work after my month off, I'm reinvigorated to follow the Howling Road project with some smaller initiatives that should have a high impact. One of the first is a proposal for a skatepark, a laser tag arena, and a climbing gym to help keep the brownie teenagers, all teenagers really, out of trouble. Ben still has a chip on his shoulder regarding them, but I think they just need to channel their mischievous energy into fun activities. They were unwitting victims in Ralston Samuels' schemes, their penchant for troublemaking used against them, and I want to show there's no hard feelings.

With the blessing of the council, I'm also amending some of the plans for the new housing development to add green spaces and traffic calming measures into sections that haven't started construction yet. Luckily, it's early enough in the process that I could redesign a good chunk of it. I want to be sure it's as safe as possible for the families moving there. I also secretly want to ensure there's plenty of space for bus stops, though I haven't wanted to rock the boat too much yet with my transit idea. I'll wait until the empty seats in the town council are filled and life in Monstera Bluff has settled down again. And then I'll sneak up on them with the most perfect plan when the time is right.

Just as life feels calmer, our daily routines with work, family, and friends normalized, Ben suggests we have a mating ceremony. "Is this common?" I ask, unsure of Whispered Folk traditions, "Your parents haven't said anything about it, and I'm sure they would have."

"They are celebrated often enough that it wouldn't be unexpected. Plus, I know of human wedding customs, and I want you to experience something similar. I don't want to take that away from you," Ben rationalizes, thoughtful as usual.

"Is that something you want, though?" I question.

"Of course, I would celebrate you in any way possible. I thought I'd start by giving you this..." He pauses as he reaches into his pocket to pull out a small box. "To symbolize my eternal love for you. I will love you and be loyal to you in this life and the next."

Opening the box reveals an emerald ring with an intricately woven gold band. It slips onto my left ring finger perfectly. "Ben, this is gorgeous! I can't believe you're giving this to me. I won't ever take it off.

And, of course, we should have a mating ceremony. I would love to," I cry as I throw myself into his arms.

I never imagined what my wedding would look like. I was never one to fixate on that. But now I can't picture anything different than what we've chosen. Ben and I decided on a ceremony followed by a catered party with a tiered strawberries and cream wedding cake for our family and friends. Something beautiful but low-key and fun. It's only been a few months since Ben's "proposal," but I'm certain we've planned a beautiful event in this short amount of time. I've chosen to include only certain wedding conventions, ones that seem the most meaningful to me.

Keeping to the tradition that Ben and the guests won't see my dress before the ceremony, I'm waiting in the kitchen with Père, who will walk me down the aisle. Our guests mingle in our backyard while a live band plays traditional Whispered Folk instrumental ballads. Clancy was overjoyed when we asked him to officiate. Even though there's no legal or religious significance to the very brief ceremony, he's taken his role very seriously. I watch out the window as he directs guests to gather in front of an arch adorned with vines of jasmine. Lucas steps toward Clancy to take his spot as best man. Rose smiles sweetly at him as she takes her place on the other side as maid of honor. I check my dress in a hand mirror one last time before we make our way outside. Maman helped me go to a dressmaker for my custom-made bridal gown, a sleeveless white square neck ball gown style with a fitted bodice. Magick will keep the skirt voluminous and grass-stain-free, which will be worth the slight upcharge so I can focus on today's more important details.

The music changes, and we exit the kitchen to the backyard. Everyone turns around to watch us. As we approach the aisle, Ben waits for me with a joyful expression on his face. He is so handsome in a sharp-looking, fitted suit tailored for his wings and tail. The midnight blue hue matches his eyes. His crisp white dress shirt contrasts beautifully with it and matches my dress. Père walks me to Ben, placing my hand in his. Ben brings it to his mouth for a tender kiss and looks me over.

"You are stunning, my belle. I will remember your dazzling beauty this day for the rest of my life," he promises.

Since Ben works in construction, we don't exchange rings. Besides, no ring will ever be as special to me as my emerald "engagement" ring. But we both agreed we wanted to speak vows to each other. Clancy clears his throat to get the crowd's attention. They're chattering again after seeing the dress and the two of us together.

He begins to deliver his speech. "Dear friends and family, today we are celebrating Benoit Garde-Pierre and Cara Bishop, who are newly mated and absolutely and utterly in love. We've gathered as their dearest loved ones to celebrate with them as they journey into the rest of their lives together. They would also like to acknowledge their beloved grand-parents who have passed. Even though they are beyond the veil, we know that their love is here with us on such an important day."

"The couple would like to speak vows to each other, to solidify their matehood, and to publicly declare their commitment to each other. Cara, would you please share your vow to Ben?" Clancy prompts with a delighted smile.

"Ben, you are my shining light in a world brand new to me. You set me on a bright path, one I never would have found without you. You've illuminated so much of my true self I didn't know I had hidden away. Every day you show me the meaning of true love. The strength of unconditional support. The wonder and inspiration to explore every possibility. You are my protector, my partner, the love of my life. I will walk beside you through eternity," I vow, tears of happiness in my eyes.

"Ben, would you please share your vow to Cara?" Clancy asks, his voice thick with emotion.

Ben's expression becomes even more earnest, his whole being focused on me, and he vows, "When the universe set our paths together, it must have known you were the one soul in this realm that would complete mine. I realize now that before I met you, my heart had always been muted, my life in grayscale. And when you arrived, Cara, you were the key needed to bring them into full color. I see the world through new eyes. I feel it in a capacity I never could before you. Your love is the kind I never thought possible. You are my fairytale ending. My greatest source of joy. My life and love are yours through eternity."

The whole world falls away, and all that's left is the two of us basking in our words of devotion.

Clancy's voice sounds distant to my ears as he wraps up the ceremony, "Ben and Cara, with your commitment to each other bound by your words, you may now kiss your mate. May you have a lifetime and more of happiness together."

Looking into Ben's eyes, brimming with love, I see our forever. Our family and friends cheer as we seal it with a kiss.

About the Author

Katie Haypenny

Katie delights in a good story, especially when it weaves in a powerful dose of swoonworthy romance. After years of work in the corporate world, she's now putting her creative skills to better use. She's often found typing away on her laptop in coffee shops, pouring her heart into captivating tales set in a whimsical, made-up little place called Monstera Bluff. Currently, she enjoys life in picturesque Savannah, Georgia, where she shares her days with her husband.

Find out about upcoming books and sign-up for her newsletter at www.katiehaypenny.com